INFALLIBLE

VOL 4

TJ SPENCER JACQUES

NOVELS BY
TJ SPENCER JACQUES

NINE NOTCHES

BURGUNDY DOUBLOONS

INFALLIBLE SERIES

This is a work of fiction created by author TJ Spencer Jacques. All the characters, organizations, and events portrayed in this novel are either products of the author's imagination or used fictitiously.

INFALLIBLE

VOL 4

TJ SPENCER JACQUES

CHAPTER 1

Wedding Reception
June 2, 2018
6:35 p.m

DERINDA

I was a bat on fire the way I ran towards the nearest exit, but I had to get out of there. In a pair of three-inch *Valentino Garavani's*, any door would have sufficed, even the service hall where the waiters and hostess appeared and disappeared.

"Help, is this the quickest way out?" I asked a server.

"Yes ma'am, down the long narrow kitchen corridor, back there you'll find a white door, but be –"

"Thank you…"

And so, I ran. "Ma'am please watch your step; the floor is damp." Her words of caution faded behind me.

I ignored the stunned kitchen staff as they tried to redirect me. *I had to Get Out.*

I found those four red letters that hung above the white door seal. I rammed it because I needed to get as far away from this reception as I possibly could, far away from the sting of my lies and wrirlpool of my guilt, and my perfect cover, and the way I wanted my life to be I ran from it all until I collided with a dry rotten fence.

I could run no further.

Yes, I told a lie, but it was the best damn lie for the life I wanted for myself, and for my child. A life free from Glenn and his bullshit. He wasn't going to hurt my daughter the way he diced my heart like onions in a blender. I was going to protect her even if it meant killing him off like a character on *The Guiding Light*.

We didn't need the drama that came with Glenn. Erasing him was the perfect ending, but the questions never ceased.

I wanted to be all my child needed.

I wanted Erica wrapped in so much love that she never felt the emptiness of his absence, but like a squeaky floorboard, the curiosity regarding her father pressed on her heart every day.

From about four-years-old, it was as if she felt his presence, and once a month Erica would ask why did God take my daddy? I would, in turn, answer her with something just as ridiculous as the original lie.

God took him because he needed more angels to watch over little girls like you.

The taller she grew the more she honed for an explanation of why God needed her father, especially considering her friends at school had active dads. *Why didn't God need their dads?* She would ask, and I would answer with another new lie.

Endless lies.

The real problems started to surface in the second grade when she began to investigate my lies by interviewing her friends, then one of them shattered her entire existence.

"My mother said that's not true about your dad being in heaven, your dad didn't love your mom, so he left." Kids can be so cruel at that age.

And yes, my brother was there for her at all *Father/Daughter* functions back then, but shortly thereafter, she started interrogating him as well. My brother wanted no part of my greasy pit. Finally, the perfect opportunity came in the form of the Gulf War, a gift of the sort that would allow me to bury Glenn deep in the desert of our lives.

Your father was a member of the Special Forces and was killed during the liberation of Iraq. My brother stopped speaking to me for a year.

He knew Glenn was alive he also knew where he lived. My entire family knew he was alive and all of them went along to get along, fearing that if they challenged me on the truth, then I would do what I've always done, run away from happy places.

"To hell with all of them," I said, "what I choose to tell my daughter about her father is none of their business. Only I know what's best, after all, I am her mother."

And yes, I knew Glenn resided right across the Mississippi River Bridge in *Algiers*, and yes, I knew about the catastrophic injury that cost him his leg, and yes, I knew he was still married to Diana. How could I not? My best friend Carolyn made it her life quest to report to me every little thing she heard or saw on Facebook. I'm not on Facebook or any other social media site under my real name, because I knew he would look for me.

I wanted him dead, not physically dead, but dead to my child.

Silly of me to think I could bury a man alive and not expect him to scratch his way back into my life. Of all places for a sighting of Erica's father, tonight was the least likely venue.

I was mortified.

When I approached that table and saw Glenn, it felt as if I'd jumped out of a 747 at thirty thousand feet, without a parachute. Not only was he there, but she was there. Tonight, was the second time that bitch Diana has been present on the worst day of my life.

She lives to torment me – she's probably laughing – I'm such a fool.

The pain of that day has never healed. It looped in my sub-conscious mind. The man who held my heart in the palm of his hands was married. It was as if someone had placed a spoon in the microwave then pressed start. My mental circuit exploded, and the smoke filled the birthing room. Erica was born in that smoke-filled room, and since then, I have suffered from chronic smoke inhalations.

Every time I think about how she held my daughter before I did, and how she married him before I did, and how she has lived the life I wanted, my heart slams the walls of my chest until all the oxygen is gone, and my lungs collapse. She held my baby first. Even in my nightmares, Diana was there, holding my child, but refusing to hand her over - no matter how much I cried. Once a month, for over thirty years, I've awakened from that nightmare.

His wife.

The one he never mentioned during those endless conversa-tions. He said *I do* to her, but no to me. What was it about me? Even his first-born child it wasn't enough? Was I that horrible of a woman? Was I that undesirable?

But I desired him.

Glenn was my first everything.

And yes, I gave him a hard time back then, but I was terrified. My mother had her own agenda for my life. I was to finish col-lege. Then on to med school, then on and on, but her plans for my life and what I wanted to do with my life were distant plans. She never liked Glenn or any other guy prior too, no one was good enough for her daughter. However, all I wanted was Glenn, no one else or anything else, just Glenn, to have and to hold.

Glenn Braxton & Derinda.

Nothing more, or less.

I wanted to be a housewife, with seven kids, who cooked all day, cleaned all day, and was up to my neck in pissy pampers. I wanted to be under him, and behind him, and on side of him, but I lacked the emotional fortitude to communicate my feelings.

When I tried, the words changed in that space between my lips to his ears. In that space, he married her.

I'm not sure why it is or how it came to be, but after he married her, I felt dirty. Shamed. Discarded. Like no one wanted me or would ever love me, and men who tried to love me, I discarded them.

Like a cigarette butt, Glenn plucked me out of the window of his life, what decent, respectable man would want me?

No matter how kind a man was to me or how eagerly he accepted Erica into his world, I constantly asked myself *what's wrong with him?* Or maybe he would leave as quickly as Glenn left? Or maybe it's my body and he's only looking to hump & dump? Or maybe he's a pervert? Or a molester? Or a rapist and a molester?

"Fuck you, Glenn. Fuck you. Fuck you and fuck this fence."

It's all out in the open. Erica knows the truth, and I am painfully exposed. There isn't anything left for me to do but leave. To Dallas, perhaps? And never look back. But I have to. The three people I love the most are behind me, in this wedding reception hall, dancing and celebrating. Like Lot's wife I must look back, I have to turn around because everything I love is back there.

Erica.

Rosa & Parks.

"I cannot leave them, I will not —"

"Who are you talking to?" It was a concerned voice.

"Myself," I know that voice.

I turn to see my only child, only feet away. A female version of Glenn, with very little from me, except for those lips. To my back is the wooden fence, and from the darkest heaven beamed a spotlight that followed me from left to right. In front of me was the one I tried so hard to protect from the pain left behind by her father.

"Mother, at a wedding reception? This is the way I learned that my father is alive, at a wedding reception?"

"My little *Carrot,* I don't know what to say –"

"You told me he was dead…dead mother… *dead*. That's what you said time and time again. How could you do that to me…?"

"I'm fully aware of what I said, but did what I felt was best for you?"

"Growing up without my dad? Grieving a father, I never knew." She whispered through tight lips.

Behind the reception hall was a three-vehicle accident, Erica, myself, and my lie. An alternative fact that was just as old as she was, born three hours apart. After I asked the hospital security to escort her father from the delivery room, I never used his name again in a sentence. That was until tonight.

"All I can say is… I'm sorry…"

"Momma you will say much more than that, maybe not here, not tonight, but I promise on Rosa and Parks, you will never see them again until you provide me with a transparent explanation."

Erica snatched my hand and closed my fist around her car keys – I'm going home alone. On the night that wonderful young man proposed to my daughter, I became the worst person in her life.

Bum-Bum-Bum-Bum!

Erica banged on the door for a member of the kitchen staff.

"Erica please forgive me, I never meant for any of this to happen" I yelled out as she stepped into a yellow beam of light. The kitchen door slammed shut, and I was shut out.

The dead has come back to haunt me. Damn you Glenn Braxton.

Damn you.

CHAPTER 2

Ten Minutes Ago

RASTA

To my right, I watched my aunt Diana sprint through the crowd towards the front door, and to my left, Erica's mom ran for a touchdown towards the kitchen. It was as if I hung my head out of the driver's side window at 110 mph - where the winds swooped across my ears and muted the world; I couldn't speak.

I tried to break the silence, but my words evaporated on my tongue. The two who remained were just as stunned as the two who vanished. Uncle Glenn always warned us that karma was as real as bad breath, and no one was exempt.

When they catch you, it will be something that was completely out of your control.

I'm now a living witness. That shit Uncle Glenn warned us about just played out in front of me, in front of all of us, and that nugget of wisdom from Uncle Glenn gave zero-fucks when it came time to expose a liar. Derinda was the liar, and the rest of the evening felt awkward.

All this time, she had her daughter thinking Glenn was dead?

My wedding reception continued around us as if we were mannequins at the mall. The same was true for Uncle Glenn and Erica, in that split second no one mattered. They were alone in a crowded room. Suddenly she fell into his arms.

How could something be so happy and sad?

Fucked up and wonderful?

I heard the lumbar section of his spine crack when Erica's arms wrapped around his body. I became his other leg and braced him upright, but inch by inch we began to drift towards a side wall. Nevertheless, I had his leg and his back, the same way he had my back.

"Daddy. Daddy. Daddy." Erica's voice was weighted with emotion. "I needed you so much. I thought you were…she told me you were…just don't ever leave me again."

"I'm here sweetheart. I didn't leave you. I was ordered to leave."

To say she was so petite, Erica was as strong as a linebacker. I needed backup. I looked around for Biyell, but I last saw him by the front door, checking on my aunt. I was losing the battle to keep Uncle Glenn upright, but thank God, Jarvis noticed my struggle. He pressed his palm in the center of Uncle Glenn's back, which was the support I needed.

Off to my right, I caught a glimpse of Parks pulling on Telly's arm. Then she whispered in his ear. Shortly thereafter, he escorted Erica daughters through the crowd towards the restroom.

Off to my left, I saw Uncle Glenn face a gut quivering dilemma. Wrinkles of anguish pinged across his forehead. This was an anomaly. He was always the one with all the answers. When you've smoked weed with a person as long as I have, you can hear their thoughts through the thickest of skulls.

Go after Diana or hold on to the daughter I hadn't seen since birth?

As quickly, as it started the hug was over. Erica released Uncle Glenn then excused herself to go check on her mother. That was ten minutes ago.

"I'll be right here when you get back. I promise." He said as Erica backed her way through the crowd.

"Uncle Glenn! Uncle Glenn" Jarvis tried to get his attention with two thunderous claps. *"Go check on your wife."*

"Huh?"

"Lady Diana – go check on your wife. She went that way!" Jarvis and I pointed, as if he didn't see my aunt dash for the door.

"You're right, I guess I'd better go check on her. Hand me my crutch under the table."

"I'll go with you," I suggested.

"No Rasta, it's your special night, no need to bulk yourself down worried about me... I got it from here." He said as the padded top of the crutch tucked in his armpit. "When Erica returns please let her know I'm out front." I watched as Uncle Glenn made his way through the dance floor towards the front door and then disappeared into a swarm of guests.

"Bruh, what just happened?"

"Dude, I think I pissed on myself, for real," Jarvis said.

"Now you know it's about to be some shit once Uncle Glenn comes down off this high. Telly has been dating his daughter. His daughter is Erica!"

"This will not end well." Jarvis' hands covered his mouth and nose. "Of all the dudes to get with, Erica ended up with the most whorish dude in our group."

"Dude, it's a tie between you and Telly."

"Fuck you Rasta, I know I did my shit, but my shit was junior varsity compared to Telly."

"Dude, you're married to your niece?"

"She's not my niece, Briana was an in law?"

"Niece..."

"INLAW."

"Change this subject – here comes Telly."

"Change the subject?" Biyell caught us off guard. "Telly

fucking over Glenn's daughter is the only subject. He better cut this engagement off tonight or it's going down!"

I yelled over the voice of Beyoncé *Who Rules the World Girls*. "Biyell what gives you the right to demand that he breaks off his engagement? Erica said yes."

"Rasta, I don't care if she said *Whodi-Who*... Telly better end this tonight. I'm not down with this at all, and if none of you are going to tell him then I will."

After looking over his shoulder to gauge the distance between Telly and our huddle, Jarvis tried to reason with Biyell.

"Biyell listen I agree with you, but not here. Not now. The way I see it is seventy percent of what happened tonight was wonderful. Rasta has a beautiful wife and Uncle Glenn found his daughter. This issue with Telly can wait."

"Jarvis the reason you're approaching this like President Obama, all cool and shit, is because I'm not fucking your daughter."

"Bruh what? Say that again?" Jarvis' chest swelled.

"You heard me the first time" Biyell index finger aimed at eye level "What if you discovered I was *fuckin* one of your daughters or your sister?"

"Or your momma, because Biyell would fuck your momma," I added.

Biyell shot me a look before turning back to Jarvis.

"Jarvis knows what the fuck I'm saying." Biyell barked with K9 teeth. "If I were dropping dick off in someone he cared about that nigga' would check me right here on the spot. For that reason alone, we need to take Telly outside and demand that he calls off this engagement tonight. Either end it tonight or we kick his ass tonight."

"Dude you sound crazy as fuck! We're not doing this tonight. I know it's urgent, but we can resolve this tomorrow."

"Biyell I agree with Jarvis, but you have raised a valid point. We're all on the same page as it relates to Telly and Erica, and it will get addressed even if I have to reschedule my honeymoon, but this night belongs to my wife. Do this for me Biyell – let's deal with Telly tomorrow."

Just as Telly approached with Rosa and Parks, he was intercepted by Erica. I was surprised to see she had returned alone. Her eyes and cheeks were rouge with emotion as she panned the table for her father, followed by the fear of never seeing him again. Without asking, she seemed to figure it out, her father was probably outside consoling his wife.

I could only imagine what was said during the brief confrontation with her mother, it was evident that it was contentious. The Erica who ran after her mother wasn't the same Erica who returned looking for her father. She was a kitten rescued from a frozen pond.

She trembled.

Telly had an expression of a kid who shitted his pants during recess, self-consciously he tried to keep his distance. Rosa and Parks became part of his diversion as he hugged them tightly on both sides. He used them as coping props. Each time I tried to get Telly's attention, he kneeled to ask one of the girls a question.

You can run, but you can't hide, your man-whoring has come full circle.

While Telly pretended to be the Step-dad of the year, I shifted my focus back to Erica who stood motionless and fragile. That disconcerted state of being without a trusted shoulder to cry on. Biyell was right, I needed to detach from this situation and find Kayla, but I was compelled to comfort Erica.

"Looks like I have the honor of welcoming you to our family, we're first cousins." I wrapped my arms around the wet kitten. "Telly brought the best wedding gift ever."

She managed a smile, then her arms thawed just enough to return the hug. "I can see the headline in Peoples Magazine now *Girl Finds A Husband and Long-Lost Father AT Wedding.*"

"It's definitely been a wedding I'll never forget...that's for sure."

To my left, I see the guests parting ways as my beautiful wife approached.

"There's my husband, I've been looking for you." Kayla gave me a peck on the lips as she continued to Erica. "It looks like we're going to be right back in this reception hall in a few months, congratulations girl I'm so happy for you." Erica's warmth and that radiant smile returned to full strength as they bounced with excitement.

"Who knew I would escort Telly to a wedding and leave with a fiancé and a father."

"…a father?" Kayla broke the hug and twisted back to me.

"Sweetie we just discovered that Erica is Uncle Glenn's daughter."

"Wait, our Uncle Glenn, is your dad? This better not be a wedding prank." Kayla shifted in my direction.

"Kayla it's true," Jarvis confirmed.

"Did I just hear you say Erica is Uncle Glenn's daughter," Briana asked as she cradled their baby. "I caught the tail end, but did I just hear –"

"Yes." We all said in unison.

"Well, aren't we going to make an announcement? This is the best news ever!" Tiffany said as she pumped a fist in the air. It's a *celabrayshunnnn*. Time for another toast!" Tiffany's voice was way past tipsy.

Before Biyell could stop her, she ran over to the DJ table, whispered in his ear, and grabbed the microphone.

"*Ummm, excuse me.* Excuse me. May I have your attention pleeeeeeeeze." Tiffany tapped the mic on the side of her champagne glass. "As you all know I am *Tifannnnnieeee'* the maid of honor. I hope you're enjoying Kayla and Roderick's bomb wedding. Earlier you all witnessed his best man proposed to Erica, who's standing ova-there, y'all wave to Erica. *Hey Erica.*" The entire reception turned and waved. Her proposal was so freakin' awesome…soon it better be me." She mumbled loudly. "A proposal at a wedding was so sweet. Don't y'all agree?"

The crowd agreed but was annoyed that she interrupted a song by DJ Jubilee right before the *monkey on a stick* portion: a definite no-no in New Orleans.

In full dramatic fashion, Tiffany fanned tears away from her eyes.

"As if this night couldn't get any better, we have just discovered that Erica is the *long, long, long, long lost* daughter of… yawl ready for this." The crowd huffed with anticipation. *"Errrrica' is the lonnnnng'* lost daughter of Uncle Glennnnn." The oxygen left the room. I swear several balloons popped. "Isn't that amazing? With this last hour remaining… let's get lit in here tonight."

Tiffany bottomed up her glass "It's a *celabrayshunnnn'* and time for another toast… cheers!"

As the room erupted in applause (followed by a twerking frenzy) my eyes scanned across the face of Briana, which interchanged between fright and panic. It was then that I realized that Jarvis had broken one of our most mandated of all by-laws, a code that was just as stern as *never snitch on your friend to his lady.* Jarvis had broken The Pillow Talk Moratorium (PTM).

P.T.M CODE - Do not under any circumstances make known to your woman, the game another friend is running on his lady. Do not discuss his affairs, his side chick, his long-term girl, his medicinal hoes, and any of the confidential information we have discussed in this room. Disclosing this classified information is the equivalent of publishing our personal affairs on Facebook. Doing so will get your ass banned from our brotherhood, and simultaneously fucked up.

Half of Briana's body stood to the right of Jarvis, while eyes stared him up and down. He broke the code, it was confirmed. Because of Jarvis loose lips, Briana knew what we knew about Telly. I suddenly became pissed off with Jarvis because Telly's personal business was still confidential.

"We'll talk later…" I overheard Jarvis say to his wife.

Just as I was about to yank his ass outside, a photographer

appeared out of thin air. She demanded we pose for group photos. We did as we were told because wedding photographers will
threaten your life if they're denied a shot. For the next ten minutes, we posed. All of us together, then just the ladies, then just
the guys. And finally, my wife with Rosa and Parks.

Once the photographer concluded her Vanity Fair pho-
to-shoot, the anger I felt for Jarvis was immediately disrupted
by thoughts of Uncle Glenn, and his whereabouts. A whirlwind
of questions consumed me.

Are they still outside discussing this bombshell?

Did they decide to leave and discuss these events at home?

*Is Uncle Glenn flat on his back hemorrhaging from the fore-
head?*

I had to find out immediately.

CHAPTER 3

7:55 p.m.

DIANA

Damn right, I left Glenn standing out there, I didn't want to hear his bullshit. I still can't believe it was her, but it was, she has one of those faces I could never forget. A face that calls your own attractiveness into question, and makes you wonder why did he pick me over her? I'm not saying it's his fault, but I can't seem to escape that bitch.

Erica is Derinda's daughter!

Are you fucking kidding me?

I have the worst luck of anyone I know. First, I delivered my husband's love child, then after thirty-four years – they're back. I swear to God, this woman his haunting me and taunting me, I know she is, but I'm not tolerating it like a bullied kid on a playground. Not today.

I had to get far away from the wedding reception even if I racked up six speeding tickets before I make it home. I've watched *The Murray Show* long enough to know that when a bitch runs in one direction, you run in the other. That's what I did, got the fuck out of there.

"Ugggggg she ruined my entire evening."

This entire day was going according to plan, no mishaps during the wedding, the bride was gorgeous, and I got my revenge on *punk-ass* Timothy.

The look on his face when Mr. Honore' lifted the veil and he saw Kayla's beautiful eyes underneath, that was worth two million dollars. And watching Rasta and Marcel perform Al Green brought me to tears, they should take their show on the road. Then came that toast Telly gave at the reception, and his proposal to Erica: couldn't ask for a better wedding. If not for that bitch. Derinda.

"Erica, that's not Uncle Glenn, that's your father. Erica, that's not Uncle Glenn, his real name is Glenn Braxton, that's your father."

Ugggggggggah.

No bitch, that's my husband and we're leaving you two in the recycle bin of our lives.

That's what I wanted to say, it was best that I did what I did and got the fuck out of there before somebody got stabbed with a salad fork. Long before Glenn saw her, I did, but I thought it was the Gray Goose kicking in. As soon as she made it to our table, my first thought was to grab Glenn by the necktie and get the hell out of there before she could speak a single word.

I'm lying.

My first thought was to snatch her by the crown of her head, drag her outside, and bloody her face. But I didn't. Because of Rasta and Kayla, but oh how badly I wanted too. For that reason and that reason alone, I grabbed my purse off the table and ran out of there as fast as I could.

Of all the people to bump into at a reception, I had to run into Derinda. I can't believe this shit. Speaking of jail, I'm about to get pulled over. The Christmas lights from hell in my rear view nearly caused me to rear-end a taxi van.

I should floor it.

I should lead this cop on a high-speed chase all the way home and jump out the car like *Fuck the Police*, either shoot me or leave me alone. But with my luck they would shoot me, then that *skank-hoe* Derinda would end up with my man.

Again.

"Dammit, I hate her!" I punched the roof of my car.

"Driver pull over!"

His ignorant-ass had to blast me on the intercom, as if I needed any more attention.

I lowered my window.

"I'm trying to pull over…*asshole!*" I didn't care if he heard me. Less than a mile from home, I veered off on Gen. De Gaulle Avenue, and onto the parking lot of Chuck E Cheese's.

I retrieved my license out of my purse, and the manila envelope that contained my registration and insurance. With all three in hand, I extended my arm out the window. The cop was a Louisiana State Police, which pretty much guaranteed four bullshit tickets in one. In my side view mirror, I observed him exit his patrol unit with all the pretentious theatrics. Slow and intimidating, with the brim of his hat covering his eyes, and fine as hell.

From the part of his face that wasn't covered under the brim, he reminded me of Don Cheadle, if Don Cheadle was a fine-ass State Trooper, with muscle ripped arms. I watched his every movement as if he was a stripper, and tonight I was the birthday girl. Halfway to my car, he adjusted his oversize holster belt until it was symmetrically aligned with his shirt buttons, but I was no longer impressed. He was on my time.

"Ma'am did you know I had to drive nearly *70MPH* before I caught up with you – the speed limit here is *40MPH*."

"Well, I'm sort of in a hurry…so I didn't notice."

"What's the big hurry?"

"I'm trying to get home, that's all."

"Family emergency at home?"

"No, I attended my nephew's wedding, and I'm dead tired."

He nearly blinded me with his ridiculous flashlight.

His eyes flatten thin as if he recognized me, or written me a ticket once before

"…ma'am have you had anything to drink this evening?"

"Why, are you inviting me out for drinks?"

He chuckled "No ma'am, but I need to know if you have consumed any alcoholic beverages?

"No, I left before I could get thoroughly drunk, but I plan to get *toe-up* as soon as I get home and kick off these heels."

He chuckled again "*Allllrightie* just sit tight for a second and I'll be right back."

Once my retinas recovered from his intergalactic flashlight, I realized I knew him. I delivered his daughter two years ago.

The wife went into labor at an intersection. I was two cars behind her dozing off at the wheel, when she began to call for help. Once her car was out of traffic in a Wal-Mart parking lot, I helped her to the back seat of the car in order to conduct an initial examination. That's when I saw a labor and delivery nightmare, one little leg and part of a butt cheek dangling between her legs. The mother's name was Shelly.

"Shelly, who's your OB-GYN?"

"Dr. Arnand." I knew him, he was the best in New Orleans for high-risk pregnancies.

"…that tells me you were seeking his care for a potential breeched birth?"

"Yes ma, ma'am we've known for some time, but we'd also hoped she would turn."

"Well she hasn't, little momma here is determined to come in the world feet first. We have to get you to the ER now."

It was then she told me her husband was in route, along with the EMS.

"It doesn't matter who gets here first, just as long as they get here soon."

After I spoke, a clinching contraction plopped out a second leg, which left her daughter suspended from the torso upward.

Nevertheless, I'd been here many times before, and relied on my thirty-five years of experience in labor and delivery.

A few Wal-Mart employees surrounded the car and made sure I had everything I needed to absorb some of the moisture. While the frantic mother tried to sneak a view of the action below, I sat there and allowed her body to do the rest.

Shelly's breech baby was delivered on the back seat of her brand-new Lexus SUV, with about twenty people gazing through the windows. Only then did the EMS and her husband arrive, we got a good laugh because that's usually how it goes.

That morning I delivered the baby and accompanied her to the hospital, while Mr. State Trooper cleared the way.

I didn't make it home until after lunch, but Glenn was Glenn, supportive, and amazingly understanding on abnormal days. He cooked another order of heart-shaped pancakes, all fluffy and buttery. I devoured those pancakes. Then I read the poem he wrote repeatedly, until my eyes could no longer support the weight of the lids.

"Ma'am I need you to step out of the car."

"Excuse me? Is there a problem?"

"Ma'am, please step out of the car."

When those Cops in the Facebook videos asked you a third time, usually a ten million views ass whipping usually followed. I was no longer interested in a high-speed chase or willing to escalate matters, so I obeyed his request. No sooner was I out of the car did he return my driver's license, and vehicle papers. Then he lifted me off my feet in the biggest hug I've had in twenty years.

"I thought that was you, I just called my wife Shelly to confirm and she confirmed it. Nurse Braxton, you are a hero in my family." I returned his public display of affection.

"And how is the beautiful little girl?"

"Bad as hell," his laugh sounded like Eddie Murphy "she has broken up everything within her reach, but other than that she's wonderful. My wife is also wonderful and it's all because of you. We stopped on your floor last week, but they told us you had retired."

"Yes, I've done my time." It was then that he pulled a card from his pocket. "My wife would love to get a picture with you."

Suddenly, Officer Tate was distracted by a commotion over my left shoulder, from that area came screams, threats, and the sound of a scuffle. He darted off without saying bye. An all-out brawl that started inside the Chuck E. Cheese's had spilled out into the parking lot.

About twelve huffing women, all paired off with a fist full of each other's sown in weaves. The altercation was none of my business, so I continued down Gen. De Gaulle towards my *English Turn Subdivision*.

Now what were we discussing before that cop?

That's right – that Bitch Derinda!

CHAPTER 4

Wedding Reception

JARVIS

B riana was like a reporter from the Washington Post, and I knew my wife would continue to fire off one question after the next, until no stone was left unturned. I tried to sidestep her, but it was too late, I was caught in the melee of her curiosity.

"Here's what I don't understand…"

I cut her off "not now Bri…"

"It will only take a minute for you to enlighten me as to how —"

"Briana please…"

Unbeknownst to my wife and the wedding guests, a quiet scandal was on the verge of erupting. We had to keep all parties calm and quarantined for the last leg of the reception but think God the evening was in the final countdown. In the center of the dance floor, Kayla waved and teased her bouquet high above her head as she prepared to toss. A few feet away tipsy Tiffany elbowed and shoved for the best line of sight.

She caught it, with help from her best friend.

"Bri, I promise. I will answer your questions on the drive home, but right now, Uncle Glenn needs me."

"Just explain –"

"Bri remember that conversation we had about picking a scab until it becomes a new sore?"

She nodded.

"You're doing it."

"But…"

"No buts, I'm simply asking for a moment to wrap up this reception. Please do me a favor and kick it with Erica until I get back." Reluctantly she agreed.

Just off to my left, I couldn't help but notice Biyell aggressively whispering something in Telly's ear. To escape the conversation, Telly turned in several directions and was obviously frustrated, but Erica was four tables away, so tempers held in check.

To my dismay, the wedding guests showed no signs of exhaustion – and the DJ didn't help with a call for a Soul Train line that stretched from one end of the hall to the other. Along the sides of the dance floor, the host staff collected dinner plates and utensils as they prepped towards the end of the wedding festivities.

With the guest on the dance floor, the pathway to the front door was free and clear, but not my anxiety. I was happy for Glenn and horrified for Diana, thrilled he found his daughter and troubled that Diana no longer felt welcome. It wasn't the typical confrontation like I would have expected – just extremely awkward.

Once I made it outside, Rasta and Uncle Glenn was seated on a smoker's bench about five yards to the left of the entrance.

"Lady Diana wasn't having any of it I see?"

"Nope" uncle Glenn replied.

"She's gone?"

"Burned rubber out the parking lot," Rasta replied.

"We were just about to head back in, but first I needed a moment out here to pull it together."

"Uncle Glenn I totally understand. By the way, that's a beautiful daughter, and grandkids."

"Thank you, as a matter of fact, I'm about to head back in and get to know them all a little better."

"Yeah, I think that's a good idea." Rasta agreed.

I pulled Uncle Glenn upright, while Rasta handed him his crutch.

"You do know they make wheelchairs for your condition," I suggested.

"*Fuck you and that wheelchair bullshit.*" We all shared a lighthearted moment as Uncle Glenn crutched towards the front door.

"Uncle Glenn if you hop past my wife let her know I'll be there in five minutes to shut it down."

"Shut it down? Rasta that *Grey Goose* just started flapping in there. I heard someone say they're all meeting up at your mom's house afterward it shuts down here."

"They can do whatever makes them happy but as for me and my wife we're going to the hotel."

"*...as for me and my wife, my wife, my wife.*" In my teasing voice, I mocked him. "You act like a little virgin husband, my wife, my wife. Still can't believe she married you huh?"

"*Don't hate. Don't hate.*" Rasta blushed "but anyway, I need to say something right quick before we head in."

"...no problem – what's up."

Rasta collected several deep breaths as he positioned his words.

"It's best I say it how I feel – my gut is telling me you're discussing our private issues with your wife."

"Huh? Where's this coming from?"

"Jarvis don't play dumb. I don't have time to break it down. I couldn't help but notice Briana's reactions when Tiffany made those announcements about Erica and Uncle Glenn. It was as if she knew insider information about Telly."

She did, and she's still asking questions.

"Jarvis what you discussed with your wife was personal and privileged to the brothers in our circle. So, I'm asking you straight-up because I have to get back inside, why are you chatting about us to your wife?"

"Rasta I'm not going to lie, I may have said a thing or two during the time I was writing the book, but that was only because my wife is also my editor. I bounced a few things off her to gauge her reaction…you know…from the female perspective. That's all."

"…and in your back and forward conversations, you snitched us out to your wife?"

"Rasta, brother, you know I wouldn't do anything to intentionally hurt you guys. The few things we discussed were related specifically to the book and that was the extent of our discussions."

"Jarvis, we don't roll like that and you know it. That's why she's so short with us whenever we try to engage her. Because of you, she has a file on each one of us."

"Rasta she's not like that. Briana is not the type to gossip –"

"**Jarvis all of them are that type!** They talk…it's what they do. What's a secret between you and Briana, is not a secret between her and her girlfriends!"

"Rasta, she doesn't have any friends…it's only one friend, a girl name Sierra. But they're not that type to spread gossip."

"The part you're failing to comprehend is, Telly's personal life, is none of Briana or Sierra's business. Why is this so hard for you to get?"

"Dude I get that part…"

"We all know Telly enjoys the sport of running game on women, and will never let Heather go, but the only people in that reception who knew that about him are members of our Madden Crew. Bruh, if your wife is in need of bedtime stories, then read the three little pigs, but don't rock her to sleep with details of our personal business. One day this little *Man Whore* seminar you've hosted for Briana will come back and bite you in the ass."

Just as I was about to speak.

"Rasta, they're looking for you. Get your ass in here." Biyell demanded.

"We'll pick this up when I get back from the cruise, but in the meantime can you keep our personal business out your mouth?"

"Damn…it's like that?"

"…that's the way it's been."

Rasta jogged down the walk-way to the front entrance and disappeared into the reception hall with Biyell.

Though I wanted to curse his ass out for the way he handled me, he was right. I had disclosed a lot to Briana. And the more I shared, the more she wanted to know. It was as if I'd introduced her to a world, she only heard of but never knew existed, the land where men were more than willing to pacify their women with money – to distract them from the truth.

And there was none Bri was more intrigued by and disgusted by than Telly. For an unsuspecting woman, his character in my novel was the monster under the bed, the thing that went bump in the night, that muddy hand that reached up from the grave, that greasy pimp with the roller-set hair she loved to hate.

The only problem was my book was an adaptation of real life, only the names were changed to protect the *Whoremongers*. But she also knew about Tamara and Tyra, Ladashia and Shameka. The things I tried to conceal, she figured it out on her own. Rasta was correct, because of the revelation she received from my book her perception of my crew had changed. Then one day she asked me.

"Jarvis, will you also take on a mistress?"

Taken aback my eyes peeled away from my manuscript.

"Why would you think that?"

"…. because it appears to be a personality trait within this group, these guys you consider your brothers. With the exception of Uncle Glenn, a mistress is that common gene. Just so we're clear, I'm not tolerating it, and if you start to resemble any of the men in this book, ***we're done that day***. As you say, *that's real nigga talk.*"

That's when transparency ended between us. That's when the soundproof wall was erected.

How could I be so stupid as to think my wife could binge watch one horror story after the next, and not question if she too was married to a Goblin? The roots of our marriage were planted in scandal-rich soil, so in the back of her mind, I knew she wondered if those chickens would one day come home to roost? How could I expose my entire crew?

Why did I tell her so much about Telly?

Because I wanted her to feel secure in our marriage, to feel, as if, I was a better man, but then it backfired. After Telly proposed to Erica, my wife wanted to run up there and snatch that mic out of his hand, but I stopped her.

"I can't watch this, I know how it ends." I heard her say in a soft resolved tone.

Then I was reminded that spiritually Bri and I come from two different worlds. She's constantly looking over her shoulder for God to show up and beat the living shit out of her for fucking Monica's husband. As for me, I feel that God is too busy to care, if I have a fornication buddy. But at the end of the day, I cheated on Monica with my current wife, then provided her with chapters of our misdeeds to ponder, categorize, and strategize.

"In other words, you're threatening me?"

"Jarvis at the first sign of any of the behavior in your book, I'm out that day. We're clear?"

"You would leave me just like that…"

"Jarvis, are we clear?" That conversation was two days ago.

Just as I made my way to the front door, I received a text from my wife. *I'm not sure where you are but the longer, I sit here at this table with Erica the more I want to tell her everything I know.*

    I broke out into a sprint.

CHAPTER 5

Inside Reception

BIYELL

R asta advised me to take my issue up with Telly after the wedding, but I had a few things I needed to get off my chest tonight. That's my dawg, and I love him, but I had to put Telly on notice. I'm not with this engagement. Not at all.

Rasta just wrapped up that garter belt thingy people do at weddings, but I've been locked on Telly. He looked guilty as fuck, and the bulk of this isn't his fault, but that's random shit for you. *Random Shit* is ignoring every warning from Uncle Glenn, brushing off his advice, only to find out that Erica is Glenn's daughter.

Like my grandmother would say.

God don't like ugly.

Seated directly behind me is Erica and Uncle Glenn. An emotional reunion that was three decades in the making. Even I had to hike it away from those two because it was getting way to mushy. But what happened here tonight was beautiful. Rasta married Kayla and Uncle Glenn found his daughter. In gaining a daughter, I hope he doesn't lose a really good wife.

Diana should be here, she should be part of this, not excluded.

Team Diana. I pressed send on that text a view minutes ago. He read it.

When Diana saw Derinda, I just knew she was going to leap on that table like Jackie Chan and kick the wisdom teeth out of her mouth. Instead, she collected herself, collected her purse, and floored it out the parking lot. That is why I call her Lady Diana – we all know what she's capable of when pissed off – but that ass-kicking fury remained hidden behind her elegant exterior. She held true to herself tonight. She left Glenn to sort it out on his own – and left us to deal with Telly.

Look at him over there with Rosa and Parks.

Telly doesn't like kids.

Never wanted any.

But Dude is winning an Oscar from those who are unaware, that this is an act. Since Derinda dropped that atomic bomb, that coward has avoided eye contact with Uncle Glenn all night. I've watched him maintain fifty feet of ducking space because he knows it's coming. That's why I asked him point blank.

"How are you going to close this out with Erica." He shot me this appalled look.

"Biyell, I haven't had a chance to take a shit, and what business is it of yours? This is my relationship with my future wife."

"Future wife? The future for that bullshit ended once Erica was introduced as Glenn's daughter. *There's no future.* Friends, but any idea you may of have of marrying Erica is a crack pipe dream."

"That's your opinion…"

"That's the rule of the game! You know as well as I do that, we don't date family and we *sho-in-de-fuck* don't date daughters."

"Bruh, this is my life –"

"Bruh that is Glenn's daughter." Telly looked past me towards the dance floor. "How many lectures have Uncle Glenn given you about Erica? Huh?" I didn't give him a chance to answer. "Are you silly enough to believe that he would approve of you marrying his only daughter?"

"Biyell the way I see it is like this…Erica is a grown-ass woman, in her right mind, and if she would like to continue with *OUR* engagement, then fuck what you think, and anyone else for that matter."

"Including Uncle Glenn? So, it's fuck Uncle Glenn?"

"I didn't say that…you did?"

"So, it's fuck Uncle Glenn…when you know we'll never sit back and allow you to fuck over his daughter."

"But it's okay to fuck over a daughter if the father is un-known…is that how it goes?"

"Look, don't use all that lawyering bullshit on me…you know exactly where I'm coming from. And to answer your question, yes it matters that it's Glenn's daughter. And no, it didn't matter before, but no one mattered before, nor did we care about the women we ran through, but now everything matters, because we're trying." Counterclockwise he ticked away from me, but like a minute hand, I stalked him.

"Telly you know me, and if I could settle down with Tiffany and wave away extra pussy on a platter, pussy I would have nor-mally eaten like a pork chop, if I could chill out, then that's your alarm clock to wake up and grow up. We're trying to fly right, and you will not weigh us down because you're still playing lit-tle boy games like *Catch kiss get a Lil Bit.* Grow the fuck up and handle this the right way."

"You mean to handle it your way…"

"Telly you know right from wrong…handle this shit the right way."

"Well since you've made my affairs your personal business, maybe you should spend more time watching Tiffany." I didn't bother to turn as he described how she was backing her ass up on some guy. "Mr. Iyanla Vanzant you better hurry over there and save Tiffany. Dude has a hand on each ass cheek. If he slides that left hand a little bit more to the right, then he's inside of that dress. Oh, snap, check her out…she's serving it to him."

At first, I thought it was another one of his deflection techniques from the courtroom until I turned around, and there she was. A woman I'd convinced myself to trust. A woman I had fallen in love with after saying never again. That same woman allowed some guy to illegally squeeze her ass, as if it were legal. It was just as Telly described, and she was looking back at him – slow grinding to Ginuwine *Ride That Pony.*

I know what I can mentally handle.

Even though that sounds like some rhetorical shit to say, here's what I'm getting at.

Whenever I'm about to fly off the handle, the first indication is felt in the lobes of my ears. I'm not sure why, and I could never figure it out, but my ears turn the color of raw liver. Then my right-hand covers my mouth in a subconscious attempt to contain my words, as my body becomes drenched in rage.

Finally, I look away, as if someone called my name. Only to refocus on that person who pissed me off. Once I'd cycled through those rapid changes in my body's chemistry, and the rapid increase in my heart rate then comes the voices.

Pimp B: *I fuckin told you! I fuckin told you! Always keep a spare bitch. I fuckin told you. Now look at you. You look stupid. She came here with you, fucked you last night, and now she's dry humping some dude. Go smack the piss out of her for embarrassing you.*

Lil Glenn: Don't listen to him Biyell, the last time you listened to him, you ended up in jail for nearly two weeks.

Pimp B: *So, he should let this slide? Everybody in here laughing at his dumb ass because of Tiffany.*

Lil Glenn: Biyell, there's no one laughing at you. Go get Tiffany. She's had one too many drinks, that's all. She's not a bitch or a hoe, she's drunk. Don't overreact.

Pimp B: *And being that she's drunk... the hoe has come out. Listen to me Biyell, Tiffany is not the one. Briana sat her sadiddy-ass at that table tonight and never moved, but not hot-cat Tiffany. You picked the wrong one, she played you Biyell, you look stupid, this shit will be on Facebook before you make it home. To rectify this bitch the way I taught you.*

"Oh, shit Biyell, she has turned to face the dude" Telly twisted the blade in my gut "you sure y'all still a couple? After this dance Tiffany will need a pregnancy test."

If you're horny, let's do it
Ride it, my pony
My saddle's waiting
Come and jump on it.

The song went on for what felt like thirty minutes. Then Rasta noticed, Then Jarvis noticed. Then Uncle Glenn, and the entire wedding party noticed. Even Mr. Honore' who walked Kayla down the aisle appeared disturbed. I'd had enough.

Suddenly the room slowed like an instant replay. In that instance, I was reduced to a referee, and after further review, Tiffany was flagged three times.

Illegal Substitution.

Taunting.

Holding.

To make matters worse, Tiffany was out of bounds, because she was my girl.

I was humiliated on my home field, in front of my team, by the last person I thought would have pulled this bullshit. She was on the other side of the room, but I could see every seductive sway of her hip, every pucker, every time their eyes locked. Then she faced him, and her arms draped over his shoulders, and his hands rested on her hips. He had my girl. She wanted him. And I was about to get ejected out of the game for targeting.

If you're horny, let's do it
Ride it, my pony

My saddle's waiting
Come and jump on it.

I see people dancing, but I don't. I hear the music, but I don't. I want to heed the advice of Lil Glenn but won't. At the midway point, the only thing I haven't decided was who to choke first.

Pimp B: *That bitch.*

She was the one who sold me on this good girl persona, the good girl who could never find a good man. I fell for it. She knew I had issues, but I was straight-up with her. Tonight, she has confirmed something that Telly once said to me

Bitches are niggas' too - stay on your toes – and do what you do.

But she's doing it in front of my face. I'm five feet away and she's still riding that pony. Just as I reached for her, Kayla appeared out of nowhere like *Glinda* 'The Good Witch of the South' in *The Wiz.* Kayla intercepted Tiffany with one arm and stiff-armed me with the other. Then she hissed at the guy.

Why are you cock-blocking me?

"Step off Josh, I'm only saying it once. You know you're married."

It was then that dude noticed me on the other side of Kayla, and with one foot behind the other, he backed away.

"Look at you" Kayla shook Tiffany by the shoulders. "I asked you several times to lay off the drinks and you promised me!"

"...I only had a little champagne, this is a *celabraaaytion.*"

"Tiffany, you're drunk..."

"I'm not drunk, I've been drunk before, and this ain't drunk."

"Tiffany Mr. and Mrs. Honore, they're right over there." Kayla pointed.

"Oops, my bad..." Tiffany slurred.

Then Kayla leaned in tightly and growled in Tiffany's ear. The only part I could hear of the music was "do I need to remind you about Tracey? Do I?"

Kayla half turned to me.

"Biyell I know how this looks. I saw it too, but couldn't get over here fast enough…"

"This how you play me, Tiffany? Like this…?"

"Biyell I'm not making an excuse, but she can't handle her liquor. Not even a little bit. I know you're angry, but she's wasted –"

"This is who you set me up with? This bitch right here?"

"Biyell what she did was wrong but she's not a bitch and when she sobers up Tiffany will feel horrible about all of this. Please, just…"

"With all due respect, because you're family now – but Kayla I don't want to ever see her again."

I then scanned the room until I found Josh standing by the open bar.

"Hey Josh, she's ready to finish riding that pony," I yelled out to him, but he longer appeared interested.

Kayla dragged Tiffany through the sea of guest who recorded the entire altercation on their cell phones. I was humiliated, Kayla was embarrassed, and Tiffany was drunk as a corner store wino.

If you're horny, let's do it
Ride it, my pony
My saddle's waiting
Come and jump on it.
"That's my jam…"

CHAPTER 6

Wedding Reception

RASTA

Yea, I saw Tiffany and that guy, how could I miss them? Slurping up each other like two recently released inmates. They had a certain type of chemistry that seemed far too effortless for a first-time connection, the type of heat that caused every single woman to reminisce about passionate days gone by.

In fact, I have seen stray dogs who were stuck together after mating, display more shame than Tiffany and that Josh dude.

Biyell saw them too.

He saw her most of all.

I imagine the calmness beforehand was the same as those never again seconds in one of those fireworks factories, shortly before the new guy exited the break room with a lit cigarette. As bad as it appeared it wasn't my place to remind Tiffany that she was in a relationship with Biyell, so I recruited the expertise of my wife. My smack brand new wife with that new wife smell was in the back corner of the reception engulfed in a conversation at a table reserved for her former volleyball teammates.

My Lord, all of them were beautiful. An assortment of heights, sizes, complexions, races, short hair, long hair, bald fade, full chest, flat chest, heavenly hips, silky hands, all drop dead sexy, with shiny lips, and sparkling eyes: just like my wife.

I nearly forgot the reason I hurried across the reception hall.

After the round of table hugs and handshakes, I requested Kayla's assistance with her dumpster fire of a friend. I pulled Kayla to the furthest corner of the room, which gave way to a full view of the dance floor. That's when she saw her best friend.

Riding that pony.

"Tiffany. No." My wife said in an airy stunned voice. "How long has this been going on?"

"…According to Telly this is her third dance with that guy, but the first dance was one too many."

"Oh my God! And with Josh?"

"Who is Josh?"

"He's married to my cousin. She's in the National Guard and had to report to base this morning." I later learned his real name was Josh LaBlanc, not that it mattered to Biyell.

"Kayla I've never seen this side of Tiffany, you have to get down there. This is about to turn ugly."

Luckily, for Tiffany I arrived just in time and managed to grab hold of Biyell. I shoved him outside. His anger would not allow him to stand still, not even for five seconds. He cursed the day he met Tiffany, and every other woman he could think of who broke his heart.

Here comes the prom night rant.

"…it's just like that bitch Lauren back in high school, had me jump through all those hoops to get a tux and limo, knowing full well her mother picked another dude as her date, but she wasn't woman enough to tell me. I arrived in the tux and limo after they had already left, her mother laughed me off their porch, that's how they do you Rasta, can't trust them, these women ain't shit."

It never failed, whenever a woman cut him deep, that prom night story would always surface. It surfaced after he caught Tamara with Mike, and it surfaced after Tyra quit him for Julian. I know Biyell isn't in a position to play a victim when it comes to relationships, but that Lauren chick is the real reason he hurt so many women, and Tiffany just became the new Lauren.

"This happens to me every time I try to do it the right way, a bitch goes there on me. For real bruh, did you see her and that dude?"

"I saw it, and the only explanation –"

"Rasta, there's no explanation for Tiffany – *a hoe is gonna be a hoe.*"

"Biyell what I'm trying to say is, that wasn't the Tiffany I have come to know nor the woman you've come to know. It could very well be what my wife said, *when Tiffany gets drunk, she's a totally different person.*"

"Rasta you can save your breath – you know just as well as I do – whatever Tiffany and I had is over."

"And the business part of your relationship?"

"We're still business partners, but after tonight that's all it will ever be."

"*And what about the ring in your coat pocket?*"

For weeks Biyell and I meticulously planned this evening, after Telly did his toast and handed the mic back to me, I'd planned to hand it to Biyell. But as always, Telly had a secret agenda. We were caught off guard. Despite having numerous opportunities to bring us in on his plan, Telly blindsided us with that proposal. That was all before Tiffany decided to grind her ass on some dude in the middle of my reception.

No exaggeration.

Tiffany and Josh were so over the top at one point, that Josh guy had two handfuls of her breast. Squeezing. Grinding. Bumping.

"Get a room." The DJ said.

How do you get so intoxicated – you forget you're in a relationship? Kayla owes me a full explanation for her best friend's behavior, and I will get to the bottom of it, but right now. Biyell feels violated and whenever he's violated, he violates. That's his rule.

"… you know what Rasta?" Before I could reply, he continued. "That James dude in there…"

"It's Josh…"

"James, Josh, who gives a fuck, he can have her because she ain't worth doing time."

"Now that much we can agree, no one is worth going to jail over."

"The one who was worth it was GiGi. That's the one I should have fought for. If only I'd tried harder, I could have won her back, but I left the door open for Julian. The reason he's in her life is that I fucked up, but I will scream it on the mountaintop, that's the one I should have fought for, she was my Kayla, my Diana, a really good woman. Rasta, none of these bitches out here ain't shit. *Ya heard me.*"

"I heard you Biyell, loud and clear, but Tyra has gone on with her life, and you're doing the same. Don't judge Tiffany based on tonight. At least give her the opportunity to sober up. Let's trust Kayla on this one. She's known Tiffany most of her life."

"Oh, that's how this works? Since you're all in love, and your wife said it, then I shouldn't trust what I saw with my own two eyes?"

"Biyell that's not it at all…"

"Rasta, you of all people know how close I came to jumping the broom with Tiffany. A woman who came with me – but leaving with him. I was this close to marrying another Tamara!"

"I don't think you should compare her to Tamara…"

"She is Lauren, and Tamara rolled into one. The type of woman who takes five hours to go to Wal-Mart, but only comes home with five bags. The kind of bitch that would have me in prison for catching her fucking a dude at 3 A.M in my garage?"

"Wait…who did you catch fucking at 3 A.M. in your garage?"

"Nobody! I'm saying for example."

"Nothing to be ashamed of, if you caught her in the garage. It happens to the best of us, that's all I'm saying. Was it Tamara?"

"No, I didn't catch anyone in the garage, I was making an example."

"...but if you did, would you tell me?"

"BRUH!" Biyell was exasperated with my sudden interest in the garage scandal, even guests leaving the reception over heard that part of the conversation.

"My point is, I know what I saw tonight and that's not the type of woman I want to marry."

"B don't finalize everything tonight, allow a few days for her to apologize for it."

"Have you ever seen Kayla that drunk?"

"No, I can't say I have."

"Exactly, a good woman is good all the time." Biyell dapped me off and said he was heading in for the night.

It hurt me to see him hurting. I can honestly say, during this relationship with Tiffany, he's been on his best behavior. Biyell completely sold out for Tiffany, even dropped $5,400 on an engagement ring, which added to his gut feeling of being played.

I'm not sure if I can put the monster back in the dungeon, Biyell had truly bought in on the *one woman one relationship lifestyle*, as compared to his former life. Just as I headed back to the reception, Jarvis and his family were leaving.

"I'll help load your gifts in your mom's van, but we're out, I have to get the family home. I'm so proud of you Rasta."

"It was a beautiful wedding," Briana said "thank you so much for inviting me and my kids. Kayla looked amazing."

After a chest hug with Jarvis, I gently embraced Briana without waking the baby.

"Enjoy your honeymoon and that lovely wife – and please post the pictures from Jamaica." As Jarvis spoke, I caught a glimpse of Briana. She rolled her eyes in disgust as Telly approached, then hurried to their van.

She knew everything, and it was just a matter of time before Erica received a phone call.

CHAPTER 7

8:32 p.m.

BIYELL

This is a good time, to be honest with myself, I'm hurt. Like a marathon runner who finished last, I've lost all expectations, and I still can't breathe. Just as I became accustomed to having her in my life every day, Tiffany pulls this stunt – in front of all my friends. I will never hear the end of this, I might as well prepare for the never-ending jokes, especially from Telly.

Biyell was so busy trying to check me, he didn't notice a dude finger fucking his lady in front of 500 people.

Telly will never let this night end, and I deserve it.

To make matters even worse, I saw the wedding photographers circling around Tiffany and Josh. That dance and that song are welded into my permanent memory of this night. Then again, I didn't deserve this, because I was on my best behavior. All for nothing.

I bet they've fucked before.

With that much chemistry, I know they have.

There isn't anything she can say to fix this. If not for Kayla, I am convinced Tiffany and Josh would have ended up in a bathroom stall, or the back seat of his car.

Why didn't I detect she was running a game?

A dog can smell a dog, but not this time, my nose was stuffy. But it is what it is. We have this business together, and the show must go on, and I can't cry over something that I never had.

Look at this pool, we did an amazing job back here. Don't get me wrong, Glenn's entire house is five-star perfection, but my favorite is this pool area. So peaceful on nights like tonight. It's where I come to think. Mainly about GiGi. I can't get her out of my head, nor do I want too.

I've loved her more than any woman I have ever held or kissed. In many ways I'd hoped Tiffany would help me get over GiGi, but I still found myself obsessing over her all throughout the day and making love to her all throughout the night – in my mind. And it hurts so bad to know that she's with the love of her life. She's happier without me. On some days I want to call and plead with her, but that ring on her finger demands respect.

GIGI is a rare kind of woman.

Take, for instance, both of my daughters are together tonight in Baker because, GIGI offered to watch Bylisha while we prepared for the wedding. At the last minute she whisked them off to the Audubon Zoo, and after that, she sent me pictures of my kids on the merry-go-round at City Park. That's what I mean by rare, she's helped us tremendously during this temporary custody transition by keeping Bylisha's mind occupied.

Abruptly, the peaceful darkness behind me was disturbed.

"Boy you scared the shit out of me, I was about to shoot you."

"Lady Diana, how I feel right now, please shoot me."

She joined me at poolside "what's going on with you?"

"I guess you're the only one who didn't see it…"

"See what?"

"Tiffany riding that pony."

"Biyell what are you talking about?" Her face tightened.

I explained the entire ordeal with Tiffany.

"I don't understand you new breed of men. When I was younger and some bozo took a dance a little too far, someone would cut in to keep down confusion."

"Cut in? There wasn't any space between them to cut in unless I wanted to have a threesome dance. I don't rock like that."

"There's always space to cut in, and she would have fallen right into your arms. That's how you should have handled it, you strut your ass over there and send that Josh dude on his way. Stand your ground and fight for your girl, instead of running off."

I felt my left eyebrow raise five inches.

"Stand my ground? Interesting you would say that after the way you grabbed your purse and was out the front door. You're faster than Usain Bolt." I cautiously teased.

"You can't compare the two."

"Oh really, how so?"

"Because I left to keep from killing a bitch, that's the difference."

"…and I left for the same reason, we spared two bitches lives tonight."

"But tomorrow Derinda might catch these hands." We both shared a much-needed laugh.

And that's Diana, she always had a way of calming me down or getting me to see things from a different perspective. As far as it goes with Tiffany, we don't agree. There's more to it than cutting in on a dance. There should've never been a dance in the first place. Kayla was the only woman with a permission slip to dance with other men, and we all paid $100 each for that honor.

"You know, I never felt like Tiffany was a good fit for me, but I did like the concept of committing to one woman."

"The problem is you wanted her to be Tyra and there's only one Tyra." Diana sipped from a long glass of something strong, mixed with orange juice. "Tyra could have been the one the entire time, but you never gave yourself a chance to be what she needed. Problem #1 is you were married when you met her. Problem #2 is you lied about it. You would be amazed at how far a man would get in a relationship if he started with the truth and remained truthful."

"I can't argue with that, I'm guilty as charged."

"Where Glenn messed up is, he never told me he was still sleeping with Derinda during our break-up period. His lie to me was he spent every waking hour *praying I would come back to him –*"

"Don't you just hate when they bring God into their bullshit?"

"I can't stand it! He wasn't praying I came back to him… he was praying for more hot-ass from Derinda." This time she bottomed up the glass until the orange drink was gone. "*Uur-rrrrrrp!* Oh my, please excuse me." Diana patted her chest to sooth the burn. "After seeing his ex-boo-thing tonight, I needed a strong drink."

"So, you didn't see any signs that he wasn't being straight up with you about Derinda?"

"Not at first, but if he would've been truthful then the sting of finding out about the baby wouldn't have been so devastating. But that's too much like right. Glenn felt he needed to keep me in the dark. And I always say, I might not discover the lie today, and I might not figure it out tomorrow, but you can bet your *black-ass* I will catch you. And that's what I did, I caught him. You know why Biyell?"

"Why Diana?"

"Because people talk and nosey people talk even more, so the rumors started to get back to me, but I didn't say a word, and I didn't show my hand. I knew deep down, on the day of truth it was going to come in a way that he couldn't lie his way out."

"And that's when you reported to work, at the same hospital, on the same day she was admitted."

"*Black-Out Bingo*, that's why I made sure the agency knew I was available that entire month and the rest worked in my favor.

A little girl was born who looked just like him from the moment she opened her eyes."

It was then that my phone alerted me that I had a text.

"That's probably your *Pony Rider*, hopefully, she's off the saddle." Dianne had a laugh at my expense, but it was so funny I had to laugh with her. "While you check your phone, I'm going to pour another drink...do you want one?"

After I read the text I replied: "yes, I will have whatever you're having."

What I thought was a text message was actually a series of alerts from my Facebook messenger app.

Tamara petty-ass tagged me in a recent post from GIGI.

Well, here it is guys, I know you're waiting for the announcement. Julian and I will jump the broom on December 15! Invitations going out this week, and I hope to see you there in eight months.

And just like that, I spiraled.

"She's really going to marry him. There's no second chance for us. It's a done deal."

"What's a done deal?" Diana asked as she returned with two drinks. She handed me the drink and I handed her my cell phone.

"Duuuh, what did you expect?"

I was at a loss for words and all I could do was shake my head in defiance of my reality.

"Biyell you knew their history, and this is her happy ending. Now if you love GIGI the way you say you do then, you would stop feeling like this is a great loss and realize that the perfect woman for this Biyell is still out there. Let it go and go find the one you're supposed to be with. It's obvious Tiffany ain't the one."

Her words cut me like a belt of razors, but it was the truth. Julian was Tyra's happily ever after, and it was time for me to accept it. The part I hate is while GIGI is living her best life, I'm cursed with *Tiffany the wino*.

"Look at it this way, it could be worst."

"How do you figure?"

"What if Derinda is the one Glenn has wanted all of these years, but only settled for me because she didn't want him?"

"Lady Diana –"

"...just call me Diana."

"No problem.... but you have to know by now that Uncle Glenn loves you more than..." She cut me off again.

"I only know what he says, and now Derinda is back in his life."

"Diana, I don't see it that way. Just because Glenn has found Erica doesn't mean he has to interact with Derinda."

"I guess you didn't notice it, huh?"

"Notice what?"

"Derinda and I? We're basically the same woman."

And she wasn't lying about that, they're almost identical. Same caramel complexion, same high cheekbones, and feline eyes, same slender build, and the same hair. To say they haven't seen each other in over three decades, it was clear why Glenn had a dilemma deciding between Diana and Derinda.

I remembered he said.

I have never been in a dilemma between a good woman and a hoe. My dilemma was having two good women and the inability to decide.

Seeing them in the same room, I could definitely understand, but I still think Diana is prettier than Derinda.

Diana's glass was near the bottom while my glass was still half-full.

"You know what hurts me the most tonight...after I ran out, as you say, I waited by my car. I wanted to see how long it would take Glenn to come after me." She bottom off the rest of her drink.

"Now come on Diana, you know that's not fair...the man just discovered that Erica was his daughter. Cut him some slack."

"...cut him some slack?" Her head bent to the left. "It was twenty-two minutes before he hopped out of that reception hall.

Did you hear me? It was twenty-two painfully honest minutes I paced back and forth before I saw his face, and there still wasn't the concern I expected. *What about me? I'm his wife, don't I count anymore?* Nope, I guess not. But it's cool, no one came to check on me."

"Diana please don't," the palm of her hand silenced me.

"Biyell the way I feel is simple, I'm too old to fight over something that's mine. If that's where he wants to be then I will hold the door open." She stood from her pool chair. "I'm going to pour me another stiff one… don't stay out here too long – the mosquitoes will eat your-ass up."

Then came another chirp from my cell phone – it was a call from Tiffany – I sent her drunk ass straight to voice mail.

CHAPTER 8

8:45 p.m.

RASTA

It was that transitional moment of an eventful day. After all the pictures were snapped, and I endured the last pinch of the cheek from my aunts, and the last slap on the back from my uncles. In that opulent hour after all of the wedding guests are gone, when it is just you and the person you married lying shoulder to shoulder on the thirtieth floor of a hotel, that's when it finally dawns.

"We're married," I said as my fingers slid inside of Kayla's.

"Yes, we're married and I'm *Mrs. Kayla Ross* for the rest of my life.

"Yes, you are, and I get to come home to this beautiful woman for the rest of my life."

"And when my body and face changes?" I felt the weight of her eyes as I gazed beyond the ceiling into the heavens.

"The beauty I'm referring to doesn't change with time or body or wrinkle, it's that inner beauty I felt in that McDonalds.

That's who you are, and the reason I married you." She pressed a heavy kiss against my sore cheek. I smiled.

"You do know this is the part where you savagely rip off this dress and have your way with me. After all, I'm all yours now." She snickered.

"Yea, I was going to get to that part, but I can't feel my legs."

"Me either!" we burst into laughter.

"Can we just lie here and count the tiles in the ceiling. We have forever… right?"

"The reason I married you #1242, we're always in perfect sync." Kayla pressed the second kiss on the same sore cheek.

That's what I loved about Kayla, she was easy to love. Doing life with her was a cool breeze. Gone were the endless qualifications that came with Ladashia and gone was the emotional entrapment that came with Shameka. My wife wanted a low-stress relationship, and I needed the same.

Strangely, she never asked how I felt about the fact that she was married to Timothy, and I never mentioned his name – with the exception of today.

"So how did it feel when you saw his face?"

"His face?"

"You know who – how did it feel to see Timothy again?"

She rolled onto her stomach and buried her face into a pillow.

"Well…?" I continued to press.

"We're talking about this… tonight?"

"Yes, we're talking about this."

"I always wondered when I would see him again because New Orleans is so small, and we were bound to run into each other, but I never expected to see him at my wedding. I have to admit, I was caught off guard, but I saw Diana and my mother fist bump, and that's when I figured it out."

"Did you feel vindicated?"

"Not really…"

"Explain."

"I didn't feel vindicated because I closed that chapter of my life. When he tossed those divorce papers across that table and waited for my signature, I left that marriage, and everything I felt for him in that kitchen. When I finally found myself again is the day, I saw you for the second time, and I never looked back."

All my life I wanted a woman to feel this way about me. Even if I were penniless, she would still feel like the luckiest woman in the world to have me. This is that feeling Jarvis wrote about in his book when he described sitting on the sofa or glued together in bed all day – shutting the world out completely. I finally have that love he found in Briana, the love that didn't make sense but satisfied every internal need. I finally have a woman who loves me, but most importantly, she likes me. I am rich.

"If I didn't have to snatch Tiffany by the back of her neck, this day would have been flawless." Her eyes thinned and lips tightened.

"I've been meaning to ask you about that. What's the deal? Why did she play my boy like that?"

"It so frustrating to explain. Since high school, Tiffany loved to drink. That's how she landed in that situation earlier tonight."

"You better know it, if I hadn't tagged you in when I did, this part of the night would have ended for you at the hospital with Tiffany, and at Central Lockup for me with Biyell."

"I like to sip just like the next person, but for Tiffany, it's *Jekyll and Hyde*, she becomes a different person altogether. I've never seen anything like it."

"…but I thought she was doing the *ministry thing*?"

"She is, and very active at her church, as long as she… doesn't drink. Part of the reason she submerged herself into the church was due largely to an incident that happened. One of those tragic times she had too much...."

"Is that the Tracey incident you reminded her about tonight?"

"Unfortunately, it is."

"What's the deal with Tracey?"

"Sweetie, if you don't mind… could we talk about this another time? I don't want to go there tonight."

"It's that serious?"

"Yes, and my wedding night is not the night to open that box, but I will. I promise."

"Not a problem…"

"On a lighter note, Erica is Uncle Glenn's long-lost daughter…"

"Shocked the hell out of me."

"But how are you guys going to handle that with Telly?"

"What do you mean?"

"Are you comfortable with Telly dating Erica?"

"No, and we will address it."

"Well, to me it would seem sort of urgent with his history and all…"

It was then that I rose on my elbows and gazed down.

"and what history have you heard about?"

"All of it?"

"…but I never mentioned anything about Telly, not once the entire time we dated. How would you know about his history?"

"For starters, why are you so defensive?"

"Not defensive, just curious…that's all. Who engaged you in a conversation about Telly and why?"

"…it's not important, forget I asked."

"Kayla…"

"…I guess I have to fess up since you're my husband and all." Playfully she pouted. "I read that book Jarvis wrote, which was very good by the way."

"So… from the book, which mentions no names, you were able to match the real person with the character?"

"Well, that and…" She turned away from me and faced the open door that led to the bathroom.

"Kayla…" I huffed.

"Promise me you will not confront her if I tell you…"

"Who Kayla?"

"Promise me first, and then I will tell you."

"Okay, I promise. Who shared information about Telly?"

"Briana. Tonight. But it was out of concern for Erica."

"So, what were you two planning to do?"

"You three."

"Who's the third person?"

"Diana."

"So, my wife, Jarvis's wife, and Glenn's wife were going to circumvent us and go straight to Erica with the truth about Telly?"

"Yes?"

"And when did you hatch this plan?"

"Tonight, while you guys were outside. So, this was prior to us discovering that Glenn is Erica's father."

"Right after he proposed, we had a *meeting in the ladies room.*"

We were on the clock to address this issue with Telly. It couldn't wait until after I returned from my cruise. It had to get resolved tomorrow. We can't have our wives getting involved, it could destroy the continuity of our brotherhood and break our group into factions. I reached for my phone to text Uncle Glenn.

Our cruise leaves on Sunday, therefore, I have the better part of the morning to have a *come to Jesus* meeting with Telly and the crew. I sent the text.

Hey, have you made it home yet?

Glenn: I'm pulling up now.

We need a meeting in the morning – urgent.

I'm already on it.

CHAPTER 9

9:05 p.m.

TELLY

Text from Heather: *Do you have something hard for me to suck on?* Yes, I do. *Heather: Will you bring it?* YES! *Wonderful! My flight arrives at 5:15* See you tomorrow.

CHAPTER 10

9:05 p.m.

GLENN

I arrived home to find a dimly lit house with no signs of life. I knew Diana was in here somewhere. I saw her shoes by the kitchen counter, and her purse hanging off the back of a chair, but she was nowhere in sight. I'd hope to find her on the sofa with a glass of Hennessy on the rocks, and a stone face, but not a chance. She forced me into a game of *hide-and- seek*, she'd made sure of it.

Time to search every room.

As I made my way down the hall that led to our bedroom, I could tell it was vacant because of the thick darkness, but I made sure. The master bedroom was ruffled, and the master-bath was still in disarray from this morning. Nevertheless, no sign of Diana.

Despite the pain in my leg and my armpit, I suffered through it and continued my search in and out of all guest rooms, but still no sign of my wife. Exhausted I made my way back to the kitchen and then on to the patio and looked towards the pool – that's when I saw her.

"Mind if I join you?"

"It's your house as much as it's mine."

"Diana, I handled things wrong tonight…"

"Really…how *so*?"

"When I was introduced to my daughter, then slapped in the face with the realization that my Erica… is also Telly's Erica, and he's planning to marry her – I blacked out. That was too much on my nervous system, far more than I could handle. When you left the room… I thought you would come right back, then you didn't return. Please forgive me, I wanted you to be a part of the moment."

"That was your moment and everything that happened tonight was meant to happen. I have no regrets, and neither should you."

She seemed a little to calm to be my wife, like she'd smoke the best weed in Colorado. I expected an argument. I expected glass items thrown at my head. I expected one of her over the top confrontations. I expected Diana, but this wasn't her. This was someone else. An unfamiliar woman who reached a resolve, a resounding conclusion, without any input from me. In the swath of time from the reception to our new home, something had changed about my wife. It's spooky and extremely uncomfortable.

Seated at poolside in a pink housecoat, with her hair tied in a polka-dot scarf and a swarm of mosquitoes was a first. She hated mosquitoes.

"Being out here has done a lot to quiet my mind, and relax my body, but I'm about to head in, it's been a long day."

"So that's it, you have nothing else to say?"

"I'm not sure what you expect me to say? You apologized for the way you handled things. I told you there's no apology needed. What else is there to discuss. Tonight, we both discovered things we didn't know, and not all of it was bad. So, it worked out."

"...I don't understand."

"...and neither did I until ten minutes before you arrived. I think it's called an epiphany."

"And what was your epiphany?"

"It's simple, there are things in life that require natural sweeteners to make them taste better. Like for instance, we received the settlement from your injury, and it made life better. You have found your daughter, and that has instantly made life better. The things we sprinkle on life that makes each day palatable, that's what this day has been about. Good night."

I tried to keep up with her as she strolled to the patio, then onto the kitchen, but to no avail.

I wanted Diana at the table with me. I wanted to introduce her to Erica at the reception. I wanted us to enjoy this miracle together. It doesn't have to be something that I experience separate for my wife, finding my daughter adds to this family – not deducts from us. But not tonight, from down the hall near the first guestroom, I heard the door slam.

She has shut me out.

I have gained something I've always wanted, and now I feel as if I'm losing the one person who made my life worth living. If finding my daughter was the additional sweetener she spoke of – why can't we enjoy this delight together?

CHAPTER 11

June 3, 2018
9:10 a.m.

GLENN

After the wonderful news last night, I fell asleep alone, and woke up alone, but not by choice. I can understand that she's upset, but I've never known Diana to leave the house without kissing me before she headed out, and I've always known her itinerary, but not today.

I'm torn.

Part of me longs to hold her.

Part of me is angry for the way she's reacting.

This nonchalant, whatever, matter-of-fact way she has handled me is uncalled for. Diana has no right to treat me this way. If anyone should have an attitude, then I'm the only one in this house with the indelible right to act shitty. Instead, I tried to reason with her and keep the peace between us, but Diana is Diana and it always has to be about her, even on a day I've anticipated my entire adult life, she has pissed all over it.

But I miss us, and for that reason, I feel stupid.

"And what exactly did she mean by there are things we add to our lives to make it sweeter? Am I not that sweetener in her life?

ding ding dong doooong - ding ding dooooong dooooong

The agonizing thoughts about my wife were disrupted by a ballad of fine-tuned cathedral bells that traveled across my ceiling. Across my spacious living room (that connected to a formal dining room) I hopped to the door, all while praying my old reliable leg didn't slip on this brand-new floor. I know this may sound strange, but I do miss my apartment, especially when someone's at the door.

In my old two-bedroom love-nest, I could always count on that narrow hallway to brace along the way, but not here. This house has taught me that bigger isn't always better, unless it involves me growing three more inches on my love tool. It doesn't feel like home, not in the least.

About halfway to the foyer, I could see through the glass in the large mahogany doors the person who rung the bell. It was Rasta. The fact that I could tell it was Rasta only added to my *Buyer's Remorse.*

I loved the surprise of the unknown guest and guessing who was at the door from the cadence of their knock, but with this monstrosity of a house. Not to mention Diana's obsession with an open floor plan, for someone walking their dog the curb-view of our house was like the window display of a furniture store. Without regard to my personal preference, it is what she wanted, and I agreed because I wanted Diana to be happy. Always. Anyhow. All the time.

ding ding dong doooong - ding ding dooooong dooooong

"*Got-dammit* I'm coming." I could hear Rasta's laughter through the mahogany doors. With a twist of the bolt lock, I let him in.

"Why are you ringing that damn bell when you have a key?"

"Because watching you boing-boing your-ass to the door is what I live for."

"Well, I hope you enjoyed it because that's the last time." We dapped and hugged.

"Good morning Teedie Diana," Rasta yelled down the hall that led to our bedroom.

"She left out early this morning, chances are she's at your mom's house. That's where she goes whenever she's pissed off."

"Uncle Glenn, I figure she would be after last night. My advice would be to give her time to recover. Last night was a lot for all of us, she'll come around... I'm sure."

"I hope so, but until then I'm preparing for forty days and forty nights of storms. Diana has always been hypersensitive at the slightest hint of Derinda, and I'm afraid that entire blockbuster at the reception sent her over the ledge."

"...which is why I'm here bright and early this morning. We need to have a meeting before the meeting."

"But I didn't expect you this early, I figured after all of that happy-cat Kayla dropped on you all night, I wouldn't see you for a month." Rasta blushed a little.

"Unc' we were so exhausted last night – we fell asleep in our clothes. I rubbed her booty four times and she kissed the back of my hand twice – that's how we consummated this marriage."

My favorite song by Luther Vandross is not one of his famous love ballots but an upbeat jam called *The Glow of Love*. That's what Rasta had this morning, and every day since West Jeff Hospital. That incandescent bulb, that phosphorescent glimmer of love was unmistakable. Even his complexion was clearer, and though he had always towered over me before he married Kayla, I could swear Rasta has grown to seven feet since he started dating her.

Joy is beautiful.

"Rasta why are you lying to me early this morning...you started humping her leg in the elevator and you know it." I teased.

"Uncle Glenn, I'm as serious as a flying cockroach in a Cafe. We were dead on arrival. And what little energy she did have was drained in making sure Tiffany made it home alone, and not with Josh."

"Least we forget to cover Tiffany this morning."

"Do we have enough time…? *Wow-Wow-Wow*. What the hell was up with Tiffany?"

"Rasta-man, that was tough to watch, but good thing you made it across the dance floor before Biyell. That pony song would have turned in to *Everybody Was Kung Fu Fighting.*"

"Yea, that's one of three issues we need to cover before I board this cruise ship tomorrow. My fear is I will return from this honeymoon to find our business partner relationship has been severed because of Tiffany and Biyell. I have to prevent this from spilling over."

"Especially since we have broken ground on six lots." I placed a cup of coffee in front of Rasta. "Tiffany and Biyell need to fix this quarrel ASAP."

"That's exactly what Kayla decided this morning, we need to fight this war on two fronts. As we speak, she's over at Tiffany's place."

"Isn't that cute?"

"What's cute?" Rasta asked from the other side of the breakfast table.

"You're doing your best impression of me. Putting out fires, all while talking sense into a bunch of nutcases and sex addicts. Just when I thought all of my talking was in vain. Where's my camera? You're acting all grown-up and shit. *Lord, you can take me right now.*" I bent in laughter.

"Call it what you want Uncle Glenn, I've invested too much time and energy in this company to have it go up in smoke over a drunk bridesmaid. Not to mention, I've never made this much money in my life."

"Hell, neither have I. This lawsuit money was a gift from heaven, but since I have invested with you and Biyell, we haven't touched one penny of that money. Fuck Tiffany and Biyell kindergarten-boyfriend-girlfriend nonsense. Fuck that."

Fuck that is right," Rasta sipped his coffee "I have momentum for the first time in life, I'm running with the wind instead of against. We're not breaking this momentum over a drunk bridesmaid."

"But not just any drunk bridesmaid…"

"You›re right, Tiffany is a drunk bridesmaid who just happens to have another classroom full of first-time home buyers. All of whom are toting around a 700 Credit Score. I agree. Fuck that." We fist bumped across the table.

"On another note, I forgot to congratulate you?"

"What for?"

"Becoming a new dad and grandfather. All in the same night. How does it feel?"

"Rasta my brother, I don't have the words. My beautiful little baby is all grown up, with two adorable little girls. The best part was hearing her call me daddy all night, and the girls called me grandpa. It's the most addictive weed I have ever smoked. I never wanted the night to end. And if it couldn't get any better, they're coming over tomorrow for dinner – which will give me today to corner Telly and get him to call off this engagement."

"…or we purge the fuck out of Telly."

"You better fuckin' believe it," I said in a deep territorial voice. "Before we kick off this meeting, you ate? I'm about to put on a pot of grits."

"I'm stuffed, we had our first breakfast together as husband and wife at the hotel. I have to admit, it was hard to chew looking across the table at a woman that gorgeous, and she's all mine."

"*Look at you, all in the bliss of Kayla.*" I teased, as I poured a cup of grits in a medium size pot, just in case the other guys wanted breakfast. "And as often as you can, eat breakfast with your wife. Get into the groove where your day starts together and ends together. Even when Diana worked nights, I made sure she had a hot breakfast plate waiting. We had a good groove for a long time."

"How hard could it be to catch a groove when you're a stay

at home husband?"

"Now that's where you're wrong," I lit the fire under my favorite cast iron skillet then cracked four eggs. "That asshole who ran me over in the *Port-A-Potty* made me a stay at home husband, but long before my accident, every Sunday I would fire up breakfast, while she turned the television on CBS Sunday Mornings. That was our thing, and every week started the same way. And before you know it, you two will catch that same groove."

"I hear you, Uncle Glenn."

"You better hear me good because you should know by now that it's not getting married but staying married. That's where the work comes in. But anyway, what was it you wanted to talk about?"

"Jarvis & Briana..." Rasta poured himself another cup of coffee.

"Oh shit...I'm all ears, let's hear it."

CHAPTER 12

9:20 a.m.

RASTA

There was so much to talk about, but so little time to cover it all. To help with the flow of the morning, I decided to tackle the items that were the most urgent. I had Erica & Telly, Jarvis breaking code with Briana, and I felt a personal responsibility for the ordeal with Tiffany, being that I had a part in those two connecting. That is the downside to being a matchmaker and why I wanted no part in Biyell & Tiffany hooking-up. When the newness of the courtship wears off, and they grow tired of faking a persona – somehow the matchmaker is the blame.

My wife was the matchmaker, which has me on the hook as well.

Something else that is bothering me is I built this house. I remember how happy my aunt and uncle were on the day they moved in, but the atmosphere in here has changed. This air is stuffy. Uncle Glenn seems worried; I can see it in his face. He's trying to function and act normal, but he's doing a poor job of convincing me.

The first signs that something is deeply troubling Uncle Glenn is when he starts burning the food. The grits have bubbled over the sides of the pot twice.

"The reason I wanted to get here before the crew is because of Jarvis and Briana."

Uncle Glenn shot me a cold stiff look "don't tell me Jarvis has cheated on Briana?"

"No, it's nothing like that, but he has cheated on *us* in a roundabout way."

"Cheated on us? How so?"

Uncle Glenn lowered the burner on the stove and stirred, but it was too late. The smell of scorched grits filled the air.

"Last night after Tiffany made the announcement about Erica, I couldn't help but notice Briana's reaction. After dragging Jarvis outside my suspicions were confirmed, he has been pillow talking our personal business."

Uncle Glenn cleared his throat "how personal."

"As in everything about us. As in she knew everything about Telly."

"Oh really?"

"Yes, everything. He claimed it was because she edited the book, but I think the breach is far more extensive. Last night I intercepted a plot whereas Briana, Kayla, and your wife were planning to have a meeting with Erica."

"Oh really? A meeting?"

"Yes, the same meeting we're planning with Telly, they were planning with Erica, and of course I shut it down, and *cursed-his-ass* out for gossiping our personal affairs. The issue that remains is the obvious elephant in the room."

"There's no elephant, and no goat, and no duck. Telly isn't marrying my daughter. Not happening."

"We agree on that much, but what's your approach?"

"There's only one approach, to tell him straight up. End that engagement bullshit on good terms, with respect, and Erica will never hear a word about his past from me. This offer ends at twelve midnight."

"Or what?"

"Or I will knock on Erica's door eight o'clock tomorrow morning and tell her everything."

"Everything?"

"Every. Fuckin. Thing. Ya heard me?"

"I can dig it."

"As far as Jarvis is concerned, how dare he discuss the confidential issues from our brotherhood. He has betrayed us. Only the people who were members of our Madden group knew the intimate details of our lives."

"I'm not sure if you noticed but Briana turns ice cold whenever Telly is around."

"I picked up on it right before Jarvis headed out. It all makes sense now. Jarvis has no right talking about our business to his wife. Talk about your own sneaky shit."

"We've become her entertainment."

"Or worse, he's trying to build himself up, by trashing us. Either way he will get called on the carpet this morning."

ding ding dong doooong - ding ding dooooong dooooong
ding ding dong doooong - ding ding dooooong dooooong

"It's open" we yelled.

In through the door came Jarvis caring the same laptop bag, but noticeably absent was his high energy, and big voice bravado. His entire demeanor was subdued like a bunch a dead beats in Child Support Court. As soon as he closed the door behind him, we both pointed to a stool at the counter.

"Good morning brothers."

"Morning…" I said while Uncle Glenn greeted him with a suspicious nod.

"Fellas let's cut right to it," Jarvis said as he placed his bag on the floor where it rested against his leg. "I know what's up and you have every reason to feel the way you do."

"…and how should we feel?" Uncle Glenn asked.

"…like I betrayed your trust in disclosing to my wife the things we confided in each other."

"…you think?"

"Rasta if I haven't learned anything over this period of reckoning, I've learned to accept responsibility for my actions –"

"Bruh, I don't mean to cut you off, but I have to," I said in a troubled voice "But you accepting responsibility after the damage has been done, doesn't minimize the fallout. Your wife has an opinion of me that did not come from her getting to know me or any of us personally, it came from you identifying who's who in your book. So, to cut to the chase – how do we go forward with you as our friend when you're blasting our business?"

"Wait, hold up now," his arms were extended and stiff. "If this is about the book, I went out of my way to conceal your identities. My book is based on our experiences, not biographies. It's fiction, and I embellished 60% of the manuscript to further protect your privacy. I even included my affair with Briana… and presented the book to you before it went live on Amazon. All of you gave me your approval to publish."

"Correct, we did give you our approval on the book because no one knew our true identities. That would have been the end of it, but you identified us with details." Uncle Glenn asked.

"To add on to Uncle Glenn question…how do we go forward with you and Briana considering she knows everyone we have ever fucked?"

Jarvis' hands pleaded.

"I get it, I do, and all I can say is I'm sorry. I truly am…"

It was then that I placed my cell phone on the counter where a webpage was displayed in my browser. I waited for a reaction, an inclination that he had prior knowledge of the website, or knew who was responsible for publishing the page, but his face was overcome with dismay.

HoeLeaks.com
It's Like WikiLeaks But For Hoes.

"When you were featured in *Essence Fest* Book Expo, someone close to me purchased your book. She was taken aback to find herself in one of the chapters, but under a pseudonym, so she didn't make anything of it, until this morning. She started receiving hits from this website. It has all of our pictures and Facebook pages. HoeLeaks.com has identified her by full name and linked back to her congressional Facebook page. Do you see where I'm going."

"Yes, I see. But who was the woman?"

"LaDeisha..."

After a gusty sigh, his chin sunk into his chest. "Rasta I never meant for any of this to happen."

"LaDeisha is working with a company called RemoveSlander. com to have the website taken down or at least scrub our personal information off the pages. The hurdle we're faced with is your book is a best seller."

"We're getting all of the hurricane, and none of the FEMA money –" Uncle Glenn said.

"...if this is over the royalties, then I am willing to split it if that would make this right."

"Nigga, did I ask you for money?"

"No."

"Did Uncle Glenn ask you for money?"

"No."

"That's because it's not about the money. It's about you benefiting from our lives in a way that has publicly humiliated us."

"Slide that phone over here. . ." Uncle Glenn demanded, ". . .and there better not have one mention of me on this HoeLeaks. com... because I'm not a hoe," Glenn said as he scrolled through the pages.

"Jarvis, I knew the exact day and time that website published, it was about three weeks ago. Out of the blue, I started to receive dozens of friend requests from women I didn't know and tagged into hate mail posts. Overnight, I became responsible for every woman with a broken heart, but I couldn't figure out why all of these women were tagging me. Then LaDeisha hits me up out the blue with HoeLeaks. What the fuck Jarvis?" I said as Uncle Glenn continued to scroll, then he stumbled on his section of the webpage.

Uncle Glenn banged the table.

"These lowdown bitches have posted all my business on this website. My home address, information about my lawsuit, my wife, it's all here. What the fuck Jarvis?"

"Guys you're acting as if I planned this…"

"This is some foul shit Jarvis, they called my house *The Honey Cone Hideout for Hoes, where average players go to perfect the art of fucking over innocent women."* Uncle Glenn eyes turned blood hot red. "Jarvis I got a good mind to douse your ass with that pot of grits."

"Uncle Glenn, please, please, you have to believe me, I didn't have anything to do with this website. I would never do something like this to you guys. You are the only family I have."

"I don't want to hear that shit, Jarvis. I need you to explain to me why in the navigation bar there's a page for Rasta, Biyell, Timothy, and Telly but none for you?" Uncle Glenn held my phone at eye level. "Where's your page?"

"I, I don't, I…"

"Jarvis the fact that all of us have a page and you don't tells me this website was created in your household," I concluded.

"Uncle Glenn. Rasta." His head osculated between us. "You have to believe me, this is my first time seeing this website."

"Then you're admitting your wife posted this?" I stood.

I've heard about websites like this, but never in my wildest dreams did I imagine I would get featured on one. That book placed us in a spotlight that caused blisters to form on my skin. It was one thing for us to know the goings-on in each other's lives, but to have Briana publish this with our faces, and the pages we appeared was a level of disgrace I have never known.

And there's my mugshot for that distribution charge, that was dismissed through a Diversion Program. And there's the Child Protection investigation when the school complained that my kids smelled like weed every morning. They even created a family reunion tree with each failed relationship on a branch, and when you clicked the branch – up popped a detailed explanation of how I destroyed a good woman.

It was like a yearbook for whoremongers, with a narrated video of how I was involved with Shameka and LaDeisha at the same time, and how I faked a suicide for attention when LaDeisha dumped me. The only people who knew I was in the hospital for suicide were the people who I play Madden with every Thursday and Jarvis was the only person constantly typing.

The website Hoeleaks.com was definitely an inside job. The only person who knew our history was Jarvis, and if he's not the guilty perpetrator, then it's his wife Mrs. Briana Napoleon.

dinnnng dinnnng dong dong - dinnnng dinnnng dong dong

"It's open!" We yelled.

"Guys I need to call my wife right quick and get to the bottom of this." Jarvis excused himself out the patio door and continued to the pool area.

"Damn, I can't get the courtesy of a *good morning* at the door? They should have never given you niggas' money." Biyell joked, but this wasn't the morning for jokes.

"Good morning B, you may want to have a seat," I suggested.

"Unc' you burning the grits? *Awwww* shit, this is serious."

Uncle Glenn hopped over to the stove and killed the flame under the scorched grits, after which he flushed down the garbage disposal.

"As I said a minute ago, you may want to have a seat for this bit of news, you might faint."

"Whoa, it's that serious."

"Yes B, it's that serious."

"Is it about Jarvis running his mouth to his wife? I figured by the time I made it, y'all would have smacked his ass around by now."

"Yes, we've covered that part, but it runs deeper than that?"

I recapped the entire ordeal LaDeisha revealed to me. Biyell clicked on his page on HoeLeaks.com and his face tensed like the onset of a stroke. His picture, his Facebook page, and a full profile, and a detailed backstory, were all featured for the world to see.

Like for instance, that Jerry Springer moment when Tamara invited GIGI to the home for dinner, was on his page. That drama when he attacked 'Big Mike' was on his page. That scene in child support court when he signed away the rights to his daughter, that letter was published for the world to see, but this time they had a name with the face. Oh, and did I mention the comments?

Fuckin Brutal, Ya Heard Me?

INTRODUCING HOELEAKS.COM
It's like WikiLeaks but for hoes.

This site was created to warn women about men like the guys featured in the bestselling book by Jarvis Napoleon. If you or someone you know has been in a relationship with any of these men, please feel free to contact us. Enjoy the comments and please share.

MzMeMyselfandCash- Three weeks ago.

I had a husband like Biyell. Confronted him, packed his crap up and threw him out. She was supposed to be my friend. She was living with me at the time. I was throwing her stuff out of my house and found the suitcase. That›s when I called her and said come get your stuff today or I›m throwing it in the street. That›s what you see in the video. Her betrayal as my friend was worse than the cheating.

GetGoneBit1985 – Three weeks ago

The one time I was cheated on by an asshole like Biyell Baltimore I didn't even raise my voice or show any kind of emotion. Honestly just packed my bags and left whilst smiling and never looked back. Best decision I ever made, never shed a tear and began dating almost immediately. If you can't see how good you had it with me then you don't deserve to have me, it's as simple as that. Yes, he tried several times to get back with me and now he's been single for a while hee hee

FuckDemFuckBoyz – Three weeks ago

Instead of getting mad at the female I would be dealing with the husband that had vows with you. She didn›t agree to vows so she›s free to do whatever. I›m not saying that makes her a good person, but I digress. Also, it›s never a good idea to have a female move into your home if you›re married. Especially if she›s cute because there will be times your husband accidentally walks in on her naked or in the shower & that seed is planted. It›s like putting a ticking time bomb beside you & daring it to go off.

ItsKadieifYouNasty – Three weeks ago

Girl run. Take him to the bank for child support and spousal support.... that mother fucka would be installing cable in his sleep fucking around with me. You hoes stupid for Biyell.

FatCatChic1979 – Two weeks ago

Tamara should have figured out when he said it wasn't his dick – thirsty ass clown. He already made a choice by having an affair for me that›s when I would be divorcing him and he›d be gone out the house, stop being a Doormat for these whorish men!

MzNOLABitchBad92 – Three days ago

It may be fun to cheat, but when you take your last breath you could get the shock of your life. Don>t do it. No beautiful girl or handsome guy is worth you spending all eternity in a hot fire, where there is no end to the pain and torment. Think about it Biyell.

PutMeDownOnIt1991 – Three days ago

Went through the same thing with my spouse and he moved in with her when I got tired of his shit. I left and after 10 years together. The Biyell type fuckface I had never married the side bitch and left her because she couldn't have kids. Best decision I ever made.

DumbBitchNoMo1988 – Two days ago

Guuuuurrrrrrl this shit on this site is a trip and a lollypop. What the purple fuck is going on when the wife and mistress seated at the kitchen table? To the Tyra/GIGI, home girl you did right. My grandmother would always say a caterpillar can change into a beautiful butterfly and fly around the world, but a dog gone be a funky dog. Do not ever settle for second best. To the other Tyra's on this page, if he wants something you are not let Biyell mangy ass go.

LovingMeSumMe4Ever – Two days ago

Kudos to Tyra for wanting better for herself, and her children. They both deserve better than this loser! And to Biyell I hope you catch something the doctors have never seen before but only your stink ass die from it.

YouAreWhoYouAreHoe14 – 16 hours ago

Part of the reason many people like the grimy men on this site cheat is because they emotional as fuck. Hormonal as fuck. Selfish as fuck. Then they discover sexual or emotional appreciation in the affair which, in turn, bolsters their confidence.» But, REMEMBER THAT EVERYTHING THAT SHINES ISN>T GOLD & THE GRASS IS NOT ALWAYS GREENER ON THE

OTHER SIDE OF THE FENCE. To Biyell and his ban of losers - may Aids be with you and you and you. Amen

IamMzWakeTFup1998 – 10 hours ago

To Tyra I say If he cheated on you with her then he will cheat on you with another. I don't understand people who are with people that are cheating, and they know it and don't care. I'm not saying that's the case, but I think Tamara knew the entire time. Please love yourself enough and value yourself enough to get someone with morals and values. Anyway, I loved the book and you should also read Infallible, somebody finally told the truth about these fucked up men.

GurlWithGun22 – One hour ago

I dated a married man like Biyell who lied all along. These dudes will lie at all cost. I was mortified after this! You know it's bad when the wife tries to warn you like the CDC. The wife said she caught him twice, once in her bed with the woman from the day care, and the second time with her younger sister. He was 100% Asshole just like Biyell. Guard your heart and watch out for these gutter ass married men!!

NOLAWifeFromThatMagnolia – One hour ago

I had a co-worker who had to commit her grandmother because she had lost her mind behind some cable dude. She said that guy was visiting her grandmother at least three times a week. Then realized something was wrong when friends started asking why was the cable guy by their grandmother so much? Then the lady started wearing a night gown all day as if she was expecting her husband to come home, braiding her hair in corn rows. If you ask me, Biyell fit the description of the dude who was fucking her grandmother. Can't no body tell me no difference.

ImSayinGurl666 – Just now

Biyell remember me, Lizzardi Street? Karma is me xoxox

CHAPTER 13

9:45 a.m.

JARVIS

After several attempts Briana finally answered the phone. She was irritated because I called her during church service, and I was irritated because she constantly sent me to voicemail. Briana and her best friend Sierra started attending a new church about four blocks away from our apartment. They grew up in her father's church, but after Sierra received that Christmas card (the pastor's family greeting minus Briana) she canceled her membership.

Having our kids grow up in Church was still very important to my wife, but I couldn't give a shit. I believe in God, but that's about the extent of it. In the *Gospel According To Me*, I cannot see paying a pastor for a free Jesus, but my wife has to have a *Church Home*, even though she doesn't have a key to that church home.' In fact, our first argument was over the amount of money she was '*Tithing*' which totaled 10% of my first royalty check.

"Briana, I know this has to be a mistake" I yelled as I inspected our account online. "You gave $4200? You wrote a check for forty-two hundred fuckin dollars."

"Yes…and watch your language in front of our children." She replied in a proud stern voice, which only pissed me off even more.

"I'm sorry but… why would you do that?"

"Because I believe in tithing, and the money was needed for the building fund."

"Wait, I just want to make sure I'm following you. . ." I stumped over to where she fed the kids their dinner. "you gave your church $4200 of the money we have worked for without discussing it with me… first?"

"I did discuss it with you…"

"No, you did not Briana…"

"Jarvis, think back to that morning I said we should give *God a first fruit offering*. You agreed…"

"I thought you were talking about a fruit basket, not forty-two hundred-fuckin-dollars."

"Well, that's what first fruit means, the first 10% goes to God. And you will not use that language in front of our children unless you want them cussing in pampers."

"Briana if they could talk, they would ask the same question, why in the fuck you would give a pastor 10% of our money," I demanded an answer, but she was more concerned about my tone. "Briana that money didn't go to God…it went in the pocket of your Pastor. Why are we financing a 'church home' when we're paying rent in an apartment?" That argument was last year, and though I disagreed with the tithing bullshit, we carved her out a salary so she could tithe off that amount.

The moment I heard her voice on the other end I went off about the HoeLeaks.com website. After I nearly blew a gasket, she finally got a word in.

"Jarvis for the tenth time, I don't know what you're talking about. I haven't created a website based off your book!"

"Briana that entire website is full of information that I shared with only you. No one knew these guys real names or the intricate details of the women they dated." I could hear my son starting to crank up in the background.

"Jarvis...what you're not going to do......... is accuse me of something I did not do." She hissed. "Because of the mistake I made with you, my name is dirt, but I've worked diligently to become a better person. It's true, I can't stand the people you call friends, but with two babies, and little help from you when you're not writing, I barely have time to check my email let alone build a website."

"So, you're saying you didn't create the website?"

"I. Did. Not. Create. That. Website. But I do plan to visit it as soon as I'm out of church?"

"Briana, this is serious. These guys are ready to drown me in this pool, I need to know for sure that you didn't have anything to do with – "

That is when she left the conversation and started speaking to God.

"Lord I'm trying to live right but I'm about to go off on my husband, just letting you know in advance..."

"Do you think, perhaps, Sierra could have?"

"No."

"You two are open about everything, what makes you so sure she wasn't the one?"

"But not that, and Sierra is a true friend in the sense that she's cheering for all of this to become a distant memory. The last thing she would do is dredge up all the dirt that you wrote in the book."

"Okay, I have to take your word for it."

"Jarvis is that all?"

"Yes, what time should I expect you?"

"You wouldn't have to ask if you were here with your family instead of by Uncle Glenn."

"I promise, next week I will accompany you to church."

"Whatever Jarvis, I'm not holding my breath. And since

you're in the devil's den – have you guys discussed the plan to protect Erica from Telly?"

"So, you're admitting that you have a running interest in Erica and Telly?"

"What I have is a concern for a woman who is in emotional danger, and I'm trusting my husband to protect her." Her words were sharp. "While the baby is quiet, I'm headed back to my pew. See you when I get home."

"And when will that be?"

"Bye Jarvis."

I reentered the house in the middle of a full-fledged argument over my fate. All of them blamed me for the website, because I was the author of the book. Recently my sales on Amazon Kindle skyrocketed. I think that was due in part to this young man named Emanuel on Facebook – the guy has a huge following.

Each night for the past thirty days, he has read one chapter of my book during a Facebook live broadcast. I couldn't pay for better marketing if I tried. The only problem it seems is the popularity of the book has sparked a curiosity about the characters, and their true identities. I never anticipated HoeLeaks.com, then again, I never anticipated selling two hundred thousand copies.

"Bruh. Bruh. Your old lady taking down this site, right? Right? What time today?" Biyell threatened me with two stiff fingers aimed in my direction, axing violently after each spoken word. The sweat that showered off the sides of his face was my cue that things were about to get physical, but my wife wasn't the guilty party, and I believe Briana.

"My wife said she's not the one who published that website…"

"What!" Biyell yelled.

"It's not her site, nor did she gossip about us to her girlfriend."

Eerily, the decimals in his voice dialed backward from ten down to one. His eyes honed beyond me, beyond the patio, beyond the pool. That's when I became concerned. Biyell's anger is like standing on the beach prior to a tsunami. At first, everything pulls back, then it all comes rushing forward with devastating force.

"And you're taking her word even though it's clear that no one else could have known all of my personal business? You're taking her word? On that website – my full name, a picture of my old cable truck, and a picture of my truck outside. I know you're all in love with your niece, but really bruh…you believe she's innocent?"

"She's not my niece…she's my wife."

"If you say so…but you still haven't answered me."

"Biyell I understand you're upset, hell I'm just as pissed because someone used my book to post personal information about my friends, and I will spare no cost to fix this, but I have to believe my wife."

Biyell cut the distance between us in half.

"I want to make sure I heard you…so help me out here. Your wife said she didn't do it and that's the end of this?"

"Biyell, I will fix this but if you're looking for someone to pin this on –that person is not my wife."

"I guess you and your wife only leaves me one option, but somebody has to get fucked up for this?"

Rasta moved from the end of the counter and inserted himself between us.

"No one is getting fucked up over something that we need to resolve as grown men. If Jarvis is saying it wasn't his wife, I don't see the reason to lie."

"Rasta, none of the lowdown shit Jarvis did when his wife was battling cancer is on this website. The reason I feel this was done by Jarvis or his wife is because all of his vile shit was left out, while everything about me is blasted on this site. And hardly any of it is true…"

"But the part about you and that grandmother was true."

"Rasta fuck you… I only fucked that lady one time."

"That's a lie…" Uncle Glenn slid in.

"If I fucked her once or nine times a week is nobody's muthafuckin' business, Ya heard me?"

"You did... fuck that old lady nine times a week." Uncle Glenn sipped his coffee.

"That ain't your fuckin business either." Biyell pointed at Uncle Glenn with two sharp fingers. "All I know is...my name better get erased off that website immediately, or it's going down in this bitch."

"It's going down outside, this ain't that black lacquer furniture, and you niggas will not break up all my fancy shit. *Ya heard me?*"

Biyell stood less than two feet from me with both fists clinched. Ready to knock me the fuck out. I wasn't in the mood to get knocked the fuck out. I backed away from him four feet. Biyell cut the distance in half once again.

"Just remember, I gave you a chance to resolve this shit the right way."

"Biyell! Jarvis! The purpose of this meeting wasn't to brawl." Rasta stood in the narrow gap between us. "LaDeisha hired a company to resolve this nightmare. The first task is tracking down who published our personal information, and the second task is getting all of it removed. She put in a call and said I could expect an update no later than Tuesday. Of course, I will be in the middle of the Gulf by then, but it would help all of us if you two would handle things until I get back, without killing Jarvis."

"You mean double homicide, because if B thinks I'm going to stand here and pluck my fingers while he's kicking my ass, then that nigga in for another surprise."

"Then let's take this outside." Biyell walked towards the patio.

"Bruh if that's how you want to handle it then let's go — but you're not going to disrespect me or my wife." Jarvis followed.

"Fuck you and your niece!"

"And fuck you Biyell..."

dinnnng dinnnng dong dong - dinnnng dinnnng dong dong

"Now that's enough, I need both of you to have a seat." Uncle

Glenn held on to Biyell's arm to prevent him from opening the patio door.

dinnnng dinnnng dong dong - dinnnng dinnnng dong dong

"It's open" we yelled.

In walked Kayla followed by Tiffany.

CHAPTER 14

Mid City
10:20 a.m.

ERICA

My mother has yet to answer her phone, but it does not matter because I plan to pay her a visit this morning. After slapping me in the face with a new reality, she has decided to crawl under a rock as if nothing happened, but I'm crawling under that rock with her. We will talk. She owes me that, and so much more.

An old fashion sit down at the kitchen table with two cups of coffee and the whole story is what she owes me, and I plan to collect, but first I must collect myself. My emotions are scattered.

I'm cautious.

I'm confused.

I'm concerned.

And *I'm complete* because I have finally been made whole. I have a caring father who has sought to be a part of my life, my entire life, and he said last night was a dream come true. The interesting part of it all is, I wasn't going to attend the wedding, but Telly insisted. The more I tried to back out of it, the more he overcame every objection I had, but late Friday night I conceded. Thank God I did.

I didn't voice it at the time, but deep down I was so resentful. For so long I felt like a tucked away secret. Telly never introduced me to any of his friends, until this day I haven't met his mother or sister, then out the blue it's *we need to attend the wedding as a family*.

Other than dinner, we haven't engaged in one activity as a family – which justified my reluctance but thank God I didn't listen to the bellowing voice of resentment, because I would have missed the greatest night of my life. Just when I'd resolved to be a *long-term-live in-boo-thing*, he proposed. I didn't think I could forgive him for that sexual escapade, the one I wasn't invited to, but last night I forgave him. Just when I thought that my first marriage was all I deserved, Telly dropped down to one knee.

On one knee for me?

This pitiful mess he met in the hall of family court?

The one who was six hours away from losing her daughters?

Yes, he dropped to one knee for me, and miraculously every systemic feeling of rejection I carried all of these years began to heal.

A man wanted me to be his wife.

A man wanted to know more about me.

It all came together in one night.

My mother could not lie to me another minute even if she wanted too, the truth was far more relentless than her deceit. I know my mother is not the first woman to lie about the whereabouts or identity of her child's father, but what kept me awake last night was how determined she was to preserve her lie. Pride mixed with vindictiveness is a toxic combination. That is what has become of the relationship with my mother.

She has never, since the invention of the cell phone, sent my calls to voicemail, and here we are this morning, I've gone to voice mail twenty-two times.

"Baby what time is it?" Telly asked with a voice scratchy from sleep.

"It's 10:34…"

"I know you're exhausted from last night, but if I recall, wasn't there a gathering of your buddies this morning at Uncle Glenn's, oops, I meant to say my father's house?"

"Yes, but I'm skipping out."

"Are you sure, because last night it seemed urgent?"

"I thought it was but it's not, I'm sleeping in this morning."

"Okay, if you say so, honey. Before you dozed off again can I ask one more question?"

"Can it wait…?"

"Not really."

"What is it?" He opened one eye.

"Have you spoken with my father yet?"

"…about what in particular?"

"About marrying his daughter… it is customary to ask for his blessings."

"No, I haven't, but that won't be a problem, I'll get his blessing."

"What makes you so sure? Last night several relationships were changed in the snap of a finger."

"Don't worry about it sweetheart, he'll give me his blessings."

"And you're probably right. But it would give me peace of mind to know for sure. So, could you still ask him if he approves?"

"…why wouldn't he approve?" His left eye joined our conversation. "What are you insinuating?"

"I'm not insinuating anything, it's just, I've never had an active father, all of this is new to me. And yes, it's been less than a day, but I do know that sometimes fathers have concerns."

"And what type of concerns would he have?"

"You know, the type of concerns a father would rather re-solve in a one on one setting with you. Being that this is my first time getting married with my father present, I only want positive vibes and energy. I know I'm going on and on but, does that make sense?"

"Yes, it makes sense, and if it would put you at ease, I will formally ask Uncle Glenn, I mean, your father for your hand in marriage."

"*Oooh* thank you thank you." My giddy moment was disrupt-ed by his cell phone. Not from a ringtone, but the buzzing in his night stand." Telly ignored the buzzing, which annoyed me.

"Are you going to get that?" I insisted.

With an agitated huff, he rolled towards the nightstand and exhumed his phone, silenced it, then reburied it in the night-stand. He must have felt my eyes asking the question because he twisted back to me and said: "It was Rasta, I'll call him back later."

"They're looking for you, I can say that for certain because your phone has buzzed constantly. I think you should go to that gathering, and while you're there you could speak with my fa-ther."

There was something about those two words my father that felt euphoric to me, it felt magical, gratifying in a way that only a fatherless child could appreciate. Just then, I realized that I had gone my entire life without uttering those two simple words.

My father.

My daddy

My Dad.

As wonderful as it feels to say, my father, it's far more com-forting to say, my dad. I have never formulated a sentence with those two words unless I was informing someone that my father was deceased: *killed in the Gulf War.* That's what I was told, and that's what I believed. My daddy wasn't killed in the Gulf War, my daddy was on the west bank side of New Orleans this entire time – wanting to be a part of my life.

My daddy loves me.

I can't say it enough, with each utterance my senses are awakened, and my spirit is reassured. I am the sum that was calculated by two variables, my mother and my father, and at the end of the equation came: Erica. I never felt a part of anything other than my mother. That's not an indictment on her. My mother is the best mom I could have asked for, but as resourceful and loving as she is, it required another variable to create me. Having a Superman wouldn't have diminished her in my eyes and wouldn't have made her any less than a Wonder Woman.

If only she believed.

For that reason, I will stand firm and demand that Telly seek the blessing of my father, and he will have the rightful honor of handing me off. I know at this point it's little more than a formality because as my mom said Telly *and I are shacking up*, but no one can fault me for wanting to get it right this time.

Another reason I would like for Telly to ask for my father's approval is that I am fully aware that they were buddies first, and last night that friendship came in contact with a rip current that dragged it out to sea. At that table last night, I also felt an undercurrent of conversations taking place around me, that was also about me but didn't include me.

And finally, I no longer take what Telly says at face value. He lost the *benefit of the doubt.* When he stepped outside of our relationship for something, I would have given him (if I knew he wanted it) but I was never privileged to the conversation. Those X-rated exchanges he had with Heather, his 'Sex Doll' as he referred to her, that's the only reason I didn't quit him on the spot. Unlike my ex-husband who fell in love with the other woman – I gave Telly a pass because it was only sex.

Nevertheless, I have a hunch that my father also knows about that threesome – that same hunch is whispering that he has concerns about last night, but he rather speak with me tomorrow about it. Telly is avoiding that meeting this morning, that's also a hunch, but this wedding is contingent upon the approval from the father of the bride. He knows Telly far better than I do.

"Telly wake up. Telly baby, your phone is buzzing again, would you like me to answer it for you?"

I knew that would wake him up.

CHAPTER 15

June 3, 2018
10:48 a.m.

BIYELL

The groin vault ceiling in the foyer is supported by two cast iron columns that spring up from smoked wood flooring. In the center of those columns is where she stood, with her fingers interlaced, in a light pink sundress with her hair, pinned in a bun. Jarvis was three seconds from needing an appointment with a dental surgeon for some of those ultra-white fake looking teeth, if she hadn't followed Kayla through the door.

Her face was naked.

Her skin absorbed the morning rays.

She was surprisingly radiant, from the lilies that covered her open toed slippers, up to her remorseful eyes. Even the smell of burnt grits and testosterone couldn't compete with her scent.

Vanilla.

Patchouli.

Geranium.

She was intentionally plain like Jane, and wore no jewelry, and her entire demeanor was deliberately deflective, a dichotomy of principles and promiscuity. What a difference a day makes.

"Could I speak with you for a moment?" her voice was frail and subdued.

I wasn't sure if I wanted to have a word with Tiffany. I wasn't expecting her to show this morning. I was still pissed. Kicking Jarvis ass was still #1 on my *things to do* list, but she looked so guilty, yet so conscience-stricken, that I couldn't ignore her. Subconsciously my eyes found Uncle Glenn.

Go on, she came here to see you. He said with a nod.

Tiffany followed me to the rear guest room, which was just across the hall from the master bedroom, a room I've often occupied while construction continued on my house next door.

Softly she closed the door and anchored it in place, while I moved to the furthest side of the room as if she was contagious.

"First of all, I wanted to say that I am so-so sorry about last night..."

I didn't nod, or accept, or express a lick of gratitude for her apology.

"If you never speak to me again, you are well within your right. You have every right to sever any romantic connection we had. You have every right to walk away from me, but I came here this morning to beg you... not to."

Her hands wrung one inside the other, as her pinkish bottom lip trembled. Her urge to hug me was so strong – I could feel her touch from across the room – but her legs were frozen stiff by the realization that she'd fucked up on a Donald Trump level.

"I don't remember all of the events of last night, after Telly proposed to Erica, everything else is a blur, but it's written across your face, you don't believe me. It also appears that I've already lost you, so there is no incentive to lie. There are some things in life I am very good at; like business and teaching first time homeowners; but there's also one thing I fail at miserably.

I am the type of person who should never have a drink, not even social. I'm not good at it. I come from a family of alcoholics, it's like a generational curse, and that's not an excuse for my actions last night, it's who I am."

It was difficult but I fought the sudden urge to run over there and kiss her and let her know it was going to be okay because it wasn't. I made zero effort to make eye contact. I didn't want to hear any more of her lame ass excuse for all the free feels Josh enjoyed. There was no coming back from that. The thought that he could have fucked her if he wanted to was all I needed to file Chapter 7 on every romantic thing we built for nearly a year: I charged her off as a total loss.

One after the other on both sides of her face, a trail of tears dripped as she searched for different ways to say I'm sorry.

"Kayla described my behavior, and how I danced, and how I'm the scandal that everybody's talking about this morning. Her descriptions didn't sound like something I would do, but I did. I shouldn't drink, but I did. I should have been by your side throughout the reception, but I wasn't. Biyell I hope you could find it..."

"Tiffany, I have to stop you right there – because here's the part that has me floored. *You forgot you had a man.* When you mentioned how Kayla described your actions last night and how you couldn't believe it, just imagine how I felt –"

"Biyell I know, and that's why –"

"Hold up, let me finish my thought. I didn't interrupt you."

"I'm sorry, please continue..."

"You forgot me, I didn't matter, I wasn't there, I was nobody to you, on one side of the room I was managing a crisis, and on the other side of the room, my woman was making out on some dude's dick. The only way to get you off his dick was to snatch you away from him. That's what your best friend did, but only after the wedding photographers surrounded you two – the stars of the dance floor. It's like this...I know I have done my shit, and hurt a few people, and cheated on my ex-wife, and committed enough sins to loan you a few, and still enter hell as a VIP, but not to you. Not during this relationship, I never did Biyell to you." A knot in my throat made it hard to swallow.

"You are the only woman I have never violated. At the same time, you are the only woman who caused me to feel lower than carpet. Tamara did it behind my back, you did it in my face."

By this point Tiffany was on the floor seated on her legs, weeping while she tugged downward on her sundress.

"Biyell I'm so sorry if I could rewind last night, if I could fix this I would, I would do anything to fix this."

"You once dated that Josh dude?"

"No, I hadn't seen him since college."

"Did you fuck with him in college?"

"No, but I think he liked me, but we've never even gone on a date."

"So, you knew he liked you, and you still danced with him?"

"I don't remember dancing with him, I don't remember him at all."

"Okay I'll let you have that, but what about Tracey? Was Tracey a dude?"

"She was my friend."

"What's the deal? Did you get drunk and fuck her man?"

"No Biyell, what I did to her was far worse."

"For a woman, what could be worse than fucking her man?"

"You would have to trust me – I did something that was so awful that I've never forgiven myself."

"Well, if it's worse than that stunt last night, my schedule is clear for this. I got time."

"I can't talk about it. I won't. I simply came here to say I'm sorry for hurting you. Hurting people is all I seem to do lately. Please find it in your heart to forgive me…"

The more we talk the more pissed off I'm getting. To think that she had more respect for the dude from college. Josh had his way with my girl last night, and the little things that I thought were a special privilege reserved for her man, like squeezing her ass, and kissing her neck, and feeling her sexy body against mine, wasn't a privilege at all, but simply: my turn. Any Joe Blow could have enjoyed the same feels and thrills with Tiffany, and last night Josh was Joe Blow.

And it's not that I'm jealous, under the contrary, I got dude beat by a mile. I'm taller and built better. He looks like life has repoed his athleticism, and now he's fallen into the mundane routine of marriage. The dreaded place where a man no longer cares that he's growing titties. Where we become unavailable and undesirable to other women, because of a wedding band. Once we start to feel unattractive, we start to look the part and let ourselves go. I'm not saying that is the issue with Josh, but he definitely looked the part.

My recurring anger would not allow me to feel compassion for her on that floor; she deserved to be down there. Alone. All one. *By her muthafuckin-self.* Because everything she prayed for in church, I gave to her. She talked all that bullshit about *Waiting on Boaz*, even gave a speech at the singles conference about *wait for him* – all the while – *I was Boaz*. I was that dude. I handled things for her, bridged gaps for her, and put in the work for her. During that period when she was conflicted, talking about *I'm practicing celibacy* I played along with that shit for two months. Two months with no pussy is a record for me.

"Tiffany, I respect you for coming here to apologize, it takes a grown woman to admit when she's made a mistake, but…"

"Biyell please spare me the other side of *but*, I know what you're going to say. I'll fill in the blanks." It was then that she stood. The sundress clung to her chest, but her hands were too damp to care. With one hand on the doorknob, she half turned to me.

"I was so depressed and lonely before we were introduced. I can still remember Rasta saying *here's $100 that's enough to pay for a six-month membership to a website call BlackPeopleMeet, take it because there's no way I'm setting you up with Biyell.* I handed him back the money and insisted that he introduce us.

Rasta was so opposed to me getting to know you, that I had to maneuver around him and asked Kayla. That's how I came to know you."

Wait until I see Rasta, I'm kicking his ass too for that.

"Here's the one thing I'll say about your friend Rasta, he loves you like a brother, but he was wrong about you. Kayla was wrong. Uncle Glenn was wrong. Jarvis was wrong. And Diana was also wrong."

Wait one fuckin minute, all of them had something bad to say about me?

"You changed, and they should consider updating their file on you because I have never been loved with such tenderness and enthusiasm in my life. It was me Kayla should have warned you about. Thank you Biyell for the dinners, and movies, and the business opportunity, and for removing my name from the list of women who couldn't find Mr. Right."

Like a slow drawing curtain on a tragic play, Tiffany stepped into the hall, savored a final glance, as the door slowly closed.

It was finished.

CHAPTER 16

Kitchen Table

JARVIS

T iffany mustered up just enough composure to bid us a good morning, then she flashed Kayla a simple hand gesture, that suggested she would wait in the car. It didn't require an advanced degree in psychology to discern that the conversation between Tiffany and Biyell didn't produce the end result she'd hoped for.

Like Mac Makeup a layer of rejection was brushed across her face.

Oh, how I wanted to wrap my arms around Tiffany, it was so sad. Even the way she slugged to the front door was sad. Her trek from the edge of the kitchen, that veered slightly left across the living room, and finally the front door, all while carrying a backpack full of regrets had to feel like a five-mile walk, at least that's how it appeared to me.

This normally bubbly woman, who was always the loudest voice, the one filled with so much laughter and cheer, had become a distressed caricature of herself. I guess it's hard to maintain a constant state of prettiness when you're splintered inside.

After the front door clicked into the locks, it became clear that *Operation Apology* was a failure. I could not speak for everybody, but I wanted Biyell and Tiffany to work – and I was fully vested in their success. Kayla & Tiffany were friends, Rasta & Biyell friends, he was a bad boy turned good and she was this innocent little flower in the hands of a beast. Last night proved a beast could sometimes self-identify as a woman.

"You guys enjoy the rest of your morning, and don't keep my husband too long." Kayla lips connected with Rasta.

"And you make sure to tell Tiffany that it's not over until the fat lady sings – last time I saw that fat lady… she lost weight." A smile appeared on her face, then again, Uncle Glenn could make a widow laugh during a funeral.

Shortly after Kayla and Tiffany reversed out of the driveway, a guy who resembled Biyell moseyed into the kitchen, looking like a guy who just lost an entire paycheck at the casino. I wasn't expecting this Biyell. It felt awkward. Unfamiliar. Like the person seated next to you on a four-hour flight from New Orleans to New York, we're in the same space, yet strangers.

Allow me to preference more clearly, I've seen Biyell sad on many occasions, but this look was something new, this sadness originated from a lower depth.

"Biyell, I know how it feels to be you right now. I went through the same thing with Monica. What I'm about to say will sound like a poorly prepared excuse, but the difference between my ex-wife and Tiffany is – Monica was sober."

Biyell reclined in a stool that wasn't a recliner. Fixated on his kneecap as if he couldn't figure out the functionality.

"Even good girls make mistakes, but make no mistake about it, Tiffany loves you." Uncle Glenn said.

Biyell released a sigh so deep he could have flipped the table.

"Big B, hear me out." Rasta walked over and placed a hand on his shoulder. "I've never had the chance to say it because we've been so busy with construction, but I am proud of you. I'm proud of the life change you made. I'm proud to call you my business partner – you have inspired me as a father. The way you and Tyra have created a safe environment for your children in the middle of a forest fire is very impressive my brother – and uncommon. I know you're hurt, I know you're angry but I'm not going to let you regress. You gave Tiffany the best Biyell you had. And for that, I'm proud to call you my brother." Rasta threw his arms around him.

He was beyond hurt.

There are those traumatizing events that happen in life that renders that adjective totally useless as an accurate description of inner pain. Hurt is a word so all-encompassing, so universal in its ability to illustrate pain that it fits perfectly in all three categories, *Adjective, Verb, and a Noun.* Biyell was hurt to such a degree that our words seemed to bounce off him like basketballs in March.

Suddenly an alert from HoeLeaks.com appeared on my phone. I gave the guys the heads up.

A picture of Biyell.

A video of Tiffany and Josh.

The caption that read "Came with him - left with him. Karma is a Bridesmaid." Posted ten hours ago, with 120 comments.

HoeLeaks.com

ShaFromThatMagnolia – Ten minutes ago

Sister gurrrrrrl, let me tell you something! You did the right thing in hauling ass away from Biyell. From what I've read he fucks over your life. I was just telling my sister the only thing that can incapacitate me emotionally is when I think a hoe like Biyell is trying to run game on me. Next thing I know I was calling in to work tryin to catch him. I got so pissed off my ends start breaking, and my weight ballooned like a bounce house, but oh, but oh oh oh when I finally caught his as and threw his shit out my house – then my hair grew down my back, I'm keeping my hair appointment, and back in my cute drawls. Don't let these men drive you crazy – as your mind goes your money goes. Protect your mind ladies. Don't let a bitch paly with you!

ColieCoFromWaLaCo – Just now

That's good for his stink ass! God don't like ugly and what goes around comes around and leaves with another man at a wedding reception. Don't feel sorry for this dog, for every woman who breaks his heart that's a down payment on five women he fucked over.

MsHelloWorld305 – Just now

I have learned everything I know about guys and relationships from reading that book and following this website. From my limited experience as I am only 16, I am quite good at getting guys to date me and ask me out. I get good guys, too. I've found that it's so difficult keeping a boyfriend, at least for me. I get that most high school guys' priorities are not a girlfriend and so you can't expect much, and I was feeling down about it until a friend sent me the link to this website! I feel like such a strong woman now and I would say a lot of that comes from learning how to identify dangerous guys like Biyell! Sorry I left this long comment, but I have found a home in the comments section of this website.

CHAPTER 17

11:30 a.m.

ERICA

I banged on the door, but she's gone into hiding. My key no longer works. I am my mother, and I know her better than she knows herself. She also knows that I'm not leaving until she answers this door. We are identical. She heard the doorbell. She heard my car horn. She saw Rosa's name on her caller ID.

Bum-bum-bum-bum-bum-bum-bum

"Momma I can do this all day," I yell, but not a peep from inside.

My mother lives in a single-family home in the Lower 9th ward, on a street called Caffin. Our family originated from the opposite end of Caffin Ave, in a section historically known as *Back-of-town*. It was literally in the back of New Orleans – predominantly Black – with a sprinkle of Native Americans – and a pinch of the poorest White families the city could spare. Oddly enough, they all lived in peaceful harmony within the confines of segregation, none had more than the other, except for my grandparents.

My grandmother was in the funeral home business, which provided us with middle-class status, but that middle class was measured according to the wealthiest African American family in the area. When it came to women who are *stubborn to a fault*, then consider me fourth generation, my mom is third, and both of us got it honestly from my grandmother.

Other than the supplies for the funeral home and Charity Hospital, everything she needed was purchased locally. My grandmother would always boast that across the street from our home on Galvez & Caffin Ave was a movie theater, grocery store, strip mall (before they were called strip malls) and a bar.

In the center of the same community was my grandmother's pride and joy, Pugh's Mortuary.

My family was practitioners of mortuary sciences dating back to slavery, it's how my great grandfather purchased their freedom. Pugh's Mortuary was handed down to my grandmother, and when it was time to pass it on, she attempted to promote my mother to her role, but my mom hated the funeral business. She was three weeks into her career as a fifth-grade teacher at Hardin Elementary, and loved the classroom more than selling caskets, but my grandmother wasn't the type of mother who gave her children the liberty of traveling new paths.

I can still hear their last argument a few months before my grandmother pasted away from a stroke related illness.

"Derinda, you think I had a choice? Do you? You can turn your nose up in the air at the family business, but you owe this funeral home everything. From the clothes on your back to that Degree from Southern University, Pugh's Funeral Home paid for it all."

"But momma, Jesse is more than capable to keep the business going." My uncle Jesse was the oldest, but my mom was her favorite child, though she would never admit it. "You asked me to become a licensed funeral home director, and I did, even though my heart was in the classroom, I obeyed you. I contribute when you're short staffed, and manage payroll, but I do not want my daughter to grow up living in the rear of a funeral home."

"How many *goddamn'* times are you going to remind me that we lived in the rear of a funeral home? Huh? There are children in this neighborhood who would have given anything to have the clothes you wore, and new bicycles, name one of those kids in this block whose father brought them a car at seventeen? Name one! You can't because you were the only one – you ungrateful cow. Derinda that funeral home you hate so much gave you the perfect life and now you're walking out on us?"

"Mother that's all in your head, I was ridiculed every day because of this place."

"This place..."

"Yes, momma this place!" My mother stumped on the thin wood floor. "Do you know what that was like to have people scared of you because of what your parents did for a living? I never had a slumber party as a child, because kids were too afraid. I learn how to jump rope by myself. I played hop-scotch by myself. Musical chairs with just one chair. Tea parties with one invited guest, but a table set for four."

"All I know is you never went without..." My grandmother huffed.

"...mother there's more to life than money and material things."

"Then try living without money and see how far you get. We didn't sit around praying things would get better, we made them better. We didn't pray for money, we made it. We never worried about layoffs at the refinery. You know why?"

"Because death is guaranteed."

"Say it again..." My grandmother demanded.

"Death is guaranteed."

"And don't you forget it." My grandmother roared. *"From death came comfort.* Sure, we live in the rear of a funeral home, but it's the biggest house on this side of Claiborne."

"Momma, I never cared about the size of our house, or color of the Cadillac, you did." My mother's words boiled in her mouth. "Every day in the funeral home... decayed a year off my life. I hate it. I hate everything about it. The deceitful scent of the lobby, the *Red Sea* carpet, the constant parade of grief, the uninviting furniture, I hate all of it. Do you know why momma? Huh? Because every funeral I planned, and every casket selected, and each cemetery plot sold, a part of me died with the deceased."

I wanted to hug my mother, but they argued on the other side of that paisley printed curtain – once stretched across, it became an ironclad door. Raw emotion hemorrhaged out of my mother like a mortal wound, while my grandmother watched her bleed out.

"You're so ungrateful," my grandmother said in a sorrowful voice. "Willie, do you see this ungrateful cow you made?" My grandmother would always look up to the ceiling and complain to my grandfather. "I told you time and time again, you're doing too much for Derinda...and you thought it would pay off, but has it? *Huh, Willie?*"

That argument was their last bout; they never spoke to each other again. My mom moved to the furthest end of Caffin, in a house grandpa left her in his will. My grandmother who remained on the Back-of-town end of Caffin Avenue in the house that was in the rear of the funeral home, where she died three months after we moved here.

But my grandmother wasn't one to lose a fight, not even in death. Before grandma died, she wrote my mom out of her will, leaving everything to my Uncle Jesse.

My Uncle Jessie grew the business from one location to four funeral homes in the New Orleans metropolitan area. When my uncle Jessie died last year, he wasn't as business savvy as my grandmother to protect our legacy: he died without leaving a will. Pugh's Funeral Homes & Mortuary Services a debt-free business which had been in our family since 1842, transferred out of the family to his second wife.

"Okay, you've left me no choice since you refuse to open this door." After two rings someone answered. "Yes, I am at my mother's home on 731 Caffin Ave. in the Lower 9th Ward. Could you please send a police officer and EMS to do a wellness check? Yes, that's correct." My voice boomed like a grade school Principle during the morning announcements. "Yes.......... yes, her car is in the driveway, but she's not answering the phone nor the door. My mother's name is *Derinda Michelle Edwards*...wait, ma'am, could you, hold just one second?"

Suddenly the door opened.

CHAPTER 18

An Open Door

ERICA

Once the door swung open, the first person to speak wasn't my mother, but a pleasant pot of gumbo with a cheeky grin, that waved all the way from the kitchen. *"Hey y'all, ya' ate?"* Mr. File' Gumbo welcomed us warmly. Therefore, the three of us followed both of them through the living room, as my mother stumped to the kitchen where her gumbo roux patiently waited. My daughters ran past me and wrapped their arms around her size ten waist.

"Nunu. Nunu," they yelled out (pronounced in New Orleans as *new-new*) but she barely spoke to her granddaughters.

"Good morning momma." My mother ignored me as she kissed the curly crowns of each granddaughter.

"Girls go practice a *Tale old as Time,* I need a moment alone with your Nunu."

"…but Nunu, do we have to," Parks whined.

"Parks, I want your third finger on the C-string – get to it."

"...but Nunu..." Rosa objected.

"Now!" A no-nonsense finger pointed the way to their room.

My daughters hugged their Nunu and shot me a look like I was the worst mother in the world, but I am immune. My mother has them spoiled to the core, which is why they love being here versus my house, and I for one am glad it's not the rear of a funeral home.

After the exaggerated hug and plea for rescue, the girls quit the act and continued to the last room in the shotgun home – the back room. Their room was a *Princess Wonderland* with enough pink and purple to overwhelm Barbie. Pink walls, purple carpet, pink and purple drapes, purple chairs under a pink table, purple tufted headboards, with pink bedding. Over by the window rested two cellos on pink mounts.

It was all my mother's idea.

The birth of my daughters promoted her to a Grandmother, but there isn't anything Granny about Derinda Edwards. The clothes in my closet look like a Goodwill 40% off Sale as compared to my mother's wardrobe. Even her kitchen is glammed out in a way I would have never thought of or could afford on my Uber salary and budget.

Because she graduated from John McDonogh High School, and their alumnus are one of the more passionate boosters in New Orleans, her kitchen is color coordinated in deep emerald and old gold trimming, with little Trojan helmets hung here and there.

It was in her kitchen my mom swayed about in her favorite emerald housecoat with a pair of matching slippers. On the counter next to the stove she had a plate of chopped smoked sausage, about a pound of blue crabs, a bowl of season mix, hot sausage links, another bowl of freshly peeled shrimp, and a pack of Uncle Ben's brown rice.

Because I knew how much it aggravated her – I diced one of the bell peppers and added it to her pot. And to really vex her nerves, I removed the lid from the large pot and added another cup of water.

"ERICA GO SIT YO-ASS DOWN SOMEWHERE AND GET OUT MY POTS." Then came the mumbling. "Before you need 911" She hissed "I didn't ask for your help?"

"Oh, your voice has returned. Sweet Jesus it's a miracle." Few things get under her skin more than *digging in her pots*.

"I never lost my voice, but I'm not in the mood for your questions."

"Momma, all I said was *good morning*. Why all the attitude?"

"…and if you ever call the police to this house again –"

"Well, you didn't give me any choice. I thought you were on the floor and couldn't get up." Only then did she stop stirring her pot.

"When I need help getting up, I will check myself into a nursing home, until then, you mind your business."

"A wellness check is what daughters do, when they can't reach people like you…"

"I don't give a rats-ass…"

Then she resumed her campaign of ignoring me as if I wasn't standing three feet away, but I wasn't having it. All of those years she lectured me about integrity and how much she hates a liar but has lied to me my entire life. I don't mean any disrespect, but my mother will get off her high horse or there will be no peace.

"Momma, after last night do you honestly feel this is the appropriate response? You made me believe my daddy was dead, now all of a sudden you don't want to talk? How is this fair to me?" I pointed at my chest after each syllable.

"Erica leave me alone."

"I will not because the way you're acting isn't fair."

"Life isn't fair, and you don't always get what you want."

"I'm not asking for a million dollars, but I would like to have a conversation with you… my mother. Why is that such a burden for you?"

"Because it is, it is a burden, and if I don't feel like discussing it, then I'm well within my rights to remain silent."

"But it isn't right, and you know it."

Mr. Gumbo had just reached the ideal boil, and from the back room, I heard the sounds of music being played on a duet of cellos.

"We're having dinner tomorrow at my dad's house. He's very excited. We're excited to."

"Well good for you..." Dish by dish she added the additional ingredients to the large pot with the roux.

Did I mention this over the top kitchen table?

In a space no larger, than 8x12 is a table that I'm sure she stole from Will and Jada Smith. The base of it is a block of Louisiana cypress, with a custom cut square of glass on top. I have a traditional refrigerator – she has one from the year 2028. Embedded in the door of her refrigerator is a television unless she decides to check her email, then it becomes a touchscreen tablet. Her washer is a front load I can't get used to because it barely uses water to wash your clothes and to start the cycle you press a play button.

She's a Nancy Wilson level diva, while I have yet to reach Mariah Carey's level. She's abreast of all the latest social media trends, and annually she buys the latest iPhone. I logged in to my first Facebook account when I started dating Telly. We are polar opposites externally but internally – we're identical twins.

Nevertheless, I'm African American, but a redhead? That has puzzled me since I was a child, until last night. I am a carbon copy of my father. During those priceless minutes at the reception, I learned that his mother was also a redhead too. Everything makes sense now.

All of my life, I have only known my mom's side of the family – after meeting my daddy – my sense of family has expanded.

"Mom I forgive you for telling me he died. I'm totally over that part. There were times I wished my ex-husband was dead, just to get him out of my life. Through that lens, I understand your reasons and actions. Here's what I can't wrap my fingers around." I stood as close to her as I could without skin to skin contact. "Why are you angry with me because of this chance meeting?"

She continued to stir as if the pot needed her more than I did.

"Momma please stop treating me this way. I've never shut you out but I'm pressing you hard this morning because I need answers for this part of my life. Why are you so angry with me?"

"Because ..." her words were carried up in the steam from Mr. Gumbo.

"Because of what mom..." I pressed.

"Because you're all I have." The stirring ceased, but the gumbo continued to swirl in the pot. "I didn't want you to meet him because you're my daughter, all mine, and those are my grandkids. I never expected to share your love with anyone, not my mother, my father, not even..."

"My daddy..."

"Not even Glenn. And... I was afraid. There, I've said it."

"Would you think I would love you any less after meeting him." Once again, her words were carried away in the brew.

"Mom answer me. Did you really feel I would stop loving you because I've found my father?"

"BECAUSE YOUR FATHER WAS NEVER LOST...THAT'S WHY."

I felt her words inside my ribcage, even the walls vibrated. Suddenly the music stopped.

"Nunu are you okay?" Parks asked.

"Yes, my little princess, I'm fine. When I finish cooking and you're done practicing, let's say we play a round of *Minecraft*?" With a huge smile, Parks closed the door. The funny part is I don't play any of the video games with my daughters, I can't figure them out. Thank God for my mother. My mom lowered the fire under her pot of rice, and then deflated onto a seat at the cypress table.

"Your father was never lost; I knew where he was the entire time. In fact, I knew as much as a woman could know from a distance, without catching a stalking charge. There were so many times I wanted to tell you the truth, but…but I always talked myself out of it…"

Condensation formed in her eyes.

"Your father was everything to me, he was my world. Careless lovers say those words all the time knowing they're not fully committed, but I was. Glenn Braxton was the breath in my lungs."

It was then that I saw the years rewind in her eyes.

It was then that I felt her vulnerability and fear.

It was then I met my mother for the first time.

Hi mom.

"You see, I had no friends. I never went out on a date until he asked me out. I never had a boyfriend. I was an awkward girl, the first time I believed I was pretty was when he told me, and he said it with so much conviction, over and over again that he managed to convince me. *I'm pretty.*"

It was then that my mom swiped a finger across her phone to unlock it, then opened another app and pressed start. Directly over my right shoulder, I could hear her high-tech coffee maker come to life.

"Your grandmother never liked Glenn, and never wanted him around. She would act so nasty to him, even though he was kind to her. My mother celebrated the day I had your father escorted out of your life, his absence was her trophy. It wasn't until you were five years old when she shared why she never wanted him around. She saw the way I looked at him. She observed how no one else mattered the moment he entered my life. Your grandmother feared Glenn would distract me from the plan she pre-arranged for my life. The cello and Pugh's Funeral Home. She was right."

Slowly she rose from her seat over to the coffee maker and poured a second cup.

"But mom, if you were so in love why did you kill him off?"

"Because he hurt me."

"How?"

"He lied."

"About?"

"Diana."

"His wife…?"

"Glenn went to my father and asked for my hand in marriage. My father gave a partial approval. The other half he had to secure from your grandma. Of course, she handled it wrong, said all the wrong things, and made him feel like the poorest hobo in New Orleans. I wouldn't have expected anything less. In the meanest, most condescending, most defecating manner imaginable, your grandmother shredded Glenn like Mardi Gras confetti."

I watched as she held the cup of warm coffee to her lips, but the sip was delayed by thoughts of the man that was chased away. Abruptly, on my mother's side of the table came the torturous sound of a steady drip, or at least what I thought was a drip: however, the floor beneath her was dry? Then came a gut-wrenching epiphany. The sound I heard, that ominous leakage, was far worse than any faulty knob on a sink – the relentless drip that smacked the floor was my mother's regrets.

"Your grandmother, Mrs. Bernice Pugh, was a skilled artist when it came to cordially insulting someone whom she felt was beneath our class level, and Glenn's family didn't own a notable business."

"And because they were blue-collar she disqualified him to marry you? You had to be furious?"

"I was, and I heard every word of her rebuke. I was just on the other side of the curtain when she set ablaze Glenn's hopes of marrying me. She said *in our world he was an immigrant, and my future was much too important to risk on a gypsy.*"

"A What? A gypsy? Why would grandma call my father a gypsy? That had to crush him…"

"She did, but he still wanted to marry me. Glenn offered to elope, but I was terrified. I couldn't imagine life outside of the support from my parents, and I knew if I married him – I was cut off. I asked your father to wait. He said when it came to a marriage proposal; *not now* was the equivalent of *no*. That's when the argument started and we broke up, then made up, then split again. During the gap between one of those breakup's – he met her. Then I discovered you in my belly, during one of those break up's."

"What did he say when you broke the news?"

"At first, I didn't tell anyone, I hid you for as long as I could underneath several *Guest Jean Jumpers* and oversized sweatshirts. When I finally told him, he was supportive but distant. I could tell Glenn had grown tired of waiting. When a man is ready to marry you that window is very narrow, and there's always someone willing to climb through it: if you leave it open."

Patiently my mother sipped her coffee and shared the most heartbreaking story of how she discovered that my father had married Diana. How his wife was the first person to hold me, and how she was forever changed by that moment. At last count, I ripped off six sheets of paper towels to catch the tears.

I felt her pain.

I felt the humiliation.

I knew the reason she hid me for as long as she could, and I accepted the reason she lied about my father. While I balled my eyes out, to my surprise my mother was as still as that cypress log.

"If you want to know the real reason, I ran away last night it was because I have never loved another, not the way I love your father. I didn't want anyone to see it in my eyes. I've had men come and go, only one you have met. There wasn't any space in my heart for a new love. My therapist said many years ago: until my daughter knows the truth, I would remain frozen. You now know the truth, and I no longer need to hide my baby."

Her coffee cup was empty, but her conscious was free.

"Since I have granted your wish, I need you to grant me one."

I sniffed and dried, then again, sniff and dried. "Whatever you need, consider it done."

My mother left the kitchen and continued to her room. She returned to the table holding a silk emerald handkerchief in her palm.

"When you manage a few minutes alone with your father please hand him this and tell him I said *Huck-a-buck.*"

"Huh?"

"He will know what it means."

CHAPTER 19

12:30 p.m.

RASTA

After two hours of pleading, Biyell couldn't get beyond the fact that another man had fondled Tiffany, and she allowed it. Within us is a switch that can turn on or off when it comes to the perceived value of a woman. Yes, it's a double standard, I admit it, but this standard has been in place since Eve. There are certain liberties a man can enjoy that a woman cannot, and I speak on behalf of the entire fraternal order of men when I confess, we are unapologetic when it comes to that double standard.

We can sleep around, but if a woman sleeps around then she's a *hoe.*

If my wife brings home a friend and says we're *going to fuck her until we pass out* – that is called a threesome.

If two men decided to have a sex party with a lone female, that is not a threesome – they *Ran A Train* on her.

If my wife discovered my mistress, then I expect her to take me back.

If I discover that a dude was dicking down my wife a few times a month, our marriage ends that night. That instant. It's over like puberty.

Why?

Because he touched her, and she allowed it. The thought of another man fucking the woman I love instantly flips that switch to the OFF position, and her perceived value depreciates to negative ten. Why?

Because we can't handle it.

I can't handle it.

The thought of my wife making the same sounds for another man that she makes for me? Spreading her legs wide and holding him by his thigh while he fills her with cement hard dick?

I can't handle it.

The image of another man bare-dicking my woman makes me angry enough to hurt both of them, but I wouldn't, because that gives the outer appearance that she still matters.

This is the reason we see so many cases where the woman was willing to forgive an affair, but not the husband, if he catches his wife in the *act of adultery*. That double standard is instantly enforced, and on rare occasions will you find a man that has forgiven a cheating wife: unless a dude bare-dicking his woman is something he could forget about or it's some kinky shit he's into.

Nah.

This is what helps me understand why Biyell is so disturbed by Tiffany's actions, the switch has been flipped. Even if he tried to work it out with her, the image of Josh with hands full of her ass will never fade away. That slow dance will live in infamy.

Every time he gets pissed off at her for whatever reason, he will hear that song by Ginuwine. If she takes too long to return from the grocery store, he will hear that song. If she has a lock code on her cell phone, or leaves the room to take the call, or ends the call abruptly when he enters the room, Ginuwine will start singing.

Even when she's sitting alone enjoying a little quiet time, in the back of Biyell's crazy-ass mind – *I bet she's over there thinking about Josh*. When Biyell pushed back I left it alone, because I already know how this ends. Tiffany plummeted from a Perfect Ten to a Negative Ten in less than twenty-seven seconds.

He said it last night.

"Bruh you know what this feels like...it feels like I had the perfect ice cream cone on a hot sunny day, and just as I was about to take a lick, Josh licked my shit. I'm not about to lick on something Josh has licked. I am Biyell....................Baltimore, I lick behind no nigga........ *Ya Heard Me*. He can have her."

Of course, Uncle Glenn tried to talk him out of that warped frame of mind, but in our world, what's warp is straight, and what's straight is sometimes warped. Nevertheless, it was still a partial victory.

Biyell is devastated, but he's not so devastated that he's stupid.

Everything I put in place business wise will continue without any disruption to our partnership. I gave Biyell the assurance that he'll never have to interact with Tiffany, and I will handle all meetings with her *First Time Home Buyers*. My wife will continue in her role as our processor of mortgages and the money will continue to flow.

But I am sad they didn't work out, I was looking forward to my wife planning a wedding for her best friend and managing all the essentials that Tiffany managed for Kayla leading up to our special day.

On another note, we have waited all morning for Telly, and as predicted, he is a no-show.

"I say we make a surprise visit to his house, he can run, but he can't hide," Jarvis said.

"I don't understand why Telly is ducking me? The sooner we can talk the sooner we can put this behind us. Run game on someone else, but it's not happening with my daughter."

"Which explains why he's avoiding you. I think Telly is set on marrying Erica, with or without your blessings."

"*THAT'S BULLLLLLL SHIT.* It'll be a wedding and a funeral. Don't let the one leg fool you, ain't shit wrong with my trigger finger."

"But what if she still wants to marry Telly..."

"*Fuck that Rasta*, I ain't trying to hear that shit." This time it was Uncle Glenn's voice trapped in the arches of the ceiling. "If she knew half of the dirt, I know about Telly, his belongings would've been on the sidewalk last night. Telly is set in his ways, he will never change, he loves to *run game* on women until they quit him. It's a sport for Telly. That's how he's wired, and I would never hand my daughter to a man who has a smoldering heap of scorned women in his past."

"Uncle Glenn I hear you. But I'm also asking that you leave a little room for Erica to make her own decisions. Certain women when it comes to certain men are willing to forgive a septic tank full of shit. Don't be surprised if she does." Jarvis said.

"I doubt that."

"Uncle Glenn, what makes you so sure?" I asked.

"Because of what I know about Telly?"

"You know about the same as we know, and I don't see how that would make any difference," Jarvis said.

"I know things about Telly you guys don't know. Heavy things I am not at liberty to say...unless. . ."

"Unless what?" Biyell asked.

"Unless he decides to continue with this crazy idea of marrying Erica."

"Can you give us a *round-about description* of this classified file you have on Telly?" I asked.

"For real, can a brother get a peek? Knowing what you know about Telly is more important than anything I'm doing today. The brethren are intrigued oh wise one." Jarvis said.

"Jarvis, take my word for it on this one, if I start talking about the things, I know about Telly, you could write two more best-selling novels."

"DAMN!" I yelled. "It's that bad?"

"At least answer this Uncle Glenn – is it a heterosexual file or a *RuPaul* file?" I asked.

"I'm not discussing it, not right now, maybe not at all if Telly agrees to stand down. Here's the one thing you can bet a kidney on, I will go to *Angola Penitentiary* with one leg, before I watch Erica walk down the aisle with two legs – and marry Telly."

After he spoke, he tucked his crutch under his arm and exited through the patio door just as a drizzle danced across the pool. We shrugged at each other and wondered who was that guy?

Even though he had just met her, his paternal instincts were fully engaged. The thought of Telly with his daughter caused a vein to swell in the center of his forehead, a vein that wasn't visible yesterday morning. I don't have any daughters, but I can definitely understand.

As a father, it's a natural instinct to protect your little girl, but something else is going on here, something only Telly and Uncle Glenn are aware of, and I will not rest until I know.

"Speaking of secrets. . ." Biyell stood and stretched "has Kayla mentioned anything to you about this Tracey person?"

"Tracey who?" Nosey-ass Jarvis wanted to know.

"Jarvis you better not ask another question in this group, because I still have a post-dated ass-whipping for you." Biyell threatened.

Jarvis stood.

"Whatever bruh, I already told you. My wife didn't have shit to do with that website. And I can ask *whatever the fuck* I want to ask. You have me confused with Josh – I'll fight your ass until the mailman pass – tomorrow."

"FELLAS. CHILL. We have other issues to discuss before I roll out for this honeymoon."

"But anyway" Jarvis returned to his seat where his fingers hovered over the keys on his laptop. "Back to this Tracey girl…

what's the deal?"

"Tracey was one of their girlfriends, that's all I managed to squeeze out of her last night."

"And whenever her name is mentioned it's always past tense as if there was a big falling out," Biyell said.

"Since I will be trapped on a cruise ship for a week, I've made it a personal goal to get the rest of the story."

All of a sudden, I heard a loud bang on the table where Jarvis sat.

"Biyell you owe me and my wife an apology right the fuck now!"

HoeLeaks.com had just updated with a page for Jarvis called *Borderline Pervert*. The comment section was twice as brutal as Biyell's page.

HOELEAKS.COM
COMMENTS

BigJudyBooty 61 – One hour ago
What kind of South Carolina back woods trailer on a flat in-bred bullshit is this? You mean to tell me the guy who wrote this book is the same character who dicked down his niece? I'm too through with this page, I need a bath after reading this post. In fact, I'm about to draw my bath water. Nasty fucker!

GrapeVineQueen1212 – One hour ago
Can't believe people like this even exist. Every time I visit this website, I'm so grateful for my husband lol

JesusComingRun777 – One hour ago
These people are cursed by the Most High for not keeping his Laws Statues and Commandments in the Bible. When they removed God out the class room it open the door for all sorts of perversion. They better check the other nieces in this family to see if anyone else has been touched. The Scriptures says he

was going to put the yoke of iron on their neck until they are destroyed, we our destroyed people and need to Wake up and return to the Most High Shalom

FuriousBitchAllDay – Just now

If he fell that hard for his niece, then chances are that sick creep have been watching her since she was a minor. To the real Monica, girl keep your head up because I know first-hand how you feel. The best thing you can do is say whatever and move on with your life. Dwelling on it will only cause you unnecessary stress. You have two beautiful daughters to care for. Don't let the negative occupy your thoughts and take away from what's most important. Protecting those girls when they're in the company of this author. Disgusting!

MrGotDatEggPlant4U – Just now

Jarvis had no business fucking his niece I don't care if she was a consenting age, only a perv would think this was acceptable. We need to get the word out and tell people stop buying his book because this is some sick shit. And that niece need her ass whipped by the entire family.

MsLovingDaQuain504 – Just now

After reading the stories on this page I feel much better about my life. I am not as fucked up as I originally thought.

RealFuckWithReal70117 – Just now

I love pussy just as much as the next man but fuck Jarvis for doing this to his wife. Dude fucking the niece and at the cancer treatment center? Bruh you hard up as fuck. If you ask me that niece was a gateway to some other illegal sex. No kids is safe around him.

CHAPTER 20

DIANA

It was that wee hour of the night, that time that belongs to the Bourbon Street drunks, the stray cats, and the levee fog in the sleepy Marigny neighborhoods. I was the only passenger on the *St. Claude Bus*, and every stop was vacant. Suddenly, Derinda boarded the bus, and despite ninety-eight unoccupied seats, she sat beside me. Her perfume was nauseating, her makeup stuccoed, her clothes were nothing more than stained rags, but her left hand was an anomaly.

It was sheen. With a Hollywood manicure, and emerald painted fingernails that were sprinkled with gold dust.

It was a hand that never pulled the black lever on a time clock, never scrubbed a spoiled pot of red beans, never swooped a mop across a muddy floor, and never had to lift a finger in life: it was certainly – the hand of a kept woman. A hand that held the most beautiful diamond ring I'd ever laid eyes on. A ring she flaunted at me. A ring she taunted at me. I was never kept.

"Do you like it?"

In great haste, I signaled the bus driver to let me off at the next stop. Instead of veering over at Desire Street, he accelerated.

"Glenn gave me this ring. Do you know why? I'm sure you do." Her words carried a stench of rotten eggs. "However, I do pity you. Glenn loves me in a way you'll never feel, and you'll never redeem the years wasted trying to get him to love you." Derinda said in a deep uncanny voice. "You were never Mrs. Braxton, nor will you ever be. But I do thank you for keeping my side of the bed... warm."

I felt the weight of her on my chest while both hands asphyxiated my throat. I ejected off my pillow in a full panic, with a face doused in anxiety, with a breath that was beyond my fingertips and each attempt to catch it overexerted my lungs. Even though it was just a freakish event in my subconscious mind, her perfume remained trapped in the cavity of my nostrils. It was then that I lost it.

I leaped out of the bed.

I twisted on the light.

I disturbed Glenn.

I didn't care.

That bitch was in my bedroom, I had to find her, I looked under the bed, in the closet, in the bathroom, in the hallway, I couldn't find her, Glenn thought I was stuck in a dream, hypnagogia is when you're stuck in a dream, I wasn't, it was Derinda, I knew it, because her drug store scent was stuck in my nose, and I wasn't going to rest until I flushed her out.

Glenn convinced me that it was only a dream, then she appeared again.

Last night at Roderick & Kayla's Wedding.

Like Jason without the hockey mask.

Bitch From Hell, The Sequel.

I know how this ends.

I've seen it before.

Netflix Remote.

Power Off.

I'm not forgiving shit, accommodating shit, understanding a

got damn thing, I'm not tolerating her or him, I don't care if she's a blast from the past or lay for a day, I swear on my mother's grave I'm out. For real, at the first sign that those two have reconnected on some romantic bullshit, I'm out. Why? Because I saw the way he looked at her.

Shortly before we moved into the new house, I strutted in front of Glenn butt-ass naked and didn't get that same Derinda Reaction. Only two men have ever gawked at me like that in ten years, and neither was my husband. His expression was beyond surprised, his heart skipped. It all played out in front of me. But I'm not going through it again. I still have plenty of hot years left and I'm in no mood to share my man, and if that's what he wants, then he can catch an Uber out of my life today.

I'm not going to be the terrified white girl in the movie who falls down as soon as she starts to run, I ran track in high school and know how to pull away.

At the next exit, please keep right at Southern University/ Metro Airport exit.

A clear sky greeted me, while a golden sun trailed me. It's Sunday morning, and I have arrived in Baker to pick up Bylisha. Tyra offered to meet me at the Outlet Mall in Gonzales, but I needed this drive.

The constant hum of the road.

The whoosh of the wind against my windshield.

The bland scenery from New Orleans to Baton Rouge.

A much-needed sedative, the same could be said of this exit ramp. I needed to get away from Glenn. I can't believe I just said that, but it's true. It's been a while since I placed miles between us, but it's happened today.

My mind is flooded with a surge of peculiar cogitations never before considered, it feels like I'm rapidly changing or better yet experiencing an awakening (where I don't understand why any of this is happening) but I'm curious. My best guess is because I saw her last night, but long before I saw her, I felt her presence. Was it all just a dream or a premonition?

You have arrived at your destination on the right.

Tyra's house was hidden on the other side of a humongous Police SUV that was as high as the roof gutters. There was nowhere to park in the entire cul-de-sac, therefore I was left with no other choice but to parallel next to Julian's patrol unit.

I entered their home to find it wall to wall packed with people. They hardly noticed me, I'm becoming used to it. All of them held a plate of food or a cup – and some held both. The houseguests were mainly women, with a few men seated at the table, and two sandwiched in on the sofa. Natalie Cole's confident voice proclaimed that This Will Be A Lasting Love, and from that smile on Julian's face – Natalie was on to something big.

Tyra zigzagged through the guests while pulling her soon-to-be hubby behind her, as they made their way to greet me. After we embraced, she made a group introduction.

I greeted them with a big wave.

The room waved backed at me. So much love and happiness compressed in one humble little home, made me miss my humble little apartment: where it was just Glenn & Diana Braxton.

Tyra offered me a plate, which I graciously accepted, and then whisked me down the hall to Braylyn's room. The girls ran to me and hugged my legs, while I kissed the top of their freshly parted hair.

"So, did you enjoy your twins this weekend?" I could tell she did.

"More than words could express." Her loving eyes couldn't separate from Bylisha and Braylyn as they closed the door to their walk-in Barbie Doll House.

"I saw your mother with her fat grandson?"

"You're referring to Momma #1?" Tyra threw her hands in the air. "I told Biyell a few days ago that my mother doesn't allow his little feet to touch the floor." She was not exaggerating. I passed her mother in the hall and the baby was on her hip.

"How was the wedding?"

"It was picturesque, a fairytale day in every sense. And congratulations again on your upcoming nuptials. How does it feel?"

"Diana, it's surreal. One minute, my life was an episode on Jerry Springer, and the next minute I am marrying the Prince of Zamunda. It all happened so quickly. But no one is more elated than my daughter."

"Who you telling? All Bylisha talks about is Braylyn."

"Gurrrl... she loves her sister."

Suddenly a storm cloud covered her sunny afternoon.

"Could I have a word with you outside?" Tyra asked.

We navigated to the front door just as another group of family members arrived to celebrate the wedding announcement. Tyra hugged each one in passing as we made our way to the front yard and continued through the chain linked gate. We ducked off in the space between Julian's SUV and my car.

"I was going to wait until later this week to give you and Bi-yell an update on our case against Tamara."

"Oh boy." I braced myself for bad news.

"As you know I transferred her case to another supervisor due to the relationships involved. What I'm about to share is for your ears only. But the case worker told me that things are not looking good for Tamara. Her custody appeal was rejected."

"But I was under the impression that she was making progress?"

"She was, then Mike moved back in..."

"Mike moved in! What! That bastard who raped her daughter? That Mike?"

"Yes, Mike the pedophile!"

"... I'm so done with Tamara."

"According to our field investigator, they're back together, she was busted in a lie."

"...and here I am cheering for her to get her life together and be reunited with her daughter."

"I was cheering for her too, but you should expect a call later this week in regards to full custody. I can say for sure, Tamara is not getting her daughter back."

"So, you're saying... there's a chance..................... I could have her permanently?"

"Yes..."

I felt my feet leave the ground. The bass drums beating inside my ears were deafening. I floated away on a cloud of probabilities. Tyra just said there's a chance I could have Bylisha full time, my very own child to raise – full time? I always make my best effort to clear my mind while someone is talking, but I couldn't help it. I need confirmation.

"I'm sorry Tyra but could you please repeat that."

"She's not getting Bylisha back, and the caseworkers have sung praises about the job you're doing..."

"We're doing..." I pointed to Tyra.

"Yes, and they're convinced that this arrangement is the healthiest for Bylisha."

"I couldn't agree more."

"Neither could I." We shared a celebratory hug.

"Any word on Biyell's parental rights appeal? It should go his way since Tamara has been declared unfit?"

"Biyell has a hearing on the 26th of July, he asked me to accompany him. I will keep you posted."

"Please, but in the meantime you and Biyell make a powerful team, and I can tell the case manager is very comfortable awarding you full custody. At first, I felt bad for Tamara, but they gave her every opportunity to get it together, and she blew it."

We hugged again.

Tyra offered to get Bylisha for me, which gave me another precious moment alone. I sat in my car waiting in an abyss of internal deliberations.

How could a mother choose a lover over her daughter?

All throughout life, especially during my career in labor and delivery, I've encountered a few situations where the mother appeared to be the worst possible caretaker, but without proof, our hands were tied. I have never known anyone like Tamara. All the mornings I cried in the tub because I couldn't get pregnant, and here is Tamara in possession of everything my heart desired. She threw it all away for dick.

No man is worth your child.

"Here's the little princess, let's get you all snapped in your car seat." Bylisha and Braylyn launched into a duet of sorrow. "Don't cry girls, Braylyn will sleep at your house next weekend. And... you will have so much fun at the zoo. Stop crying... okay. Be a big girl for your mommy... I mean... auntie Diana." After double checking her snap-lock on the car seat, Tyra closed the door.

Before pulling off, we hugged once more and that's when she asked me about him.

"Soooooo, I saw that Tiffany had a thot flare-up, Tamara, made it a point to tag me in the video on Facebook."

"She also tagged him in your wedding announcement. Tamara's messy-ass is worried about everything but the right thing. But that Tiffany has been the talk of the wedding for all the wrong reasons"

"He didn't deserve that."

"I hadn't seen the video yet, because I left early, but I ran into him later that evening. He was in pieces. What pisses me off the most is he gave that relationship everything he had, became a brand new Biyell. Tyra, you wouldn't have recognized him he was on such good behavior. *I did my best to cheer him up. I hope he doesn't regress.* The man he is today deserves to be happy."

"I agree." Her eyes gave me a sneak peek into her heart...she still loves Biyell. "Even though he threw me in a spin cycle, he's an excellent father, and I was happy for the majority of the time we were together. I pray he finds the right woman and they live happily ever after."

After another embrace, we were off.

I looped around the cul-da-sac, and a few red lights later I was back on I-10 headed east to New Orleans.

Bylisha wasn't much company, by the time I drove past the exit for LSU, she fell deep into her mid-day nap. Tyra and I talked about quite a bit in that brief period of time, but the main thing that penetrated my sub-consciousness is when she mistakenly referred to me as *Bylisha's mommy.*

I have never been called mommy.

I've touched thousands of crying babies, and not one of them cried for me. I've never had a child tree hug my leg until now, and I loved it.

It doesn't matter if I hadn't given birth to her, birthing a child isn't an indication of a loving mother. I could give Bylisha everything her little heart could crave, plus safety.

For a pervert like Mike to molest a child, he has to first obtain the opportunity to molest, the space to violate, and the exclusive access that's indicative for an atmosphere of rape. All of the before mentioned comes into play when there is a breakdown in the parenting structure, or when parents become trifling with their child's overall safety.

Not this little girl in my rear-view mirror.

I wish a *mother fucker* would try it.

I was never molested because I was surrounded by my brothers, who kept watch over me and my sister like we were the future heirs to a throne. That's the same level of protection this child will have. A whole new world where a pervert will never gain the opportunity to harm her. A peaceful home where a child is free to be a child and a pre-teen girl could adjust to her new body without a bunch of men thinking pervert thoughts like *That little girl is gonna be fine when she grows up.*

A home where she could transition through her teenage years without falling prey to some statutory perv like Mike. Where she could reach my age and boldly say, *no man has ever violated me as a child, teen, or adult.*

"Lord thank you for the men in my life, and even though my

daddy was a rolling stone, his presence covered us. He protect-
ed us, and he taught my brothers how to shield the girls in our
family. Lord thank you for surrounding me with real men. And
one more thing Lord, everything you did for me, do it again for
Bylisha."

"Your mommy."

It has a nice ring to it.

I am a mommy, and soon I will have the official paperwork to
go with the child. There is so much I want to teach her from the
lessons of my life, and now I've gained the access and liberty to
love her unconditionally. Even though it's not a done deal yet, it
doesn't matter – you are my daughter from henceforward.

Bylisha, welcome home… forever.

Love Always.

Mommy.

CHAPTER 21

BIYELL

I love pussy. The End.

CHAPTER 22

3:31 p.m.

BIYELL

I could sum up my entire life with those three words: *I love pussy.* Three more words: *I really do.* Three more: *I want some.* Even as far back as I could remember, which was my first time sliding inside of that magnificent cubbyhole at fourteen years old, since then I've been hopelessly addicted. It was also my first time experiencing an orgasm, and it freaked me out so much that I leaped off the girl and ran home to inspect my dick.

At first, I thought it malfunctioned because I couldn't stop the white stuff from gushing out, but now, the white stuff is the trophy I award some really good pussy. Did I mention how much I love it? Oh my God.

Yum. Yum. Yum.

I love everything about good pussy, the way it feels on my fingertips, the U-shape of a thick pussy in panties, the way it looks when it's doing absolutely nothing, on a table, on the floor, on a chair, I don't care. I can't live without it.

It's essential.

It's my medication.

It's my oxygen mask.

I could eat some good pussy all day and never come up for air. Real nigga talk. I wish there was an All You Can Eat Buffet that only served one dish, *a hot plate of honest pussy.* I would arrive two hours before the doors opened and would not leave until I lost all feeling in my tongue.

If I were elected to Congress, I would draft legislation to give pussy a Federal Holiday. Kids wouldn't have school, everything would close in honor of *Good Pussy Day*, and I would fly in some brothers from American Samoa to do a Haka dance, in honor of our new holiday.

I know a few Samoans, they enjoy it just as much as I do, so they would be more than happy to participate.

And to prove how serious I am about my holiday, I would commission Stevie Wonder to write a song called *Happy Pussy Day To You.* Like the *MLK Holiday*, men who love pussy would march in cities around the world, holding big-ass banners, with bold pink letters that proclaimed: ***We Love Pussy, It's Delicious.***

I didn't lie to you, it's my crack-rock.

It's the reason I don't understand gay dudes.

Don't get me wrong, to each its own, and my life is so jacked up – I would be the last to judge, but I have to ask – why don't you want some? Have you tried it?

Have you ever watched a thick sexy woman slowly spread her legs and with her index finger flick you a wet invitation? Have you ever stepped out of the shower after a long day, and were pleasantly surprised to find your woman on her stomach – warming it up? I have so many questions for the gay brothers. Like, have you test driven some good pussy? Have you ever reclined in it? Well, I have, and I ranked good pussy in the Top 3 things God ever created.

Chicken.

Water.
Pussy.
Amen!

Tyra had the best pussy I ever had; she was the Undisputed Champion, until last night. I couldn't sleep, so I called her over. For the second time that night, she gave me some. That made my day. I call her Tesla because she is self-driving on a dick, the best hands-free nutt ever. Then she quickly recharged that dick for a final lap.

Tesla got it out me three times last night, it's been at least ten years since that happened, but I was also excited to see her. After the way Tiffany handled me, I needed Tesla to make me feel better. Selfishly, I used her, but she wanted me to use her. It was all about me last night. I needed that.

She whispered.

"That's it baby, take it out on that pussy. I brought it to you. Whatever you need is inside of there, go get it baby, that's it, beat that pussy with your hard dick, now cum for me, dump it baby, I want every drop."

That is all I remember.

When I stumbled out the bed to piss, she was gone. Maybe that's all I need? A woman like Tesla who's more than willing to take care of me without all the deep emotional traps. What makes her so perfect for my current state is Tesla can't be with me every day even if she wanted to. She's married. Sneaking dick is all she can handle.

And peep this, what makes this arrangement even sweeter is, I no longer feel like fucking three different women every week, *ain't nobody got time for that.* For now, Tesla can replace Tiffany and take me where I want to go until I decide to either trade her in or hold on to her as a Classic.

The one thing I know for sure is this marriage thing is not for me. I'm finally honest with myself.

I don't trust women.

I love freedom.

I love pussy.

I get bored.

But I don't like being alone. I don't like sleeping alone. I don't like waking up alone, and I definitely hate having sex alone. *Ain't nobody got time for that.*

Some men can do the marriage thing with no problem, I am not one of them. I've accepted that reality. Tiffany got my best effort, and she was the last hoop I will ever jump through for some pussy. I have to be honest with myself, at the end of the day that is all I wanted: to monopolize her pussy.

When it became apparent that I didn't have a lock on it – I no longer wanted her. Not for the role of the *Queen of my Kingdom.* Hell Naw, to the Naw Naw.

For a security clearance that high, she has to be Michelle Obama level of committed, supporting a nigga through a campaign for the *Louisiana House of Representatives,* a fancy title that paid peanuts, but it didn't matter because she's down for whatever.

Could you imagine Michelle Obama drunk on the dance floor with some dude name Josh?

Tiffany was prettier than Tyra, but what good is pretty if she's a magnet for random dick? How about Tiffany's face on Tyra's body? Hmmm, now that's the perfect woman. She's someone who would make me change my mind about marriage. But Tiffany's face, with Tyra's body and Tesla's nutt sucking talent? I would stalk her ass like Sylvester from Bugs Bunny.

I Tawt I Taw a Puddy Tat.

Like a bodyguard at the *B.E.T. Awards,* strutting in front of her, shoving nigga's out of the way. No lie, after she takes a piss, I would hand her the tissue. I would put a house arrest bracelet on her ankle that called the cops if another bum name Josh came within ten feet. Shit would get hostile real fast.

I'm as serious as a 72-hour notice to vacate. She wouldn't have any problems out of Biyell Baltimore. *Believe Dat!*

By the way, while I'm sitting here daydreaming about Tesla, the fellas are still trying to figure out who published that website. At the edge of the counter – Uncle Glenn continued to speed dial Telly.

"Oh, oh… I see the cat & mouse game we're playing, but I got something for his ass." Uncle Glenn huffed as he reached across the counter for the charger cable. "

"I bet he has forgotten the last conversation we had…the one where he casually stated that Heather flight arrives around five, and he agreed to pick her up from the airport."

"That was prior to last night, and us meeting your new baby momma. *But it's a whooooooole new… worrrrrrrrld.*" I song.

"You're got damn right, yesterday changed everything. Not my daughter. Fuck that Peabo Bryson."

"If her flight arrives at five… then I say we meet him there at five. *MSY Airport* is not *Atlanta's Hartsfield-Jackson*, it's only so big?" Jarvis suggested.

"If that's the game plan, then you brothers have to fill me in later. I have to blaze out. My wife has sent five texts begging me to come home." Rasta stood and collected his keys off the table.

"*My wife. My wife. My wife.*" I teased in a whiny voice. "He up that girl's ass like a thong, ain't been married 24 hours and has said, my wife, 24 times since I got here. He can't even formulate a sentence without saying *my wife, my wife.* BRUH, we know you're married. Fuck!" The room burst in laughter at Rasta's expense.

"Wait, Lenny Williams trying to cap on me? With your lonely-ass? Talking about *you've never been in love like I've been in love - you get lonely - oh-oh, and I cried, I cry cry cry cried oh-oh-oh, ohohoh oh.*" Rasta punk ass sang on one knee. "Don't hate because I have a wife! You were the one who let Josh Deebo you out your pussy."

Yea, he got me, but as soon as they stop laughing, watch how I bounce back.

"Here I am leaving the reception with my wife, that's right

nigga' I said my wife, only to have Josh squeak by us with Tiffany on the handlebars of a 10-speed. He peddled away with your pussy. Meanwhile, Biyell was pouting like *my grandma set me up with that girl."*

"*Mannnnn* fuck Tiffany," I said over the laughter.

"That's what Josh did, he fucked Tiffany," Rasta yelled above the laughter as he dapped his way out the door.

Jarvis tried to get us to refocus. "Fellas, we have to get this website taken down or this will ruin me." He warned.

"Oh, now you're getting off your ass? It just became urgent huh?"

"Biyell even before I discovered my name on that website, I wanted this page taken down."

From his wallet, Uncle Glenn flicked a $20 bill across the table in my direction. Confused, I picked it up.

"What's this for?"

"It's for a box of *Menopause Solution*, they sell it at Walgreens… you're hormonal as fuck today."

"Okay okay, it's crack on Biyell hour."

"It comes in a pink and white box, it's good for hot flashes, and shit like that."

"Fuck you, Uncle Glenn."

Then Jarvis flicked another twenty-dollar bill "Get two boxes."

"Whatever bruh…"

"I'm with Uncle Glenn, you're going through *"The-Change"*. All that bitching and hating."

"Yea, I took an L last night, but this is a best of seven series. Real players make plays, Ya Heard Me."

"Took an L? Took an L? Nigga, please. Josh dunked on you with his nuts in your face!" Jarvis clapped his hand after each word for added emphasis. "You're hating on everybody because of Josh," Jarvis said.

"Dude I'm not worried about Josh, you clowns are the ones constantly bringing up his name…"

"Because he jacked your main lady, that's like Josh barging in here and stealing Uncle Glenn's refrigerator full of meat. You know how serious he is about his specials from the meat market. How far do you think Josh would get before Glenn beat that bitch with a bat?"

"As soon as he touched the handle on my icebox – Josh would've been a dead *mother-fucka*."

"Exactly, Uncle Glenn! But Biyell let a dude come in his house and pack up the refrigerator full of meat, all the can goods, *niggggga* opened your bottom cabinet, took all your cleaning products, then went in your bathroom, not the guest bathroom, but your wife's bathroom – took a shit, then dried his hands with your good towels, the ones on the rack, the decorative towels, the ones for *lookin'* only, and after all of that, he walked out the door with all your shit while you sat on a *sofa called Hurt.*"

"Keep running your mouth…watch I knock your teeth out." I threatened, above the thunderous laughter.

"All I'm saying is the next time some dude name Josh touch your refrigerator… handle it like Uncle Glenn –"

"Beat that bitch with a bat …" Uncle Glenn said in a Don Cornelius voice.

"Exactly!" Jarvis laughed aloud.

I had no choice but to join in. Jarvis punk-ass was funny and dead on. I had no comeback. Nevertheless, laughter was also our way of dealing with painful setbacks, we tormented the person until his defenses rebooted, and he rejoined the fight.

"If we're going to catch Telly in the act then we should leave now," Jarvis suggested as Uncle Glenn hopped down the hall to change clothes.

"Uncle Glenn, bring your fancy hand-held camera. I plan to jump out on Telly like an episode of *Cheaters.*" Jarvis suggested.

"When I jump out it'll be to kick his ass if he doesn't stand-down," I said.

dinnnng dinnnng dong dong - dinnnng dinnnng dong dong

dinnnng dinnnng dong dong - dinnnng dinnnng dong dong
"It's open!" We yelled.
"Whose ass you're planning to kick?"
It was Telly.

CHAPTER 23

New Orleans
August 15, 1998

KAYLA

Our graduation from Dillard University was back in May, but all summer long, I've busted my butt in Atlanta at a volleyball training camp. Tonight, is the first and last chance we have to celebrate our academic achievements as a trio. It's bittersweet. Our streak of attending the same school has come to an end, and my emotions are scattered.

Tiffany was accepted into Tulane's MBA program. Tracey will follow her mom into the legal world by graduating from Southern University Law in Baton Rouge, and eventually settling into the prosecutor's office. And being that my life centers in front of a volleyball net, I'm blessed to transfer my scholarship (with two years of athletic eligibility) to Georgia Tech, where I also plan to pursue my MBA.

"What is taking her so long?" I complained.

"Kayla, you should know it's all about Tiffany. She always

has to make a grand entrance even if it's McDonald's." Tracey said as we drifted back and forth on a porch swing at Tiffany's house.

Tracey was the only one in our crew with a steady boyfriend, but Josh Leblanc is a sick puppy because she's moving to Baton Rouge. We asked to use his car tonight, but Josh was full of more excuses than Bill Clinton. He could be such a moist booty sometimes but thank God for Tiff's mom!

She saved us from club hopping by way of public transportation, or even worse – dropped off at the party like three high school freshmen. Mrs. Arceneaux rented us a *Sebring Convertible* for the night, it's parked in the driveway – patiently waiting for us – with the top down.

My gaze at the shiny convertible was disrupted when Tiffany's mom bumped through the screen door hip first.

"Where did the time go?" Mrs. Arceneaux asked as she handed us some lemonade. "It's a lot cooler in the den, are you girls sure you don't want to wait inside for Tiff?"

Mrs. Arceneaux was a curvy mom with thick roller set hair, Oil of Olay cream skin and a permanent cheeky grin. Due to the air quality within her salon, over the years her voice had grown raspy from exposure to fumes released from harsh chemicals like Jheri Curl and No Lye Relaxers, but her voice was ever the more pleasant to my ears.

"Thank you, Mrs. Arceneaux, but if we're in the same room with her - then Tiffany takes even longer with the multiple wardrobe changes."

She chuckled. "That's my daughter, you know her well."

"Tiffany, you hurry your tail up! Got everybody waiting around on you. Don't you change another outfit. You hear me?" Mrs. Arceneaux called out to Tiffany as the screen door closed behind her.

It seems like only yesterday.

I was that stringy girl in the 5th grade, sitting alone at the lunch table, relentlessly teased by the permed hair girls, because plaited hair was forced upon me. My mom couldn't care less what the other girls thought of my pre-school hair-do, but I cared, and desperately wanted a perm. At the beginning of the sixth-grade school year, the only other girl teased because of her hair was Tiffany Arceneaux.

A child better stay in a child's place.

That was more than just a saying, but a threat. No one was threatened more than Tiffany.

To drive home the point, her mom tied thick cotton ribbons to the bottom of each plait. The multi-color ribbons hung off her shoulders like depressed worms. I felt sorry for her, but Mrs. Arceneaux was an authority on Womanish, and hated when little girls acted womanishly. Any inkling of the behavior was dealt with immediately, and that's how we became best friends, our mom's parenting styles were similar and equally suffocating.

In sixth grade, we were two displaced nerds who didn't fit in anywhere but somehow, we connected, we communicated telepathically through those fat dookie plaits with braided cotton ribbons.

Then two weeks into the school year *The Plaits* added a third member to our lunch table, Tracey Honore.

Tracey transferred to *Thomas Edison Elementary* from St Maurice Elementary, a predominantly white Catholic school. She did not fit in the parochial setting and was a fish out of water in the urban setting. Not only was Tracey bullied because of her plaits, but the lenses in her galaxy glasses gave her a signature look that no one envied. And on the rare occasions, when she smiled, I could see rubber bands intertwined in her braces.

The Plaits vs The Spritz.

That was the name we branded the popular girls, and the more they tried to intimidate us, the more we fought back. We were as close as three girls could be, we were in fact, sisters.

Here we are today, three tall beautiful college grads, all with beautiful natural hair. As for me, I wear two cabbage sized afro puffs, because it intimidates the hell out of opposing centers on the volleyball court. Tiffany wears her hair bold like Erykah Badu. Tracey on the other hand, she loves micro-braids minus the synthetic ends, and all those years she suffered through braces – produced a flawless smile.

Tracey is attractive but doesn't believe it. I think she's still tormented by The Spritz girls even though most of them are either pregnant or two kids deep. Nevertheless, I have made it my personal goal to tell her as often as possible, like yesterday, when we were at *Dress to the Nine* clothing store in Lake Forest Mall.

"Tracey, if you're not going to do anything with that face then can I borrow it next week? I've tried everything to get Eddie's attention, but nothing seems to work..." We tiptoed over the dressing room stalls.

"Oh, whatever Kayla, if I only had your legs." Tracey was first to view herself in the large dressing room mirror.

"I may be the tallest, but from the moment your mom traded those glasses for contacts, all eyes have been on you!"

"You're exaggerating..." She frowned at the outfit.

"I'm not. Tiffany will you tell this girl she has it..."

"Whatever, she's alright for a white girl." Tiffany teased.

Tracey's vanilla complexion ranked her in a top tier of a category guys lusted over called a *'Red Bone.'* Tracey couldn't stand to be called *red*. On our way out the mall, a group of *wanna-be* thugs approached us.

"Say red, say red holup holup, let me holla at cha Lil-red... holup." A guy blinged his double deck of gold teeth.

The three of us locked arms with Tracey and hurried towards the food court exit. The faster we walked, the louder they flirted.

"Aight. Aight. I see how you wanna be Lil red, but what's up with tall mama?" His friend asked who was no taller than my navel. "Don't be like that tall momma." We locked tighter and hurried toward the food court. "You're stuck up too? Well, fuck y'all then." His voice chased us across the food court and out the back door.

Of course, Tiffany and I found it funny, we giggled all the way to the car, but for Tracey, that sort of attention was like popping all ten fingernails at once.

Even when the more respectful more polished guys from St. Augustine High would flirt with us, Tracey would always fade to the back or walk a half block away until I caught up, but not Tiffany. She loved the attention, she couldn't resist a flirtatious guy, and her Beeper constantly buzzed with guys. Unfortunately, I would later discover that one of those constant beeps came from Josh.

Tiffany's Josh.

CHAPTER 24

3:55 p.m.

DIANA

Unexpectedly, the clouds mourned in great sorrow, and unleashed a downpour that worked my windshield wipers to exhaustion. "Thank God for my automatic garage door," I whispered to my sleeping child in her car seat, only to awaken her when I came to a rolling stop in my drive-way.

"Look at this shit," I banged the steering wheel "of all days to block the garage door... they would pick today." Jarvis and Biyell's vehicles hogged the entrance to my side of the garage.

Bylisha awoke from her mid-day nap crossed and confused. Looking around for her sister and little brother. Strangely, she hasn't cried for her mother not one time since I received custody, and likewise, I haven't mentioned Tamara. When she's in the mood to talk, we'll talk.

"Look at the rain, it's pretty."

"And it's cold, but this rain isn't stopping anytime soon. Bylisha we have no choice but to run through the rain. Are you ready to run?"

"Yes, let's run in the rain." She replied in a elated voice.

Once inside the house, we quickly made our way to my bedroom to find dry clothes, and that's when I heard the sounds of large dogs. Huge dogs. The size of Rottweiler's. The sharp toothed barking came from our patio.

With Bylisha trailing close behind we entered the kitchen unnoticed.

"Princess, would you like to eat in your room and watch your favorite show?" Of course, she nodded. While Bylisha fell into a *Baby Shark* induced coma, I grabbed a bag of chips and slid into the seat closest to the patio door, a discrete area where I could hear them, but they couldn't see me.

"So, it was all cool until it was your daughter. That's how this goes?" Telly scoffed at the hypocrisy.

"*Mutha-fucka,* you know that man tried many of times to…"

"Biyell, I got this! Telly… how many conversations have we had about Erica prior to me finding out she was my daughter? Huh? So, don't come with that bullshit."

"…if you let me get a word in… all I'm trying to say, Uncle Glenn –"

"Telly I sat quietly for twenty minutes and listened to you try to run the same game on us you run on women, do I look like a hoe to you?"

"Unk' why you're going there."

"Telly do I look like a hoe to you?"

"No Unk' you don't look like a hoe."

"Then why are you trying to play me like a hoe? You haven't stop fuckin around with Heather and even if you did, there would be another Heather. I figured that out years ago. You will do you until your dick falls off, but you will not run that shit on my daughter. This is not up for a vote or debate. I called you all morning in hopes that we could work this out like a gentleman without getting into gangster shit..."

In the thirty-five years of our marriage, plus to two on and off years we dated, I've never heard Glenn speak in that tone. Normally, if his nerves are calm, he could stand perfectly still on his good leg for ten minutes with no problem, but when he's pissed, his nerves become overactive and his equilibrium is thrown off. That's when the pogo bouncing starts.

In a circle, he bounced.

Left to right, at first.

A quick break.

Then repeated.

With an unlit cigarette dangling out the side of his mouth, a Heineken in his right hand, he jabbed violently at Telly with an index finger. In the middle of those two, but totally bias was Biyell.

In the center of the patio was a portable fire pit that we carried in and out to prevent rust. To the right of that portable pit, seated on a wicker bench, was Jarvis and of course his laptop. Across the fire pit, the three of them spat fire at Telly who tried his best to shield his face from the flames. Resting on the wall next to Jarvis was Glenn's crutch, but he didn't need it.

"The reason you feel so strongly about our engagement is because I confided in you about my personal life, but if you were just meeting me, and your daughter introduced us today, you would hand her off with a full tank of gas and a loaded food stamp card. Do you know why?"

Vexed, Glenn and Biyell didn't answer but simultaneously folded their arms.

"Because I am the top three percent of all Black men, Ya Heard Me."

"Three percent? *Nigga please.*" Biyell laughed aloud.

Telly pounded his chest. ***"Black. Educated. Lawyer. Athletic, Heterosexual. Single. Available. No Kids. I could go on all day."*** Telly brushed off his shoulders while, Jarvis and Biyell shooed.

"I didn't come here to argue, I came as a friend and a brother to ask for your daughter's hand in marriage."

"Telly you're here because Erica forced you. You had every intention of avoiding me as you have avoided my calls since last night."

"Even though I ended things with Heather, your position hasn't changed?"

Glenn inhaled a few deep breaths, downed his entire Heineken, then lit his cigarette.

"Telly what I'm about to say I mean from the bottom of my heart." He leaned over the pit as far as he could without falling. "FUCK NO. Ya heard me? *FUCK NO*!"

"So, it's like that?" Telly slipped through the middle of Glenn and Biyell and headed to the door, but Glenn wasn't done.

"This is my daughter we're talking about. Do you think I want her with a man who fucks over good women… just for the hell of it? A man who didn't try to win the challenge because he has to maintain a spade hand of women, *two and a possible*. As broke as you were at the time, the one who needed the money the most… creeping in the middle of the night was more important than making a lifestyle change for the better. Even knowing you like a book, I believed in you so much – I was willing to pay you for simply trying."

Jarvis typed as if Jesus asked him to write this down.

Telly nodded in disbelief, even though he disagreed.

Biyell waited for a cue to throw a punch.

Glenn's voice calmed to a more diplomatic tone. "Telly, gaming women is what you love to do. You'll never grow out of it. Some men don't. My brother is sixty-eight years old, with a wife of forty years, and a nine-month-old baby by a thirty-five-year-old mistress. Some men will bounce from woman to woman until they die. You remind me of my brother. When you're eighty years old in a nursing home, Ms. Barbra from room sixty-nine will catch you with Ms. Shirley. But not on my daughter."

I guess Biyell felt his instigating services was no longer needed. He took a seat next to Jarvis. I could feel the heat of contention seeping under the doorframe. They had reached an understanding, but not a resolution. Telly was still set on marrying Erica and Glenn was dead set against it.

"But you do understand that I'm here as a courtesy and will still marry Erica?"

"But you do understand the courtesy I've extended to you, would've allowed you to save face."

"So, you would break the code, and snitch me out."

"Do they sell… white toilet paper? Is Kermit The Frog… green? Did Ike… slap… Tina? Did Michael Jackson –"

"Uncle Glenn! He got the point…" Biyell couldn't hold a serious face.

"As long as we're on the same page. Cancel this engagement, blame the proposal on the Gin & Juice. You're an expert at lying, I'm sure you can come up with something."

"I can't do that, I love her, and I love those girls. I may not be the best man… in your opinion, but she feels otherwise. Telly turned towards the patio door.

"Because she doesn't know you! Even now, you're lying your ass off."

"Whatever Glenn…I'm headed home."

"Telly I was born at night, not last night. You're not going home. Within the hour, you'll pick up Heather from the airport. Her fight was delayed. ***Don't play with me,*** I know more than you think I know."

"Glenn, you only know what I wanted you to know, and anyone could've guessed that the flight was delayed."

"Here's where you fucked up Telly." Biyell reclined like actor Bill Duke in *Menace II Society*. "Never try to sell a lie to a liar. I don't believe you, none of us believe you, because you're lying. That's where you fucked up."

"*Mannnn*, I'm out of here, neither one of you know anything about me, you only think you know."

When Telly touched the patio doorknob, Glenn uttered a name that froze him solid.

"I know about Reebie…"

I watched Telly's jaw dislocate. I watched him turn pale like a bag of rice. I watched Jarvis and Biyell shrug at each other. Jarvis fingers waited patiently. Apparently, the brotherhood wasn't as transparent as they once thought.

Who was Reebie?

Why the sudden mention of her name caused the Rottweilers to hush? The room was still dangerously silent, but the space between Telly and Glenn was deafening. How was Reebie associated with Telly? How was Glenn able to gain knowledge of her? Why was she a secret from the group?

"I'll catch y'all later." Telly continued to the door.

"Don't fuck with me Telly. I will bring your world crashing down. You're on the clock."

Telly greeted me with a wave on his way out the door, seconds later he backed out of my driveway just as Bylisha entered the kitchen.

"More juice."

I folded my arms in defiance "More juice what?"

"More juice pleeeze."

She's so adorable it's hard to look at her and not smile.

"That's more like it…" She followed me into the kitchen just as the guys exited the patio.

"Daddy-Daddy-Daddy." She leaped into his arms. Biyell bench pressed her to the ceiling.

Biyell hugged me and then Jarvis, afterward their attention shifted back to Glenn.

"Care to explain this Reebie person?" Jarvis asked.

"Please do, because when you said that name – dude looked like he had just seen *The Ghost of Bitches Past.*" Biyell blurted. "Bragging about he's the top three percent, that *Fucka'* turned white as 2% milk when Uncle Glenn said Reebie. Who is Reebie and why is this the first time we're hearing about her?"

"It's not for me to say right now, but it is in his best interest to erase any thought of marrying Erica."

"Well answer this, is Reebie pregnant?" Jarvis asked.

Glenn hopped over to the refrigerator and twisted another Heineken, then back to the table.

"*For-real for-real* Uncle Glenn, you have to give us something." Biyell pleaded as he saddled Bylisha on his shoulders.

If he hasn't called off this wedding, you will know everything there is to know about Reebie by the time the bacon finish popping in the grease. Ya heard me?"

"We heard you." They said.

"*This tea is delicious,*" I whispered.

CHAPTER 25

August 15, 1998
6:42 p.m.

KAYLA

E arlier this evening my mother bombarded me with that question again. You know the question; the one no mother would ever dare ask her son, unless she questioned his sexuality. That fingernail popping backwards sort of question. That disparaging intrusion of privacy.

She leaned against the bathroom doorframe and cornered me with her curiosity. There was no escaping her inquisitive hunger nor could I blame her. If I were my mother, I would've asked the same question. Without the hubris undertone. Without the ominous overtone. Without the insinuation that I was to blame. Not one single guy in Atlanta asked me for my phone number all summer. Was I the blame? Hell no!

Mom it's not my fault that these 1998 guys are pussies and piss their pampers the moment I make eye contact with them.

That is what I wanted to say, but I held my peace. No need to slip into a spat that could cause me to run late for the only outing I have had this year. Done in the bathroom, I side stepped my mom and made a hard left towards my bedroom, but she was in high pursuit.

"Soooooooooooooo, have you met anyone special... lately?" She asked with a twisted smile.

That question.

The question that isn't a question but an indictment.

The question that concluded: I am the lone reason I'm single. Something is wrong with me. There has to be, because it is the only reasonable explanation. Pretty, but lonely. Attractive, but solo. The *cute-model-type*, but not the *marrying type*. I guess.

"Soooooooooooooo, been on any dates lately?"

"Momma... I'm going out tonight."

"Yes, that much I figured, but Tiff &Tracey hardly constitute as a real date." She moseyed into my room as if invited. "Kayla I surely expected you to follow in my footsteps. Kidnap the heart of the finest Alpha Phi Alpha man on campus. That's how I met your father you know..."

"Yes, I know, you've only told that story fifteen-hundred times."

"Because I'm trying to push you off the fence."

"Momma, I'm not on any fence? Where's all of this coming from?"

"From me, I'm encouraging you to get out there. Test the waters a little."

I have tested those waters and nearly drowned in four feet.

Gingerly she commandeered the edge of my bed, where the vanity provided an unobstructed view of my every expression.

"But the summer is still young... you know? Morehouse College isn't that far from Georgia Tech. I hear there's a lot of single guys at Morehouse, the kind that will make a good husband one day."

Exasperated, I sprung from my vanity chair over to the closet, with each step I felt her ruby smile on the back of my neck.

"Momma, *waaaaaay back* in the day when you attended Dillard University," I pointed behind me to 1984 "marriages were arranged in freshman orientation. Things are much different now."

"Is it, really? Or maybe we were more versatile in our campus activities. For instance, able to play sports, and court at the same time."

The promenade around the true purpose of our little chat just ended. "How is it humanly possible to spend two full months in Atlanta, and still come home single?"

"Momma, please, not tonight. I don't have time for it…okay."

"Soooooo, you're short on time I see? No wonder. All of your available time away from volley ball is spent mall bumming with *T&T* instead of that guy who was gaga over you." A lone finger tapped against her tempo for what felt like a week. "What was his name?"

"Momma you know his name…"

"For some strange reason his name has slipped my mind. The really nice-looking guy, real tall?

"Tyrone momma, his name is Tyrone Weaver."

"Yea, that's the cute guy…Tyrone Weaver." My mother wanted me to say his name, because Tyrone was her handpicked, favorite potential suitor of all time.

"*I think you better call Tyrooooone---.*" She whined in her Erykah Badu voice. "Yum, yum, what a delicious looking pudding pop he is." Her neck rolled in delight.

"Will you chill please," I stumped in embarrassment.

"Well, he is." Cautiously, she gazed over towards the living room where my father dosed in his recliner. "You should call him and ask if he would like to tag along."

I huffed in anguish "I'm not calling Tyrone. And besides, I haven't spoken with him since graduation day."

Tyrone's father was the Warden at Orleans Parish Prison, and my mother managed his bundle of investment properties. Unfortunately for Tyrone, his dad strategically mapped out the next ten years of his life in preparation for a city council seat. My mother also knew his mom from her days at Saint Mary's Academy, and if my mom knew *your people,* then all that remained was the formal engagement announcement.

And she was right about that whole *pudding pop* thing, dude was Blair Underwood handsome, only taller. But little did she know – I had already disqualified him – not for his conservative republican aura. I am a sports junkie. Tyrone is a political junkie. The problem is he doesn't know how or when to turn off politics.

Don't get me wrong, he's a really nice guy, but he lacks the romantic experience to know that on the first date, a discussion about how much he loved George Bush for the republican nomination was a definite turn off. An evening with him was like trying to have an intimate dinner with Dick Gregory.

My mother stretched the yellow-coiled phone cord across my bedroom. Suddenly I heard the distinct chime of pressed buttons. With hands still damp from styling gel, I snatched the phone before she could press the final digit in his phone number.

"Momma...chill. Please –"

"Well, I'm just trying to help."

"I don't need your help."

"I think you do...because you're two months shy of twenty-two, and I have yet to meet one guy or wave bye-bye from the porch as he whisks you off into the evening. As a loving mother, it's my indelible right you know. Which leaves me no other choice but to ask." Her chest swelled from compressed reluctance. "Kayla are you...are you –"

"Am I what? Don't go silent now, am I what?"

"It's just, I don't understand your way of doing things, and it has me a little worried –"

"...about what momma? I've never known you to search for the perfect words. Bluntness is your tiara. Get it off your chest, what are you so worried about?"

"Are you more interested in women than men?"

I knew that was her gut feeling but I wanted to hear the words slide off the tip of her tongue.

How did I become a gay suspect?

Because I can't get a date?

I'm the problem?

Flabbergasted!

Long before my mother asked if I was gay, I heard that question ricochet off the walls in her cluttered mind. It was in the quizzical way she stared. The dead silence after one of my less than fulfilling replies to one of her intrusive questions. The plastic grin that greeted Tracey at the door. Armed with a misguided hunch, I have been bonded romantically to my best friend. That hurts.

Why?

I have no one.

Not even the person she suspected, not in the least.

"Kayla, before you answer. Just know... I would love you *none-the-less* if you are in fact...gay. I mean, it would crush me and destroy your father because it's not what we had planned for your life, but we would love you none-the less. I hope you understand how difficult this is for me, but as your mother, I have a right to know if my daughter is gay?"

"No... I am not gay," her chest deflated in relief.

"That's music to my ears, but are you sure? Kayla I'm not here to pressure you or make you feel as if you have to –"

"MOMMA, I'm not gay! I...am not gay." I pointed at the bridge of my nose. "If I were gay, I would have told you a long time ago –"

"Lower your voice... before you wake your father. I didn't mean to upset you, but if you're not gay, then this thing... with you and Tracey...and the excessive amount of time – "

"Tracey? Tracey? This thing with Tracey?"

Momma, are you fucking serious? That's what I wanted to say, but I caught the words in the roof of my mouth.

"All of my life you policed my every interaction with boys, made me scared to death of getting pregnant, and now, all of a sudden, you're Ms. Match Maker? Just like that, you're worried that I could be a lesbian? Do the *lez-boom-boom* with Tracey, who happens to be in a relationship by the way, but it's the only thing that makes sense to you."

My mother gazed into my closet, and then out into the hall and then back to the closet.

"Kayla, I didn't mean to upset you but, but –"

"For the last time. I'm not gay…I'M CURSED."

It is truly a curse.

I am the spitting image of her.

My mom at 39 years old is still Essence Magazine gorgeous, with her yogurt skin, wind sensitive hair, hazel eyes, and cushiony lips. I stole it all. Except for the hair. Thank God I got one trait from my dad's side of the family. At Dillard, my Afro-puffs became my look and allowed me to blend into the bustling herds that roamed the campus – somewhat – if only I were more like Tracey.

Her eyes, even though she is blind as Ray Charles.

Her height, even if I had to forgo my volleyball scholarship.

Her shape, even if I had to purchase an entire new wardrobe.

In the meantime, I will have to make due with these lanky legs and bulky shoulders.

Like I said, I'm cursed. I may not ever have a real relationship, and mother will always think I'm dry humping with Tracey. Fuck it. As long as my self-esteem can get a sabbatical from my mother, everything else will work out. Hopefully.

That heated exchange transpired less than an hour ago, and here I am on a porch swing, with my favorite person, looking every bit the happy gay couple. Oh well, fuck it. If I were into girls, it would definitely be Tracey. She is *Velvet Rope Sexy.*

Maybe I am…

The Jackson Barracks bus rumbled through the night like a ghost ship, eagerly searching for a passenger. Trailing the bus was a gale-force sauna that blow-dried the styling gel between my afro-puffs – it also caused beads of sweat to drip off the sides of my neck, and in the mist of my frustration, my pink chiffon blouse started to soak across my chest.

I feel sweaty.

I expected to get sweaty tonight, but in a club.

Better yet under Tyrone, if by chance I bumped into him. Under Tyrone is a good reason to sweat, but not on Tiffany's porch. Not waving at neighbors with our damp armpits. Not feeding the Ninth Ward mosquitoes. But with all things considered, there wasn't anywhere else I'd rather be than right here with Tracey. She needed me. I needed her.

In the same way, a deer sought comfort amongst its own kind. It helps knowing someone is always looking out for you. That was not the case with *inconsiderate-ass Tiffany.*

"What is taking her so long?" I huffed, while Tracey made that jaw & teeth sucking sound, as her eyes rolled away from the screen door. With each minute that perspired – my patience dripped down the center of my back.

"Girl… it's too damn hot out here. Let's wait inside?" I simmered.

"Nah, you can go. I'd rather chill out here." Tracey said as her eyes gazed into each passing car. She was consumed with an approaching cold front (a blizzard) that would more than likely ice her relationship with Josh Leblanc.

"Are you expecting him?"

"No…not really."

"Seems like it," I said to the back of her head as she focused in on the next car to boom down Chartres Street. "Tracey if you're not up for this tonight, I understand."

"I'm up for it…and besides, this will be our last time together until Thanksgiving. I'm sure as the night unfolds – I'll find something else to occupy my mind."

"Or better yet…someone else?"

Tracey sucked her teeth again, rolled her eyes again, then bottomed up the last of her ice cubes.

She wasn't the only one who needed distance from their thoughts – my mind was still engulfed in the argument with my mom. Wincing over the things she said. Grimacing over the things I should've said.

Momma, instead of obsessing over my sexless life, you should focus on that dead-ass marriage you have with my father. But I held my peace because I enjoy biting into delicious apples without the assistance of dentures.

And the sad part is my parents actually think they've fooled me with their arrangement of convenience. The thrill has been gone long between them for at least ten years.

Why stay together just to be together if you're not together?

Children or no children if I ever end up with a man who no longer wanted me – I am out that day.

Therefore, we drifted, in the desert heat of August, with Tracey's mind on Josh, and my mind on my mother's insinuations and innuendoes. We drifted, in a bassinet of uncertainty; only confident in knowing it would take more than miles to break our bond. Even our sighs were in perfect sync. In between the booming cars was silence, and the electrical hum of a street light.

The only other sounds came from the squeaky joints of the porch swing, and a determined mosquito that buzzed in the space between us like a gossipy co-worker.

Why are we sitting out here in this humidity?

Is this what my mother was referring to?

Why am I questioning my sexuality?

Do I like Tracey in that way?

Could I be...gay?

Above our heads four moths discoed around the porch light, while Tracey and I did what we've always done, wait around for Tiffany. That is what we've become, two ladies in waiting, except one of us has a man, and the other one is a suspected dyke.

"So how are you two going to survive the distance being that he has opted out of college completely?" I asked because misery loves company.

"I don't think we will," she pouted "he's convinced that I'm going to Baton Rouge to date other guys."

"Tracey...there's no way Josh could be that insecure..."

"He is, and I've explained repeatedly that I'm only going to be *right up the road* in Baton Rouge. But to Josh, Baton Rouge is like I've moved to Oklahoma."

"Tracey, I'm so sorry to hear that..."

"To answer your question, I don't think we're going to be a couple after tomorrow."

With each passing minute we waited on Tiffany, my girl Tracey spiraled at the thought of losing her first love. I knew then that if Tiffany didn't hurry, then Tracey might start crying, which makes me cry, and I wasn't having that.

Just as I touched the handle on the screen door, Tiffany made her grand exit, followed by her mom with a Polaroid instant camera.

After a ten-minute pose-off, we waved at her mother on the porch, as she fanned the photos. The night was young, and we were off to connect with all of our friends who were also leaving the nest.

Tiffany drove; I was the director of the itinerary in the passenger seat, while Tracey held down the back seat. She waved royally to all of her subjects at each red light.

"Woooooooo-hooooo" Tiffany yelled as we zoomed across the St. Claude Bridge with her braids flapping in the wind. "Oh yea, Tracey, I almost forgot to tell you...Josh called while I was getting dressed."

"Why didn't you tell me, we were right outside?" She yelled over the wind.

"I asked him to hold on, but before I could make it out to you, he hung up."

The wind that whisked over the windshield swooped us all the way back to grade school, to a time where we could communicate through our plaits. I half turned and made eye contact with Tracey. I heard her every thought.

I knew her body language.

Her head shook from left to right. Finger pressed against her temple. Nostrils flared. Right arm cradled across her stomach. Tracey was pissed. Her boyfriend was too cozy with Tiffany. She never gave Josh Tiffany's phone number. This wasn't a good start to our evening.

"Tiffany, why are we stopping here?"

"Hello, the sign says." Tiffany pointed at a New Orleans Daiquiri sign.

"I don't drink daiquiris, and neither do you." Once again, I half turned to the backseat. Tracey shrugged. "You shouldn't drink & drive, that's not a good combination."

"Kayla or do you prefer Mother Dearest?" She shot me a smirky look. "It's just a frozen drink with a shot of gin. It takes more than a shot to get me drunk. Okay!"

"Tiff when did you start drinking?"

"I wouldn't call it drinking, but I like daiquiris, what's the big deal? Lighten up."

It was about ten minutes later when she returned to the car and placed her 16oz in the center cup holder, then we were off. Once we arrived at the house party Tiffany headed straight for the table, the one along the back wall, with the fancy punch. She helped herself to two cups.

We left the house party around eleven and headed to the gateway of New Orleans East known as *Gentilly*. In this snoring side of town, we'd planned to finish the night at a popular hangout for twenty-year-olds: *The Big Easy Night Club*.

Immediately once we entered the club, we caught the attention of bullish dudes who tried to impress us with blinged out jewelry, and gold teeth that glowed like strobe lights. I could tell from Tracey's vibe – she hadn't gotten over the revelation that Josh and Tiffany had a separate friendship. *Girls Night Out* ended for her with that portion of the conversation. It was obvious that the only one in the group having the time of her life was

Tiffany. By midnight Tracey and I were done, but not Tiffany, she was just getting started.

She backed it up and bounced it from one guy to the next, I'd never knew she enjoyed being fondled by that many strangers. Then the DJ made a special announcement.

"Where are my sexy ladies, I need only the hottest of the hottest on the dance floor – we have a special guest here tonight and he heard about these New Orleans Red Bones – he came down here just to meet you." Without knowing who it was, Tiffany twitched and switched to the middle of the dance floor with about six other girls.

"Fellas before we bring out our special guest, we need to narrow it down to the hottest Red Bone in the club tonight – there could only be one." The men in the club roared at the idea of voting for the prettiest girl.

"She's not a Red Bone," I whispered to Tracey. "You're much lighter and much prettier."

"Who cares, I'm ready to go home."

The DJ strutted behind the row of contestants like Kiki Shepard from *Showtime at the Apollo* and held his hand above the head of each one, the girl with the most applause won. Three of the girls were eliminated, leaving Tiffany going head to head with a girl that resembled LeToya Luckett, who should be the lead singer in Destiny's Child.

"Tiffany, why did you run your ass up there? You don't stand a chance. That Destiny's Child look-alike will win this hood pageant with ease." I mumbled.

Tiffany won.

"This is so fucking degrading! I would call my dad for a ride if she wasn't so tipsy." Tracey said.

"I agree, we can't leave her. As soon as *The Miss Hood of American Pageant* is over, we're out of here."

The DJ's voice blared.

"Now that we've crowned the hottest of the hottest Red Bone in the club tonight, it's time to bring out our special guest. Please welcome Epic Recording Artist Ginuwine!"

The music started, the club lost their minds, and little did anyone know *Ginu-fuckin-wine* was Tiffany's favorite singer. She drove us crazy with that pony song, and her alter ego.

A stripper name *Taffy*.

For over a year, we listened to her fantasies about Ginuwine and all the X-rated things she would do to him if they were alone. Her fantasy entered the dance floor, and it was just Tiffany and Ginuwine."

"Oh no…" Tracey murmured.

"This can't be happening," I said.

But it was.

In front of a packed house, it happened, he happened, and Taffy happened. The seductive stripper moves she practiced in my living room, for an audience of two, she performed those same moves with flawless choreography.

At one point, while grinding behind her – Taffy pulled up the back of her jean skirt. When he moved around to the front of him, Taffy guided his hand to her inner thigh. Basically, they had as much sex as you can have without genital participation.

It went on and on.

The crowd was stunned into silence.

"That was a setup! She's probably one of Ginuwine's back-up dancers." The runner-up complained.

"I think that's the girl from the actual Pony video." Another contestant said who wore a mini skirt so high I swore I saw her Tampon string. Not that I was paying any attention.

"I knew it, that is her." The tampon mini skirt girl said.

They both were wrong, it wasn't the dancer from the video, it was Taffy, also known as *Tiffany Arceneaux,* a founding member of our trio, but not anymore, tonight she was a Professional Pony Rider for Ginuwine.

When the song ended, the club went berserk for the special guest, and he went berserk for Tiffany. I observed Ginuwine whisper in her ear, then she nodded, then he kissed her on the lips.

"Not on my watch..." I spoke across the room as if Ginuwine could hear me. She wasn't one of his video models, she wasn't his to kiss, and she wasn't going back to his hotel. Tiffany was a member of *The Plaits*, and we always leave together.

"Let's grab her and get the hell out of here now! Right now, Kayla. Move."

With me leading the way we rush the dance floor just as the DJ cranked it up again, but Tiffany was in a purple haze of ecstasy, and refused to leave the dance floor.

"I have your purse let's go." I pulled her by the arm.

She backed out of my grip.

"I'm not ready to leave."

"Yes, you are, let's go." Once more, she pulled away.

"Tiffany we are not leaving without you. Stop causing a scene." Tracey demanded.

"How about you two bunk bitches catch a cab." Arrogantly, Tiffany tried to shoo us way. "*I'vvvvve* been invited to the *VIP Section* for a private party."

"Like hell you are!" Tracey said.

Tracey rushed Tiffany and started dragging her off the dance floor. Before Tiffany managed to free herself, I straight jacked my arms around her from behind and lifted.

"Hey Ginuwine, you better get down here – they are stealing your dancer." The DJ said as we shoved our way through the crowd and out the door.

Once outside we looked like wasted tourists on Bourbon fighting with a bouncer, but Tiffany was the only one drunk. Talk about acting a complete ass. We were parked directly across the street from the club, but Tiffany resisted arrest for nearly an hour. Suddenly the sound of gunfire ring out in the club and all the patrons ran for the door at the same time. It was then that Tiffany chilled with the bullshit. We made it to the car through a crowd of people who were determined to live, but in the chaos, we were blocked in by a promo truck from Q93 FM.

The girl who resembled the Destiny's Child lead singer. The one who stood next to me during the performance and complained that *The Hood Pageant* was rigged, she caught a stray bullet in her throat.

We hauled ass away from that club.

On the way home, the ride was quiet, but tempers were still boiling. I was perfectly okay with only the sound of the wind combing through my hair. I had a headache. Tracey could not sit straight. We'd never had a fight, not amongst ourselves.

At a glance, my arms appeared as if someone tried to draw a football field with a red marker. At a glance, Tracey's chin and neck appeared as if she'd been locked in a closet with eight violent cats.

"Bitches always gotta be jealous." We heard Tiffany say under her breath.

"Bitches? Jealous? We just saved your hot ass from getting gang raped or as they would have called it…*a train*. You always have to be the center of attention." Tracey snapped.

"Hey, that's enough" I yelled over the voice of Lauryn Hill, by the way, she was right; *some guys are only about that thing that thing.*

"Hey knock it off! We're only a few red lights from home, let's calm down and zip it." I yelled.

"That's what I told Josh," Tiffany whispered.

"Come again, what did you say?"

"Tracey, you heard me the first time…you may be blind as a bat, but ain't shit wrong with your ears."

"Pull over, pull the fuck over right now." Tracey unbuckled at the Poland & St Claude intersection.

"No, your *bunk-ass* wanted to go home, so I'm bringing you home, **Right… the fuck now!"**

The car accelerated.

Up ahead was the ever active, always making you late for school, aggravating as hell: St. Claude Bridge. The same bridge we crossed five hours ago as loving sisters, bonded by 15 years of friendship and academic accomplishments. It was that bully of the Lower Ninth Ward, with its banging bells, its infamous flashing light that dared you to beat the four lowering traffic arms, and the impatient air horn from tugboats. Tiffany accepted that challenge.

30mph

35mph

40mph

45mph

50mph

Before I could scream slow down, the fancy punch and dai-quiris in her bladder accelerated us to sixty-five miles per hour. Up ahead as you approached the drawbridge, the road veered slightly right. The fancy punch and daiquiris wouldn't allow Tiffany to swerve slightly right with the lane. We pinballed between the guardrail and the median, before ramming head-on into the center petition. The center petition didn't budge and inch.

Tiffany's seat belt and the airbag did its job.

My seat belt and airbag did its job.

It was then that my mind reeled in reverse to the intersection at the foot of the bridge on Poland Street, the one where Tracey unbuckled her seat belt, and attempted to leap out of the convertible. I couldn't remember if Tracey re-buckled, but I figured she would've once the car started accelerating.

She hadn't.

The last image of my best friend was her smacking the damp pavement after descending from thirty feet up, after her head collided with the steel lift beam on the bridge. The following day the paramedic who was first to arrive on the scene of the crash, visited my room at Charity hospital. He informed mom that Tracey was dead before she hit the ground.

I was the first Plait.

Tiffany was the second Plait.

Then came final the Plait, Tracey Honore.

In addition to losing Tracey that night, I also lost my volleyball scholarship. My injuries included severed ligaments in my right knee from the impact with the dashboard, and a torn rotator cup from the seat belt. Tiffany on the other hand, walked away from the crash without a scratch, was voted the prettiest girl in the club, and I almost forgot;

She got to ride that pony.
If you're horny, let's do it
Ride it, my pony
My saddle's waiting
Come and jump on it

CHAPTER 26

4:10 p.m.

RASTA

She left me. In the middle of our conversation, without excusing herself or the minimal courtesy of goodbye: she vanished. In the click of a mouse, before I realized it, I was alone in the room, once occupied by newlyweds. Not *Gone With The Wind*, but rather, *Gone With The Memory* of someone she deeply loved. And so, she left me. Departed, yet near, here, nonetheless there, on the sofa, but so far away. I now know where she goes on those suspiciously quiet days: she visits a dear friend.

August 16, 1998, the day the sunset on Tracey.

She was weary from this recent visit, and it was quite apparent that my bunny-eyed wife had descended into a lamented shell of the woman I married yesterday. It was all my fault.

I should not have picked this lock, not the day after our wedding.

I should have given her the liberty to make a formal introduction, at a time of her choosing. I should have never pried open that can of grief, but I so desperately wanted to meet Tracey – I placed my need to know above her personal space.

Then again, is it solely my fault? A name I heard for the first-time last night, on the dance floor, had reverberated in my mind for twelve consecutive hours. It was how I knew Tracey was more than just an old classmate – a volleyball teammate – a salon acquaintance: *Nah*, it was so much deeper. Their souls were connected, and the two assholes who are truly at fault for opening this can of grief is none other than her surviving best friend Tiffany, and that dude Josh.

That Dance.

That Song.

After she expressed the intimacy of their bond, and the events leading up to her deaths, I was compelled to apologize, but remain convinced: if I had not conjured up the memory of her friend, then she would have remained a mystery.

Nevertheless, it was nice to meet you, Kayla has told me so much about you. I'd only wished we could have met under more pleasant circumstances.

"Thank you for opening up, I can tell she meant a lot to you."

Kayla didn't reply but continued to sigh and cradle herself.

"If you don't mind me asking, how did you and Tiffany's friendship survive that night?"

"I wanted to kill her, but my busted knee and shoulder would not permit it. She was arrested that night for driving under the influence. Tracey's mom (who was an assistant District Attorney) made sure Tiffany was prosecuted to the fullest. She was held in jail on first-degree manslaughter, but after a hearing, her charges were reduced to reckless endangerment, unauthorized use of a motor vehicle, and negligent homicide. Mrs. Honore' wanted blood for blood but had to settle for ten years' probation, five years revoked driving privileges and a host of other knick-knack fines, that in no way pacified the loss of life."

"For the most part, she got away with it."

"Not even close." Kayla folded her arms and reclined. "Tracey's father sued Tiffany's mom in a wrongful death case because the convertible was rented in her name. He won a five-million-dollar judgment. Her family lost everything."

"What was everything?"

"Tiffany's mom owned one of the best hair salons in the city but had to surrender the deed to satisfy the judgment. A few short months before the accident, her father had just expanded his collision center, in which he used a rental property to secure the loan. In the end, they were left penniless. And Tiffany lost her scholarship after the story aired in the local news that night. Once she became a convicted felon, she lost all interest in continuing her education."

"Because you can't get *Federal Aid* if you're a convicted felon."

Kayla nodded.

"How did you two reconnect?"

"Because I loved her just as much as I loved Tracey, but in a different way."

"A different way?" She nodded again. "How so?"

It was then that Kayla shot me a look of discomfort, followed by a blank stare. Even though I was guilty of trespassing, I was smart enough to know that I had better tiptoe from this point forward. Thankfully, she continued without any additional arm-twisting from me.

"I still wanted to kill Tiffany, but watching her parents suffer through devastating losses for her mistake was excruciating. Despite the absence of Tracey, over the years our families grew very close."

"Which explains why Mr. Honore 'gave you away yesterday."

"Correct, I was also the one who asked him to have mercy on the Arceneaux family. To continue to garnish them for every penny wasn't going to bring his daughter back: he agreed. After a few months had passed, the garnishments ceased, and the property was returned."

"Just like that…?"

She nodded.

"But I don't understand, what was in it for Mr. & Mrs. Honore'?"

"Tiffany had to vow, in memory of their daughter that she would never drink again."

"Oh no…"

"and…"

"Go on…"

"I vowed to Mr. and Mrs. Arceneaux that I could be held accountable to make sure Tiffany kept her end of the deal. And I also vowed to name my first daughter after Tracey. The Arceneaux's were moved to tears. That's the main reason the property was returned."

"Sweetie, baby, I'm honored you've allowed me into this corner of your world and shared the details of that arrangement." I blew her a kiss from across the coffee table. "Kayla, thank you. If there is anything you would like to know about my past, I will match your transparency with the same open doors, I promise."

A radiant ray broke through her clouds.

"I never told anyone the full story of that night or the heated words that were exchanged in the moments before the crash, but you're my husband now, and last night my friend… hurt your friend."

Her friendship with Tiffany made sense. I now had a deeper understanding of why her behavior seemed so out of character, her sobriety was broken with that first toast.

Then the champagne toast for Erica and Glenn, then two turned into four, and the fifth glass sipped her back to 1998, to the night she had a dance with Ginuwine before her world slammed into the St. Claude Bridge. Suddenly my mind fell on Biyell. Could he find it in his heart to forgive her after I explain the Tracey mystery? Probably not, because no one forgave him. Once Tyra discovered Tamara, she never gave him a second chance to make it right.

It was over.

Shut down like K-mart.

Indicted and convicted like Bill Cosby.

I traveled the short distance around the coffee table and kneeled. Next, I laid a tender kiss on the top of her scarred knee, the one I often wondered about but never asked. Then I kissed the ten-inch line on her right shoulder, the one I assumed was a battle scar left over from a deadly fight, with a cheap bra. Then I placed the palms of my hands gently on the sides of her face and turned her lips to mine.

For about five minutes at least, I kissed my wife until her eyes softly shut, and she felt safe again. Only then did she cease to cradle herself. She started to hold me instead, and the kisses continued. Not the selfish kind puckered during the prelude to sex, where the expectation of pleasure is paramount, but the cozy kind, the reassuring kind – loaded with contentment and commitment.

"Thank you…" She said once we resurfaced for air and our foreheads connected.

"What for?" I whispered.

"For making me believe in men again. I didn't know there was anyone like you still available. I'd lost hope in love. Then you appeared in the same place I lost you, like a mirage of a man that was beyond my reach. Every day I asked myself, *why does he love me? Out of all of the women, why did he ask me to partner with him in love and happiness?* You are so custom designed for me that I often curse my first marriage. The only reason I married him – I felt the clock was about to expire, and everyone around me except Tiffany was married. If the truth is told, I had a fear of being an old maid with rumors circling me. *She can't keep a man because she's gay."*

"Kayla no way? You're shitting me! You felt pressured to get married…because of potential rumors?

She raised her right hand "That's the whole truth and nothing but. So, I said yes to the first person who'd asked. After that marriage fizzled, I lost faith in love, men, and …God."

"Seriously, I've learned more about you in this one morning, than our entire engagement. Hi, my name is Roderick." I teased. "I definitely didn't know you went through a period where you hated men."

"It's not that I hated men, but I hated the shit men do to us. Losing Tracey came with a lifetime of hurt feelings, the last thing I needed was a synthetic man like my ex, but that's what I got – Timothy." Her voice rumbled like approaching thunder. "Then came you. Mr. Roderick Ross." Her face sparkled with sunshine. "You restored me. But I should've waited for you…"

"Kayla I wasn't out there, not this guy you married. The only reason we're here right now is because Uncle Glenn kicked in a door with one leg, and DeShonta paired me with a man named Levi."

"Your roommate in the hospital…?"

"Yes Levi, because I was broken, and if you would've married me broken, eventually I was going to demolish you. That's what broken men do, we break women. West Jeff was an intervention of someone who didn't believe he had a mental problem. Do you remember the early days of our phone conversations, when you asked a million and one questions…?"

"Yes, I remember those questions, but I should get a pass. I was paranoid…okay."

"Paranoid? You were scared to death of me – you were shaking like a bowl of Jell-O."

She giggled "I wasn't that bad…"

"Kayla, that first week, I thought my name was NIGGZILLA – that's how fast you ran from me."

She slapped my shoulder in laughter "well obviously not fast enough." Kayla flashed her wedding ring "you caught me."

"Yes, I did, my best catch ever. But I still struggled to get a grip on you, then it all changed one day you asked that question. Once I answered you. Only then did you relax. Do you remember that night we walked down Magazine Street?"

"I do, but I asked so many questions during that time. Help me recall."

"Roderick are you happy with Roderick?"

"Oh yeah, now I remembahhh." She said in her Betty Wright voice from *Tonight is the Night.*

Caught off guard I laughed too "that was the first time I sat down and pondered on it..."

"Then you said yes, *I'm happy, because of my relationship with my sons, and I've fallen in love with myself again.* You apologized to those you hurt and forgave yourself. You said happiness had been achieved prior to meeting me. Then I was like, *why are you interested in a relationship with me, if you don't need me.* Then you said..."

". . .your job is not to make me happy, because that's not fair to you. I want to celebrate my happiness with you. And your only requirement was to..."

". . .like you, because our marriage has to be built on *Love & Like.* Whenever I stop liking you then the hayride is over."

"Wow, you remember..." I was impressed.

"I did, because my ex...and please forgive me for constantly comparing you two, but he placed so much pressure on me to make him happy. You were the first person to ever say, Kayla, you're not..."

"...the director of entertainment and happiness...just chill and be the girl. Be my girl. *That's all I ask of you.*"

"Then you started to sing That's all I ask of you. I surrendered to you that night, on Magazine Street. I knew then you were the one." She wrapped her arms around my neck, and we kissed. "Roderick...I'm so addicted to you because I like you, I like you just as much as I love you."

"And I love you too... Kayla."

I love her Eskimo kisses.

"There was a reason I constantly bugged you while you were at Uncle Glenn's house."

"Oh my God, that's right...baby forgive me." I had hijacked

the conversation. "What was it you wanted to talk about?"

"That because of you I might get the chance to make good on a promise."

"Huh?"

Kayla pointed at the center of her chest.

"Reach inside my shirt…" She stretched the crew neck of her Dillard Volleyball T-shirt outward.

"Huh?"

"Just do it…stick your hand in my shirt. A little deeper. Keep going. You're getting warmer. Bingo."

Over the years, I've slid my hands in many bras. Lace bras, satin bras, little bras, *Big Bertha size bras*, even lying bras, but this was the first time I retrieved an object out of a bra.

With two lines.

"I made a vow to Tracey's parents and –"

I cut her off "Kayla are you telling me –"

"Yes, there may be a little Tracey in my belly."

An astonished feeling robbed me of my breath. "We're expecting a baby…"

"Yes baby, The Plaits are back."

"THE PLAITS!" I yelled as I pulled her up to me and squeezed the air out of her lungs. "Thank you, Mrs. Ross, for the best wedding gift ever!"

"And thank you, Mr. Ross, for helping me keep my word. My word is my bond."

CHAPTER 27

New Orleans MSY Airport
6:55 p.m.

TELLY

I have calculated every possible angle, scenario, and *what if* – for the life in me, I can't figure out how he discovered Reebie? Unless, unless, he's having me followed.

Nevertheless, why would Glenn have me followed, if he didn't have a dog in the fight prior to the wedding reception? He wasn't that invested in my relationship until the news broke that I am involved with his daughter. The one thing that is for sure is he better mind his *got-damn* business.

The flight delay with Heather was a given, but Reebie? Where is he getting his information? *Calm down Telly, stay calm. You have to stay calm.* My hands trembled. *Breathe Telly, you have to breathe.*

How.

N.

D.

Fuck does he know about Reebie?
How?

What has pissed me off the most is I don't like when someone tells me what *I better do.* Normally I would've told him to go *fuck himself,* but I can't because he has me by the nuts. And I like my nuts cuffed just as much as the next man, but not like this. Glenn is dragging me by the nuts, and I can't fight back. I don't like it one bit. I don't like being told what to do. I tell people what to do, and not the other way around.

It's best Glenn stay out of my business.
Erica is a grown-ass woman!
Who does he think he is?
Heather, please hurry.

Glenn gave me until tomorrow or he will tell Erica everything. What exactly does he know? Who am I kidding? He knows everything. The question that remains is how? How? Who told him about Reebie?

If I wouldn't have invited Erica to the wedding reception, then none of this would've happened. Wedding receptions have a way of intermingling circles, and I keep my circles separated and scattered.

But no.

I had to fit in with the crew, and buy into all of this *commitment nonsense,* knowing damn well I'm not built for that life. Now I'm being forced to do it or let her go, and I don't want to. I love Erica and I also love Heather. I can't see myself being happy with just one. I need Heather to get through my day. She listens like no other woman I've ever had, I mean, she listens like there isn't another person alive but me.

I love that.

Heather is solely focused on me and only me. No kids. Zero distractions. Financially set from that life insurance policy, and all she wants to do is please me. I love that shit!

Sure, when we started out, it was just fucking, but that's how love takes root in me. The more I'm in her, the more I want to be in her, and listen to her moan that seductive melody. Here is the best part.

Heather nurtures my sexual appetite. We've had so many threesomes I've lost count. The only rule is she picks the girl and time. Heather is irreplaceable. There isn't another. And she accepted Erica.

But I love Erica just as much. But in a different way.

And for full disclosure, I have considered leaving Erica, but Heather is older, and I'm not sure how long she can maintain this level of sexiness. On the other hand, Erica is not aggressive at all, not even a little. Sometimes I just want to fuck! That's it.

Not make love.

F. U. C. K.

As in, I'm on my lunch break, and she offered twenty dollars' worth of noon-day pussy on sale. Not make love but fuck, as in bend her over the kitchen table, or on the hood of my car. With no resistance or hesitation. Because she's in it for the twenty dollars.

Not with Erica.

Hell no.

Surprises and spontaneity is not her thing. Like that time in *River Bend Park*. The girls had a recital dinner performance under the stars. The entire time we picnicked, all I could think about was submarining my tongue deep inside of Erica. On the low, I even tried to slither my finger under her panties, but her mother was parked on the blanket next to us – peaking and blocking my hustle.

Once the recital was over Rosa & Parks rode home with their grandmother leaving us alone to star gaze and smooch. The more the crowd dispersed, the hornier I got, until finally – on our way to the car I made my move.

"Telly…you're joking, right?" Her body tilted left.

"I'm not, I want you. Right now, on side of this tree…" I unzipped my slacks.

"Outside?" She pointed at the old oak tree. "Right here?"

"Yes... right now." When my dick ejected out of my pants, it was red hot as the inside of a toaster. "No one can see us, and the moon is all the light we need...." I attempted to draw up her skirt.

She swatted my arms.

"...*ummm, do I look like a hoe to you?*" Little did she know at the time – that's her dad's favorite question once he gets pissed off.

"No, but can we pretend you are." From the waist, I reeled her to me and tried to whisk her around. "Twenty minutes for twenty dollars?" Offended, Erica broke free. "If I were to do it, trust me, it would cost you way more than twenty dollars." Erica left me standing at the tree, with a dick harder than chrome rims. "When we get home, you can have anything you want, but not outside by a tree like two dogs. What in the hell has gotten into you lately?"

DICK PILLS

That's what has gotten into me.

DICK PILLS.

Last month Uncle Glenn gave me ten of his prescription dick pills. My shit has never been this hard in my life. And I sure in the hell have never been this aroused. About five minutes after popping my first blue pill, I felt all the blood in my body leave my legs and rush straight to my dick. I sat up on the edge of the bed in disbelief.

"Woe, woe. Look at this mother fucker." I greeted a dick I've never seen before. "Erica! Erica! Come walk around here. You have to see this..."

"See what?

"Stop asking questions, and comes see this..."

"Telly just tell me... what is it?" She huffed in frustration.

"I can't describe it; you just have to see for yourself." Erica moseyed around from her side of the room.

When Erica made it to the foot of the bed, she saw it, a painfully swollen anaconda.

"Well hello…" she whispered, "you really missed me I see."

"I think you better run," I said in a deep serious voice.

Until this day she still can't figure out how I've gone from wanting sex once a week, to chasing her around the house the moment I enter the kitchen, but this is Erica I'm referring too. Sex only happens after her hour and fifteen-minute bath, and never before. She doesn't like to have sex with a sweaty cat, and here I am thinking *sweaty pussy is the best pussy.*

The following week, same time of night, same park, same tree.

"Heather, I'm horny. Fuck me"

"Right now? Out here? Right here?" She pointed.

"Yes, turn around. Pull your skirt up."

Heather gazed over my left shoulder than behind her, the coast was clear.

"I thought you'd never ask."

It was that simple, and that satisfying.

Heather gave me what I asked for and enjoyed it just as much. Glenn was right about one thing, if not this Heather, then I will search every corner of the earth until I find another one just like her. *That's a fact jack.* Once you have been to the mountain of pussy, you can't settle for anything less.

Which is why, the day after proposing to Erica, I'm parked on the first level of the parking garage at New Orleans International Airport, with a clear view of the baggage claim. At 6:30, I observed a trickle of travelers racing towards the conveyor belts to retrieve their luggage. There was no sign of Heather. The silence inside my car was disturbed by a call from Erica. I had to answer.

"Hey, hey…"

"What's taking so long? My dad said you left almost an hour ago."

"Wait, you called Uncle Glenn?"

"No, I called my father…"

I didn't like the feeling of this, how's she's so free to call him.

182 / TJ SPENCER JACQUES

I don't care if he is her father, I feel as if she has trespassed into my personal space.

"He said you had to pick up a colleague, but you never mentioned a trip to the airport. Who are you picking up?"

Fuck. Fuck. Fuck.

I get it, I see his strategy. Glenn is leaking snippets of classified information in order to apply more pressure and scare me into ending my relationship with Erica. *Glenn it's going to take more than snitching to get me to break it off with Erica, it's over when I say it's over.*

If I confess to Erica, it'll strip the power he has over me, but nine times out of ten, I will lose her. Erica is Uncle Glenn's only heir.

"Telly are you there? Did I lose you?"

"Sorry, my face accidentally touched the mute." I lied. "I was saying... as soon as I drop him off, I will be on my way. I apologize, but this was a short notice request."

"I was asking who are you picking –"

"He's here now...I'm doubled parked. Erica, I'll call you right back."

I ended the phone call just as Heather exited the baggage claim with her luggage. Over the chorus of bitchy horns, I called out to her a few times before we made eye contact across the four bumper to bumper taxi lanes.

She was dressed in all black, a color she wore for me. It makes her look ten years younger, not that I have an issue with her age. Black stilettos, black slacks, pink blouse, black blazers, and noodle colored hair that she constantly brushed away from her eyes.

I will confess this much, I am madly in love with Heather.

What started as a Craigslist ad for a sex club date has evolved into a friendship that I have never experience with any other woman. Heather is the only woman I have never lied to, never felt the pressure to, never wanted to. She loves this Telly. The Telly I introduced from day one, the Telly who thought he was in love with Megan, only to discover that I was little more than an appetizer, but when it comes to Heather, I am the seven-course meal prepared by an exotic chef.

With intense determination I was willing to risk getting ran over by a Dodge Caravan full of tourists and luggage, nothing mattered but Heather: three days was the longest we had been apart. One more lane to hurdle. Her sparkling blue eyes and radiant pink lips tempted me to walk across the hoods of several White Fleet taxis.

Finally, my lady was snugged in my arms.

"I don't want to ever miss you that much." Heather released the handle of her suitcase.

"Oh really? *Then...make me a Believer.*" She serenaded me.

"Not bad for a girl from Slidell. I'm impressed."

"You mean a girl originally from *across the canal.* And besides, your favorite Luther Vandross song is the best love song ever. It made me miss you so much."

A three-minute kiss ensued.

Once our lips separated, Heather re-gripped her luggage. With my *other wife* tethered to my arm we cut in front, and behind cars, across four airport lanes until we finally made it to my car. I set the climate control to wintery freeze, but there was no cooling Heather.

"God, I hate this center console," in a single motion my zipper was down, and her legs folded under her knees in the passenger seat. "How's a girl to please her man with this bulky thing in the way." Heather punched my armrest in the face. "Your next car will have a classic dick sucking bench seat." With rapid smooches, she kissed the side of my neck.

"Heather, we've had this discussion before, it's hard to find a car with a bench seat up front."

She pouted "then find an older car, that has a bench seat. That's an order."

"Consider it done captain." After a determined tug, Heather freed my dick and started to stroke me soft and slower than an office clock on Monday morning. Then she gave me that look. On the radio was Janet Jackson's *Would You Mind*. Heather didn't. The stroking and kissing continued until a minivan parked on her side of the car and shitted out seven kids. Of course, one of them noticed us.

"Heather, Heather..."

"God... I've missed you so much." she moaned.

"Heather, baby. . ." I thumbed to the right "we have company."

When she turned, the face of a pre-teen boy was plastered against the glass. His devilish little smirk suggested he knew what was up, that was until his mom snatched him away from our car.

"Close call, I was about to go snorkeling."

"Speaking of snorkeling, how was your reunion in Miami?"

"It was boring and long. All I could think about was you. I wanted to catch the next flight out four hours after I arrived. I can't stand being away from you that long."

After two hard lefts, we zoomed down the service road that merged into I-10 East, while Heather manually shifted the transmission with my prescription pill dick.

"But enough about my boring trip, how was the wedding."

The more I recapped what happened last night the less she stroked. My dick became bewildered and frustrated. It was a serious moment, and a serious conversation, but pill dick refused to deflate. Like a fat microphone waiting on Jill Scott, it stood there patiently.

From Kenner to the New Orleans East elevated high-rise, I presented just the facts in a way that left very few questions other than.

"Are you fuckin serious? Erica is Uncle Glenn's daughter?"

"She's the spitting image of him."

"Holy fucking shit Telly! Holy shit! Glenn knows about me, I remember one day when you were sorting out all of that mad-

ness for Biyell – you made mention that we were together. That call ended when you said *fuck that cake test.* I never knew the meaning behind that, but holy shit. Telly, he will expose us."

"I know, he's made that clear. I don't break it off by tomorrow then he will tell her everything."

"Telly, this is awful…" The air inside the car was icy cold. "What are you going to do? Wait, before you answer that let me say this: I knew this day would come."

"What do you mean…?"

"I never planned for you, or meant for us to be long term. I had zero expectation of us going beyond the first month. To be here with you right now is more than I ever dreamt of…"

"Hold up, are you canceling me…?"

"No, that's not what I'm saying."

"Then what are you saying…" Before I knew it, we were in Heather's drive-way.

"I guess, what I'm trying to say is, my time with you has given me so much happiness, it was like being on a magical carpet ride, but I'm a big girl, and a lot tougher than I let on. I know that all joy rides must come to an end. If this is the end of the ride then I want you to know that I had a blast, and I will always love you. Maybe in another life…perhaps?"

"Heather, I didn't say it was the end. Come on, you think that I could kick you out of my life that easily? It has been a whirlwind since last night, I'm still trying to figure it out…"

"Telly you're trying to figure out how to keep us both. There is no way Glenn is going to stand-down knowing what he knows. I can't say I blame him. Sounds like he's given you a chance to end things with Erica in a respectable manner, but I've gotten to know you. You love me. I feel it." Her eyes began to water, as she turned towards the passenger window.

"Telly I see it every time our eyes connect. What you feel for me is deeper than anything I've felt in my marriage. But I love you just as deep. When you feel the way I feel, then you want the best for your lover, even if that means letting your lover go. You are my perfect lover. Being that you can't leave me, I'm giving you an out. I wish your marriage to Erica is filled with all of the joy you have given me."

For the first time was difficult for her to look me in the eyes, so I walked her to the door. "Just in case I don't see you again, thank you for the happiest year of my life." She kissed me, entered the house then tenderly closed the door on me until I was gone.

CHAPTER 28

8:35 p.m.

RASTA

My ex-wife called and said my sons wanted to see me before I left on the cruise, they'll be overjoyed to have a sister, but we decided to hold the news about the baby until we made it back from our honeymoon. Oh yeah, by the way, Kayla and I made love for the first time as a married couple. A full day after we said I Do, we just got around to consummating our marriage.

It was better than our first time, and I didn't think we could top that night, but we just did.

It wasn't the cliché sex where I tossed her around the room, knocked the flat screen off the stand then fucked on it, not even close. Today we had an honest session of sex. That face to face, deep, talkative, show me, turn over, tell me again, in my other ear, really, right there, ooooh baby, don't move, hold it, not yet, there it goes, that kind of sex.

Good thing I saved that Viagra pill from Uncle Glenn, I really laid it down.

That Tony Toni Tone Anniversary dick. That Mother's Day dick. That don't expect this all the time dick. That Benadryl dick. She's still stuck to me. Don't tell her I told you, but Kayla snores. I mean for real. Not a cute Smurfette kind of a snore, but more like dragging a transmission across the floor kind of a snore. Like she's been working at a shipyard all night snore, like Marcel the Walrus. But she's my Snoring Beauty, and I love her.

If that guy who saw me trying to hang myself had not gotten involved, if Uncle Glenn didn't get there in time, and if that ER nurse hadn't forced that charcoal down my throat, yesterday wouldn't have happend and I wouldn't have this beautiful wife, and a baby in the oven: thank you, Dr. Morton.

#21. Don't sweat the small stuff – it's all small stuff.

#22. My past doesn't control my future.

#47. My happiness comes from within.

I want the same happiness for Biyell. I reached for my cell phone and shot him a text.

What I learned today about Tiffany helped me to understand last night, and for that reason alone, I think he should give her another chance. Tiffany's not a bad person, she's human and we've all made mistakes. Right?

Right as the charger connected with the bottom of my cell phone, Biyell called.

"Biyell lend me an ear, that's all I'm asking."

"Rasta, I appreciate you bruh, I do, but I don't know about Tiffany."

"But you have to admit…you're starting to miss her already? You tried to play it off this morning, but it was written all over your face."

"I do miss her…and hearing what happened to Tracey put's a lot into perspective…"

"How so…"

"When we first started dating, I noticed Tiffany always de-clined when I offered to buy her a drink. At first, I thought it was because she was scared, I was going to put the date rape dick on her, which offended me, but much later into the relationship; after we had sex; she still wouldn't join me for a glass of wine. I wrote it off as church-related bullshit, so everything you've said makes sense now…"

"It was the toast that got her."

"No shit…"

"Biyell you know as well as I do, that we all have made our share of mistakes, and if you could find it in your heart to give her a *Get Out Of Jail Free Card* on this one, I think she'll be forever grateful."

"Peep this… I forgave her earlier today when she asked for forgiveness…"

"Then why stonewall her like that?"

"Because I forgave her in my heart, but my brain is telling me to cut her loose and never look back."

"It's because her mistake played out in front of everybody."

"Nah, that has zero to do with it…"

"Biyell I know you, it's the public embarrassment you can't get over. Your manhood has been put on blast, but now that we know the truth, Tiffany's behavior had nothing to do with you. Like you once said *sure, I fucked up, but we all fucked up.* I think you two will become a power couple if you give her another chance." There was no rebuttal.

No one sets out to feel stupid, and for a man like Biyell, feeling stupid is a deal breaker. Adding to the uphill haul is humiliation, but I will not give up. We were two happy couples that just happened to be *kick-ass business partners.* That's the reason why I'm committed to *Tiffany & Biyell's* relationship.

In the past, I struggled as an entrepreneur because of my poorly thought out gambles, and the lack of rainy-day support. In the four of us (including Uncle Glenn) for the first time, I had that support and the brain trust to beta test ideas. I know it sounds selfish, but it is hard as hell to find a productive team like the one we've formed, and that positive harmony we have is worth fighting to preserve.

In the rare silence that accompanied his undivided attention I pressed forward.

"Biyell we're in our forties now, and forty-something is way too fuckin old to still brag about quick flings and side pieces."

On the other end of the call I heard a tapping sound, which hinted I was on speaker while he replied to a text – but I stayed the course.

"Bruh, I miss Madden night, but not the way it was, where we aired weekly infomercials on how to fuck hoes and get away with it. Biyell that part of my life is over, and I thank God Uncle Glenn challenged us to **Be Better and Do Better.** I don't want my wife to ever wonder if I have a mistress because you have a mistress. I left that Rasta in West Jeff Behavior Management Clinic. Ya heard me?"

"I heard you Roderick Ross. Now hear me." Biyell cleared his throat. "I feel everything you're saying, and I don't think Tiffany intentionally set out to hurt me, but even unintentionally still hurts, my nigga. And I do appreciate you going the extra mile for me, but I've concluded that the married life is not in the cards. I'm not good at that fairytale shit, real talk. I agree, we are getting too old. I'm also too old for a *saved-sanctified* bitch who would drop drawls for any dude whose name starts with the **letter J and** has a cup of Hennessy. At forty-two years old – I need to focus on the things that I do well…"

"Pussy hopping around New Orleans like a horny goat?"

"I didn't say that…"

"Then what else is there? Huh… Biyell? What else dude? This is the part where you have an addiction relapse –"

"Addiction…?"

"I didn't stutter *muthafucka*… I said your addiction. *Three-married-women* a week. Mrs. Monday, Mrs. Wednesday, Mrs. Friday. And one grandma from the bingo hall."

"Fuck you, Rasta…you keep bringing up that one grandmother."

"Dude this is me you're talking to… you know as well as I do…you can't lie to a fuckin liar bruh. Don't act as if I don't know your triggers. Tiffany squeezed that trigger last night and shot herself in the thigh, but I'm asking you, for me, please don't go back there big dawg."

"Too late…" He laughed out loud.

"Come-on bruh?"

"… I smashed one last night."

"After the reception?"

"Yup, she brought me some?"

"Who is she…"

"Let's just call her Tesla."

"Tesla? Like the electric car?"

"Yup, hands-free my nigga, hands-free, better than GIGI."

"Oh no…"

"Oh yes…"

15. I cannot control the behaviors of others; I can only control my own behaviors.

16. I am not responsible for making other people happy.

9. I can stay calm when talking to difficult people.

"Hold on B, don't hang up, that's Uncle Glenn calling."

I clicked over to a frantic voice on the other end, a voice I recognized as Uncle Glenn, my phone confirmed it was Uncle Glenn, but I've never heard him freaking out to this degree.

"Rasta, please meet me at University Hospital, it's an emergency – it's bad, really fucking bad –"

"Wait, slow down, slow down…University Hospital? Why? What happened? Did you fall and couldn't get up?"

"No, I'll explain when you get there. It's serious. Please Hurry!!!

The called ended while the phone was still pressed to my ear. I quietly eased from under Kayla's arm, and threw on some clothes. Before leaving, I kissed my wife on the forehead, then sent her a text.

Uncle Glenn called with an emergency. He asked me to meet

him at University Hospital. I didn't want to wake you – when you get this text, call me and I'll fill you in. I love you.

Like a cool breeze on a summer's day, I hear the voice of Dr. Morton for the second time, coaching me through an hour of high anxiety, with a list of responses that have become my spur of the moment coping medication.

49. I can stay calm under pressure.

28. I can handle whatever comes.

35. I am strong.

46. I am wise

Once the elevator made it to the ground floor, it dawned on me that I never switched back over to Biyell. On the way to my car, I made several attempts to call him back, but each time I was sent to voicemail. I'd figured he was probably on the phone with Uncle Glenn – adhering to the same urgent demand.

Get here as quickly as you can… it's bad. Really fuckin bad.

CHAPTER 29

10 Minutes Earlier

ERICA

I was just about to place his bowl of Gumbo in the refrigerator when the headlights in the driveway turned night into day. In the span of time from his car, to the kitchen door, I reheated the bowl. The timer beeped just as Telly moseyed over to kiss me on the cheek. He slouched into his usual chair, the one that gave him the best view of Rachel Maddow, but his political fix was the furthest thing from his mind.

I was even further.

This wasn't my Telly, this was a hologram that was broadcasted from a land *far far* away, where there were no major highways, no reliable cell signals, and if you needed a doctor than chances are you died in route. Who are you and what have you done with my fiancé?

"So… things didn't go well with my dad?"

His reply was a sigh.

"I have to know, what did he say exactly?"

Another sigh.

"Telly…"

"Erica…it didn't go as plan, okay."

"I figured that much –"

"Then why are you asking questions when you already know the answer?"

"Because you're answering with one word, and not giving me the reason, he objected…"

"I guess he based his entire decision on the man I was, the one you already knew about, and not the man I am today. Before things got out of hand I left. He's dead set on belching up everything I've ever done, and I'm not having that."

His eyes were those of a child who was chased by a German Sheppard, and barely made it home.

"How about we start over from the top." In mid-stride, I reached for his arm. Once he turned to face me, I guided his lips inches away from mine. "You talk, I'll listen…okay?"

He nodded, then sighed up to the ceiling.

"Well…to make a long story short…he's demanding that I call off the proposal."

"Don't make a long story short, what did he say specifically?"

"He thinks I'm still involved with the woman from the threesome…"

"Heather…?"

"Yes…Heather."

"…are you?"

"What is this? Gang up on Telly day?"

"If you consider asking questions ganging up on you then I guess you're right. I need clarity. Why a person who has known you longer than I have is adamantly opposed to us getting married? Stop with the victim crap and put yourself in my position."

"Erica, I don't know, I'm not in his head. I can't read his mind. Glenn is trippin' hard…."

"Oh really? You have no clue. Telly, listen to me." I advised in a cold steel voice. "What you're not going to do is give me a half ass explanation about something that could impact not only my life but my daughters."

"Look, I'm tired. Let's pick this up in the morning."

"Fuck the bullshit…Telly are we getting married or not?"

"From the kitchen to the bedroom, I don't remember calling the wedding off."

"Well, it sure in the hell feels like it…" I hissed. "Telly I promise on everything I love, this is the last time I will ask this question. ARE WE STILL GETTING MARRIED?"

Embittered, he stood with fist pressed into his hips.

"Erica…that decision is not entirely mine to make…"

"How so? Help me understand. Wasn't it entirely up to you when you proposed? Now all of a sudden… it's not your decision to make? I'm not with this. After the confusion with my mother, I at least would like to know for sure, beyond a shadow of a doubt, that it's Telly & Erica, and right now this feels fickle as fuck. Talk to me"

I followed his eyes across the bedroom where he gazed at the top of a chest that posed in the corner. Displayed on top were several pictures of Telly and the girls at a Second Line parade in Treme. I could hear the clattering of sprockets in his mind – this was the moment – I felt it the pit of my soul because he never made eye contact with me – only with the portrait of my daughters.

He's contemplating leaving me.

He's searching for an exit.

He's cornered.

Normally when Telly displayed this type of agitation I would concede and revisit the matter at another time that was more emotionally convenient, but not tonight. It was my life and the structure of my home that blew in the wind. Telly would have to be emotionally inconvenienced.

"TELLY" I startled him out of his internal deliberation "if it's not entirely yours to make then what has changed?"

I watched him go in and out of the closet, in and out the washroom, in and out of everything he could think to create distance from my question, and that's what pissed me off. I didn't matter. I was irrelevant.

He had the attentive patience clients, and accommodated their inquiries, but for me, he couldn't answer a simple fucking question. I will not concede to his frustration, and I don't give a shit if he gets angry – this will get sorted out tonight. My girls are at my mother's house; therefore, I will get as loud as needed to get to the truth.

"Telly, you're walking away in the middle of our conversation?"

"Erica…it doesn't matter if we talk or not your father will tell you everything you need to know tomorrow."

"That's it, that's the reason you're acting this way. He gave you an ultimatum, didn't he?"

Telly continued across to the shower.

"Didn't he? What will he tell me? I want to hear you say it, not my father."

"Just know that I love you and I never wanted to hurt you…"

"Telly I don't want to hear that shit, not right now. I want to hear you say what my father is forcing you to say." I yelled from the door seal of the bathroom, as he tested the water temperature.

"He doesn't want us together and will do or say anything necessary to end our engagement by this time tomorrow." He yelled over the downpour. "It doesn't matter if you hear it from me or Glenn, you will know the answer to every question. The only question that will remain is if you still want to be my wife on the other side?"

"On the other side of what?" He stepped into the shower and closed the frosted door. "On the other side of what Telly?" I stumped over to the shower, opened the door and twisted the water off. "I will only ask you one last time…what will I know?"

Telly brushed me aside, closed the shower door.

I clutched the first thing my hands touched which happened to be a ceramic toothbrush holder. It felt like a glass baseball.

With the power of *ten thousand Oprahs*, I threw that ceramic jar at the shower door.

The explosion of the glass was just what I needed to regain his undivided attention – to show him I'd had enough of his ducking and dodging. Enough of snooping through the locked compartments of his life. Enough of stumping my toe in the middle of the night on the bed frame of truth.

It was then everything slowed down, even the noise became distorted, and motion reduced to fifteen frames per second. Glass shards charged at him like a thousand knives, and I watched the laceration patterns form across his torso. Accidentally his feet gave way and he fell. On the back wall of my shower, there was a little bench where I would often enjoy the therapeutic massage of the water pressure.

The back of Telly's head connected with the little bench.

The blood gushed in a steady flow like strawberry syrup cascading of a hot stack of pancakes. At the base of the shower is where his body crumpled, and remained, motionless. It was then that I let out a scream that I couldn't hear. I had to get to him. To save him. I jotted across the glass carpet floor without care or regard for the bottom of my feet.

Off the rack, I grabbed two large towels and joined Telly in the warm crimson pond on the floor of the shower. His eyes were stretched, and still. His arms were heavy and limb. His head was saturated, and disjointed. The area where he injured himself was gruesome and iridescent, soaked in shades of velvet, cherry, and a deep burgundy only *Mary Tudor* could love.

I held one of the large towels to the back of his head with pressure, but it was not enough. I then tied the other towel tightly around his head like a huge bandana, but it wasn't enough.

I panicked.

Life continued to flow out of him with the fury of a flash flood. I slapped his face *"Telly, stay with me baby, Telly…….... Telly. Oh God please. Somebody help me!"*

My voice traveled to the sink and back empty-handed. After I ended the call with 911 and was assured that an EMS was headed my way, I then made a call to a person I needed now more than ever.

Please answer.

Please.

Please.

Please.

"Hello…daddy, I think I just killed Telly."

CHAPTER 30

University Hospital ER
10:47 p.m.

UNCLE GLENN

It is a statistical fact that traveling by air is the safest form of travel there is, far greater than trains or automobiles. I've always found it miraculous how an object that large routinely defies gravity, and reach altitudes near heaven, but sadly, it's the sudden impact with the ground that creates the mass catastrophe. Yesterday my daughter was above the clouds at forty-five thousand feet, without a tremble of turbulence.

In the amount of time it took to *Cha-Cha Slide* she had a fiancé and a father, then came the sudden impact with the ground. Smack.

Parentally, the advice she received was the best advice for my child, and it didn't take years of experience as her father in order to spring into action. I'm here because that's what she needed, someone to hold her while she agonized over her mistake. After she told me what happened – I'd succumbed with remorse. I was the one tightening the noose around Telly's neck.

Nevertheless, it was an accident.

A crazy-ass accident.

If my daughter could roll back the hours, I know she would handle things differently, but couples argue, and some even get physical – Erica didn't mean for any of this to happen. She only wanted his attention –not for him to slip and fall. Simply, a freakish accident.

Diana and I had just ended a bitter spat when I answered the phone. Immediately I hopped to the patio for privacy, and like an air traffic controller, I found the nearest airport to make an emergency landing.

"Sweet Heart calm down. It was an accident. If the police have to question you, do not mention anything about a tooth-brush holder. Do not attempt to move him. Place the jar on the sink and open the front door for the EMS. Do you understand."

"Yes, daddy...but, but I didn't mean too. *Please God, don't let him die, Please.*" She prayed in between sobs.

"Erica, I know you didn't mean to, but our main focus right now is his status. I'm on my way." The EMS beat us there, so Biyell and I continued to University Hospital.

She wore a blue pair of stonewashed Jeans (like the kind women once sported in the 80's) and a black New Orleans Saints jersey that was three sizes too big. The name on the back of the jersey said *CROWD NOISE*. The jersey and the Bananarama jeans were both covered with Telly's blood.

From the very first glimpse of my daughter, I was force to except two realities. Erica has my entire face, and Biyell's assumption is probably right. My gut bloated with trepidation.

Is Telly dead?

"Uncle Glenn, if all that blood oozed out of his head, I think we need to mentally prepare ourselves for the worst." Biyell whispered in a hopeless voice.

"There's still time on the clock Biyell, it may take a Hail Mary pass to win, but the game is not over until it's over."

Biyell lips pulled tightly to the right side of his mouth, like the rapper *Conceited* from the famous Facebook GIF. With the same pursed-lip reaction, he found a seat in the furthest corner of the ER waiting room...

The good news is Erica trusted my advice, and the EMS recorded exactly what they encountered.

A slip and fall in the shower.

According to the *Home Safety Council* at least six-thousand people a year die as a result of slip & falls in the shower, I looked it up in route to the hospital. When Biyell and I arrived, Telly was in surgery and we hadn't received an update in over an hour. This is one of the cases where no news was good news. The down side was with no positive news, left with only the tragic images in her mind, Erica became more unhinged by the minute.

"Daddy I didn't mean to…"

"…shhhhh Erica, I know you. You pitched a jar, it scared him, and he slipped. You didn't shoot him or stab him. It was an accident that happened during an intense argument. It happened. Shit happens. Stop beating yourself up and let's concentrate on saving his life."

If there was still a life to save, I thought. It's a known fact within my circle that I didn't want Telly to marry my daughter, but he was still one of my closest friends, as close as a brother.

Incidents like this, makes me regret that commitment challenge, and how it affected so many lives in the worst way. I hate to say it, but some relationships are better kept as secrets.

Who am I to change something that has gone on since biblical times, people fuck around, it's what they do, whether I am guilty of it or not, adultery & whore mongering will continue long after the worms have eaten out my asshole!

It is what it is.

Here's another situation that would have never transpired if I wouldn't have opened my big mouth. But if I hadn't opened my big mouth, then Timothy's scheme would have never guided Rasta to Kayla, which resulted in a wedding reception, and the unveiling of my blood connection to Telly's live-in girlfriend.

Perhaps I was right?

But it doesn't feel right.

When men do the right thing there's normally that warm and fuzzy feeling that accompanies a good deed, but not today. I don't feel warm or fuzzy, only regret. Even Biyell had his heart broken by the least likeliest of women any of us would have ever suspected. For what it's worth, Rasta says there's more to the Tiffany story than what transpired last night but it's all water under the bridge at this point.

"Unc, Rasta said he's parking and will be up in a second. Telly's sister and Mother are also on their way up."

Erica raised her head "mom and sister? But I thought…"

"Just roll with the flow tonight, if he pulls through this there will be plenty of time to sort out any misunderstandings."

It was then I realized that he never introduced my daughter to any members of his family. Erica was a tucked away secret just in case things didn't work out. If she was never introduced, then no one will ever ask him *whatever happen to ya-girl.*

Such is life for women trapped on a flat planet called Telly, where females are nothing more than continents separated by a sea of lies, which allows him to jet set around his globe.

"I've been asking to meet his mother for over a year, and this is how we meet…" Erica murmured from the ledge of Telly's world.

"Everything is going to work out my dear, let's keep our minds focused on Telly pulling through, that's our main concern."

Deep down I was pissed because I knew of every occasion when Telly played her like a Kenny G saxophone. In many ways, Telly was right, it was all shits and giggles, until I discovered it was my daughter who was getting played.

As men seldom consider, that woman is someone's baby girl regardless her age. We never stop to think "I'm mistreating someone's daughter." This time it was my daughter.

For all the times I wanted to correct them but held my peace.

For every mischievous story I listen and laugh.
For every ironclad alibi I provided for them.
Karma wanted me dead or alive.

In fairness to me, I did try to point Telly in the right direction, but the moment one of the women opted out of his triangle, he replaced her with a quick run to Wal-Mart.

According to Telly, there are plenty of single women in Wal-Mart on Saturday mornings.

He called it *Swipe Cat,* and the first part required a partial introduction near the produce, then stand quietly behind her in the checkout. Before she could manage to swipe her card, he would swoop in like a super hero we called *Food Stamp Man*, and assertively swipe his card.

I could not make this shit up if I tried.

"That's all I have to do Uncle Glenn" Telly would brag. "Before I could punch in the pin, I would hear the dead bolt lock sliding off the pussy. Unlimited my nigga unlimited. It's amazing how much ass you can get for two baskets of groceries."

But anyway, where was I?

"Hey guys any update on Telly's condition?" Rasta and his wife were winded and panicked.

"Not one word since he arrived." I handed Erica off to Kayla and we huddled in the far corner of the waiting room.

"Sorry for taking so long but just as I was about to pull out the parking lot, Kayla called. She wanted to be here, so I waited." Rasta appeared frustrated. "Any word? I don't get how he slipped and fell that hard?" Rasta asked.

"It could happen…" I quoted the statistic again.

It was then that Biyell and Rasta recognized the two ladies who had just entered. The one with the flour hair looked like Mariah Carey, plus twenty years, but the gorgeous woman with her, resembled the current image of Mariah. Even though the younger woman wore a navy-blue full-length dress, the large white belt that hugged her waist gave clues. Sister girl was fine as fuck.

"Telly was the only reason I never went after Phaedra fine-ass, but since he broke code first... I just might."

"Dude chill-out..." Rasta barked at Biyell as the two ladies approached.

"Hello Mrs. Ned, hi Phaedra." They embraced with the kind of hug reserved for old friends from the neighborhood.

"We just left the nurses' station and there hasn't been an update." Phaedra voice cracked like a distant thunderstorm.

"That's pretty much the same news we received, before we were herded in this waiting room."

"Don't none of you worry, I've already received word." Mrs. Ned said. "And you must be Uncle Glenn? I'm Telly's mom."

"Yes, I am, and this is my Daughter Erica."

"Oh my, you're the beautiful young lady we've heard so much about?"

"Nice to meet you... ma'am. Wish it were under better circumstances."

"There's no time like the present. Do you mind if I ask you a question?"

"No Ma'am." I felt Erica's body tense up under my arm.

"Do you have a relationship with our Lord and Savior Jesus Christ?"

"Momma, please!" Phaedra's cake batter complexion turned rich as strawberry jelly.

"Oh, Phaedra it's no problem, yes ma'am I do. My grandfather was a pastor."

"And who was your grandfather?"

"Rev. Pugh of –"

"My lord today, I thought I recognized that face, Pugh's Funeral Home."

"Yes ma'am..."

It was then that my body tensed up because I recognized Telly's mom. Ned's Grocery Store on Caffin Ave.

The Ned family owned just about every business in the neighborhood, except the funeral home. Sunny, her husband ran a mechanic shop, there was another family member who owned a life Insurance company for Colored Folk as they called it back then, and Mrs. Ned's sister was one of the first female doctors, Dr. Phyllis Ned-Cain.

She was the smartest person to ever graduate from McDonogh 35 high school and received a full ride to Howard University. The next time we saw her it was for the two-block long second line parade to celebrate the opening of her clinic.

"Are you Derinda's daughter?" Mrs. Ned asked as she gingerly found a seat.

"Yes, ma'am I am." Erica was astonished, and when she said Derinda, I felt a little bit of urine *skeet skeet.*

"This world is too small, I've known your family all my life. Your grandmother was my best friend, we jumped rope together since knee high to a door knob. Our families were close as two families could be without being related. I guess you can say we're just like family. The last time I saw you... right before your mother moved on the other end of Caffin. And the last time I've seen your mother was at your grandmother's funeral."

I pulled my Saints cap as far down as it could stretch, down to my chin if were possible. I wasn't ready for Mrs. Ned to recognize me quite yet, because her best friend hated my po-ass.

"The family of Telly Ned?" A doctor requested our attention.

"I'm his sister and this is his mother Mrs. Althea Ned."

"Do I have your permission to speak freely as it relates to Mr. Ned's status?"

"Yes, you may." His mother replied.

"I am Dr. Martinez. The head of the Neurology Department here at University Hospital. Your son is in recovery after surgery to treat a six-inch impact injury in the back of his head, where the spinal cord merges into the skull." Dr. Martinez pointed to the injured section on a diagram. "When your son arrived, he hardly had any blood pressure and was seriously depleted. If not for the pressure applied to his injury, Mr. Ned would have bled out."

"Is my brother going to live?" Phaedra asked.

"He's nowhere near out of the danger zone, but he's stable."

"Is he alert?" Phaedra asked.

"He isn't..." By this point Rasta and I had ushered Erica back to her seat. "Currently were running test to determine the severity of his D.A.I –"

"DAI...?" I inquired

"Yes, Diffuse Axonal Injury. Commonly associated with a traumatic brain injury, such as the one Telly suffered when he fail backwards. Currently, he's in an unresponsive state which isn't anything we induced, but his condition upon arrival. Please keep in mind we're still in the discovery phase, and his diagnosis is subject to change. Just rest knowing we're running more test to better understand his condition."

"How long is my brother likely to remain in a coma?"

"It's hard to say, some patients pull through the following morning, others typically 3-5 days. Anything longer, then I'm afraid...well let's just say – that's a different discussion."

It was then that Jarvis arrived breathing like a thoroughbred.

"I have his condition listed as *critical* while we monitor his brain activity and we'll have another update for you in a few hours or so." After a few more questions regarding the coma state, Dr. Martinez vanished down the hall.

Erica and Phaedra heavy emotions drowned out the waiting room television, while Biyell and Rasta struggled to update Jarvis. Telly was unresponsive and it just became real.

"I know who you are?" The thin voice said, "You're Percy's boy, aren't you?"

"Yes, ma'am I am."

"Please Lord don't let my Brother die...please lord."

"Phaedra you hush all that nonsense, what did I tell you before we got here?"

"You, you said, God has sat him down, but he will rise up again."

"And when did I say he'll rise...?" Mrs. Ned asked in a firm voice that was fortified with faith.

"In three weeks."

"Look up here Phaedra, do I look troubled?"

"No momma…"

"…am I crying and cutting up –"

"No momma."

"When you see me crying, that's when you cry. Now get up off that floor." In the same breath Mrs. Ned turned back to me "I told that boy *a many of days*, if God can't have you, no one will. My son will be alright, he just needed to take a walk with the lord that's all. Telly was running wild like a crazy man. When he rise up in a few, some of you will not recognize him." Then she opened up her purse which was actually a bible on the low.

It was then that we heard a commotion from the nurses' station. A frantic female voice paged Dr. Martinez to Room 289, while another doctor sprinted pass the waiting room and disappeared into Telly's room."

Phaedra stood watch in the middle of the corridor, desperate for an explanation or cause for the urgency.

"Momma I just heard a nurse update the status on my brother…he has coded." Phaedra went down to the floor for a third time, and slick-ass Biyell was more than happy to attend to her.

"Oh Phaedra, I got cha…I got cha!"

"I can't lose my brother, momma I can't. Please Lord. Please." Slowly and delicately Biyell lifted Telly's sister and cradled her in his arms over to a couch."

"Stand down Biyell…" I whispered as he carried her past me.

"This is the last time I'm gonna say it…doctors will give a report, but I have already received peace, and heaven is not ready for him. He will get up when it's time to get up and not a second before. Now hush it up." Mrs. Ned turned to me "I remembered your grandma Fannie, she had the best mustards in the entire ninth ward, yes it deed. The best mustards black dirt could grow."

208 / TJ SPENCER JACQUES

CHAPTER 31

JUNE 6, 2018
10:25 a.m.

ERICA

Everything in this room is white or teal green and the worst kind of quiet. The only sounds coming from Telly are the rhythmic tones of the computer that's monitoring his brain functions, and the only other sounds are the cushions beneath me, my sorrow, and my sniffles.

I have only seen my daughters once since Sunday, but I have peace of mind. It's times like this my mother becomes my everything; she always knows exactly what to do and say. She is so strong, and I need to borrow some of her strength. I've hardly left Telly's side, other than to bathe, and when I'm not here Phaedra is, we cover in shifts.

Waiting for a wink of an eye or flick of a finger, but seventy-two hours later, Telly is just as lifeless as the day the EMS lifted him out of the bloody shower. The tubes are everywhere except his ears. His doctor said patients with mild cases of *Diffuse*

Axonal Injury show improvements in their vitals within three to five days, but Telly has shown no signs of life, and that time frame has come and gone.

Unlike Mrs. Ned, I have little faith.

This is my entire fault.

He asked me to wait until tomorrow, but I had to have all the answers right then and there. What has gotten into me?

I was happier when I did not suspect that he was cheating on me, but after I saw the pictures from his weeklong birthday celebration, I questioned everything.

I questioned myself.

Why didn't he ask me?

I would've been willing to fulfill his fantasy within reason.

This is the second man who automatically assumed I was not that type of woman. My ex-husband married that skank from his extramarital affair; she was one of his call center reps. On a random workday around lunch, I decided to surprise him at work with a little desktop loving. That was before I spotted him reclined in his car: napping.

He was not napping.

She was snacking.

That dick hungry bitch munched on my husband like *TLC's My 600lb Life.* And she knew he was married, but she didn't care. I remotely unlocked that passenger door, he saw me first, but she didn't.

"HOE…" was the only word I could muster.

I snatched her mouth off my husband so violently, I thought her neck snapped, but a *Dick-Hog* has nine lives, and you have to kill all nine to keep one away from your husband. Neither of them was worth a prison sentence, and I love my daughters more.

But that wasn't the end of it, it never is. Around eleven o'clock that night, just as I settled in my bed alone, she called me from his cell phone.

"It's late… do you know where your husband is? That's right,

your husband is next to me, sound asleep." Her laugh boomed like Dr. Evil while I levitated out of the bed.

"Girl… fuck you and keep him. I'd rather have the garnishments out of his check." I pressed *End Call* so hard I nearly cracked the screen on my phone.

Like a tornado, I blew through the house to the back door and pitched my wedding ring as far as I could. After a bitter divorce, she became the new Mrs. Drago. Then Dick Hog came after my kids.

I knew it was her instigating him to sue me for full custody because the $1330 a month plus medical insurance garnishment, was sodomizing his checks. And she almost got away with it, if not for Telly. That pretentious cunt got the man, and I got my name refunded.

For what it's worth.

I'd plan to suck his dick.

I didn't know I was on the clock.

But I've never been that woman, a woman like Dick Hog or the white bitch Heather. When I tried to act out my thoughts, a firewall blocked my forward progress, I felt slutty or even worse, I heard my mother's voice.

It doesn't take all that to please a man, if he's seeking a whore then point him to the door. For real, I absorbed dating advice from a woman who never maintained a successful relationship with a man for a full year. Had a date on New Year's Eve – single by Thanksgiving: my mother.

But was it really too much to ask?

Like the time when Telly wanted to spice things up a little, so he asked me to have sex in the park. Just as I was about to say yes, I glanced over his shoulder, and on the levee I saw two women speed walking in the dark. They were engulfed in a gossipy conversation, but my first thought was what if they glanced down here and notice Telly humping me on side of that oak tree?

Those women would think I was the biggest whore in New Orleans.

In the world outside of my head, those women didn't know me, and didn't care. In my paranoia, I was more concerned about opinion of strangers – so much so that I missed the chance to create a special memory with Telly. The following month is when I discovered that white bitch Heather, the one he referred to as his *Silicone Sex Doll.*

He begged me not to leave him.

"Erica it was just sex, that's all it was. I'm sorry, I know it was wrong, but I feel like there are things that I can't bring to you. Things I want, need and daydream about. I guess if you were a man you would understand. I didn't want to put you in an uncomfortable situation. I figured a win-win would be to hire someone to carry out those fantasies. In hiring her, I wouldn't have to bother you. That's all it was, just sex."

Whaaack

It was right there that I tried to slap the nose off his face. At first anger, then came hurt. Since then his words have reverberated in my head.

There are things I can't bring to you.

I didn't want to bother you.

I hired someone.

In the silence that preceded that tight finger slap, I left my body and stood on side of us at the foot of the bed, arguing just above a whisper to avoid my daughter's bionic ears. I am sick of treadmill relationships. Running my ass off, but not getting anywhere.

I'm tired of the *I-love-you's* during the first trimester of dating, but in the third trimester it's – *I'm bored with you.* I had every right to leave Telly, but I didn't, because he was the second man to outsource his *fantasies.*

I wanted to hurt him – badly.

I wanted to cheat on him, the way he cheated on me, but I couldn't bring myself to sleep with another man, not even a one-night stand, I couldn't do it. The fact that I thought about it revealed the toxicity of our relationship.

Like that day I dropped him off at the airport – when she picked him up at the same airport three minutes later. That's what her text read. *Erica is three cars ahead. Walk in the terminal then come back out. We should line up precisely.* He did as he was told. She owned him. I was an eyewitness.

That secret cell phone told the whole story, I saw them together, in those thirty-second video clips, recorded at a bed and breakfast in the French Quarters, when he should have been in New Jersey on business.

Whaack!

That was the second slap.

In a furnace of infuriation, I planked in front of Telly with eyes hot enough to sear the skin off his face. A measly slap wasn't satisfying enough. I let him off the hook, but I didn't want to leave him. I wanted him to stay but severely pay for hurting me. I also wanted to hurt myself for allowing it to happen for the second time in five years.

And now the truth.

I pitched the jar at the shower door, because I'm tired of losing men.

Change comes hard for me. A creature of conservative habits. Set in my ways. If only Telly had the patience to peel back the curtain door and hear my real thoughts, not the filter crap I say after it's been funnel through *Derinda's Good Girl Rules & Etiquette.*

It's all her fault, I think she wanted me to be like her, filled with more pride for having done it alone, rather than to share the glory with a man.

I'd rather have both.

But…

My self-defecating rant was disrupted by soft knocks on the door.

"Guys you are so sweet."

It was my dad and Biyell, one with an arm full of breakfast and the other with magazines and a novel by my favorite author.

"How did you know?"

"It was your most recent post on Facebook," Biyell said.

"Recent as in seven months ago."

"Hey, like I said…your most recent post said you were waiting on the follow up to *Burgundy Doubloons*. Here's *Nine Notches* until then." I thanked him with a hug.

"Guys excuse me for a moment…it's Rasta calling." Biyell continued his call in the hall. After about ten minutes, he sent my father a text saying he would be back for him, just as the nurse entered in to check Telly's monitors and replenish the clear plastic bag that dripped into his vein.

Once another nurse joined her, she asked if we could relocate to the waiting room until his morning examination was complete, which we kindly obliged. Before we could fully take our seats, we noticed a herd of white jackets smiling their way into Telly's room. Many of them had twelfth-grade faces, which left little doubt - Telly was their neurology lecture for the day.

"So how are you holding up kiddo?"

"The best I can…never would have made it the other night without you."

"And that's why I'm so proud of you."

"What for?"

"For trusting me, I know that had to be difficult for you in such a stressful emergency." His arm across my shoulder squeezed me closer to his side.

"Not really, it felt as natural as falling off my bike, and having you dust me off." *Dammit, why did I use that analogy?*

A painful silence ensued.

We both felt the totality of time that was stolen from my childhood. My father's chin lowered to his chest like a vintage drawbridge over a lazy river, that too was all my mother's fault. She had to be every woman when I really needed a mother and father, but it didn't matter one bit what I wanted because in the end, she didn't need him to raise me, and that part was true: but I needed him. The single mom to the extreme – amped up on hardcore feminism – that's the story of my life.

A single parent by choice.

My mother was the one who removed the training wheels and ran alongside my bike. When I fell and scraped my knee, she was the one who encouraged me to try again. If given the chance, I know my father wouldn't have missed a single day, not one field trip or doctor's appointment.

His breath was deep and slow, and I was in complete solidarity with his sudden wave of sadness. My mother had robbed my father, and the punitive damages were extensive. Abruptly he broke the silence.

"Have you noticed any positive changes in Telly?"

"None."

"Flickering eyes?"

"No."

"Not even a twitch in his lips?"

"I would've noticed before those monitors, I watch him all day. I don't know what I would do if he doesn't pull through. Only our second argument and this happened."

"Which tells me this most recent argument was sparked by the meeting we had this morning?"

There was a long hard pause, the kind where I wished his shiny forehead was the surface of an iPad, where I could swoop my finger forward to the next thought.

"I will say this, we were at a stalemate." My father leaned back in his chair but never withdrew his arm from my shoulder. "It was quite a confrontation as you could imagine, with Telly gripping the rope on one end, while I held the other. You were the center of this rope. I was on his case every week about making sure he honored you, this was before I knew his Erica was… my Erica. Today was our first falling out, prior to this our only disagreement was over something called the *Cake Test*. Don't trouble yourself trying to figure it out –"

I had to cut him off "would that be a chocolate frosting cake, yellow inside?"

"The one and only."

"I knew it was some sort of test…"

"Well, you passed with flying colors." He smiled proudly.

"Did you give my mother the cake test?"

Suddenly, his leg heel tapped as if it had somewhere to be without him.

"Dad did you…?" He didn't answer, but the pattering intensified. "My mother failed didn't she." In not answering me, he did. "That reminds me, I was going to give you this at dinner tomorrow but…well you know."

From a zipper pouch in my purse, I handed my dad the handkerchief. I could tell he knew what it was before it touched his hand.

"My mom also wanted me to say –"

"Huck-A-Buck."

"Yes, she said you would know what it meant."

"It means…"

"I love you." He said.

"Correct, it was the way your father and I said I love you if we were in a crowded room or in the presence of my mother."

It was my mother, my father, and me. The greatest family that never was. For the first time since birth, the three of us shared the same space, inhaled the same air, and exhaled as a family. A frozen frame in the cinema of life, a Season Greetings card from the Braxton Family that was never mailed.

We.

Us.

So normal.

So natural.

It was then that I understood why some couples stayed together for the sake of the child. I totally got it for the first time, it is for this feeling. This warmth in my chest, this safety, this sense of wholeness and value, and never having to force what doesn't fit. For the first time, I felt that I was created in love.

I represented the legacy of that love.

When my mother entered that waiting room wearing a satin floral crop top, and squeezed in a pair of mid-rise skinny jeans, I knew then that she also longed to experience this moment – at least once in her life. Instead of guesstimating, she came in the *name of Telly* to compete.

The atmosphere became electrified.

The hairs on my arms and neck spiked from the voltage. I was that path of least resistance. I was that conduit. Both in and through me, I allowed every current they stored for over thirty-five years to flow freely without breaking *Ohm's Law*, or any rules of marriage, adultery, or fornication. With all of the safety precautions in place, my mother tested her theory in front of a private audience. She still had the power to turn him on at will, and I was there when the light began to spark.

Feeling like three was a crowd; I excused myself out to a bench in the hall where I said a little prayer for Telly and one for my parents.

"…and lead them not into temptation."

Amen

CHAPTER 32

June 9, 2018
9:10 a.m.

RASTA

One week plus a day, that's how long it's been since Telly's accident. Things are not looking good and visiting him has become even more difficult. That serenade of endless beeps and chirps' rings in my head for hours after I leave his room, and if I try to avoid visiting him, the beeps and chirps echo even louder.

I never thought I would miss the sound of his voice, but I do. As you probably anticipated, my wife and I decided to use the insurance option for emergencies to reschedule our honeymoon cruise until a later date. How much later?

Who knows?

Damn, I miss my dawg.

About five minutes ago I ended a call with LaDeisha and the crisis management firm RemoveSlander.com. They were able to remove our photos from HoeLeaks.com but requested a little more time to track down the domain owner.

"The internet accelerated us into the future and has made the sci-fi movies of the sixties our daily reality, but the internet is also the Wild Wild West when it comes to privacy." Tyler, the Brand Manager explained during our video conference. *"Anyone can post just about anything, and unfortunately people will accept it as fact. In fact, the burden of proof is on the accused rather than the one who posted the lies. We have two teams on this project. One to eliminate any political threats prior to campaign season and the other to protect the online reputations of the men linked to the book."*

LaDeisha was in D.C. where she spent most of her time fighting for her district. Surprisingly, the tech company was also from New Orleans, part of that Silicone Valley migration that started ten years ago and has resulted in Caucasians taking up residence anywhere they can find, even if the area was once the hoodest' of the neighborhoods in the city: Gentrification is as real as funky breath.

Tyler felt pretty confident that his investigators could have an accurate trace on that IP address within a week, and *motion of discovery* mailed to the hosting company by the end of the month. This was the portion of the meeting that was of the most value to LaDeisha. She intends to take legal action against the site owner if any of the content jeopardizes her chances of getting reelected.

"Rasta, after that call with Tyler I feel much better than I did last week. I have become obsessed with that website, sometimes I refresh the page for hours on end and there's always a new comment." Jarvis appeared relieved.

"That's what happens when the Queen of Gossip Wendy Williams mention's your book in her open segment. Why talk about your book but not invite you on the show?"

"Who said they haven't?"

"Really? Why didn't you accept the invite?"

"They reached out last week but we had too much drama going on to even consider it."

"Dude you turned it down? You can't turn down exposure that big, interviews equal money. Do you have a publicist?"

"Other than my wife, no?"

"You meant to say, other than your niece."

"See there, that's what it's like, even if they don't say it, they're thinking it..."

"I'm just fuckin with you *oh sensitive-ass-Lil-boy.* I know the whole story behind you two. Hell, I was the main one in the crew excited to hear about each encounter with the niece. I mean, Briana."

Jarvis' neck was redder than a box of Fruit Loops, but I figure he was used to the public scrutiny by now. He wasn't and knowing that he was also a recovering whore I seized the moment to do a quick assessment.

"When was the last time you slept with someone other than Briana?"

"Since I've been married?"

"Yes?"

"Why are you asking me this?" Jarvis shot me a perturbed look.

"Answer the question..."

"I will, once I know where this is coming from?"

"Jarvis, do I look like a *baby momma?*"

"No..."

"Then stop avoiding! Answer the question."

Jarvis reared back in his chair and squinted across the room at Kayla's mortgage license. Time to turn up the burner under the jambalaya.

"Jarvis who have you slipped off with? And don't lie to me. Come clean."

"No one, but..."

"...but who... Jarvis?"

"No one but *theeeese nuts?*"

"Haha funny, so in other words touching your own nuts makes

you sweat like the black sheriff *In The Heat of The Night?"*

"Bruh, I'm sweating because it's hot in here."

"Jarvis, you're sweating because – you're lying your ass off.

Jarvis wiped his face and forehead with the sleeves of his shirt. I had a roll of paper towels but I'm not wasting good paper towels on Jarvis. "Confess and you might get a lighter sentence."

"Monica."

"Boy, I know you lying." I leaped out of my chair.

"Have you ever known me to lie on my dick?"

"Dude Monica? As in EX-WIFE MONICA?"

"That's the only Monica I know besides the singer."

"Jarvis, you like getting stabbed in the neck with stilettos huh? You like pissing out blood huh?"

"No, not at all, it just happened."

"So, in other words, you are the title of your book? Monica didn't just happen, some thought, and planning went into *"falling into the same hoes."*

"You're right, I can't argue with that. She was in town last week trying to sell rental property she hid from me during the marriage, but the title clerk sniffed out that lien Telly placed on our first home – she was busted. I had to sign the title, or the sale was dead."

"Did she cut you a piece of the check?"

"To my surprise, she gave me half of it to place in our annuity for the kids. After that kind gesture, I was no longer in fight mode – everything changed. She was originally going to catch the dinner flight to Atlanta, but after we shared a few celebratory margaritas..."

"Monica decided to stay overnight?"

"Yes, the next thing I know we were in a room at the top of the Sheraton Hotel downing more margaritas, and reminiscing." Jarvis showed me a selfie of the two of them, with the New Orleans skyline in the background.

"...reminiscing turned into kissing and kissing turned..."

"Into fucking…"

"The next day was your wedding…it happened again."

"JARVIS NOOOOO."

"Yes…"

"How when we were together all day?"

"During the reception."

"Nigga' how did you pull that off with a wife at the reception?"

"She rented one of those vans where you can press a button and the back seats fold down. In that cargo area was a twin-size air mattress."

"Boy no…"

"Yes, and it was unlike any pussy she had given me during our marriage."

"Jarvis, she wasn't fucking you."

"Huh? What are you talking about?"

"It wasn't about how much she missed you, how sexy you looked at the closing, this is still about Briana."

"I disagree, since then we've been on very good terms."

"Did she mention how her cancer treatments were going?"

"Now, that you mention it, no she didn't."

"Did she look thinner than she did this time last year?"

Jarvis whipped out his phone and dredged deep into Monica's Facebook photos. Side by side, I watched as he scrolled back through hundreds of her positive postings about beating cancer. After five minutes of rewinding through nine months, he landed on the date we searched for, the one that aligned with my gut feeling – a photo of Monica in Havana with a pink bandana on her head. She stood in front of a window that gave way to a breathtaking view of a Cuban shore.

The sockets of her eyes were dark as closets around midnight. Her jeans lied about her weight loss, and her shirt was a co-conspirator. Monica posed with a side view of her body with one arm raised in grandeur, but her body was as translucent as the glass in the large terminal window.

"I was with Monica for two days and it never dawned on me..."

"Jarvis. Dude. My Dawg. Monica went to Cuba as a last resort. right before the Trump Administration closed President Obama's gateway to cancer curing doctors over there."

"She looked nothing like this picture a week ago. Other than a bald fade hair cut Monica was the Monica I married."

"That's what she wanted you to see, but you were so busy trying to fuck her that you failed to notice."

"Oh fuck."

"Oh, fuck is right, whatever treatment she received in Havana cured her, and you, Mr. Hot Dick Willie, may have just fallen into a trap."

Jarvis hurled to his feet and stampeded to the door in a bull's rush of anxiety, apprehension, and agitation. In the selfie picture from that room in the Sheraton Hotel, Monica appeared just as healthy as I am, but had more muscle definition. He fucked up majorly, and it just hit him.

"Jarvis wait up... I'll walk you out." Once we made it to his car, I offered him a word of caution. "I know you just crapped in your pants but hear me out – do not contact Monica accusing her of setting you up."

"But that's what it was...a fuckin setup. She constantly snapped selfies, saying it was something to treasure on those days when she missed our marriage."

"What kind of selfies Jarvis."

"Enough pictures and videos to last for an hour. Fuck!" He paced away, then returned, then paced away again. "Dammit, how could I be so stupid. She could send these pictures to my wife..."

"Did she hand you the camera and asked you to video her while she sucked your dick?"

"Fuck fuck fuck fuck fuckidy fuck fuck...she did."

"My dude, she just reenacted that session you and Bri had in Houston."

"I am so fucked..."

"Jarvis you are penitentiary level fucked."

224 / TJ SPENCER JACQUES

CHAPTER 33

June 17, 2018
2:10 a.m.

DIANA

When I discovered it, I was minding my own business, doing what I've always done, gathering his clothes off the bedroom floor. At first, I didn't give it a second thought, figured it was just a silk emerald handkerchief tied in a knot: then I touched it. In my hand was everything I suspected and feared, and all the things I wondered, the things he partially confessed and barely answered. Glenn lied to me.

Looked me deep in my eyes and lied, and the inscription inside this band is the proof.

Huck-A-Buck Derinda.

I fuckin loathe her name.

I prefer, that bitch.

For two consecutive years, after the day I delivered his daughter, I asked him repeatedly.

"Do you love her?"

"No way near the way I love you." He lied.

"Were you planning to marry her?"

"I only had plans to marry you." He lied.

"Why me and not her?"

"Because you're all I've ever wanted. I knew it would have never worked out with her because Mrs. Pugh hated me. Diana you have to believe me, I'm where I want to be, and with the woman, I plan to be with until I die." He lied about everything.

He doesn't know it, but I can hear him.

When he's seated out there by the pool in the same chair *that I......that I..........* *well, that's not important now.* Nevertheless, I can hear him, maybe not as clear as you're hearing me now, but clear enough to tell that he's enamored by the voice on the other end of the phone. He has seduced the person on the other end. Sometimes it's his daughter, and sometimes it's the person whose finger was fitted for this ring.

I can distinctively decipher, and he took me for a fool.

When it's his baby momma, the love of his life, every five minutes a new episode of their conversation would lead off to *remember when?* Followed by a laugh, or *how could I ever forget.*

Never has there been four words that have torn my wounded heart to shreds like *how I could ever forget.* Each time he said it the nerve endings in my chest squealed in agony. Just as the soreness would subside, he would say it again – *how could I ever forget.*

Some many times over the course of the last two weeks I wanted to jump through this bedroom window, fly through the air like in that movie *Crouching Tiger Hidden Dragon* and kick his ass in the back of the head – then watch him fall face forward in the pool.

While he struggled to the edge of the pool (because he can't swim) I wouldn't lift a finger to help. Instead, I would ask him point blank – what is it you could never forget? I would water-board his ass until he told me the truth, then leave him.

Is he that excited over distant memories?

Where are you two traveling to in the back corners of your minds that's so treasured – neither one of you have forgotten? How come all of the blissful days we've enjoyed during this marriage wasn't enough to max out the memory card in his brain? The reason *you could never forget* is because my husband acted more like a Motel 6, he kept the lights on for that bitch all of these years.

During sex when he closed his eyes – did he run to her?

I didn't just find this ring, I've had it for nearly two weeks. Like a fool, I've waited for him to acknowledge that this ring was in my house, but he's carried on as normal.

It's obvious, it's right there in my face, when I'm home with Bylisha, he's at Telly's bedside with his first family. The reason he's there all day is forty percent Telly, and sixty percent to see that bitch.

As I sit here clutching this ring in my left hand, my right hand couldn't take it anymore and decided to go rogue. An uppercut to the side of his face sent half of his sleeping body over the side of the bed. The rest of him quickly followed.

"DIANA, WHAT THE FUCK," he yelled from the floor "why did you punch me? What's your problem?"

"Who me? A problem? What makes you think I have a problem?"

"Because my lip is bleeding and I'm on *the flooooor.*"

"Glenn, I don't have a problem, but you do." I tossed the ugly-ass ring over the side of the bed.

A guilty sigh was all he could manage.

"That's been in my house for nearly two weeks. I waited for an explanation. Not a word Glenn. Not a single word about that ring. For nearly two fucking weeks, I've watched your behavior change. All of the phone conversations by the pool. All of the constant texting. I saw the *mother-fuckin cell phone bill –* you've sent more texts in these two weeks, than you've sent during our entire marriage. And don't tell me all of that was updates on Telly's accident."

"Diana, I apologize for not telling you, I was going to get around to it."

"Interesting, I've become something that you have to get around to, work in, or better yet, address at a more convenient time, but you talk to her all day every fucking day. *Ain't that some shit.*"

"Diana that's not what I'm saying" he managed to sit upright "I've been so worried about Telly that I'd figured I would deal with it at another time, that's what I'm trying to say."

"So, when you're sitting poolside on your cell phone giggling your ass off, is that also about Telly?"

"So, you're eavesdropping on me now?"

"Our bedroom window is a short walk to the pool I don't have to eavesdrop I can hear you through the wall. Those are some wonderful conversations you're having, wish I could join in. I like to laugh too, just as much as you do, can a sister get a three-way?"

"Hey, you got me." He raised his arms above his head and surrendered. "At first, it was to get an explanation for why she lied to my daughter. After that, a few of those conversations were two old friends catching up."

"Just two old friends. Catching up. What could go wrong with that…"

"Diana it was just a few phone calls, and she returned a ring."
"Glenn when you tell a lie you have to remember the lie."
"Diana I'm telling you the truth."

"Correction, the truth is you proposed to her, prior to proposing to me. The truth is you only married me when you couldn't marry her. The truth is she's still in love with you and has never loved another. The truth is, I'm not going to sit around like an asshole, bracing myself, for what I know is about to happen. The truth is, fuck you because I deserve better."

"Diana please calm down for a second" he kneeled in a prayer posture on side of the bed "you're making this into something it's not. I'm where I want to be, and who I want to be with.

You're right about the conversations, inappropriate on my part and will not happen again, but you're wrong for thinking I want something more with Derinda."

"STOP SAYING HER NAME IN MY HOUSE!" With both claws. I launched at his eyes and lips, but he flew backwards out of my reach.

Every time he says her name, I feel like I should uppercut his ass again. It's not just the sound of her name it's the way he says it *Derrrrrindah Derrrrrrrrrindah...*

It's like the tearing sound of the vulva during all-natural childbirth. The screeching wails of a mother who realized it was too late for that epidermal.

I hate that name.

I hate it, even more, when he says it. I know to say her name gives him pleasure, I can tell. He conjured that bitch up in his mind just to torment me. I know what this is, it's a plan to aggravate the fuck out of me until I eventually say *fuck you Glenn and fuck your deranged, love-struck, stalker bitch from the eighties.* She wants you that bad she can have you.

"Diana, baby you have to calm down I don't –"

"You know what? That's the first thing you've said that made sense to me. I need to calm down." I made my way to the bathroom and slid into my pink house coat.

"Thank you, Diana, if you're calm, we can work through this."

"That's right, If I'm calm, we can work through this, here's how it's going to go," I spoke in the space between the bedroom and the door. "Like you, I also received something special that came at a time when Telly's recovery was everyone's main focus, but it was no less precious indeed. That night I was going to tell you was… the night I found her engagement ring in my house. Tamara has been stripped of custody and I am now the legal guardian."

"Diana why didn't you tell me…"

"For the same reason you didn't tell me, that's what this marriage has become, something of convenience. I didn't sign up for this, not to live constantly looking over my shoulder or at you by the pool *keke-ing with your bitch*. After the adoption is complete... I want a divorce."

"Diana..."

"Shhhhh, you will grant me this divorce when the time comes, but now is not the time. I will continue to live here until you obtain another residence."

"THAT'S BULLSHIT...you can't kick me out of my house."

"Fine, then we'll live here until I build another house, but you will not mention a word of this until the adoption is complete."

"I'm not going along with any of this, and you're not leaving this house! We can fuss until you lose your voice. You can even sucker punch me a few more times, if it makes you feel better but you're not leaving me. Not over a phone call with *Derrrr- rindah –*"

I advance towards him with my fist cocked. His back rammed against the nightstand. The lamp tumbled.

"I'm sorry, I'm sorry, I didn't mean to say her name again, but look at you Diana, look at us, this is crazy. We've never gotten physical like this, this is not us, let's get help and save this marriage. Have you even discussed this adoption with Biyell? He is the father. Remember?"

"I planned to have a conversation with Biyell, but he did sign away his rights, remember? In the same manner. I plan to sign away my rights to you, I want a divorce, that part is not up for negotiation."

"I don't agree."

"You will..."

"Diana, there's no way you can force me to agree to these terms."

"Your login is **Braxton1966** and your password is **TheBraxtonFive.** The same thing that was placed on them – was also placed on you. As I said, you will give me everything I ask for." I allowed a minute to lapse before leaving the room to finish the night with my baby. Glenn didn't say another word. His lips were paralyzed.

Huck-A-Buck that!

CHAPTER 34

June 17, 2018
8:30 a.m.

ERICA

His mother was here last night till around ten o'clock, and I truly enjoyed her company. At times she mentally slips off a little, but just when you think she's out to sail she says something so profound it leaves you in deep thought for the rest of the day.

"Erica do you have a relationship with the Lord?"

"Yes, ma'am I do." I left off the part about my grandfather because memories of him awakens decades of additional memories for Mrs. Ned, but she remembered.

"Since that cold December day when your grandfather laid holy hands on him, I have ministered and encouraged that knucklehead boy of mine. One thing you have to know about him, if nothing else, Telly will give you the desires of your heart, just to get exactly what he wanted all along." From out of her purse she unrolled a peppermint and handed me one in the same motion.

"Telly went on to graduate at the top of his seminary class and law class. Then came that devil of a hurricane, old hateful nasty Katrina. She wanted New Orleans all to herself. That heifer of a storm blew us to every corner of the south. For a while, he was preaching in a little town called Rayne, right outside of Lafayette. For his first Pastor's Anniversary Service we were all set to drive in from Houston to hear him preach, and out the blue Telly quit the church. Just like that, it was the craziest thing in my seventy years on earth. That boy has ran from God every day since."

"Ma'am, Mrs. Ned, are you telling me that this man, in this bed was a pastor? Telly?"

"And a pretty good one at that...when they voted him in as the pastor that church didn't have enough members to fill a Popeye's, but after a few months, he told me people traveled from miles to hear him preach."

I never knew Telly was into church or even God for that matter. On Sundays, I remember asking him on occasion if he would like to come to mass with me and the girls, his answer was always no. Emphatically no. After a while, I stopped asking. It wasn't a big deal if we had different religious views, most couples do these days, but I was starting to feel that he was a low-key atheist.

Telly was a Pastor?

I wondered what happened?

My pondering was interrupted by a soft knock and a cracked door, after confirming that it was okay to enter, I was happy to see Rasta.

"Good morning, I knew I would find you here." He handed me some breakfast.

"Phaedra will relieve me in a few hours to catch up with my girls, they need a break from their grandmother."

Rasta and I made small talk for a little while, then I figured now was my best opportunity to inquire more about Telly's prior life as a pastor.

"So, in a conversation last night with Mrs. Ned, she shared

that Telly was once involved in the ministry." Rasta's eyes nearly rolled out of his head. He didn't volunteer any information. If I wanted to know more about this side of Telly then I would have to flood Rasta with questions, and hopefully he would answer a third.

"Telly told me he knew you longer than any of the guys, why did he leave the church in Rayne."

"I think it's best he tell you when he's feeling better. "

"Rasta, please help me understand more about this area of his life. It's not like I'm asking you about a mistress, I know how men could be when it comes to keeping their brother's secrets. Mistress and flings are trivial; I want to know more about his life. I'm fascinated by this spiritual side that he concealed from me. Why?"

"Erica, I really prefer Telly tell you in his own way." I gazed over at Telly in the bed with all the bells and whistles connected, then back at Rasta.

"Here's what I will say, as you already know, not everyone who stands in a pulpit is called to take on that responsibility, but that wasn't the case with Telly. The church grew from thirty members to three-hundred almost overnight, the problem for Telly is most of those new members where young attractive women like yourself." Rasta tried to end the conversation right there but I pushed him forward.

"The young, single pastor from New Orleans...that alone came with a basket of issues....of biblical proportions."

"Did he fall for one of the women who joined the church?"

"Of course, he did and was head over heels for her. After a few short months they were engaged, then married at the courthouse before any of us could get there to witness it."

"But... but I never knew he was married?"

"Did he say he wasn't, or did you assume he wasn't?"

When I thought about it, in the beginning, I hardly asked him anything about his previous relationships, I was just happy to meet a man who wasn't married and could formulate a sentence that didn't sound like *Trap Music*. Telly asked all of the questions, and I provided all of the answers. Three dinner dates later we were a couple.

"The reason he never mentioned it is probably because it's a chapter of his life that he buried, for reasons I fully understand."

"Please explain."

"Telly wasn't what people referred to as a full-time pastor, the church wasn't big enough to support him financially, but he had a law degree and with that law degree, he still maintained a portfolio of clients. Many of his clients from New Orleans were scattered as a result of Hurricane Katrina, and with that batch of commitments, came weekly travel around the state. On one of those trips out of town, the church secretary asked him if he liked his new truck – the one parked in his driveway. A shiny white Ford F150 Limited."

"Oh no…"

"Of course, he hadn't purchased a new truck, and of course the wife wasn't answering the phone when Telly called, and of course the description of the truck matched the head of the assistant pastor. In a rage, he hurried back a day earlier than he originally told his wife."

"Did he catch them?"

"No, nor was the truck there, but for Telly he didn't have to catch them in bed – just the thought of her cheating on him was more than enough to end the marriage."

"Wait, so he ended his marriage over a phone call about a car in the driveway?"

"Ended the marriage and quit the church without saying goodbye. He headed back to New Orleans and never looked back. I tried to talk some sense into him, but I'd never seen him so angry, and with the help of his law buddies the marriage was annulled."

"Just like that…"

"Just like that, as crazy as it sounds." Rasta's head shook in disbelief.

"Did she ever get the opportunity to explain the truck in the driveway?"

"As a matter of fact, she did, about four years later she cornered him at the courthouse, and convinced Telly to give her five minutes of his time."

"She drove here…to talk… after four years apart?"

"…for four years he avoided her, it was a desperate measure, but it worked."

"Was there an explanation?"

"You know there had to be, and the church secretary who called him to report the truck in the driveway knew it, but she was dangerously in love with Telly. That new F150 truck was in the driveway because one of the Elders, a church mother, had just passed away. The church mother lived next door, but with the surge of grieving family members, parking was limited, so the assistant pastor parked in Telly's driveway, then waited with the family for the medical examiner."

"That's horrible, the marriage ended because of that ominous phone call which gave the impression that she was having an affair."

"Well, it all backfired on the secretary because he left his wife and the ministry. Erica, my dawg was one of the good guys when it came to church, not like a lot of these guys who are in for the money. His greatest fear in life is catching a man having sex with his woman, and unfortunately, that secretary pulled that trigger. I can put my finger on the time that Telly lost all trust in women, and it was that church incident. Even hearing the explanation didn't help much because he never apologized for it. His wife didn't answer the phone because she was next door at the prayer vigil standing in for her husband."

"Rasta, I feel so bad for her."

"I did too, and it wasn't until I spent some time with mental health professionals, did I come to see that many of my issues with commitment are connected to post-traumatic stress syndrome. Emotional trauma doesn't end when the relationship ends, in many cases, the ills are felt for years afterward." Rasta raised his wrist to eye level.

"I know you're busy but thank you for helping me understand this man I love so much." We stood and hugged. Rasta can I ask one more question before you go?"

"It depends on the question."

"Mrs. Ned believes this has happened to Telly because he ain't living right, and refuse to do right by Reebie" who is Reebie?" Rasta hugged me for the second time and back peddled. I followed him.

"Come on Rasta don't leave me hanging. Who is Reebie?"

Defiantly he nodded "I have a meeting with Jarvis...Erica, I'm sorry, but Telly will have to explain that one." And with that being said he hurried down the corridor and made a left towards the elevators.

As if not to disturb his rest, I slid into the teal green recliner next to his bed with my novel, but I was too distracted to read. A pastor. A husband. A mystery woman. With my book resting on my chest, and my eyes locked on my fiancé – I whispered.

"Telly I know you can hear me, who is Reebie?"

CHAPTER 35

June 17, 2018
9:30 a.m.

UNCLE GLENN

Wynton Marsalis brilliant trumpet announced the airing of my favorite show on CBS, but I can't stand to hear it this morning. I reached for the remote and powered off the television. It was Sunday morning everywhere but my house. Back in our old apartment, Sunday was a time for Diana and me to catch up on the week and indulge in each other. It was the most anticipated day of the week for us, a day where we relaxed, while Jane Pauley provided an exclusive tour through the arts. If our week didn't start with Jane Pauley and Wynton's trumpet, our week was doomed.

That was the Braxton's home.

This is now.

"Guess it's time to break this routine and find another one."

Diana was out the door at 8:45, not a kiss goodbye, not a note on the refrigerator, not even a bye nigga. Was that too much to

238 / TJ SPENCER JACQUES

ask considering mere strangers enjoy the niceties of courtesies? We have arrived. We are here. This is the bottom floor of our marriage. It's cold down here. Contentious, but thank God for Bylisha.

Before Diana could twist the doorknob, she broke away and leaped into my lap.

"See you later paw-paw…"

Diana folded her arms impatiently by the door as Bylisha hugged me.

I have yet to see the child wear the same outfit, and whatever was purchased for Bylisha, was also purchased in the exact same color and size for Braylyn. If a strand of hair is out of place, out comes the brush and comb, around her little nose, snot doesn't stand a chance, and Bylisha is already registered for dance.

This child has given Diana life.

To my dismay, she has expressed zero interest in developing a relationship with my daughter and granddaughters, silly of me to think the more the merrier.

dinnnng dinnnng dong dong - dinnnng dinnnng dong dong

"It's open…" In came Biyell, he's my ride to see Telly.

"I could've been a rapist who loves one-legged black dudes."

"Oh well, guess I'm raped…"

"Don't think I haven't noticed, your lazy-ass is hopping less and less these days. *That's all I'm gonna say.* Done moved over here by the *De-luxe apartments,* and now you are screaming out it's open. That's how it's gonna happen to you. That amputee pervert is gonna rape your ass."

"You don't believe that shit yourself."

"Are you hungry? I got some hot donuts for you…" After removing five for himself, Biyell sat the box on the counter.

"First you threaten my asshole, now you offer me donuts? What the *SVU, Ice T, doom dooooooom…* kind of night you had?" Biyell laughed out loud as he sat the donuts on the table.

"I saw my baby and Lady Diana zoom pass on the bridge, without you, again, what's going on?"

"Nothing at all…she on some bullshit today."

I made my best effort to turn on a swivel as he moved around the kitchen, but not fast enough. He saw it.

"DAMMMMMMN! UNNNNNNK' The fuck happened to your face?"

"It's a long story…"

"And I have all day" Biyell tried to touch it, but I swatted his hand "seriously what in the *whole grain fuck* happened to your face?"

"I fell…"

"You fell? On what? A straitening comb?" He leaned in closer than necessary to examine my bruised eye socket and jaw. "Glenn…bruh, what really happened to your face?"

"She punched me…"

"He who?"

"No…she punched me."

"Glenn ain't no way a woman hit you that hard."

"Diana did, while I was sleep."

"No way Diana did that…no fuckin way?"

"What do you mean there's no way she could have fucked up my face like this…didn't GIGI knock your eyeball out?"

"Yeah but that was with a brick."

"Well, this was with her hand…"

"DAMMMMMMN! UNNNNNNK… her hand?"

"Bald fist."

"Uncle Glenn… I am the Tom Brady of fucking up, you had to do something on the Super Bowl level of fucking up. Bruh, have you seen your eye?"

"Nah, not yet."

"Uncle Glenn… this *whooooole* side of your face" he drew a circle with his finger "looks like she just punched you thirty seconds ago. Uncle Glenn…. this *whoooole* side of your face is *Fifty Shades of Purple.* Uncle Glenn …. the only thing missing from your face is Prince singing Purple Rain. Uncle Glenn…. this *whoooole* side of your face… looks like she kicked your ass with a can of commodity grape juice.'"

"Biyell I don't need your shit this morning…I have a lot on my mind."

"Correction, you have a lot of shit going on with your eye. I would take you to the hospital, but I'm scared I might get the charge."

"I'm straight, don't worry about me – the swelling will go down?"

"When…? When do you suppose that's going down? The side of your face looks like afterbirth, and you think that's going down?"

While I was distracted by something Diana said, I noticed he was also quiet. Biyell is like one of your kids, the really bad one, the one you check on if it's too quiet down the hall. With a sneaky smirk, he slid his ass into a seat at the breakfast table, and shortly thereafter, my cell phone started to buzz.

GROUP TEXT WITH IMAGE

Rasta: *Uncle Glenn I'm on my way! Did you get a good look at the dudes who jumped you?"*

Rasta: *Why were you on Claiborne and Washington Avenue?*

Rasta: *I'm coming to pick you up – I need you to point them out. On my momma, those Fuckas' will pay for this – Believe dat.*

Jarvis: *Got my gun…I'm not too far from you, I'm on my way. Come point them out Unk!"*

Glenn: *I did not get jumped at the corner store by five dudes… I'm okay. Ignore Biyell.*

Rasta: *then what the fuck happened to that whole side of your face?*

While I recapped the way I was abruptly awakened in the group text, Biyell nearly choked on a piece of donut. I couldn't lie about the injury, Biyell's photo snitched a thousand words. The truth is, it was Diana who punched me in the face, and I can't say I blame her. The truth is, I was so caught up – I forgot how sensitive she was to anything related to Derinda, even the mention of her name.

"Big unk' I don't know what's going on with you two, and I'm not trying to get in your business, but whatever it is that has you taking these ass-whippings, you need to fix it." Biyell downed the last of his milk.

"Not sure if this is something, I can fix…"

"Everything can be fixed… if you're willing to put the work in."

"Biyell I have always shot straight from the hip with you, so let me come out and say it."

"Oh no Lord Jesus, Uncle Glenn done caught the Gay. Lordie, he done caught the Gay all over his body Lord. Uncle Glenn is now Aunt Glenn, and we need you, Lord. I turn Auntie over to you. Heavenly father, help him find peace in his new walk." Biyell said in his grandmother's voice.

"Biyell, fuck you with that shit." Biyell bent in laughter. "You may not know it or not but I'm back on speaking terms with…" I looked around for my wife *"Derrrrinda."*

"You mean all the *keke-ing* you do out by the pool? And that ridiculous smile on your face every night we leave the hospital? You mean to tell me, your giddiness over Derinda has caused a problem? Who would have thought Diana would've noticed…? Such a strange occurrence…mighty strange." He heckled in that grandmother's voice again.

"Unk' the entire hospital knows the back story of you and Derinda. It's been like two teens sneaking off to suck face. Not saying you have, but that's how it looks to us. I totally understand why Diana tried to put a dent in your forehead…"

"Biyell I didn't know it was that obvious, and I tried to apologize for it but, but…"

"Bruh, the reason your eye looks like tomato paste is because you're high risk, a threat to her emotional stability."

"Now that's where I disagree, my conversations with Derinda are totally innocent, a little more than *old friends* catching up. She has filled me in on all the years I've missed with Erica, that's it, and now Diana is checking out of my life, just as they are checking in. I don't feel that's fair to make me pick between the two."

"See there…right there" Biyell wiggled a finger at me "that's why you got punched in the face."

"Why am I having this conversation with you of all people? You're not trying to see my side."

"Sounds to me like it's more about Derinda, than it is about Erica, and you can't blame her for not trusting you two. If I can remember correctly, you're the dude whose wife discovered he had an outside child – when she cut the cord off his mistress. You're one unique muthafucka. *Ya heard me?"*

"For the one-hundredth time, Derinda wasn't my mistress, after she failed the Cake Test and declined my last wedding proposal we broke up. I did not cheat on either one, but I did use one to get over the other one."

"And the Tylenol chick was Diana?"

"…that's a cruel way to categorize her, but yes, she was."

I can't say that I've ever ceased to love Derinda, how do you stop loving someone you love? What I ceased to do was express how I felt about her, and once I fell deeply in love with Diana, then it became easier to suppress those feelings for Derinda. Then I went through a long period of anger for the way she shot-putted me out of my child's life and hid her right under my nose.

Biyell moved to the living room and turned the television on the NFL Network. "Do you still love Derinda?"

"I can't lie…I do."

"Would you leave Diana for Derinda?

"No."

"But if Diana leaves you, then chances are you and Derinda are **Reunited** like *Peaches & Herb?"*

"I wouldn't automatically run to –"

"Bruh cut the shit! If Diana leaves you… are you going to be with Derinda? Yes or No?"

"…that's not a fair question."

"*He will…*" Diana stood in the seal of the door that led to the garage "if that's the answer you're seeking."

"Oh shit, Good morning Lady Diana."

"Good morning and Tyra said hello." Biyell bolted to the patio door like a bomb threat. *That scary bitch.*

"How long have you been standing there?" She tossed her purse, keys, and cell phone on to the sofa, where they hid in the valleys of the seat cushions.

"Long enough."

"Where's the baby?"

"You didn't just hear me tell Biyell… Tyra said hello? Tyra is taking them to the aquarium, so I met her halfway, and now I'm back."

"Diana, I have not cheated on you. I have not kissed or had sex with anyone, other than you. And you haven't touched me in over a month."

"*I'm glad you're counting…*"

"To treat me like this over a few calls is not right… but if you want to throw everything away, all the years we have together, all the work we've put into this marriage, all that we have accomplished, you're throwing it away? Over this miscellaneous nonsense? This is how you treat me?"

"*YESSSSS INDEED…*" She hissed. "You have the nerve to make this about you? After toting around her ring, then bringing that bitch engagement ring into my house, you're making this about you? Have you lost your mind?"

"But you're making it about her –"

"Glenn Fuck you… and Fuck Derinda and fuck…*Err –*"

She caught the final fuck firmly between her lips but not the part that whispered out.

"Don't stop there" I braced myself up from the table "finish it, you were about to say fuck Erica and my grandkids. *Weren't you? Weren't you?*" I could smell the brake dust in her breath she wanted to say it so bad.

"Don't stop now, you're on a roll. Keep dealing out the fuck-you's. This is about Erica too. You selfish witch."

"Witch? Who *in-the-fuck* are you calling a witch?"

"You…because the way you're acting is downright evil."

Her breathing sounded like steam shooting out the bottom of an iron. She paced in a circle while punching one hand into the other. But I'm as serious as fart in an elevator, *she better keep her hands to herself. For-real for-real.*

"This is about me loving someone else just as much as I love you. You've never had to share me, not one time during this entire marriage. You hate my daughter already? But I made you into this spoiled brat monster!"

"No, don't you stop, you're on a roll. Get it all off your chest."

Diana slowly inched towards me and I slowly hopped towards her. As the space between us decreased so did our care and compassion for one another. I was pissed, I didn't give a shit, it was whatever she wanted it to be, she harbored animosity for my daughter and my grandkids. With less than ten feet separating us, I figured if it was her intention to tear us down, then I'm swinging the sledgehammer.

"Where I made my mistake – after you tried to quit me the first time, I should have held the door open."

"Oh really."

"I didn't stutter…and if I had to kiss your ass to stay, then it meant I had to kiss your ass all the way. That's all this marriage has been, Glenn kissing Diana's ass. Glenn making sure Diana has a hot meal. Glenn making sure Diana is comfortable. Let me ask you one question when was the last time you cooked for me?"

"This is not an argument about food!"

"Okay let's take food off the table…when was the last time you did something special for me?" I heard the hum of the central air unit, I heard the television out on the patio, where Biyell tried to drown us out. I also heard the sound of my neighbor cutting his grass, but not a word from Diana.

"The reason you can't answer the question is that you don't

do shit for me, I am the one who caters to you. If you're planning to leave me because of a few conversations I've had with *Derrrrindah.*"

Shwoom! She nearly caught me.

Shwoom. Shwoom. Another left and a right.

Shwoom. Strike three, a final swing and a miss.

Her right fist whistled past my ear then her left, but I ducked each time. Then with the audacity of all the pissed off women in the world, Diana launched at my left eye, but before she could make contact, I manage to restrain her.

"That's why I called you a witch – only a witch would try to take out the only eye I have left. If that's how you want this to play out, then no more Mr. Nice Nigga." I growled.

Since she hated her name, I started screaming it so loud I heard the paint crack in the ceiling.

"DERINDA-DERINDA-DERINDA-DERINDA-DER-INDA-DERINDA....DERRRRRRINDAH, DER-FUCKIN-RINDA!"

My hands snapped tight around her wrist like handcuffs. I'm not one to hit a woman but this *mean-ass-bitch* has disrespected me for the last time. All of the non-violent years we've enjoyed has gotten shit twisted in her head. Just because I have never hit her, doesn't mean I'm incapable. It was then, for no explainable reason other than to add to the volatility of the situation I started sing Lil Wayne – real loud.

"And I ain't ever ran from a nigga and I

Damn sho' ain't bout to pick today to start runnin'

Look honey, I ain't never ran from a nigga and I

Damn sho' ain't bout to pick today to start runnin' get money!"

I know her, she wanted to get in a lick right there, but I vice gripped both wrists and pushed her flat against the wall.

"Let go of me…let me go!"

"I plan to let you go…don't worry. I'm letting you go for good."

Over to my right, I could see Biyell scary ass bolting through the door, unsure of what to do or who to help.

"Since you don't want me, and since you hate my daughter for no fuckin reason at all, and since you're determined to get a divorce, then let's get this party started right. We can go to the courthouse tomorrow morning." I released her wrist "and if you put your hands on me one more time, **I WILL KNOCK YOU THE FUCK OUT – TRY ME"**

Diana gazed into my eyes – I was hotter than a cremation. She did not try me.

CHAPTER 36

June 17, 2018
10:30 a.m.

JARVIS

During the entire call with the crisis management rep from RemoveSlander.com, I was distracted by the same frightening thoughts that have kept me up all night. What if Rasta was right? What if it was all an attempt to get back at me for cheating on her with Briana? The excruciating part of this epic fuck up has been my attempt to anticipate Monica's next move.

Every time Briana's phone rings, I'm wondering if that's Monica on the other end. Every time Briana received a text, I'm wondering if it is a photo of me eating Monica's pussy or a video of Monica with a mouth full of my dick, but for the most part, it's been quiet.

I sent Monica a text the other day to say hi, and she replied with a kissing Emoji, followed by three hearts. About an hour later she sent another text.

Can't stop thinking about you. I miss us.

I miss us too.

Then come visit me...sooner than later.

The next day I arrived in Atlanta around ten that morning, she scooped me up from the airport; ten minutes later, we fell on the bed in a hotel room that she had reserved and waiting. Monica and I locked up for two hours, by 6:15pm I was back in New Orleans. Why did I go? Because I was excited, and horny, and turned on at the thrill of sneaking away to Atlanta for a lunch fuck with Monica.

The other reason?

I wanted to test Rasta's suspicions and surprisingly, she never snapped a photo the entire time. Why did she take so many photos when we were together in New Orleans but none in Atlanta?

Maybe I'm paranoid?

Could it really be that simple to cheat on Briana or was it something I missed about Monica? Here is what I do miss, I missed the Briana before the babies. Don't get me wrong, she still the sexiest woman most men would see in a month, and she still has a walk that makes me want to pounce on her, but all of that sugar and spice from the beginning has dissolved into *Similac.*

This marriage has been beautiful and boring, loving and lackluster, rewarding and regretful all packed into one apartment. I know that sounds horrible to say, but I have never expressed any of this to Briana because she's over whelmed. Gone are the seductive panties, the random blowjobs, those days when she would purr from the bedroom.

Hubby stop typing and come fuck me... please.

It's all gone with no guarantee of an encore. If we have sex, it's because I asked for sex, and that's what I regret. In pumping her full of kids, I'm missing out on the things that made me want to hump her in the first place.

It was almost as if Monica could smell the mothballs of boredom.

Now that I think about it, she didn't have to work that hard to get me in that hotel room, I wanted to be anywhere but that apartment. I feel horrible for admitting it, but it's true. I've never had so much fun in the back of a van, I enjoyed every second with my ex-wife. She was the break I needed from the mundane life of shitty diapers, and my exhausted wife. I was willing to take that risk in the same way people travel to casinos and take risks with their paychecks. I gambled because I am frustrated.

I also wondered if the pregnancy was the main reason, I married Briana? Am I with her because I love her the way a man should love a wife or was it a case of the dog with the swollen penis?

I got stuck in her.

"Hello Jarvis, anybody home?" Rasta knocked on the desk. "Does next week at the same time work for you to view the law suit filing?"

"Yes, that works for me."

A few minutes later we signed off the call with Tyler about the attack website.

"Man… that's great news!"

"Which part?"

I'd zoned out at the top of the call.

"Jarvis you didn't hear one single word, did you?"

"I was in and out."

"Lying your ass off, you were in Atlanta with Monica and you know it."

"True dat true dat, so tell me what I missed."

"They located the address for the owner of HoeLeaks and the hosting company said they will comply with a court order. Once this asshole is served, Tyler feels they will deactivate the site, but if they fail to comply, then we will have them in court within a month. Either way it goes, by this time next month this will all be behind us."

"And not a minute too soon because the day Monica gets a hair up her ass, she could destroy me."

"And whose fault is that?"

"I know, I know, but why did it feel so good?"

"Do you really want me to answer that?"

"Please…."

"The reason it felt so good to cheat on your wife with your previous wife is because you have a mental disorder."

"A what?"

Rasta shaped his hands into a bullhorn.

"I said you have a mental disorder that's preventing you from being happy. The woman could have been Mrs. Black America, it would not have mattered because you are mentally ill."

"Get out of here with that dumb-shit Rasta! I may have my issues but none of it qualifies as a mental illness. *Fuck what you're talking about dude!"*

Rasta pretended to catch a buzzing fly.

"Got it."

"…what?"

"Part of your mental disorder – which is that reaction – right there. When I placed you in a category of mental illness, you became instantly offended. You want to kick my ass… huh? That's why I used that exact verbiage, for the shock value, but even you can't explain your actions. How does a man go from calling her his evil ex-wife to *we fucked in the van outside of your reception?"*

I didn't have a response.

"Exactly, you can't explain why you didn't decline her flirtatious behavior. The sad part is Monica knew she was going to fuck you when she boarded that plane in Atlanta, and you proved to be nothing more than a *Thot.* Something is dislodged in your brain."

"So, you spend a few weeks in a mental institution and now you're Dr. Phil? There wasn't anything mentally ill about my actions other than wanting some hot cat. Not the sky-blue Wal-Mart panties, but some sizzling pussy in a hot pair of panties."

Rasta pretended to catch another fly.

"Got it…"

"Got what Dr. Phil?"

"The same excuse you used to justify fucking Briana when you were married to Monica. Different woman, same you, same shit, until you realize it's not the woman in the ugly panties, it's the mentally ill dick in the woman." You are the problem, It's You!!!!

"Whatever Hood Shrink."

"Call me Hood Shrink all day, but the issue you have is obvious to me, you need a clinical psychiatrist. Your actions are a danger to yourself and others."

No sooner than he wrapped up that ass chewing session, his phone buzzed – it was Biyell. Something to the effect of Uncle Glenn just had an ugly fight and Diana and he's grabbing an *Extended Stay* until his house is done.

This can't be happening, not to Glenn and Diana. They were once the happiest couple in our circle. The kind of couple that gives your marriage a goal to reach. If they fall apart then I have lost all hope for this thing called marriage.

"I'm on my way, hop Uncle Glenn to the pool, and stay there with him until I get there."

On the way out of Kayla's office, we crossed paths with Tiffany. Today she was dressed in funeral black. After Rasta greeted her, she shot him a look that wondered if he'd made any progress.

"Just leave Biyell to me, he will come around and you two will never leave each other's arms again."

"I so appreciate you for helping me, I don't want anyone else but Biyell, please express how badly I would like to see him. He's still not taking my calls, and his new voicemail says *if you're looking for me, I'm enjoying my new Tesla.* But he doesn't have a Tesla."

"Tiffany try not to read too much into that voicemail or any of his actions right now. Leave Biyell to me. I know it doesn't appear that I'm making progress, but I am." Rasta gave Tiffany an encouraging hug on our way out the front door. In the car, my seat belt clicked at the exact time a text message alert demanded my immediate attention. The text was from my wife.

How could you...

CHAPTER 37

June 17, 2018
11:05 a.m.

RASTA

It was three Thanksgivings ago, the last time I heard my mother tell one of the tails of walking home from O. Perry Walker High School with her sister, and how they had to fight the girls who lived in the Fisher Housing Projects. The story never changed, and the family ever ceased to laugh. In fact, it actually was a little bit funnier every time.

How growing up she never had a solo fistfight, because Aunt Diana would always jump in before she could throw a single lick. In her Wanda Sykes voice, my mother reenacted.

"...then Diana yelled... *you finna hit who? Not... my sister?* Before I could drop my book bag, Diana hit Big Belinda ten times in the face: *pop-pop-pop-pop-bitch-pop-pop-pop-pop-bitch-pop-pop-bitch-yah-bitch.* The fight was over."

I knew my aunt had a legendary set of hands, but the last thing I wanted to hear was she used them on Uncle Glenn.

While sitting at the traffic light near the foot of General De Gaulle & Woodland Drive, where Intercostal Canal Bridge ushers you to the exclusive English Turn subdivision, I noticed a black Mercedes sedan approaching at a high rate of speed: it was Aunt Diana. Leaned forward on the steering wheel as if her windshield had fogged, she zoomed passed us.

When I entered the home, Uncle Glenn was slouched on the sofa while Biyell was nearest to him in a chair he borrowed from the kitchen table. They both greeted me with a nod. I tried to be sensitive to the situation, but *that eye, though.*

"Uncle Glenn, Uncle Glenn, look up at me... now smile."

"Smile at you...why?"

"I need to audit your front teeth?" Uncle Glenn flashed a middle finger. To call my attention to the cheekbone area under his eye, Biyell drew an imaginary circle with his finger. It was as if Mike Tyson had beaten Uncle Glenn in the face for practice.

"Look right here Rasta...the whole side of this nigga's face looks like a rotten pork chop!"

Laughter exploded out of my tight lips.

"Rasta that may be true, and I know it looks funny as hell, but I will laugh last, you can *believe-dat"*

"...but that last lick nearly killed you," Biyell said.

"All bullshit aside Uncle Glenn, why are you two in here trying to kill each other?"

"Rasta, I know she's your family and all, but I'm tired of Diana and her *bossy-ass* attitude. For too long I allowed her to disrespect me, but she's gone too far. If it's a divorce she's after, then it's a divorce she will get."

"Now slow your roll Uncle Glenn, no one is getting a divorce...you two will work through this."

"Rasta there isn't anything to work out, she has called off the marriage over a few phone calls..."

"Annnnnnd?" Biyell demanded a full confessional.

"...and a ring that Derinda returned."

"A ring?"

"The engagement ring I gave her over thirty years ago."

"Annnnnnnd?" Biyell asked.

"…and I forgot to tell her the ring was in my pocket."

"Let me guess, my aunt found the ring?"

"It wasn't like I was trying to hide it, nor have I cheated on my wife. Diana would have probable cause to harass me if she caught me dicking her down in a hotel, but to threaten me with a divorce because of a returned ring…"

"Annnnnnd?"

"Annnnnnd my ass, I haven't done one got-damn-thing that warrants this reaction from my wife."

"And what about all the *haha-hehe* between you and Derinda?" Biyell asked.

"*Haha-hehe* isn't the same as *fuck-me fuck-me.* If she wanted out of the marriage, then all she had to do was ask for a divorce, but don't pick this simple shit to declare war on me. I am too good to Diana for her to treat me like this. If she doesn't want me, then there's always someone who will take me faster than you can fart."

"Who…Derinda?" We asked.

"Rasta and Biyell, will you two stop bringing up Derinda. It's not about Derinda? If I wanted her, I could have her…"

"Annnnnnnd how do you know that?" Biyell asked.

"Because I know it, there are certain things a man knows, and I know if I wanted her, she would come to me right now.

"I dare you…tell her to come right now and watch Diana knock your left eye out. You will be the *Disability MVP* in this bitch, **blind, crippled, and crazy.** Call her, I dare you." Biyell tossed Uncle Glenn his phone, but he quickly tossed it back.

"I didn't think so…talkin all that shit." Biyell reared back in laughter.

"Rasta, I have not acted on it, but it's there."

"That is why we're here and your wife is gone, she's exercising her right to tap out. That dog bit her the first time, now she knows that dog bites." Biyell said.

Like three hamsters inside of a wheel, round and round we spun, only to have Uncle Glenn side-step all responsibility for his role in their marital problems. His behavior is also closely related to Jarvis in terms of mental health issues, whereas Jarvis commitment to his wife is contingent upon constant praise and sexual reinforcement, Uncle Glenn has developed a sudden case of blame deflection, and an unhealthy emotional attachment to another woman.

It feels like everyone in my circle is having problems in their relationship, which leaves Kayla and me – as the lone *Happy Couple* after dethroning Glenn & Diana.

My aunt isn't willing to compromise, and my uncle isn't respecting boundaries, which is the ink on the divorce papers. This is the point I tried to convey to Jarvis this morning, before he became offended at the suggestion that he should speak with a clinical psychiatrist. It doesn't take Al Bundy to see that the shoe fits him.

There is something causing all of my friends to struggle when it comes to relationships, and it has little to do with an addiction to random sex. I know it's a long shot, but hopefully I can get them to see the benefits of spending a little time with a mental health professional. I know where I made my mistake with Jarvis – it's time to try a different strategy with Uncle Glenn.

"Uncle Glenn, I would like to schedule an appointment for you with my therapist, what's a good day for you?"

"Therapist? Like a psychiatrist?" His face wrinkled as if my breath was foul.

"*Potato-patata*, what day works for you?"

"Here's a better question for you, why do I need to see a shrink when it's Diana who's battering me? I wasn't fuckin with her. She kicked off all of this bullshit!"

"Uncle Glenn I see your point, I really do, but I still feel that you can benefit from a little one on one with someone who's clinically trained to help you process your feelings."

"Rasta, ain't a *mother-fucking-thing* wrong with my processor, it's Diana who should go sit on a couch. Diana is obsessed with Derinda, fighting her in dreams like a crazy woman. I don't think about Derinda half as much as she does. I'm not the crazy one in this marriage."

"Uncle Glenn no one is calling you crazy I'm simply…" he cut me off.

"I may not be the smartest kid in the class, but I damn sure ain't the dumbest. If you're suggesting that I go, see a psychiatrist then –"

I cut him off "Uncle Glenn that's not what I'm saying…"

"Hell, if it ain't" he grunted off the sofa and searched for his lighter, then mumbled under his breath. "This nigga has sat in my house, and called me… crazy? How in the fuck am I the crazy one? *Huh, Rasta?"*

"Uncle Glenn, he never called you crazy. Rasta simply suggested that you see his therapist, that's all," Biyell clarified.

"What about sneaking panty pictures of your customer's lingerie drawer while you're in the bedroom installing their cable isn't crazy? You never thought to seek a shrink for that?"

"Wait, wait, hold the fuck up!" Biyell arms stretched between them. "How did you…"

"And you, Mr. know it all," I could feel the heat steaming off his index finger "how many European Brothel videos you need to look at… just to beat one dick? Huh? Did you tell your shrink about that shit?"

"Dude, how in the fuck do you know about that?"

"Serious shit, how do you know about those panty pictures?" Biyell was mortified.

"Oh no," Uncle Glenn plummeted to the sofa and covered his face.

His good leg started to hill tap off beat on the wooden floor.

Biyell paced on an angry trail from the patio door back to the armrest of the sofa and then repeated. From my chair, I bent in Glenn's direction and waited for an explanation, of how he knew something so personal and private. Neither one of us denied Uncle Glenn's accusations, I was cold-busted, Biyell acted cold-busted, but how did he come to know that I had developed a fondness for underground *Czech porn.*

It was during the time when I was between women. I'd lost my appetite for the one who wanted to fuck me, and the one I wanted to be with puked at the thought of fucking me.

My porn lineup is no different than most guys. First, I would start with the 'cum swallow videos' and if that didn't make me cum then I'd check out the threesome section, if that didn't do it, then the BBC Snow-bunny isle would normally give me what I needed to beat it off, but one night in particular: they all failed me.

So, yea, I admit, I frequent the roleplay section of Pornhub that included video clips like *stepmom and son*, then *son and grandma,* then I collided with some weird shit called *Cuckold* (that grossed me the fuck out) only to finally stumble on *The Czech Sex Rooms.*

In this wonderful section is where I got what I needed every night, it never let me down. It's a large room where these women waited on tables behind a wall, with their bodies exposed from the waist down. The men would enter, and it was like a pussy vending machine: you can figure out the rest.

Sure, I watched every video in that section, at least twice a week, but in my defense, I was trying to wean myself off Shame-ka, and beating my dick to brothel videos became my metha-done. All of which was my personal *mother-fuckin-business.*

But who told Uncle Glenn?

What I choose to watch while beating off is my personal business as long as the video I'm watching isn't a class A felony.

"Uncle Glenn, I'm asking you as nicely as I can, how do you know what porn sites I watched?"

"…and my little game I played with the panty drawer? *How bruh? HOW???*"

Uncle Glenn started to speak but he never lifted his head to face us.

"Early this morning when Diana and I were having our first heated argument, she reminded me of a login and password to an account that I'd forgotten about…"

"What type of account?" Biyell asked.

"**…shhhh,** let him finish," I said.

"I'll start from the beginning, back when I presented you guys with the challenge. I asked each of you to turn in your cell phones. Then I issued brand new phones. The phone swap was a symbolic act that represented a clean slate, but little did you know, on the phones you received was corporate spyware. It was my way of verifying who was being honest about living a committed life."

"That's *fuuuuucked up.*" Biyell screamed.

"Unk' tell me you didn't"

"I did, and though I only spied on you the first two weeks, I did listen to some of your calls, and I had access to all texts and pictures. As long as your phone was powered on, I could hear your conversations, on or off a call."

In the center of the coffee table was his laptop. Uncle Glenn logged in to the spyware site and enlarged the spy history. Next to each one of our phone numbers were little files. When he opened those files, everything was there. Text conversations, those panty pictures Biyell had snapped in the bedrooms of his customers, and about 129-page views to the brothel site. I also saw where he ended all tracking.

My privacy had been violated.

My trust was contaminated.

"Unk' this is so fucked up on so many levels bruh. You have been spying on us all this time?" Biyell said before he snatched the laptop and began to open the files next to his cell number.

"Biyell I have no reason to lie, for the first two weeks – I did. With two million dollars of my money on the line, it seemed like a good idea. Then I felt bad about it and stopped, not to mention most of you were already disqualified. I fucked up, and all I can do is ask for your forgiveness." His plea for forgiveness fell to

260 / TJ SPENCER JACQUES

the floor like bowling balls.

We were pissed at the one person we respected the most.

Uncle Glenn had betrayed us.

Suddenly I felt molten anger upsurging from my lower abdomen, and a furnace blast vented out of my nose. I wanted to choke him, I wanted to curse him out, I wanted to make him feel what I felt, instantly. Then I heard a cool voice whisper a new combination of numbers.

#28. I can handle whatever comes.

#11. This difficult situation will soon be over.

#15. I cannot control the behavior of others; I can only control my own behaviors.

"I see where the surveillance of our phones ended, but I also see where you started monitoring Telly. That makes no sense. He was never part of the challenge, and he kept his phone?"

"That's true, but around the time you went to jail for that incident at Tamara's house —"

"You mean when I caught her with that nigga in my house..."

Despite being wrong as two left shoes for the tapped cell phones, Uncle Glenn still snapped back on the Tamara incident.

"It wasn't your house and we've covered this bullshit a million times." "It was my fuckin house and that mutha-fucka had no business sitting on my —"

"BIYELL, I DON'T GIVE A FRYING FUCK – IT'S OVER!" I yell into the space between them. "Uncle Glenn... continue please."

Anyway, like I was saying – Telly asked me for the phone to conduct business for you but I had a hunch he was up to something."

"... so, you put that FBI shit on his phone too?" Biyell asked.

"My gut was he wanted an additional phone to cheat on Erica, and my gut was correct."

"What Telly was doing was wrong, but this right here" Biyell pointed to the files on the screen. "I don't know how we go forward from this."

"You have every right to feel that way. Once I started spying on him, I couldn't stop. I guess like Briana, his world of lies and deceit became my entertainment, that was up until your wedding reception when Derinda formally introduced me to my daughter."

"So that's the other reason you're so opposed to Telly and your daughter?"

"That's why Telly ran out of here so spooked when you mentioned Reebie," Biyell asked.

"I had no idea who Reebie was so yes I became fascinated and listened in on his every call. Then this morning Diana abruptly informed me that she installed the same spyware on my phone."

"and heard every conversation you had with Derinda?" I asked.

"Every single call, even though I'd never cross the line into anything inappropriate, there was still endless calls between us. I know you're angry and disappointed, as I am angry and disappointed in myself, but today I have lost a wife and now my closest friends. Please, please forgive me."

"Are you going to do it, or do you want me to?" I asked Uncle Glenn.

"I'll do it."

Biyell handed Glenn the laptop and watched him delete all of the files and permanently deactivate that account.

After that, we each handed him our phones and watched over his shoulder as he deleted the spyware. After receiving his scrubbed phone, Biyell bolted for the door. I felt the urge to do the same, but I was also concerned about Uncle Glenn and didn't want to leave him alone in his current mental state.

"Uncle Glenn I'm not going to lie, this hurts bruh. Like, I have never felt this naked and this exposed. What you have done unto others, has now been done unto you. Being that my aunt cracked your password for this spyware, she not only spied on all of your private little secrets but also our personal lives."

"I can say that for sure, she appeared more interested in my conversations with Derinda…"

"Come on Uncle Glenn, you know damn well that if she was able to spy on you – she opened every folder on this account. She knows everything about us. You said it ended two weeks later, and I believe you, but for this reason, you have to seek help. The cesspools you've opened in your marriage, and the way you've betrayed the brethren, are all symptoms of something far deeper than spying on cell phones: you spiraled into perverted voyeurism. You listened to us having sex. Now, I'll ask you again, which day are you available to meet with my therapist?"

Suddenly the room began to spin, and my breakfast sought the nearest exit. It was not the bombshell of the tapped cell phones that brought on the abrupt case of nausea; it was something far more sinister. Not wanting to regurgitate all over Glenn (even though the thought did cross my mind) I excused myself out to the pool instead. After about ten minutes, I gave in to the possibility that never appeared plausible prior to this morning.

Could my aunt, Mrs. Diana Braxton, be the creator of Hoe-Leaks.com?

CHAPTER 38

June 17, 2018
12:05 p.m.

JARVIS

For the past hour or so, I've tried to burn as much time as possible before I faced Briana, but I could stall no longer. When I entered our apartment, I could hear the sound of a lullaby coming from my bedroom, blended with the sound of rage typing.

With little guesswork, I knew the lullaby meant both of my kids were deep in their mid-day nap, and the person typing was my irate wife. It wasn't until I closed the front door did the familiar clacking cease. Then it resumed for a while longer, before pausing again after a hard pound on a single key. A few seconds later, I heard her move in my direction like a loaded down tree hauler.

Our first initial contact was a stare off from across the apartment. Neither of us made any effort to cool the desert between us, nor did I want to be the first to speak. In allowing her to go first, it would give me the opportunity to assess the damages, without volunteering more information than she already acquired.

Biyell taught me that.

"I'm listening." Briana ended the silence but barely.

"What for?"

"Your *move-out* date?"

"I don't understand, why would there be a move out date?" I shot her a confused look.

"Since you're fucking Monica, then I need space to adjust to my new life as a single parent. Again, when are you moving out? If I may suggest… the sooner the better."

"Briana, I know you're upset with me right now, but I have no plans to be with Monica."

"So, you're into one-night stands? I see…well, I'm not sticking around for that part either. How long before you're gone?"

"I'm not leaving…"

"Then we're leaving. I'll find us somewhere else to live."

"Briana, please, you're acting as if I've run off with her or would abandon you?"

"Jarvis, I don't know what you would or wouldn't do. What's for certain is you slept with Monica. The photos of you two uploaded this morning to HoeLeaks.com."

Briana stood there with her arms tightly folded, as I whipped out my cell phone and headed straight to that website. On the homepage, under my name, there it was.

AUTHOR JARVIS NAPOLEON CAUGHT HAVING SEX IN VAN

There were no photos of Monica and I having sex in the van, however, there was a photo of me entering the van, then a close up of steamy windows, then a final photo of me exiting the van and zipping my pants.

Just as I was about to dispute her version of the van incident, I continued to scroll down. Someone followed Monica back to her hotel. The same person snapped a photo of her getting out of the rental van and adjusting her dress. There were also video clips to accompany the still shots.

I was majorly fucked.

Once I calmed down, I realized that none of the pictures were taken from her phone, but from someone else who watched my every move. If Monica wanted to do me in, all she had to do was post those selfies. I was convinced that Monica wasn't involved. This was the work of a paparazzi asshole and time was running out on my marriage and career. I had to stop the bleeding.

Kill the investigation with a confession.

Biyell taught me that as well.

"First of all, I am sorry. I come to you with no excuses, only regrets for my actions. I had a moment of weakness and, and, I had sex with Monica."

"A moment of weakness? Jarvis how many moments of weakness have you had with your ex-wife?"

"Briana that's not really important, what I would like to do is move forward from here and –"

"You don't dictate to me what is or isn't important. Every damn detail is important. Everything you did with her is important. So, let's hear it, how many moments of weakness have you had with Monica?"

"Just that weekend, it happened twice, but that was it." Her body shifted in place. Her arms untwined and rested on her hips. Her lips pursed.

"Briana, I'm lying. There was one other time… "

"When?"

"…in Atlanta."

"Jarvis… when did you go to Atlanta?"

"Last week, I flew in and came back the same day. It was the day of the seminar at Loyola. I never made it to the seminar, I lied. I'm sorry."

"Just to have sex with Monica?"

"………………………yes."

"So, your first time was the weekend of the reception. Once in a hotel, then in the van, then you flew to her, on the day you lied to me about a writing craft seminar at Loyola?"

"..........................yes"

"Wow, my sister said this day would come, and it's here." Briana dusted her hands.

"Briana, this is the God's honest truth, after a few celebratory drinks, the rest spiraled out of control. I'm begging you not to leave me. Please, give me a chance to fix this. I know I fucked up. You have every right to pack up my kids and never look back, but I'm begging you. Please, please, don't leave me. Don't leave our home. I can and will fix this."

Defeated, Briana lowered to the sofa.

Her face descended into a dullness that reminded me of commercial carpet. Her disgust was iridescent, and cycle through a range of emotions. **Vexed. Fury. Disillusion. Animosity. Pensive. Pissed.** Her voice sounded dehydrated or better yet, sedated with a heavy tongue.

It was then that my palms became sweaty, and my fingers started that uncontrollable twitch, and a mist appeared on my forehead. I tried but failed to beat down the strongest urge I face on a daily basis.

How pitiful of me, that even in the crisis of this hour, I wanted to power up my laptop and capture every painful indention in her face, and every raw emotion she exuded. It is who, and what I am. I am a writer, and writers write stuff, even their own misfortunes and misdeeds, so much so that, I feel a certain obligation to reward my readers with the raunchy, realness of my reality. I can't help it even if I wanted too.

I wanted to write Briana, right now, at this very minute, in this mood, with that embalmed expression, those pin-point questions, and the finality in her face, but not now: that would be inappropriate and insensitive, and inexcusable. Such were my actions with Monica.

Nevertheless, this romantic thriller with all of its suspense and pre-packaged dialogue was happening to my life in real time, and why should I have to suppress the urge to do that one thing I love to do more than anything else – that one thing I love to do more than squeeze a thick ass? Because it's inappropriate, and insensitive, and inexcusable. Therefore, I'll stand here and ignore the voice of my oldest companion, the one that's urging me to write this down, the one that's reminding me that I am a writer.

I am a writer.

A horrible husband.

I am a writer.

A disconnected father.

But none the less, a writer.

And that's the real reason I slept with Monica, I wanted to experience the scenes I've embellished every day. I wanted to inhale the scent of forbidden sex and describe it in every secreted detail to the point that it's too edgy for the editor, and too racy for a reader. I wanted to be the man in my new manuscript, the story I have kept hidden from Briana, the novel about my fantasies. Deep desires that she's too exhausted to fulfill.

That's the reason I slept with Monica, it wasn't about the sex, I did it because I wanted to give my fingers a fresh voice and watch the words fly on to the page. That's the excitement that Briana once ignited, and that's why I'll do it again if Monica opens her legs for me.

"Jarvis," an airy voice called out to me. "I asked you a question…"

"I'm sorry, please ask it again…"

"Again…do you love Monica more… than me?"

"Briana, rather than engage in a conversation that will only make matters worse, how about –"

"Do you?"

"Briana…"

"Jarvis the only reason you're still standing, and breathing is because I talked myself out of it. Originally, I was going to wait over there by the window. When you entered the doorway, I'd planned to stab you in the chest."

I followed her eyes down to the floor. On the side of her foot was a large stainless-steel knife. The knife normally hung out with a gang of ten in a rack, unless their services were needed. The one that sat next to her foot was the alpha male of the gang, the wide, pointed fucker, and he still appeared willing to carry out the hit.

"I was going to plunge it in your chest... up to the handle." She said in a resolved voice.

"Even now, the pain I feel after watching those pictures and reading those comments about my husband, I've concluded that you still deserve a knife today. The reason you're still alive and well, is because of my children. I have no one to care for my babies. Isn't that amazing, how those precious little kids saved your life."

Mechanically, her head oscillated towards me, then slowly away.

"Considering that I denied myself the gratification of watching you bleed out in the doorway, in this pivotal hour, the best way you could express your gratitude for sparing your life is to answer my question."

She was going to kill me – I could tell from the hard swallow in her throat, and the shrinkage of her eyes.

"Do you, Jarvis, still love your first-wife Monica?"

"I do."

"Good, we're making progress. It's a two-part question please bear with me. Do you love Monica, more than you love me?"

"Not in the same way I love you...It's different because you're my wife–"

"But the internal conflict you were confronted with was loving two good women, like the scenario you wrote about in *Stop Falling Into Hoes*"

Fuck.

Fuck.

Fuck.

She had me cornered. She was my editor. She remembered that passage.

When I was younger my grandfather gave me a puppy, and during the house-training phase (when the puppy urinated on the floor) my grandmother would drag the puppy over to the urine, press his nose in the spill, pop the puppy five times, then tossed him in the backyard. Each time the puppy wet the floor she would add an additional lick. Eventually, the puppy figured it out and barked at the back door when he needed to relieve himself. After which, he was allowed back in the home.

If you are in a relationship with a whorish dog, there may come a time when you have to drag that dog over to his own piss and pop his ass.

Listed below are the TOP 10 ways to train a dog/man that he cannot shit all over your house.

8.   *EVACUATION PLAN:* *It is okay to forgive him, but before you give him another chance, make him aware if it happens again you will leave him that day. Explain how you plan to leave, and the rules of engagement if children are involved. If you plan to remain in the domicile, have him sign your evacuation plan. Once he has acknowledged your plan (with signature) only then do you entertain a conversation about reconciliation. He can never claim he was blindsided, because your plan is a living breathing document. The best time to present your Evacuation Plan and obtain signature is during those pleading hours, when he's begging for another chance.*

9.   *DOCUMENT THE PAIN:* *Write him a letter explaining in detail how his actions have affected you, why it hurts, and your real-time thoughts about him as a man. Discuss the letter with him in detail to ensure that he understands how his actions affected you and placed the family in peril. Every ninety days,* *for a full year, you should have a contract renewal meeting with him to evaluate and gauge if you would like to continue your relationship.*

__10. CANCEL THE CONTRACT:__ Leave him and start accepting applications again for another man. Make him aware that you're going on with your life and plan to date other men, just in case he happened to see you out and about, or word gets back to him. The best time to cancel his contract is after you have executed your evacuation plan and given yourself at least a ninety-day grace period.

The comparison of men to the behavior of dogs is fitting because some do require training on how to exist within the confines of a healthy committed relationship. If you're reading this book as a single individual, then I advise you to never assume your potential partner knows the meaning of monogamy. Most black men grow up in single-family homes, where they've never witnessed a successful marriage. Be proactive and have this discussion a few times a year.

For those women who are dealing with repeat offenders, if he fails to figure it out, then you have an outside dog who should never step foot in your home.

Yep, I wrote all that bullshit, and now it has come back to bite me in the ass.

"Briana, I know what I wrote in the book, and you know how it is when us writers start writing, some of that stuff, you know...I mean you can't take everything in my book literal. It was for entertainment purposes –"

A finger pressed against her lips.

"That's not what you said on the stage at Essence Book Fest, I was there. I facilitated your book signing table."

"Yes, I remember but –"

"What you wrote, and I quote: *my book came from the observation of men like myself, and each page will help women protect themselves from emotional devastation.* You went on to say, *that some of these men are permanently damaged, and love falling into hoes. There's no help for some of us, because we have metamorphosized into monsters, and the only safe option for a woman in that unfortunate scenario is to run like hell and never look back.*"

"Briana, I know what it says, I wrote it, but this is real life and...our situation is different..."

"Jarvis, there is no difference, and you can't wiggle from under the weight of your own book. I'm not going around in circles with you, not doing it. Nope." She internalized. "...and besides, you have admitted that you still love Monica – where does that leave me?" I could only shrug because I did not have an answer.

"What am I to do with that bit of information? How do I plan a life for me and my children knowing that the love you have for me is not exclusive?"

"Briana... please don't take it that way, I love you as my wife..."

"She was also your wife."

"But you're the woman I'm married too and –"

It was then that she retrieved her phone from the back pocket of her denim shorts and read a message I assumed was from her best friend Sierra. Casually, I noticed her mood deescalated to the eerie calmness of a cop who suspected I was driving while intoxicated.

"Briana, I love you, and I love my family. I don't want to lose my wife..."

"Jarvis, being your wife equates to monopoly money, it has no value once the game is over. Mrs. Napoleon is merely a title, other than the last name for my children... it's basically worthless. She fucked you on the first date, and with very little effort invested. You're still wrapped around her finger. She owns you. She's in your head. I shouldn't be surprised or caught off guard.

I stole her husband before she had a chance to kick your ass to the curb, but she had first dibs, therefore she has every right to fuck you. Whenever. Wherever. I guess? Did you hear how fucked up that sounded? That's what it's like being married to you, constantly looking over my shoulder for that day and time, I have to pay for the man I shoplifted. But my aunt and I are even now, wouldn't you say?"

"...Bri, Bri, baby, please. It's not like that Briana, it may feel that way to you, but it was just sex, I'm not going to lie, I just wanted to fuck, that's it. It will never happen again. I promise."

"Oh, it will happen again in this marriage, I'm already preparing for it..."

"Briana, I promise on my children, this will never happen again..."

"Shhhh...*Jarvis-Jarvis-Jarvis,* I wasn't making reference to you when I said it will happen again..."

"Now, wait now, slow it down a bit Briana, we can fix this okay but there's......."

"You said you made love to your wife in a rental van because you *wanted to*......... as you said, so I've put out a few calls and tonight I will need you to babysit."

"You need me to baby sit...what?"

"Yes, babysit. Like you, I'm now in the mood to fuck someone. After all, isn't that how this works? When we're in the mood to do something, we do it, and think about the consequences later? After reading your book and the comments on that amazing website HoeLeaks, I've gained so much clarity. The only way to have any level of sanity with a man like you is to declare this marriage open."

"WHAT...?"

"I'm not done... hear me out. There's no reason to fuss and fight, we're no longer exclusive. My EVACUATION PLAN is to audition new men until I find something better – or you get tired and leave – either way I win."

After she spoke, I received a text alert notifying me of a purchase for $19.99 to POF Merchant. When I Googled the name POF Merchant, I was perplexed to discover that thousands of people had searched the same phrase.

What is POF?

Plenty Of Fish Free Dating App

Single? Find dates on POF and meet singles near you.

"Briana you're going out with a guy from Plenty of Fish? Don't walk away while I'm trying to work through this…Briana!"

My words fizzled before reaching her ears. Quietly she entered the bedroom, restarted the lullaby, and opened the sliding doors to her closet.

Did Briana say she was in the mood to fuck?

CHAPTER 39

June 17, 2018
4:05 p.m.

ERICA

I thought I saw him smile for about three seconds, or maybe five, the duration is trivial, I believed he smiled for me. Not a full smile like the day nurse who comes in every hour on the hour to check him, and adjust him, and replaces the plastic bags of life. Not quite a full smile, but just a little twinkle of light.

Telly there's a beautiful red-head on side of your bed and if I were you, I would wake up. The day nurse always interacts with him as if he could hear every word. Maybe he can? I wasn't sure which one of us she flirted with more today, we take turns basking in her compliments.

She has wood-grain skin and warm autumn eyes. Her hair is a different weave or wig every other day, but always professional and neat. Her nails are plain, but her lashes constantly wave. I bet she was prom queen or a dancing doll for Southern University, she exuded a certain loftiness.

We are about the same height depending on her hairstyle, but she's a few pounds thicker, with a much bigger butt. She tried her best to hide it, but in the center of her forearm are two Mardi Gras masks, one smiles, while the other pouts. I've never seen her sad, even after a twelve-hour shift.

Her name is Crystal, how fitting.

You have to lower your visor as she approaches because her smile says hello from a block away, and her energy is just as high. Her mother could not have selected a better name if she tried.

I wonder how she knew?

Crystal is one of those radiant personalities who backpedals when they say goodbye, more concerned about your cheerfulness than her own. As Crystal wiped, replenished him, and flirted with him, I didn't mind one bit. Even with all of the tubes, and this medieval medical bed – he's still the sexiest man I have ever kissed.

"Can I count on you to watch Mr. Man until I get back with some fresh pillows and a pamphlet Dr. Martinez left for you?" I nodded as she backpedaled into the hall.

I wonder if Telly would prefer Crystal more than Heather? I wonder if Crystal would consider it? Wow, I think I've just become that type, and I'm not freaking out about it. It was then that I rose to his ear.

"Oooooh Telly, if you decide to wake up, I may have a special treat for you…I think you'll like her." I blushed as I reached for my cell phone. Reclining comfortably in my chair once more, I could have sworn I saw him smile again, or maybe I wanted him too so badly that I smiled on his behalf.

Posthumously.

Speaking of flirting, Biyell stopped by this morning to get an update on Telly, and Telly's sister.

"*Soooooooooo,* is Phaedra coming this morning?" He asked with a ravenous grin.

276 / TJ SPENCER JACQUES

"She called late last night to say I could expect her right before dinner." I have a feeling he will pop up here again around dinner time.

The hilarious part of it all is Biyell likes Phaedra, but I think she's more attracted to me. She hardly bats an eye in his direction, but when it's just the two of us, then she relishes in my face the entire time. Smiling, touching my arms, my hair, intensely interested in every word I have to say; a curvaceous body that's starved for my attention. I'm not 100% certain she's gay, but I've never received so many compliments from another woman.

She invited Kayla and I to a cruise when all of this is behind us, I might just take her up on that offer.

The only down side of the day came from the usual suspect, Dr. Martinez. The status update this morning was the same generic gibberish designed to separate me from my hope and rob of me of my pennies worth of faith. I listen to Dr. Martinez, but I no longer hear him. He goes out of his way to dampen my spirits and douse my daydreams of Telly ever living a normal life, but I never asked Dr. Martinez for the truth.

For once I welcome all of the hyperbole in its purest form, I wish someone would burst into this room just one time and tell me an old fashioned lie, the greatest falsehood ever told.

Where are all the really good liars when you need one?

I need a world renowned liar like Donald Trump to barge in here and disrupt the staleness of this room with a bald mouth lie – while I backflip and cheer. You can do it, Dr. Martinez, be that liar who saves the day. Just say it. Open your damn mouth and speak something that contradicts your years of med school, your battle field experience in Iraq, your endless nightshifts in the ER, just this one time, as a favor to a guilt-ridden bride to be – for the love of everything exaggerated – LIE TO ME.

Tell me we're walking out of here together.

No news is not good news, and whoever said that never heard the percolation of faith nor the seepage of expectancy. I have come to feel that no news is evidence of bad news because unlike good news, bad news is extremely patient.

"Here's a folder with the pamphlet Dr. Martinez left for you." Crystal handed the folder to me and moved to the other side of Telly to replace his pillow. "He prepared a list of long-term care options for you to consider. I'm very familiar with the entire list, so if you have any questions please don't hesitate to ask."

When I opened the folder and my eyes fell on the first pamphlet, it felt as if someone had dropped a piano on my head.

"HOSPICE CARE…" My breath departed. Crystal made her way back to my side of the bed just in time to catch me.

"Has anyone ever told you that you're much prettier when you're not crying so damn much?" She held my hand firmly. "It's not as bad is it seems, I've had numerous patients miraculously recover in settings far away from this place. One was awakened by the sound of his favorite football team defeating Alabama, after eight years of losing. No matter here in this hospital or in your living room, he's still in our care, and I'm not to quitting on Mr. Ned. Stop crying and be strong for Telly, that's what he needs right now. As long as you're still fighting, then I'm fighting beside you."

It wasn't much, but Crystal gave me more than I had last night, and twice as much as this morning. Telly's projected discharge from the hospital to hospice is June 27th which gives me a week to prepare my home for him.

I'm not his next of kin, Dr. Martinez assumed that I was.

What if Phaedra or his mother decides to transfer his care to their home? Do I have any rights to object? What if Mrs. Ned decides that I can't be trusted to care for her son? After all, I'm the reason he's here.

Just as my pressure was about to reach stroke level ten, someone drummed a tune with their knuckles. I invited them in.

"What if Telly wakes up and the first thing he sees are those swollen red eyes? You would scare him half to death." My mother said.

"Ma'am, I just said the same thing to her." Crystal said as she

278 / TJ SPENCER JACQUES

released my hand. "I'll be back to check on you in an hour... okay?" She whopped me playfully on the shoulder and twitched out the room.

"Hi momma" I slouched "what time did he pick up the girls?"

"About ten minutes ago, I think Disney World is just the thing they needed. I wish I was going with them." She pulled me into her bosom until my eyes dried, then busied herself with the fresh flowers.

There was something foreign about my mom this past week, and even in my somber state of mind, I couldn't help but notice. Perkier, bouncier, jollier, and giddier than ever. There was even a noticeable change in her daily wardrobe choices, gone were the *I am woman hear me roar* pants suits, which gave way to *I'm a delicate little flower* full-length dresses. I can't remember ever seeing her wear pearls this much and free-flowing hair. My mother was suspiciously happy, and that was very disconcerting.

After she replaced the water in a vase of fresh lilies, she got to her primary reason for visiting.

"Have you spoken to your father today?"

"No mother I haven't, but I know you have."

"Only in text, but I'm sure I will hear from him soon. He normally calls around this time of day."

"Normally, am I to assume that my parents are close friends again?" My mother gleamed like Crystal. "When you two converse, what do you discuss?"

She blushed "A little of this and dab of that, mainly updates on friends from the neighborhood, and of course...the three of you."

"And what else?"

"What else could there be?"

"Mother I know you better than you know yourself, and I can tell when you're *excited*."

"*Excited? Who me?* Now that's a bit of a stretch."

"Here's a better description of this new you...alluring, attracting, anticipating, and agreeing."

"Who me? Anticipating what? Whom, am I alluring?" Her hand fanned the peak of her cleavage.

"Mother..." I puffed.

"My little carrot, you're reading far too much into my new lease on life. I know what you're hinting at, and you're wrong. Glenn Braxton is married to Diana Braxton, and I would never hop across her fence."

"But are you enticing the bull to hop Diana's fence instead, and graze in your pastures?"

"I'm doing no such thing."

"Mother..."

She scooted her chair closer to me "I'm not, but if he enjoys our conversations, and those conversations never wander into forbidden areas, then I don't see the harm in that..."

"Mother, he's married."

"Erica, I was aware of that before you."

"Technically, we discovered he was married at the same time, but moving on. I know how you feel about my father, and I must compliment you, this has been a smoother adjustment than I anticipated, but let's continue to walk this slowly. Agreed?"

"Are you assuming that we're going too fast?"

"Not exactly, but you two have a transaction history, and I am the receipt. The one thing I have learned from watching you two is there's no expiration date on true love. The more you interact with him the more you're going to enjoy the feeling..."

"It feels wonderful." Her fingers comb backward through her bangs. "I can't lie. I won't pretend. It feels like we've never lost contact. It feels like I have found the part of me that was missing. Over the years I wondered if his voice had changed, but it's still the same voice I fell in love with years ago, back when I had to sneak the phone under my blanket just to blow him a kiss goodnight. It's the same voice that asked me to marry him...........the same voice that said keep the ring because he was moving on. You once asked me why the cello over all the other instruments? Why did I force you to play and later my granddaughters?"

"Yes, I remember, and still wonder."

"...because playing the cello was the only way to hear his voice, and I wanted you to recognize the pitch of his affection." She then walked over to the large window and conversed with her reflection.

"He's a rarity you know? Sonorous. Lustrous. Poignant. Sensuous. A *Kallo Bartok cello* professionally tuned. I missed his voice. There, I said it."

It was then that my mother's cell alerted her that there was another text. I felt her exhilaration from across the room. There was that smile again as she brushed a lock of hair behind her ear.

I gazed at a motionless Telly, then back at my mom in all of her ardency, and then woefully, back at Telly. It was then that I was punted back in time, twelve months and a day to be exact, when Telly seduced me in a text. That's all he had to do, send a one sentence text to perspire me in passion, and soak with desire.

I want to feel the softest part of your body on my tongue tonight.

I read that text 20 times, and each time I inspected my body for the softest place. It was where it had always been. That's how we created our love. We expressed our unfiltered thoughts at the moment of conception, and that steamy text continued until that night I shattered the shower glass.

I wonder if my mother just received the same type of text? What else could explain that luminous complexion? My father has said something to my mother that has given her hope. The same hope I long for.

"Is that a text from my father?"

"Maybe it is or maybe it isn't ..."

"I know it is...only he has that effect on you. Care to share."

"I'm not sure if I can."

"I'm his only child therefore if it isn't anything inappropriate as you say, then you could share it."

She returned to her seat next to me and held the phone close to her chest.

"Mother, now I'm really curious, show me?"

My mom held the phone where I could read it and not touch. It was far too precious for my fingers. After I read it, I was touched, but also concerned.

You are the only person outside of my daughter who still considers me a good man. I have fallen from grace.

My mother collected her purse, keys, and then kissed me on the forehead, as she texted her way out of the room.

Mrs. Diana Braxton, I hope you can hear me you're going to need a taller fence.

CHAPTER 40

June 17, 2018
8:05 p.m.

JARVIS

That uncontrollable desire to write has been drenched like a camp fire, my nerves are too bad. All throughout the day, she avoided my touch, my questions, and any attempt to reconcile. I am invisible. Despite her best effort to appear unruffled by my fling with Monica, I could feel her anger each time she walked passed me.

When she moved to the kitchen, I stood near her, she relocated. If she was tending to my kids in their room, the moment I entered the room, she collected them both and carpooled to another room.

That is the current climate in our apartment, and just about what I expected – with the exception of that dating profile. Briana paid for that Plenty of Fish profile with money from our account, which makes me fifty percent owner of my wife's booty call page.

Using the same app, I created a profile out of curiosity just to see if she had really created a dating page and there it was, my wife in the same t-shirt she had on earlier, the same yoga pants, and a pink cap.

WANTED: A New Netflix Partner

Yes, I'm definitely easy on the eyes, but I'm not perfect and can be mean AF. I'm Very Unique, Beautiful, Smart, Very Confident, Very Observant. Love to talk, sing and dance. Did I mention I was Very attentive? Looking for someone who is not too busy for me. I won't tell too much more, chill with me, and you'll get your answers. I also enjoy spending time with my kids, watching television, and making money.

Five Things About Me?

1. I'm one foot out the door with my current situation, and not looking for anything serious.

2. I will not agree to commitment based on a false sense of security.

3. I won't promise you what I don't know.

4. If something physical sparks between us, it's because I wanted you, and not because of your superpowers.

5. I hate liars, so be straight up with me, tell me what you want, and I'll let you know if it's going to happen or not. I reward honesty - so don't come at me the wrong way.

One more thing: please do not be offended if I do not respond, it is most likely because my inbox is out of control.

In my lifetime, I have experienced variations of pain, like finding out I wasn't the father of a child I've loved since infancy, but the pain of reading that profile was a different level of excruciating. Reading Briana's profile made me wish she would have followed her first mind and buried that knife in my chest up to the handle. A quick death would have been more humane than reading this post on Plenty of Fish.

At first, I thought she was blowing off steam, the sort of thing a woman would do to make a man jealous, but then she started to dress, white blouse with skin-tight jeans, then an hour ago her girlfriend came to pick up my daughter, and I was the sitter for my son. Then Briana prepared the bottles for the evening. Then it fully registered.

My wife had a date.

Her husband wasn't her date.

It wasn't up for discussion, and there wasn't anything I said that convinced her otherwise. The more I pleaded with her the faster she applied her make up. Once she finished preparing the overnight bottles, I cut her off in route to the bedroom.

"This is not happening, you will not go out with some guy you met and think I will tolerate it – that's not happening."

"Let go of my arm." She growled.

"You disrespect me and think it's some kind of joke? I suggest you take off those jeans and let's finish the conversation, that is the only way to fix this, not hooking up with some dude you exchanged a few messages with."

"I said let go of my *fuckin'* arm, now!" She jolted out of my grip.

I reached for her again but this time she slapped my hand away. That's when I grabbed her by the collar of her blouse, and man-handled her over to the sofa, while she swung and scratched at my arms and face.

"Get the fuck off me."

Nose to nose I howled.

"I said you're not leaving this house."

"You try and stop me…"

"Briana, I'm not playing with you, keep trying me. Try walking out of that door."

"I don't want you any more…I'm fucking done."

"After everything I gave up for you, this is how you disrespect me? I lost everything, and now you're going to fuck some dude. Is that the thanks I get?"

"If your plan is to choke me then do it now because as soon as you release me, I'm getting the fuck out of here. I was the one who gave up everything, my sisters, my cousins, my mother, *my, my, daddy!* All for a weak-ass dude who wasn't worth it. I got what I deserved but so too will you. Now get the fuck off me." Her teeth broke the skin on the inside of my forearm. I had little choice, but to release her collar. Then came the voices.

Jazzy J: *Smack the piss out of Briana.*

Lil Glenn: Don't hit her, you better not hit her.

Jazzy J: *Fuck Lil Glenn, smack the piss out of her while you have her pinned down. That's a Bold bitch right there... created a dating profile? If you don't kick her ass from this day forward, you're the hoe in this marriage!*

Lil Glenn: You are not a wife beater.

Jazzy J: *This bitch is tryin to handle you – you have to choke her-ass out for disrespecting you!*

Lil Glenn: Jarvis you brought this hell into your peaceful home, you set these events in motion. You will not physically abuse her.

Jazzy J: *If you knock that bitch teeth out, she'll cancel that date – I promise you.*

Lil Glenn: She's not your property, you have destroyed this marriage. Be a bigger man, do not threaten her with violence and give her time to cool off. It's the least you can do.

A battle raged within me, and I knew this was the type of altercation that would define the type of man that I am. To hit or not to hit?

I'm not a wife beater.

I sat to the furthest end of the couch and watched as she stormed into the bedroom, then the bathroom door flung open, and five minutes later she stumped over to the closet wearing only a bra and those jeans. Next, I heard the sound of a hanger snapping as she snatched off another blouse, this one was the same color as the scratches on my arm.

"Briana I'm not going to stop you from leaving if that's what you want to do, but this isn't right."

She exited out the bedroom with her purse swinging off her shoulder and her car keys in hand.

Over by the counter, she wrote a note, slapped the pen on the counter, then placed the note on the refrigerator. It was instructions for my son's Eczema medication and evening feeding regiment. After one final trip to the bedroom to kiss our sleeping son, she marched like a North Korean soldier to the front door.

"Briana… if you do this, then you're no different. The way you feel about me is the way I will feel about you. Don't become what I am. That's not how you get even."

With one hand on the doorknob, she paused, something I said finally penetrated through her fury.

"I never set out to deliberately hurt you. I never paraded women in front of you. I fucked up, but I didn't do it in your face. Briana, you are a good woman, stay that way. Don't expose yourself to my disease, where you always need a third person to co-sign your worth. This morning Rasta told me point blank that I am mentally ill. At first, I took offense, but he was right. I have a mental health issue that requires immediate attention because I am a danger to myself, and others. Whether you want this marriage or not I need to get help, but don't sleep with some guy just because you're angry with me. Help me get help."

It appeared she was contemplating her next step because her eyes were fixed to the ceiling.

"Briana, in your profile post you expressed how much you hated liars, as you should, but I never lied to you. When you confronted me just now, I told the truth because I've felt horrible since that night. Please, Briana, come sit down next to me and let's attack this the way we've attacked every devil we faced, let's create a plan to have a happier marriage. Let's start going to church together. I'm so sorry I hurt you. Please cancel that date. Please."

She did not respond.

She did not release the doorknob.

She did not take her eyes off the ceiling.

I suddenly felt a warm moist sensation around my collar. When I inspected the area, my fingertips were bloody. I saw myself in that Exxon restroom in Shreveport after Monica attacked me. I saw myself abandoned on side of the road bleeding from the face and neck.

I have incited another woman to violence.

What the fuck is wrong with me?

Why am I back here again?

It was then that she half turn to me in that rouge blouse, rouge lips, and those hips, that were a gift from back to back child-births. Not even for the wedding was her make-up that vogue, and bold. Something has to be mentally off with me to cheat on a woman this beautiful, it doesn't get any better than this, and once she gives me this chance to fix this mess, I will never end up here again. I listened intensely as she cleared her throat to speak.

"After you change his diaper, the *Boudreaux's Butt Paste* is in his diaper bag."

Briana opened the front door, pranced out through the door, then slammed it. As she disappeared into the night, I was left with that echo.

The only way to have any level of sanity with a man like you is to declare this marriage open.

I'm in the mood to fuck someone.

CHAPTER 41

June 17, 2018
8:35 p.m.

BIYELL

While in the shower at the Hampton Extended Stay, I left the door cracked for her to come in and make herself comfortable. I decided to give Uncle Glenn and Diana some privacy to work through their issues, and some additional time for his face to heal without me laughing my ass off.

Their guest room was mine when needed, and they never asked me to leave, but I felt awkward being there especially considering everything that popped off this morning. Nevertheless, their altercation still consumed me throughout the day. Was Uncle Glenn really going to hit Diana? How would I have handled it if he would've? Who do you help in that situation?

A)   *The woman who's landing one hundred jabs a minute?*
B)   *The dude on the floor with one leg?*

Had she finally picked and pried until Uncle Glenn said fuck it? I know when I'm about to cross that line of *fuck it* because I always hear Uncle Glenn's voice.

Whose voice does Uncle Glenn hear?
Who walks him back from the ledge?
Who is Uncle Glenn's...Glenn?

I wish someone would have talked sense into him about tapping our phones, that was straight hoe-shit, but now that the smoke has cleared and no one won the money, it was pretty ingenious. I would not have trusted me either if I were Uncle Glenn. I had too much shady nonsense going on. I was still torn between Tamara and GIGI and could not decide one way or the other.

I would not have trusted Rasta either because he loved LaDeisha but was financially dependent on Shameka.

I would not have trusted Telly 'Crowd Noise' Ned because in a former life I think he was a street hooker, better yet, a white girl junkie who sold blow jobs two for ten dollars. That Horny-Horny Hippo. Telly does not know when to quit, that is probably why his ass is laid up right now. But I love him. I pray for him every day.

"Damn I miss my dawg."

And I wouldn't have trusted Jarvis because he fucked his niece, even if she was niece by-law, niece is a niece *muthafucka.'* But I judge not. But it was still fucked up. That's all I'm saying. And I never would have trusted Timothy because I didn't trust his chubby pretty boy-ass before the challenge.

Woe! Woe!

It makes sense now!

Glenn was calm during that *Tootsie Saga* because he knew. If he would have let it be known that he knew, then it would have blown his cover.

I still hate that he put me on blast. I know it was wrong, and it was only a phase, but I only checked the panty drawer, if the customer gave me the *I would fuck him* stare. I could learn a lot about a woman by getting a sneak peek at her panties.

If she had more sexy panties than *maw-maw* drawls, but no husband? Then I knew to proceed with caution because she's playing for keeps.

If she was married and all the drawls were maw-maw, but she still shot me the *I would fuck him* stare, then I knew she was bored with hubby and willing to play for at least two years.

If all the drawls are maw-maw and she's not giving me the *I would fuck him* look, and she doesn't have a man? Install the cable box and quickly get the fuck out of her house. She *ain't the one to play with.*

That is how I made the determination that Tesla was perfect for the taking. The top two dresser drawers were stuffed with panties so ugly she probably bought ten packs from Ace Hardware, but in the third drawer that's where I struck gold. In the third drawer I saw a little something that told me periodically she feels sexy, maybe once every other month, but it happened from time to time. She had a few lace panties on the left, a few satins in the middle, on the right was the jackpot. The leopard prints. That is when I started to do that thing, I did to all of them.

Lick my lips when she looked my way.

Lock eyes with her every chance I got.

Listen and repeated when she spoke.

Lay a soft imaginary kiss on her lips.

Leave a personal contact number.

Learn her mannerisms and taste.

Like what she likes and love it.

Laugh, laughing, laughter.

Lean into her space.

Last but not least, lust for her in a way that's so deep that it soaks those Ace Hardware drawls from five miles away. That's why she entered my room ten minutes ago, she felt me in her panties all day.

Sometimes I would close my eyes and takes several deep breaths, as I exhale, *I would say I need you, come to me, I want to love you more,* and after a few minutes she would send me a text or call. It is voodoo dick without the dead chickens, it is sexual and spiritual, it is how I got into her bloodstream.

It's that thing I do.

I dried off in front of her while she relaxed in the bed under the plush comforter. Her breast reflected the LCD from her cell phone. She settled on Mint Condition in her Pandora lineup, I love Mint Condition. The skin on her arms, cleavage, and neck sheened in anticipation, and her lips were naked and aroused. With my every movement she fell under my hypnotic control.

I made the most of her undivided attention.

With the patience of the IRS when they owe you money, I was slow. Methodically, I dried one section of my body at a time, first my neck, while my dick played peek-a-boo from behind the towel. Then I dried my abdomen which forced her eyes up to my chest. And then my back. Tesla stalked my dick as it swung from left to right, with each swoop of the towel. Once I was done teasing her, I slid the top layer bedding out of my way and bullied her legs open. Her heels came to rest on my back.

"I daydreamed about your body all day and here you are."

Just as my moist tongue was about to lift her clit, Tesla pulled me up to her lips.

"I want to return the love. It's about you tonight."

"Biyell I appreciate that, and maybe later if you still have the appetite, but I had a bad day… I need this." She rubbed me against her warmth, then slid me in.

Her body fully adjusted to me thanks to those three days a week sessions. What was a cramped uncomfortable space, I remodeled in a more spacious floor plan: my custom designed man cave. The fit was perfect.

"Fuck me like I'm your bitch…" She whispered.

"Are you sure? It could get a little rough?"

"I've been a bad girl today, punish me."

By this point, my dick was as hard as a can of Afro-Sheen, and I gave her exactly what she wanted until she tapped out about thirty minutes later. I ignored the taps and forced her to escape from under me. To the left of me, she panted and peddled her legs. I was out, but still deep inside. One hand covered her face while the other handcuffed her kitty.

"...oh my God, that dick, those arms!"

"Are you okay?" I pretended to be concerned, but deep down I was laughing my ass off at the way she convulsed and sizzled like bacon.

"Biyell, you dope dick mother fucker." She said in between breaths and sweats. "I am convinced, your entire body is one big dick. That's what it is, I've figured you out. You are a walking, talking, veiny dick. Your hands, lips, legs, chest, equals one big dick, because you have fucked my entire body. Who sent you? Huh? Who sent you? I surrender." I tried to compose myself until she was done but the last woman to react like this was that older white customer, Mary Brown.

"You- naughty-muthafucka... you." Her fist pounded on my thigh. "Why did you fuck me like that? Haven't you heard that this is what makes a bitch like me burn up your car? Do you want me to burn your grandmother's house down to the ground?"

I laugh out loud. "Please don't."

"Then you better quit while you're ahead. Dick like this is how a bitch like me ends up on Facebook... taking a bat to the ass of your car. This dick right here." Tesla shook hands with my dick.

"Okay, then I will stop fucking you like that..."

"Then you'll leave me no choice but to burn down your grandma's house when I can't find you. Comprende?"

"Si, senora."

"Oh my God...did I do all that?" Modestly, she pointed.

"I think so. because I hadn't..."

"Oh my God I'm so...I've never...oh my God, I must get a towel, and clean you up." She started to twist away, but I restrained her.

"Don't..."

"...*but-but*, it's all over you."

"And I love it." I pulled her back to the pillow and chuckled as she covered her eyes.

"I don't know what's going on with me tonight. I feel myself losing control of my emotions. I need to control this. But I can't because I want you inside of me every day, loving you endlessly, and I can't, but I want to, and that's not healthy, at least, not in my situation. I have a husband, and here I am with you, but with you is where I want to be, if only…" I cut her off.

"Listen, relax and enjoy me. We have all the time in the world, well maybe not tonight – you have to get home, but we do have all the time in the world emotionally. This works because you're all I can handle right now. After that Tiffany incident, I decided marriage is not for me. I need someone who will take care of me the way you do, and if you can't be with me every day, then, for now, it works. Okay."

"But what if…"

"Let's not discuss if's"

"But seriously, what if I decide that I want more, and I become completely available for you – will you at least consider it?"

"Consider what?"

"A life together?"

"I'm not sure, but if it happens then it was because you changed my mind."

"I know this is hypothetical pillow talk, but I can't believe these words are coming out of my mouth…wow. We've only been intimate a few times…"

"Seventeen…not that I'm keeping track."

"Whatever, Mr. Seventeen." Her smile was the prettiest thing I'd seen all day.

"Yesterday I had a panic attack at the thought of getting free to love you, only to have someone scoop you up before I had the chance to tell you." She rolled onto her side and began to kiss the bulk of my shoulder.

"Scooped me up? Someone like who?"

"I don't know…Tiffany perhaps? I mean, you just admitted that you were seriously considering making a life with her, and deep down I do feel you should give her a chance to make things right, but selfishly I want you to stay pissed off and scorned."

I chuckled "So you think I'm scorned?"

"I'm surprised you haven't burned her grandma's house down to the ground…" She teased.

Rudely, Maxwell's This Woman's Work was interrupted at the peak of the song by a text. Our love session was cut short by her motherly duties, and I had no choice, but to accept it. Before she slid into her lace panties, Tesla slid on top of me and then twerked me inside of her, but she didn't move, nor did she want me to move.

"I know it's early in this thing we've gotten ourselves into, but do you feel that?"

"That grip?"

"More like, that hug."

"Yes, I feel it."

"Whenever you need it, I will bring it to you. Don't call Tiffany, call me. Okay?"

"Deal."

The tables turned, and now the rabbit had the gun.

Whereas I dominated her with brute force, she dominated me with her ego stroking words. I was in her bloodstream, but she was in my mind. I never again wanted to feel the weakness I felt for GIGI, but it was starting to happen. The more she whispered, the more my eyes rolled to the furthest place in my head. Hands-free Tesla was about to park me again.

"I have a feeling we will be together. I do, and it's crazy, because our moons are so far apart, but soon they will intersect in a way that's so powerful, so cementing, that we couldn't return to our former worlds if we wanted too."

"And you're able to tell all of that from this fit?"

"No, I'm able to tell from this…"

Without permission or warning, she rolled off then sucked me into her mouth. "Feed me."

I fainted.

Once she was fully dressed, I reached for my key fob next to the lamp and pressed the button two times to lock it. Tesla chirped two times as she closed the door.

It's either going to be Tesla or *loose booty-ass* Phaedra.

CHAPTER 42

June 17, 2018
8:45 p.m.

BRIANA

I want to go on this date, and then again, I don't. This version of me is the Briana he earned, and the wife he deserves. I didn't ask for much. I just wanted to be happy. Unlike most women who drag their husbands into unrealistic mortgages and car notes – I just wanted him, in our little apartment, our children, our home, our home-based publishing company, our takeout food, and that's all.

That was my happiness.

I was the one who demanded the least, expected less, and gave more, but in return, I'm the only one left holding a gift bag of stale air. My entire consciousness, the foundation of my sense of security, and everything that I am rested in believing one thing above anything else: after all that we've gone through – Jarvis would never hurt me.

I believed that with every tendon in my body, I truly felt that the storm that nearly killed us would be the one repellant against all pests, but Monica buzzed her way back into my life. She landed in my soup.

What hurts the most?

Monica told him when and where, and my husband was there.

That's the part that has me in this car tonight, instead of at home, giving my kids a bath, and squeezing the last ump of energy out of my exhausted body to please my husband. That was my typical evening, but not tonight. On this unusual evening, Briana Napoleon is sitting in the parking lot of *New Orleans Food & Spirits*, fifteen minutes late, watching the guy through the large window, thinking to myself *I don't want to do this, not now, not ever.* I'm not this type of woman, but I have no one worthy of my faithfulness.

I am married to myself.

I was escorted to the table – he stood to greet me. Jarvis is tall, but he's taller, with skin that could work twelve hours in the sun, and not burn. His name was Carl. I did not meet him on that Plenty of Fish dating app, he was my boyfriend in college. I figure there was no greater punishment for Jarvis than to think I trolled the internet for sex. He deserves a woman who trolls for sex.

"Welcome to *New Orleans Food & Spirits*, my name is Haley and I will be your waitress." She was a lightly toasted woman with a body that was on the thinner side of BBW, but someone that I could tell would make a really cool friend, if you saw pictures of your cheating husband on the internet.

He ordered lemonade, I ordered the same. After Haley *The Waitress* scribbled in our drink orders, her thick calves hurried her over to the bar. Back in college, Carl could not keep a job, and gifted me a reason to break up with him every month, but I entertained him until something better came along. I thought Jarvis was the upgrade, but I was tragically wrong.

What if every time you turned on your television, there was your ex? That has been my life for the past three years. Carl is a local action news reporter with a legion of groupies that would fill up the Superdome.

"So, *Mr. Sexiest Anchor Guy* in the city, how have you been?"

"Miserable since someone nominated me for the sexiest anchor in the city."

I nominated him last year.

"... you know you're enjoying the attention, it's all you ever wanted."

"Not true, you are all I've ever wanted."

"Whatever Carl..."

"It's true."

That button up shirt was losing the battle to contain his chest and his arms in that suit jacket were one sneeze away from busting out, that's new. I could see why so many women voted for him, his face makes me feel safe, that's new.

"When I received your text asking if I was available for drinks, I thought it was a prank, or someone had hacked my phone. I waited for over three years for a text from you."

"Maybe I sent one a year ago, but it was buried under all of your admirers."

"There you go" he blushed "always thinking I have more women than I actually have."

"...maybe not as many as I assume, but we can agree that you have multiple?"

"Wrong again, this is one of the few times where I'm taking a little break from the relationship thingy. The last one ended in an insurance claim on my car, and she tried to set my grandmother's house on fire. It was crazy."

"Man, you must have really hurt that young lady. Did she catch you in bed with someone? Pelicans game? The mall? Where did you get busted?"

"Nope, she didn't catch me. She was married."

"You...were a *boo-thang* for a married woman? Get out of here"

"Sure was, and everything was cool in the beginning, but feelings crept in…followed by crazy. Which caught me off guard – she was an older woman, so I never expected her to fall so hard."

"It happens to the best of us."

"So…what about you? Who's you're boo-thang?

"Excuse me? I've been married for over two years."

"…*and what can I get you guys for an appetizer?*" Haley The Waitress pranced and smiled at Carl.

"…just a garden salad with some ranch dressing. That's all I'm craving."

Suddenly my Hoe Detection Security System flashed a warning – *Haley The Waitress s attracted to men with dark complexions.*

"And what about you Mr. Carl Nash, *what are you in the mood for,* I mean, hungry for? Can I start you off with some wings?"

"Yes, I think I'll take some wings and a glass of …"

"Orange Juice…" I said.

"Yes, a glass of orange juice."

With the menu's in hand, the waitress winked over her shoulder at Mr. Nash as she faded into the bustle of the restaurant.

"You better not start with me…" He warned with a finger. "That's the spotlight attention that comes with being a local media figure."

"I hear *yah*, Mr. Nash." I reached in my purse and retrieved a pen and sticky note, after which I handed it to Carl.

"…ha ha you already have my phone number."

"That's not for your phone number, I would like an autograph to frame." I never witnessed a chocolate man turn red in the cheeks, but it just happened.

He separated my fingers from the pen and sticky note but held my hand inches from his lips. Then tenderly kissed the back of my hand. I needed that.

"So, you were saying, before the waitress licked the side of your face."

"You mean, the part where I grew impatient waiting on you to become single again, so I started working out in preparation for the duel…"

"The duel?"

"I'm planning to challenge your husband to a duel…"

I burst into laughter and caught the attention of the two tables just to our left.

"Carl, a duel?"

"Desperate times require desperate measures, so I'd planned to challenge him to an old school fist fight in the middle of the street: the winner takes you home."

Now I was the one blushing uncontrollably "You would fight him over me…would you?" Carl slid his cell phone across the table.

"Call him right now – we can do this tonight…"

"I see your *holla game* has improved since you originally stepped to me." my eyes rolled.

"Game plan, is more like it."

"Good Game…" I smiled.

"I heard about Dallas…" My smile faded to black.

Just as he said Dallas, *Hot Girl Haley* returned with my garden salad in one hand, while she balanced a tray of wings on her forearm. This time, I didn't mind her excessive chatter or those flirtatious eyes that never blinked: Carl knew about Dallas and I needed time to collect myself.

"Thank you, Haley, that's all for now." He shooed her away from our table. "Now back to our regularly scheduled program. Dallas."

"Wasn't Dallas an old television show on CBS, with JR. and Sue Ellen?"

"Yes, and Dallas was also why you married Jarvis."

"Keeping tabs on me I see…"

"In my job title is the word investigative, but that's not how I found out."

"So how did you find out?"

"I rather not say…"

"Carl…"

"It's a source, sorry but I can't…"

"Carrrl." My bottom lip poked.

"Not fair, you know I could never resist the lip."

"Carrrrrrrrrl." The lip poked and puckered. He caved.

"I was following up on a lead that involved a youth pastor, and an underage girl, when I was approached by your mother. She remembered me from our time together. People beg me to kill stories all the time, but your mom's behavior was…was weird. She didn't sit well with me."

"…You don't have to sugar coat it for me, my mom is churchy weird, but what was it about her that was weirder than the last time you spoke with her?"

"For starters, she was more concerned about protecting the youth pastor, and never expressed any empathy for the victim. Immediately she mentioned you, and how sometimes young girls develop attractions for older men, then use their youthful bodies to seduce those men. And that's when she told me everything that happened that day in Dallas, and even eluded that the teen, in this case, could have been influenced by your favorable outcome?"

"Excuse me…my favorable outcome?"

"Jarvis married you."

As he spoke, I brutally attacked the cherry tomatoes in my salad, stabbing them repeatedly. I felt a slight air of vindication watching the juice ooze out the bottom. Half of the cherry tomatoes died for my husband's sins, while the others were bludgeoned in memory of my mother. For how she covered for the assistant pastor who raped me, and how she's still protecting perverts. In my parents' marriage that was her unofficial role within the ministry, she was *The Fixer.* The list of things she fixed for my father was never-ending.

Molestation by ministry staff issues she fixed.

Accusations of affairs involving my father she fixed.

Lesbian rumors involving my sister Erin she fixed.

Rumors of a gay sex tape involving the choir director she

fixed.

And that other daughter we heard about who was my age, **she fixed that too.**

And I never believed that it was because of her love for the ministry, but a matter of survival. The lifestyle she'd become accustomed to was contingent upon the survival of the ministry, and in her world, my father was the ministry.

Anything that posed a threat to his reputation she paid off, blackmailed, quarantined, and in my case banished.

"I don't mean to cause offense because I know that's your mother, but I lost all respect for her that day. It was like a silent threat to kill that story or she was going to drag you down with them. So, I iced the story."

"If you don't mind me asking, what was the name of the youth pastor?"

When he said the name, my hand froze in mid-stab, it was the same assistant who raped me. They rehired him.

"That's how I learned of Dallas and..." His words softly faded out.

"Dallas and what else did she tell you?"

"The website your husband has been featured on...the one with the photos of him and Monica. She emailed me the link. The subject: HERE IS A REAL STORY JARVIS IS A WHORE-MONGER. Briana I'm so sorry you're going through this. I tried desperately to protect you from your mother's smear campaign, then your husband goes out and –"

"Carl it's okay...thank you for always having my back and thank you for a wonderful evening." With my purse under my arm, I kissed Carl softly on the cheek and headed for the door.

As I turned, I caught a glimpse of him settling up the check. Soon he would catch up to me, I know him. Walking through the waves of dining room tables I felt naked, like each one of them had seen the HoeLeaks.com website, they watched the video of my husband making out with Monica. I felt like this was all part of my punishment for sleeping with Jarvis.

No one cared that she treated him like shit, and no one cared that she got pregnant by one of her colleagues; my life feels like the worst scandal in the history of infidelity. Just as I pressed the unlock button on my key fob, Carl spun me around.

"Before you go, I wanted you to know that I will always come when you call. I still love you. I know when we were together, I was scatter-brained, and couldn't make you any promises, but that was then. When things finally came together for me, the first person I wanted to share my life with was you – the one who stuck by me when I was broke as fuck. The one who encouraged me and forced me to take those journalism classes. Since you quit me, I haven't found anyone like you, because there isn't anyone like you…"

"Carl, haven't you noticed? I'm married with two kids now… I've totally fucked my life."

"But it doesn't have to stay fucked. Come back to me. Get away from this dude, and all the juvenile lies that comes with him."

"Carl …I can't."

"Yes, *You Can!*" His voice boomed across the parking lot. "Come back to me and let's live a new life, where you could put it all behind you. I can love you far better than he can, and I will provide a happy home for those babies. All I'm saying is think about it, okay. You had issues with me, but cheating on you wasn't one of my issues, because no one compared to you. The one thing I know about men like Jarvis is, they can't help themselves when it comes to their greatest love, and I don't think it's you. But for me…you are *THE GOAT.*"

"Thank you for dinner Carl, I have to get home."

Then a memory waltzed into my mind for reasons I couldn't explain. Jarvis and I had just finished making love and capped the evening with a little pillow talk before we dosed. He was worried about Biyell because her ex had returned with a vengeance and made Tyra and offer, she couldn't refuse.

Whorish Baby Daddy vs. First Love?

She ran to Julian and never looked back. At Uncle Glenn's house warming, she said the last time she felt safe – was with Julian. Carl is my Julian, this could be my last chance to feel safe and loved.

"Briana before you go there's one more thing…" In the clutch of his large hands, he squeezed me by the shoulders.

Don't pull me close to you. Carl don't. I'm married. I can't kiss you. This isn't right. Two years. Two kids. Two years. Two kids. Two years. I am marr…

It wasn't that he ignored my rejection, my brain never sent the message to my mouth to object, therefore, those words never reached his ears, because they were never uttered. Without a second of hesitation or a second thought, Carl reeled me deep into his pictorial wonderland, as I watched his lips float down from heaven, like a feather from an angel.

I kissed that angel, it was good.

CHAPTER 43

June 18, 2018
8:50 a.m.

BIYELL

My dick was still stuck to my leg, but it's cool, because her fragrance still permeated from the pillows. I think I'll bask here for a while. All throughout the night every time I shifted or rolled, the scent of flowers bouqueted between the sheets. For the past twenty minutes, indiscriminate thoughts shuffled through my brain.

I need a shower.

Tiffany has another sale.

Tesla said my entire body is a dick.

I've never been called a dick in a complimentary way.

When I'm ready to settle, I should take her from her husband.

Can't believe I'm having thoughts of busting up Tesla's marriage.

My brain emailed my bladder.

Standing at the toilet my nose agreed with my dick that I

needed another shower, but it was good pussy, so I was feeling like, it would be bad luck to wash it off prematurely, without allowing time for her juices to soak into my pores.

When it comes to a life-changing sexual experience – every time I take a piss, I want to be reminded of how she made me feel, how her pussy ministered to my manhood and triggered that feeling of weightlessness throughout my body. I know, a hopeless romantic. Nevertheless, my dick vetoed that thought, but it still felt like the right thing to do, not the shower, but the part about leaving her love cream caked on until tonight.

Overruled said the dick.

"Ahhhhhhhhhhhhhh what a woman you are," I said in a yawn and a stretch.

After I showered and dressed for my morning inspection of potential properties, my mind fell on Telly. I think I should start my day at the hospital. I might get lucky and run into *loose-boo-ty* Phaedra. I think Erica is blocking me, but it's cool. If I don't get her now, I will get her later. For an innocent conversation that is. But not this morning – too much shit to do.

It was twenty minutes after when my cell lit up.

"What's up Rasta?"

"Hey, have you heard from Jarvis?"

"Not at all. I gather he's late for the conference call?"

"A complete no call no show…I may have to start without him. What time are you headed over to check on that house on Apple Street?"

"As soon as I leave Telly, it's my first stop. Why what's up?"

"A certain somebody may have a customer for Apple Street, you know, that super selling real estate chick who keeps fresh money dropping in our account. I can't recall her name right now, but you know the one I'm referring too, really beautiful woman, looks just like Ciara Level up, and she's single from what I hear…the guy she was with is still acting like a *Lil Bitch*, instead of locking her down. But I also heard he could be on the *Low Low*… so that makes sense."

"…bruh fuck you, your paw was on the *Low Low.*"

He laughed so loud I had to hold the phone away from my face.

"For real Biyell, you're going to let Tiffany walk?"

"Rasta, the only reason you're minimizing what happened that night is because it didn't happen to you. You know damn well if you would have spotted Kayla humping on a dude's leg like a broke dick dog, tables would have flipped, and chairs would have flown – so cut the shit."

"So, you're still in your feelings, huh?"

"Let it go Rasta, Tiffany and I had our time to shine and she blew it. Meanwhile, *ole-girl* was here last night…?

"The Used Car girl."

"Tesla nigga it's Tesla. *Put some respect on her name.*"

"Uncle Glenn would always say, *let your dick dry off before you dive into another woman.* Can I ask you a question?"

"No…" But he asked anyway.

"Is this someone you're –"

"I said no you cannot ask me a –"

". . .planning to settle with or just a weekend bang?"

"Bruh, are you deaf?"

"But you heard the question…"

"It's like this, I could see us together, but she has to get completely free…"

"Biyell, your willing to delete Tiffany because she danced with a dude, but you have no problem sharing a woman with Mr. Tesla? This is the life you want? Help me understand."

Just as I sat in my car, I saw an alert from that HoeLeaks.com website, and a call was coming through from Uncle Glenn.

"Rasta, I need to hit you back, it's Uncle Glenn."

"Stop lying, and answer me…"

"Bruh this Unk' I will call you back." I switch lines "Uncle Glenn, good morning to you."

"You got a minute?

"Sure do…"

"Brother, I am reaching out to each one of you individually to ask for your forgiveness… for the whole cell phone thing. I was wrong and wanted to come to you as a man and say I'm sorry."

"Uncle Glenn… I was over that on yesterday, apology accepted."

"I feel awful for thinking that was a good idea."

"Uncle Glenn, you've always had my best interest at heart."

"Biyell to hear you say that… means a lot to me…"

"I was more pissed off you found out about the drawls. I repeatedly tapped the left side of my chest like; *Scotty, Scotty, Glenn knows about the drawls, beam me up out of this bitch Scotty…do it now Scotty.*" Uncle Glenn loves Star Trek so, he laughed his ass off on the other end, but I was humiliated as hell to know he knew. "Next time don't blast my freaky shit out in the open like that, pull me to the side. *Ya Heard Me?*" Uncle Glenn laughed on the other end.

"I heard you."

"How are things going with you and the wife…?"

"Like America & ISIS." He said in a defeated voice.

"No improvement from yesterday? None?"

"None, like two strangers sharing a Bed & Breakfast. She's blaming me for the reappearance of Derinda. Suggesting that *I conjured her up.*"

"I'm with Diana on this one, you probably have a pair of Derinda's panties tied around a key chain… huh? You buried it in the back yard… huh? You think yawl got a soul tie… huh? You still giving her the sweet eye… huh? You tryna' give her that turkey neck…huh?" I screamed in louder.

"You mind your fuckin business, before Josh jack your ass again."

"All jokes aside Uncle Glenn." I shifted to a serious tone. "I know there's a lot of history between you three, but it does seem like an overreaction on her part. I'm not one to hand out marriage advice, but sometimes a little time apart can make a woman miss what she had."

"Or she'll go fuck someone else…"

"Uncle Glenn get out of here with that garbage. You know your wife is not interested in being with anyone else. This is about those conversations she overheard with you and Mz. Derinda: with her fine-ass."

"Watch yourself, Lil Nigga."

"See there, that's why you just failed Baby Momma 101 right there, still guarding the pussy." I laughed because he was busted.

"Biyell you're wrong, just as wrong as this pot of gumbo that spoiled on the counter, with one hundred and fifteen dollars' worth of meat and seasoning."

"Nigga what?"

"I just poured it out…"

"The big pot?"

"The big pot…"

"Mannnn, fuck this Uncle Glenn, you have to get your life back together. Shrimp and Crabs died in vain all because you and Derinda fine-ass playing Indiana Jones – constantly digging up old shit. So busy catching up that you blew up your marriage."

"Watch yourself Lil Nigga."

I heard Uncle Glenn chuckled simultaneously as another notification from HoeLeaks.com flashed across my screen. While Uncle Glenn tried to justify why he's right and Diana is wrong, I clicked the notification link and nearly dropped my phone.

"Uncle Glenn I need to call you right back…"

CHAPTER 44

June 18, 2018
9:30 a.m.

RASTA

*T*hanks *for calling you've reached Jarvis Napoleon, chances are I'm writing a kickass scene and missed your call – please leave me a message or text and I will call you right back.*

Our call this morning with Tyler from RemoveSlander.com was originally scheduled for nine, but LaDeisha had a fire to put out on her congressional end, and Jarvis wasn't answering his phone. I decided to continue on with the briefing and planned to update those two later in the day, but I could not shake this uneasy feeling I had about Jarvis. He was one of those guys who never let a call go to voice mail, dude is too nosey for that, he answers all calls by the second ring.

My meeting concluded with good news, but no one to share it with, that's when my wife tapped the door.

"Come in sweetie."

She entered with a cup of coffee, a bowl of fruit, and a face that lit my world. It was only two hours ago that I watched her dress for her morning workout, and just as the yoga pants snapped over the booty, I said *thank you lord, I owe you one.* I've never felt like this, like I've won a prize every time she's near me. And don't get me wrong, it's not all physical, but a big portion of it is.

No apologies from me.

I listened to Uncle Glenn, I implemented his advice, I gave my dick time to dry off before I dived into someone else. I gave myself time to be single and used that time to focus on a few broken areas, thanks in part to West Jeff Behavior Management. They deserve a medal of honor for saving the women of New Orleans from a high-risk asshole by locking him up for nearly 90 days. Then came *sexy-ass* Kayla.

When she sat the coffee on the desk, I tried my best to slide my fingers inside those tights, but no luck.

"You better stop..." She slapped my hand "before you start something, we don't have time to finish." She tried to wiggle out of my reach.

"Who doesn't have time? ...just say the word *BAAAAYBAY* and watch I fast I reschedule everybody." I pulled her to my lap.

"You can stop spitting, I already said I do,"

"I will spit game at you for the rest of our lives..." I sucked her neck.

"Stop-stop-stop, you know we don't have time," she leaned far way "you have an appointment with Biyell and Uncle Glenn to view that flip." My hand slid deep between her legs. "I have a conference with Tiffany about a potential buyer at eleven, and an appointment to buy two tax liens after lunch, so please, please, Roderick. Stop." She evicted my hands from between her legs. "How did the call go?"

"The calls went great..."

"There was an additional call?"

"Yes, I had a brief chat with Erica. She informed me that they will transfer Telly to hospice after his last run of tests next week."

"Awww baby I'm so sorry, I know how close you guys are."

"It's like my world stabilized, but everyone around me lives are falling apart. At first, I was the one in pieces. And I want to help them, but to suggest they do what I did to stabilize their lives, wasn't received well at all."

"It's never received well by African Americans, especially men, but recent trends are showing a perception shift. Did the PR guy have some good news?"

"*That's right,* I almost forgot." Kayla leaped off my lap and sat across from me on the little couch just in front of her desk. "The company who owns that website has been identified."

"...a company owns that site?"

"Yes, and being that the domain is registered to a company, we're launching a *Gawker Bomb?*"

"That Hulk Hogan lawsuit? The one that put Gawker out of business for publishing private sex content of him and his ex-wife?"

"Yes, we have a similar situation."

"How so?"

"Jarvis..."

"How so?"

I hesitated. She noticed. It was the code, my first impulse was to protect the code, even though this was my wife, and the website had already published those salacious videos, I still hesitated. I was still doing it, that thing we did when we covered for each other, that thing that caused me to chew Jarvis ass out. Subconsciously, I was still willing to protect the code.

"Jarvis had a fling with his ex-wife but didn't know someone was following him." I still had the window open in my browser. Kayla saw what was out there for the world to see.

"Jarvis-Jarvis-JARVIS!" She shook her head in pity and pumped her fist in the air. "What were you thinking...?"

"He wasn't, that's how he fell into the same situation he wrote about, but scorched earth can still produce beautiful flowers."

"I can't see how? Once his wife gets hold of this he's done?"

"A lawsuit has been filed on behalf of Jarvis…"

"But wouldn't all of the success from his book qualify him as a public figure?"

"And that's what the owner of Gawker thought, but Tyler said when you publish content of this sort with a headline, you could be held accountable for damages."

"How much are you guys suing for?"

"Without any input from Jarvis we decided to sue F*elProof Media* for twenty million, and the good news is the owner of the site was served. Tyler was also able to expedite a hearing for the 10th of August."

"Yea, that's how you do it, drag them in court and make them pay."

"I'm surprised you never viewed the site, not that I have anything to hide, but I figured you would."

"I haven't viewed it because I really don't care."

"Even if half of it is true?"

"My guess was the majority of it is true, but none of those posts are an accurate description of the man I married. That's the old you, and the man you are today wouldn't do those things to me. I believe that in my heart." An alert on from her phone announced it was work out time.

"Time to go hit it. Any idea of what you would like for dinner?"

"Anything on the menu at Popeye's."

Her eyes rolled.

"Nice try, but we agreed no more fried food for a year."

"Kayla, Popeye's represents 60% of my diet…"

"Forget I asked, I'll select us something tasty…see you at dinner."

I met her halfway for one more hug and kiss.

"Do I have to give up the biscuits?"

"No Popeye's Roderick." She stomped the floor.

"Okay, Okay, I'll see you tonight for more of that flavorless health food – *ptooey, ptooey!"*

Another Kiss.

Another hug.

I'm stable, and joy is beautiful.

#20. I will enjoy myself while catching up on all I want to accomplish.

#40. I can make healthy choices

#39. Today I choose joy

#13. Other peoples' opinion is just their opinion

CHAPTER 45

June 18, 2018
9:32 a.m.

UNCLE GLENN

I just ended my morning call with Erica, and the news is all the same as it related to Telly, *no movement, slight brain activity, more tests to run*. Even though most of our getting to know each other has taken place over the phone, I've learned so much about her in these past two weeks. Her strength is what has impressed me the most, the way she stands guard with Telly day and night, he's fortunate to have found a woman like Erica, but when he wakes from this coma – my position is the same.

Over my dead body.

Welcome to my world, where I swing between two Glenn's, one on the left who braces for the death call every time the phone rings, and the other who fears if Telly recovered, then my daughter will marry him. If only she knew him as I have come to know him, and heard his conversations, Erica would realize she dodged a bullet. Somehow, I will get her to understand, but that is a conversation for another day. This morning Telly is a non-threat as long as he's sound asleep, the greatest no win, if there ever was one.

"And good morning to you too," I said to Diana as she walked past me in my recliner on her way to the kitchen.

"Good morning *Unccccle Glenn.*"

"Good morning little princess, did you have fun with your sister and brother yesterday?"

"Yes, *fun fun fun.*" Bylisha ran to the kitchen table were a bowl of cereal awaited her.

Suddenly, I heard a violent disturbance in the kitchen, where utensils wailed in pain, plates protested the excessive force, and the large pot once filled with gumbo – received an ass whipping that was intended for me. But what's done is done, and my worst fears have come to fruition, I am in a dead marriage with a woman who hates me.

Last night I slept in one of the guest rooms, while she slept in our bedroom with Bylisha. I often wondered how couples ended up sleeping on different sides of the house, now I know. It mirrors a broken finger on a child that was never medically treated, as the child aged that finger continued to grow – but crooked.

Just like our marriage, crooked.

Last night I tried to reset us.

I sent her a text asking what she would like for dinner, but Diana never replied. She's very good at this part.

The Quiet Part.

That is how she fights dirty, by walking around me, by me, over me, and through me, without uttering a single word. I would rather we cussed each other out, and flushed our system, instead of this disrespectful silence. I always wave the white flag first, and she knows it, but I care. I miss her.

In front of the coffee pot, she watched the cup fill.

Her body was draped in her favorite housecoat.

Her hair was tied in a polka-dot wrap.

Her slippers – plush and pink.

"I would like us to work through this, and I believe that we can if you could just... meet me half way."

My words bounced off the back of her polka-dot wrap. "Diana, talk to me..."

"Glenn, leave me alone."

"Diana, come on..."

"Glenn I'm not for it this morning, not in front of Bylisha... leave me alone."

"Diana, I understand you're angry about the phone calls, but you've listened to those calls, and not one of them ever crossed the line. The extreme of a divorce because I didn't tell you about the ring? You have blown things way out of proportion."

She added sugar to her coffee and stirred.

"I cannot help it if someone still has feelings for me. Would it make you feel better if I shot her? How about that? Since we're going to extremes, tell me what would make you feel better... huh?"

To avoid me, she moved to the opposite side of the center island, kissed Bylisha on the forehead, and continued to the patio. I followed her.

"Have it your way, I'll leave you alone, but remember... I came to you. Even though I feel this is all *dumb-shit* that you've welded together, I was willing to drop my end of the beef and give it one last try, but that's it, Diana." She slurped her coffee again and gazed into next week.

"If this is the way you wanted it, where we become enemies, then it will be this way until the divorce is final. Just know one thing: I'm not leaving my house." I pointed down at Diana, while she continued to slurp in perfect peace.

"My leg bought this fuckin-house, so if you're that disgusted with me, then you leave." I hopped towards the door.

SLURRRRRRRRRRRRRP

"And another *mutha-fuckin-thang* ...you can delete my number out of your phone. Don't call me for shit! I wouldn't care if

a bunch of crack-heads stumped your-ass in the project court-yard, don't call me, because I'm not your man *no-fuckin-mo*...
Ya Heard Me?"

SLURRRRRRRRRRRRP

"That's what you better do...look out that window. Get used to it. Get some practice at looking for a husband. Get a book on how to look for a nigga: *For Dummies*. Because you will need it. Do you Know why? Huh? I said, do you know why Huh? Because Glenn Braxton will be *gone gone gone*! And on that day, your hateful ass will realize what you had on the beautiful sunny day when I walked out –"

"You meant to say...hopped out?" *Slurp. Slurp.*

"Go to hell Diana."

"This coffee is delicious."

SLURRRRRRRRRRRRP

CHAPTER 46

BRIANA

O nce my eyes closed, we were back in Freshmen orientation, two quirky 18-year-olds, fresh out the nest, green as *Spinach*, yellow as *Summer Squash*. He asked me for a stick of my gum, then he asked if he could walk me back to my dorm, but he never asked if he could be my boyfriend: somehow, I knew he would be. I was alone with a man for the first time since I was sexually assaulted, but it felt natural, and his tenderness was just what I needed to unwrap the bandages of rape.

In that kiss, I was reminded of the first time our lips touched in the backseat of his car – I saw our first apartment together – our first pillow fight. That kiss caused me to scrutinize my better judgment and own the brutal truth that when it comes to men, I'm simply cute, but not acute.

I'd rather chase after Jarvis, than grow with Carl. An assessment so skewed – I've decided to fire myself as *CEO of Briana LLC*.

Terminated because of greed and stubbornness.

Terminated for believing Jarvis was the man I wanted Carl to be.

After our lips separated, I accepted full responsibility for this BP Oil Spill that has become of my life and decided not to burden Carl with the laborious task of disaster recovery. This is my mess, I made it and I alone will clean it up. I was wrong for leaving him.

I was so unfair to Carl.

Then karma skip traced my address.

By the time Jarvis made it home, my eyes had succumbed to drought, and I was emotionally dead, but once again, it was Carl who triaged his way back into my life: he found a woman worth saving.

"The night is young…get in your car and follow me."

"Carl I can't…"

"Yes, you can…"

"I'm married now…" I said in the tight space between his lips.

"You're married to a sheet of paper from the courthouse, but unfortunately, your husband isn't married to you, and no matter how hard you try, Jarvis will never be anything other than Monica's husband."

How did he know?

I have felt that way for two years.

I agreed with Carl but continued to resist. "Come home with me, leave him. Three years ago, Jarvis stole you – that was my fault because I wasn't financially fortified enough to secure you, but I am now, and will not lose you again. When you called me, I knew something was wrong. You were scared and –"

Abruptly, a gleeful voice dislodged the hypnotic hold of his voice and created a pathway of escape. "Oh My God, thank you so much for the tip, Mr. Nash…" *Haley The Waitress* winked at me in envy. As he greeted the server once more, I stood a few paces off to the side of Carl and became a fly on the wall within his world.

"Not a problem Haley, you were excellent…enjoy the rest of your evening." His smile was nourishment to a withered lily, and accidentally, a seed of possessiveness took root deep inside my heart: a silent bloom of jealous pedals.

"Before you go, do you mind if I get a picture? My sister will never believe you sat in my section …I hate to ask, but we're sort of like…*Carl Nash fans*…we voted for you at least two-hundred times each." She blushed in my direction "I'm not trying to be rude, but do you mind?" She assumed I had the right of refusal, so I played along.

I granted her request with a nod and a smile as if this sort of notoriety was normalcy, but it wasn't, and there were no visible signs that he was perturbed, but he was – I know him. Nevertheless, Carl selflessly leaned into her and flashed that fluorescent smile, as Haley snapped six pictures in a row.

He's such a sweet guy. So humble and kind. Long before he became Carl Nash, way back before the tailored Brooks Brother's suit, there was that mahogany skin and the smile. He still has the most beautiful parts that I discarded like an empty bottle of eyeliner. What was I thinking to walk away from that smile? That's right…I was infatuated with Monica's husband.

After the photos, she thanked him again for the tip, then backpedaled to her car. Carl immediately pulled me back to his chest, as if there had never been an interruption. To the casual eye, I imagined we were the silhouette of the perfect couple sharing a romantic embrace, but it was all an illusion of happiness, starring a displaced shadow that was about to vanish in a puff of smoke.

"Carl… I really have to head home, thank you so much for –"

"*Bri-Bri-Bri…* I was saying…when you called me earlier today, I also knew tonight was my one opportunity to free you from the endless humiliation of **Life with Monica's husband.** Briana… look at me."

The pitch of his voice deepened, in the same way, news anchors transition to a story about a homeless woman, who died of hypothermia. Deep canals appeared in his brow – lines I failed to notice when he lowered to kiss me. Even the tenderness of his touch was gone – replaced with the grasp of a Fire Fighter pulling me out of a burning building. I did as I was told, I gazed deep into his eyes and for the first time in years – I listened.

"You deserve better, don't waste your life trying to prove something to a man who's still in love with his wife. When you ended our relationship, you said do not call you until I have gotten my shit together. My shit is together. Come back to me. Why go home to a man who you love more than he loves you? Be with the one who is crazy about you."

"…but, I'm a *stay at home* mom with back to back babies."

"I know…"

"…but…but, I still love Jarvis and I'm still his wife…"

"I know…"

"And knowing I still love my husband…I mean Jarvis… you still want me…?"

"Over time, the feeling you have for him will matter less than they do now. A better question for you is…"

"Yes Carl, I still love you…I don't understand it, but I've never stopped."

"Don't feel guilty for loving me, you have two kids, and you love them both, so it's possible to love more than one person. In the four years, we were together, I never hurt you, not the way he has crushed you. The question is which man gives you the best opportunity to be Briana again? As for me, I miss Briana. Do you?"

It was then that my head rested on his chest.

"Briana, it's not about sex, I want you to follow me so we can map out how to transition you, back into you. Let's go on a scavenger hunt for Briana. That's the reason you called me this morning…" I nodded.

"I needed to get far away from him…"

"Briana, in his book, the one you're listed in as the editor, author Jarvis Napoleon wrote about having an *EVACUATION*

PLAN & CANCEL THE CONTRACT: *Leave him and start ac-cepting applications again for another man.* Briana, I'm here to evacuate you, do not try to ride out this storm, this is Hurricane Katrina."

Carl quoted a passage I meditated on for weeks after Jarvis wrote it. I needed an evacuation because my husband placed me in harm's way, he doesn't have my best interest as a priority, and if it came down to evacuating Monica or getting me out the eye of the storm, Jarvis would leave me at the mercy of Red Cross.

"Okay, how about Los Angeles?" Carl held me by the shoul-ders and shook me a little. He remembered how much I loved L.A.

"You always dreamed of living on the West Coast and pursu-ing a career in screenplay writing. If I remember correctly?" I nodded again. "Briana, I have a job waiting in L.A. and they've just upped the offer. Come home with me, let's share a bottle of wine, and talk about it for the next two hours."

I nodded again and followed Carl home.

That was last night

The time now is 7:20 a.m

To my surprise, my house key gave me permission to enter, even though I'd expected him to change the locks. Jarvis was still in the same place I left him. On his chest sound asleep was my baby, but the swollen sacks under his eyes convinced me that, he was the one who cried throughout the night.

It was such a sad scene.

A wife returning home after being out all-night doing God knows what, and a husband home alone, worried, angry, and hurt, but I didn't give a fuck.

Jarvis returned from the baby bed to find me in the refrigera-tor taking inventory of the bottles, the feeding was to the exact. On the television was Robin Roberts and Michael Strahan. I still wore the clothes from yesterday, but I didn't give a piece of fuck about that either.

"So, I don't get an explanation?"

"For what?"

"Briana I'm not playing this little game with you, where in the fuck have you been? Do you know what time it is in the mother-fucking morning…?"

"I told you yesterday, I was going out. Now if you don't mind, while the baby is sleep, I need to get ready for the day."

After a quick glass of juice, he blocked my path to our bedroom.

"Is this the part where you choke me again? If it is, then let's get it over with."

"No, but I would like to know where have you been and why you think it's cool to come home the next day? Did you fuck someone you met on the website?"

I didn't answer, but I was thinking if he came any closer to my neck, he would have the answers to all of his questions.

"This is how you handle me? This is how you disrespect my house? Our family? This marriage? It's taking everything in me to not hurt you right now."

"Everything in you didn't stop you from choking me yesterday, why would everything in you prevent you from doing it now? Everything in you didn't stop you from flying to Atlanta to fuck Monica, you know why? Because there isn't anything in you."

"Don't act as if I've abused you…I grabbed you by the collar, I never laid a hand on you."

"I said it yesterday and I'm saying it again, I studied you, the men you hang around with, and the only way to deal with a man like you is to become you, if just for a day so you can know what it feels like to get fucked over."

"So that's what you were out doing last night? Hooking up with someone you met on a sex-app?"

"…but it was okay for you to fuck Monica?"

"I didn't say that…"

"Not in words, but in your actions…it was said loud and clear. Now I'll make this just as clear… Jarvis, you were the man of this house. Jarvis, I followed your lead. Jarvis, I submitted to you and allowed you to set the tone for this marriage. Once in possession of the most precious gift I had to offer – my trust – you went on to define what type of marriage this was going to be, you made decisions that violated the sanctity of our bond, you engaged in sexual acts with your wife. Jarvis, all I've done is repoed my precious gift, and adjusted my life accordingly."

"Briana, since yesterday I've apologized a hundred times, I offered to seek help and even gathered a few referrals for marriage counseling. I can fix this… if you give me a chance."

"No…"

"Excuse me…"

"No…I'm not interested."

"What do you mean you're not interested."

It is true, what they dish out they cannot take. As women, we have allowed men to create the double standard, benefit from the double standard, and change the rules as they see fit. If I wanted to make love to Carl, I could have but that's not what he wanted. He missed my voice. We talked all night until I fell asleep in his arms, and this morning I awoke to a new perspective of love and respect. Carl respects me.

I feel zero guilt.

I don't feel afraid or ashamed.

Jarvis' eyes are watery, but I don't care – *fuck his feelings.*

"Mr. Napoleon I'm not interested in giving you a chance or therapy, or counseling, or anything of the sort. The only couples who benefit from those services are the ones who haven't lost all respect for each other. You wrote in your book, and I quote:

"Adultery is an act of disrespect, and there isn't a therapist alive who can make a man respect you."

"Briana… I made one mistake, and you take this position?"

"Correction, you made three mistakes in one month."

"…but, but, I'm willing to fix the things I need to fix to be a better husband."

"Then Monica might appreciate that, I'm not sure how Nile

Biggins, you know HER HUSBAND, would feel about your little triangle. He doesn't strike me as the type of man who's willing to share, but that's none of my business. As for us, we're over. We're getting a divorce. This apartment is in my name; therefore, I prefer that you look for a place to live immediately. The kids, like the publishing company, are community property, and you can see them as much as you like, let me know what works for you, but make no mistake about it, we're done. So, either clear out of my way, or I'll call the police to move you. What's it going to be?"

"BRIANA, I AM YOUR HUSBAND! You can't leave me like this, after all that we've been through…"

"Jarvis…*sweetie-pie*…*sugar-cakes*…*honey-bun*, a few minutes ago I deliberately referred to you twice as Monica's husband, and you didn't correct me either time. Now get the fuck out of my face, I need to pack."

HOELEAKS COMMENTS
AUTHOR WIFE CAUGHT CREEPING WITH ANCHOR CARL NASH

The wife of Best-Selling Author Jarvis Napoleon is not sitting around waiting for the book to happen to her, new exclusive video! Would love to get your comments about the video of Briana Napoleon and Carl Nash.

BoujeeGirl504 – Four Hours Ago
I feel bad for that young woman. Yea Its very easy to criticize her, but I have heart especially for people like her who married a dog. I hope everything works out for her.

AlphaMan06 – Four Hours Ago
I guess in I'm the judge she lost her rights to any of his money. And if I'm Jarvis I'm making thanking that anchorman because he got you out of paying a whole heap of child support. That's the Brightside.

TrustNoHoe2019– Four Hours Ago

When my girlfriend cheated on me, I simply told her to pack her stuff and leave. She tried to explain why for about 2 months then I changed my phone number. Then she came to my home and apologized to me, but I had moved on. I promised that day I will never ever trust a bitch unconditionally. I'm Out!

GrindingGirl24_7 – Four Hours Ago

Wtf she ain't no real wife just a hoe in wife's clothing. Smfh men are always trying to find a wife in a hoe and then get mad when she does hoe-ish things. At least wait until you're divorced! Kissing another man in the parking lot of a busy restaurant? WTF. Then slept at the anchor man house, hoes just as ruthless as these hoe-ish men. Jarvis can't get mad at no one but himself, because when you met her she was a hoe so what makes you think anything will change? Dumbass. LOL

GotIvy4Cheap – Four Hours Ago

Thot! Straight fucking thot! Sad this is how most females are these days no loyalty in their DNA, and if you're a man reading this your woman has cheating on you too. None of us niggas are safe, this is a thot epidemic! Time to call in the military to stop these thots from infecting the good women. There's still good ones, but all it takes is one thot friend and you have an outbreak of hoes. That's why when I see a good lady being fucked over I tell my home boys you stupid as fuck because good women are endangered, most girls only out for themselves on some real hoe shit...shout out to all the real loyal women out there and to these thots – we're about to round you hoes up.

BriceGirlGoState – Four Hours Ago

When black men say this is why they don't date other black women, after watching this I'm starting to get, I totally get it. I'm not saying you're wrong for not dating black women because hell, my boyfriend is white. But don't blame this kind of fuckery on ALL of us. All black men aren't dogs and all black women aren't hoes. Jarvis drove her into his arms. I think it's cultural and maybe it's time more Black women to give white guys a try. It's working out for me, no baby mamas, no cheating, no fuckery. WINNING.

WakandaQueen504 – Three Hours Ago

All these men on here bashing black women listen up……………………………………FUCK YOU!!!. Most of you sick fuckers on the down low any way! That's why your mama been single since 1987. Did she cheat? Is your mother a whore? Lol You all look stupid to categorize an entire race of women because y'all made bad choices on who you decided to date. Like my grandmother use to say, everything that look good isn't good. I am a black woman that has never cheated on my man, not even a little. @BriceGirlGoState the first time that white boy Brice has had his fantasies fulfilled he will call you a nigger so loud it'll blow that cheap weave out. She can be black, white, Asian, Hispanic, anyone of those things and still cheat on your black ass simply because that's just who she is. If it wasn't hard for you to get in her pants then guess what, it won't be hard for the next man or her first boyfriend. Jarvis wife was wrong, but she doesn't represent me or any of my sisters.

SayYes2Weed2019 – Three Hours Ago

@WakandaQueen504 you need to shut the fuck up, you know these hoes ain't shit because you're one of them. Hoes can be anything on the internet, cat fishing like you hold it down for a nigga. Man shut the fuck up y'all ain't nowhere near like the women back in the 1940s, I be wishing I could go back in time and get a faithful woman then bring her back here to teach these bitches how to act. The woman in this video is a true representation of women today.

DeltaBride1988 – Three Hours Ago

This is sad all of it!! This is not a black woman's problem it's a women's problem. Women of this generation are not the same as your mother because they've watched their mother be hurt and broken by men so they don't have enough faith in God first off or men to be faithful. But in black women's defense it's 20 single loyal over looked single black women out here forever one sloppy slut like the one in this video. And trust me she didn't just jump up one day and disrespect their union like that. Have you forgotten that it was her husband's how to hoe guide that inspired this wonderful, marvelous website. Kissing a side dude like this is wrong and nine wrongs don't make one right. Maybe Briana should write a book and acknowledge she's out here down bad as fuck. This is a L for Briana, not women, not black women.

TMfromBAMA – Three Hours Ago

That's what I'm talking about, that's how you do it Briana! Married or not I would have fucked Carl Nash too, on the same date. Fuck these bum as black men, fuck'em all. I caught one dude back in high school and then I graduated. Bitches still letting these niggas run high school game, all you hoes kept back. Cheat on that mother fucker first, then wait for him to catch up. I just told a nigga name Byron the other day – we can go out, we can fuck, but that's it. I ain't shit to you.

RodieRO – Three Hours Ago.

You @ThisByron I think I found ya girl. This Her? TMfromBAMA?

Drop&RollEggPlantFire – Three Hours Ago

Bitches out here still falling for the same magic tricks, after Jarvis told you how the game works. Long Live Biyell!

BAMAMAN – Three Hours Ago

@DeltaBride1988 is a hoe that's why you mad or you did

something.

ThisByron – Two Hours Ago
@TMfromBAMA this Byron, hey this Byron. That's how you do me? Put all that fancy loving on me and now you're not answering the phone. Hey @TMfromBAMA this Byron. DM me. Call me. Why you blocked me?

IBroughtIt504 – Two Hours Ago
To them men on here trashing black women, keep in mind unless you're President Obama, your momma is a black woman! Is your mother a hoe? I'm definitely not a hoe. I have morals and common sense. I'm engaged, employed, in school, no kids. My sister is married with 2 kids by her husband. My mother also is happily married oh yeah all three of her kids same father. Just stating facts. When white people say all niggas are lazy and on welfare you same mothers want to protest, then get on this website and call all black women hoes. Can't label an entire race of women so take several seats and keep it moving.

FreeMyNiggaRayNagin – Two Hours Ago
Its always that one that wanna bring up yo mama....Jarvis aint fucking their mamas. He fuckin this trifling ass hoe.

BerniceCateringNOLA – Two Hours Ago
@ IBroughtIt504 Gurrrl thank you for pointing that out. Your statement was nothing but the truth. And everybody wasn't born to a single mother...some of our parents where actually married and together...that does happen u know. I'm glad Jarvis got exposed maybe he'll think about that with the next woman, but I doubt it. Jarvis will do that shit again. I bet that on my last dollar.

AqueenToBe 1990 – One Hour Ago
Right, I've never cheated on my hubby, not even when were

*bf/gf, I've been faithful for 8 years and will continue to be be-
cause it's not hard. There aint shit out here worth cheating with.*

LetMeTestifyHoe – One Hour Ago

*Honestly my mom did cheat on my pops lol he caught her with
my football coach. Same coach was fucking all the moms on the
team, that's how I got to play QB, mom broke him off a piece.
Now, I got a full ride and a shot to make the NFL. To women like
Briana I say a little bit of pussy given to the right nigga could go
a long way – so Do the Rite Thang with your pussy.*

TalkDatShitttt – One Hour Ago

*I'm here to defend the woman in this video. Fuck Jarvis and
fuck these illiterate niggas making untrue blanketed statements
about all black women. Reading comprehension is key and 75%
of you idiots lack the skill. My only advice is trade up for the
new model nigga, one that's educated, and isn't a convicted felon. These black men represent all the crime and drugs in our
communities, black men are our main enemy. If we make too
much money, they intimidated, if you don't make enough money
then you're considered a Save A Hoe Project. Briana did right,
trade in for the new model because I don't have time to put two
of these nigga's together to get one light bill paid. Ain't Nobody
Got Time For That!*

IaintGotIt4U – One Hour Ago

*They are not bashing black women. Black women are beau-
tiful. But this whore is trash and should be dealt with as such.
How could you even try to stick up for a woman like that? She
could at least have the respect and decency not to do that in the
streets. This is fuckin disgusting along with Jarvis, I'm not up-
holding that simple minded ass dude either. A serial killer could
bait Jarvis in a dirty white van with a piece of pussy. Black men
like that make all of us look fucked up.*

BePatientBruh – One Hour Ago

My wife died two years and here I am trying to raise three daughters by myself and dude had a good woman? We were married 16 years now I'm trying to find someone but all of these women have been dogged out. What I do now is play a little game where I asked them about their ex then time how long she talk about him. That entire list of issues represents the damage the ex-dude caused. Most of that damage is irreversible and unsalvageable. Guess I'll be single a while longer.

TMfromBAMA – One Hour Ago

Hey @BePatientBruh I just sent you a DM, check your inbox. Wink wink

TakeWheel&CarJesus – One Hour Ago

I've never cheated on my husband or any other man. Hell I can barely keep up with one relationship how the heck can Briana juggle 2? And on top of that...For every person you sleep with.. u have slept with 10 of the people they slept with b4 you... Now that's scary...Carl Nash better get checked out at clinic...#ijs

BAMAPelican4Ever – Just Now

There's a lot of ignorant assholes on here that think all black women are thots, so I guess if they're black, then females in their families are thots as well. What is wrong with you young men today? And it's a shame how young women can carry themselves with no respect, but what I like to see are the ones who do respect themselves. Hats off to you my strong black sister .... #RESPECT

9THwardSoldier – Just Now

Here comes the feminists to defend this hoe in 5.4.3.2.1 LOL

AhitBitchHolla – Just Now

So many women out there claim their baby father ain't shit, but they should be mad at themselves for getting pregnant for a nigga who ain't shit. You thought a baby was gonna change him? He wasn't shit when you fucked him – that's the who reason you fuck him. You are who you fuck.

This generation is full of thot bitches and hoes and bitches with side bitches. I have only dated black women, and ran across a few who were fucked up. So to classify those were in fact fucked up, does make you feel a certain way about black women in general. But I also never gave up, but found a black woman worth my time. My queen. Married almost 20 years this year. But went through a lot of worthless black chicks to get her. So my point is simply, it's human nature to assume the worst of people. We do it every day. It's not a black women thing it's just facts. But this bitch in this video who's married and tonguing down a dude could have handle that better.

ThisByron – Just Now

@TMfromBAMA this Byron, hey this Byron. Pick up or DM me, this Byron.

CHAPTER 47

June 18, 2018
12:50 p.m.

JARVIS

This can't be my life, this can't be my wife, this isn't happening, and if it actually happened, then there's a reasonable explanation. Not my Briana, no way, no how, because she loves me too much to go there, this has to be some sort of cruel prank.

That was the voice of denial at five o'clock this morning, but that voice was quickly silenced by a bold header, on a website from hell.

**BREAKING NEWS: ANOTHER HOTLEAKS.COM
EXCLUSIVE!
WIFE OF AUTHOR KISSING ANCHOR CARL NASH**

It was not a case of mistaken identity, the video of them standing by her car was HD quality. The kick in my face came when the video zoomed in and I saw the way my wife looked at him right before the kiss, with those 'save me' eyes, I knew then it was over. Last night my wife spent the night with Carl Nash, and there isn't anything I can do or say about it.

I'll walk it off somehow.

I inquired about Carl a little over a year ago, when I saw her voting repeatedly for him in a Hot Celebrity Contest, but I didn't make anything of it because Jada Smith is everything. Then I received an anonymous email from Briana's old church circle and ignored that as well. I figured it was her mom's messy ass, at it again: but the devil told the truth that time. He did show up at their church looking for my wife, and he waited for me to screw up.

It's too late to open the EX-FILES now.

Dude was forty steps ahead of me.

It was a nice head fake – make me think her date was with a random guy, but the entire time, it was her true love. I had to hear it from Monica of all people, in the middle of the morning. Then around nine this morning Biyell called, then Uncle Glenn, followed by Rasta. All of them were overly concerned that I might harm her. Each one basically said the same thing.

Don't do anything stupid Jarvis and think about your life and your kids.

Why would I do something stupid?

What's done is done.

Winner takes all.

Jazzy J: *But you still should have stumped that hoe on principal. You can't let these bitches walk all over you like this, hanging out all night, fucking a nigga name Carl Nash. What kind of a name is that for a nigga anyway... Carl Nash? But nooooo, you listened to Lil Glenn, whose life is all fucked up. The same Lil Glenn who's letting a bitch walk all over him. My nigga, I can't fuck with you anymore. In fact, I've lost all respect for you, old pussy-fied-ass nigga. I'm out.*

Suddenly she entered the house for the second time with both of my kids and her friend Sierra. She also had the same overly concern expression as if her life was in danger, but it wasn't warranted. Her friend stood frozen near the front door. Briana walked past me to the bedroom without saying a word or turning a hair in my direction. This time the feeling was mutual. This morning I felt she was something worth fighting for, at twelve noon – I was offended she still has my last name.

"*Cummy bitch...*" I said in a voice only she could hear.

My daughter reached for me, and Sierra walked her over. My kids are too young to notice what's about to happen to the only home they have known. We're going our separate ways, that much was implied from the sound of packing and the long zip of suitcases.

And every time I thought about saying something civil, that video of their kiss in his driveway replayed over and over like a *Time-Life* commercial for 24 cd's, stuffed with sucky love songs from the eighties: that kiss screamed loud as fuck – like Michael Bolton. We were done – sealed with a kiss. Paparazzi watched her drive away, and she rubber necked until he was out of view. The person who followed them captured it all, and for that I'm grateful.

Briana stormed past me again with an overstuffed suitcase in one hand, and my son on her hip sucking a pacifier. She handed my son to Sierra, then headed outside. She returned to the bedroom for two diaper bags and two bulging carryon bags. When she returned this time her friend was given the okay to wait in the car, so I kissed my daughter then handed her off to Briana.

"I will give the apartment manager my 30-day notice." My eyes were fixated on the refrigerator.

It still had the residue of a happy home, with *to do notes,* messages, and photos of my immediate family. Our counter was still crowded with washed bottles that sat upside down on a towel, two feeding chairs waited for two babies, our kitchen table chilled just below a wall graffitied with selfies of Briana and me.

"With everything that has taken place I don't feel that this is the best time to discuss visitation. Let me know when you would like to see them, and I will do my best to meet you half way."

If this was all just a dream then this has to be *Sleep Paralysis*. I'm wide awake, but I can't move, and things are happening to me that is out of my control. This is what it feels like to have someone slip *Rohypnol* in your drink, which renders you defenseless while they violated your body. If I look at her, I'm going to rush over there and pitch her through that window, if I respond to her, chances are, I will call her every *slut bitch* I can think of. So, I sat there motionless, while she walked out of my life.

"I...guess that's it, okay, that's all I can think of, for now, I'll see you around." Followed by the click of the door locks.

In the grand scheme of things, I know it's the pot calling the kettle a hoe, but I'm entitled to my feelings, and *she's a hoe.* That sums it up. *If Carl could fuck you that quickly then I never had anything, to begin with.* I'm fucked up and she's, just as fucked up, and maybe that's why we connected: we're both sexually gullible.

Mr. & Mrs. Hoe.

Suddenly there was a knock at my front door. Briana wouldn't have knocked because the bitch had a key.

"It's open."

In hopped Uncle Glenn, Rasta, and Biyell: worried – as if I dropped a wide-open touchdown to win the super bowl. They encamped as close to me as they felt needed.

"Talk to me, young man..." Uncle Glenn sat next to me.

I shook my head in astonishment.

Rasta sat on my left side and fist bumped my knee.

"Jarvis, I know how this feels. We're hurting with you. You stood next to me, you watched LaDeisha flash a wedding ring. You were also there the night I was released from the hospital. I am living proof...you can and will get through this..."

"And I just went through it too, it stings like a mutha-fuc-ka. Tiffany waited until I fell for her before she pulled a stripper move, but every time I walked up behind her and busted a Bounce Beat – I couldn't get a piece of twerk out of her big booty-ass. Got to the reception? Bitch became the Michael Jackson of twerking. Bitch moonwalked and twerked at the same time. Real talk…"

"Biyell that's impossible." Rasta could not hold his laughter.

"Rasta, y'all should have given Tiffany a trophy and a 2pc & a biscuit, and an outfit, for all that ass she popped on Josh."

"But anyway," Rasta tried to recapture the serious tone, but like a single finger raised in a Baptist Church, it was gone. Only Biyell could make a man laugh who just watched his wife and kids walk out the door. Then the seriousness of the moment returned like a bad case of acid reflux.

"Fuck, this hurts."

"As it should hurt." Uncle Glenn placed a hand on my shoulder. "This wasn't a hat you lost or car keys, this was that treasured chance to raise your kids with a beautiful wife. It should hurt." Uncle Glenn's voice in times like this, became the father I never had.

"Prior to our arrival we expected sixteen cars of police, and the medical examiner van parked in front of your door, but the fact that she's gone without incident: takes a lot of growth. You still have a long ways to go but you handled it the right way. You fucked up, owned up to it, and respected her decision. All it takes is a split-second emotional reaction to land you in *Angola State Prison* for the rest of your life, I should know because, I nearly had one yesterday – if not for Biyell."

"*Mannn,* I appreciate you guys… for checking on me, but I'm good. There's something about seeing your wife on video with another man that could turn a lovely lake into a dry desert instantly. I made a mistake and she followed up my mistake with one of her own, it is what it is."

"Jarvis, you missed the meeting this morning, but Tyler was able to get us an expedited hearing date, and they're going to obtain a court order to have the salacious videos removed, while we pursue our damages. With the exception of Uncle Glenn, who was never a major feature on the site, all of us have a case including LaDeisha, but we're only pursuing her claim if we run into issues getting the website removed."

It was then that my cell phone alerted of a series of texts messages sat in my inbox. The massive mudslide that had become of my life, continued to wreak havoc.

TEXT 1: *My husband saw the video of the website and started to trash our home. He has broken and smashed everything but me and the girls. Our daughters are terrified.*

TEXT 2: *I left with the girls in a hurry! We have to get out of Atlanta because he's on a warpath. He has left several messages threatening to kill me. Problem is we left with the clothes on our backs. We need to get our belongings and move back to New Orleans.*

TEXT 3: *I'm scared*

TEXT 4: *WE NEED YOU!*

TEXT 5: *I LOVE YOU!*

CHAPTER 48

June 29, 2018
7:50 a.m.

UNCLE GLENN

When Percy Sledge recorded that timeless love song, the *B-side* should have featured a second rendition: *when a woman loves a man.* My daughter loves Telly and I know this to be true – we had to pry her fingers loose from his bed rail, but she had to go. Only she could prepare her home for Telly's long-term care. That was two days ago, and today is his transfer day – she pulled it off.

Her home was now equipped for Telly's medical care, and Biyell oversaw the rewiring of her electrical sockets, the only thing that remained, was the discharge procedures.

In Erica absence, Phaedra, Rasta and I split the bedside duties, in other words, it required three of us to maintain the sitting regiment that Erica willingly sacrificed. Even Rosa and Parks adjusted to life in a hospital room with *Mr. Ned sound asleep.* Her description was perhaps the most accurate summary of Telly's new life as seen through the eyes of a child.

Maybe I should write that song?

When a woman loves a man.

It's the perfect love song but the wrong man. My feelings about Telly have not changed. Even if he opened his eyes right now, I would be elated, but would still protest their engagement. Erica doesn't know him well enough. She does know some things, from what I heard when I listened in on his calls, but she doesn't know the extent he would go to preserve his lie.

All of the shit that Telly had going on was part of the reason I ended my surveillance of the other guys, he made their lives look like an episode of Mr. Rogers Neighborhood. But not Telly, from the moment I handed him that phone he called two women within five minutes and told them the number was his new primary contact.

And then there's that Reebie situation.

Then there Jarvis who's tried to hold down the dumb shit department until Telly is off sick leave. The day Monica told Jarvis she was scared and needed his help – she picked him up three hours later in Atlanta. He secured the home while she packed. Mr. big bad husband who threatened to blow her brains out was surprisingly cool calm and collective once Jarvis arrived.

Jarvis prayed for a reason to kick his ass since he found out about Lyric, and the fact that he was at the divorce hearing – any reason would have sufficed. Thank God everything went smoothly and Biyell picked all of them up from the airport the following morning.

Yesterday Jarvis told us that Briana has moved in with Sierra, and HoeLeaks.com posted another video: out on the town with Carl. I can't make any sense of it other than Briana was the one who edited his book, therefore she had a lot of time to prepare herself mentally if Jarvis had a relapse, and that plan involved running like her weave was on fire.

Who would have thought?

And while all of this madness is going on, Telly is knocked

342 / TJ SPENCER JACQUES

the fuck out.

On another note, the sub-contractors told us they're on pace to finish Biyell's home by Labor Day, but he could start living there as early as next week, while they wrap up the trim. I hate the fact that he no longer felt comfortable at my house, and opted for the extended stay hotel, but things are dark between Diana and I: this appears to be the end of the road.

And if it is, then I'm okay with that and plan to live out the second half of my life with someone who respects me. Diana doesn't respect me.

It is, what it is.

Here comes Erica, looking all wide eye and bushy-tail.

"How did my king sleep last night?"

"I couldn't tell you because I was knocked out too." My daughter slapped my arm. "No kidding, if Telly would have got up and walked out of this room, I wouldn't have known until his catheter popped out and he screamed. But I slept my ass off on that little sofa sleeper. How about you? Please tell me you got some rest?"

It could have been the makeup, but she didn't seem as weary.

"A little bit, but even in my sleep, I'm at his bedside."

"Speaking of which, what are you doing here? We ordered you to man the fort at home until we got there…"

"I know but once my mother came to pick the girls up for music lessons, I'd rather be here with you and my king."

Every time she referred to him as *my king* it felt like bed bugs crawled down my back and started nibbling on my ass. But it's best that I hold my peace. I may not have to be the bad guy after all. I had a chat with one of the nurses last night, and they believe Telly will remain in a vegetated state for the rest of his life. The doctor, on the other hand, feels that over time his brain may heal and reboot. I see no signs of that happening."

"Did I ever tell you how much I thought about you over the years?"

"Yes daddy, every time you see me…"

"In that case, then one more time wouldn't be a bother." I managed to steal a smile. "With every birthday I wondered how tall you were? How well you were doing in school? Even tried to guess which high school you would have attended. Then as the years added up it became more difficult to predict your life, but I never gave up hope that I would see you again. Can I ask you a question?"

"Whatever you like…"

"Anybody ever told you that you look just like your daddy?"

"They do now…" She smiled again. "I'm so happy my mom buried that hatchet and released her animosity. What a long time to hold a grudge."

"You can say that again…it felt like I lost ninety pounds when your mother stopped hating me."

"She didn't hate you, because my mother never said one negative word about you. You became an off-limit topic, that's all, but never spoke ill of you…"

"Tell me more, but this time, say it in my good ear…" I leaned over to Erica.

"And you better not repeat this because I will *deny-deny-deny,* but lately my mom has gone Glenn crazy."

"Really…"

"I kid you not, she has enjoyed reconnecting with you, and I don't ever think I've seen her this happy. Speaking of which, how are things going at home…?"

"That depends on who's asking?"

"Your only daughter?"

Do I tell her the truth? That Diana and I have had our last romantic breakfast together or should I sugar coat it? She has a right to know the truth.

"This is not a very good time for us and from my point of view, it isn't getting any better."

"It's because of my mother huh?"

"I wouldn't say that…"

"Daddy, I am a woman too, we process a situation like the

one you're in very quickly. So come out with it, I'm a big girl?"

"Throughout this marriage, Diana was threatened by your mother. The day you were born has replayed in our home more than a rerun of *Good Times*, and your mother's name wasn't always mentioned but it was implied. My wife has never let it go, and I shouldn't have expected her to. For thirty-four years, I have gone to a teller to make a withdrawal of trust, but Diana's account was in the negative. I should've asked myself that day, how much of my life am I willing to commit to earning someone's trust... who has none to give?"

"Daddy I'm so sorry to hear this, of course, I had no idea."

"It's okay, and whatever will be, *will be,* but I can't continue to live as if I have cheated on her when I have been fearfully faithful to her. Faithful to someone who has never forgiven me. It's time to forgive myself for the years wasted in a futile effort to make her feel secure. It's time to forgive myself."

"Daddy since you brought up forgiveness, as you know, Telly and I had a horrible fight that night you rejected our engagement."

"Yea, about that –"

"Daddy... sorry to cut you off, but if I may?"

"Please continue..."

"All the days I've sat in this hospital has given me endless time to think, the solitude of this room has been a blessing in the storm. When you relieved me the other day, on the way home I asked myself, *what unknown act could I possibly discover that would make me call off our engagement?* And I made a mental note of the things I knew like, the Heather woman, and his playboy lifestyle, and the Reebie situation that everyone is so tight-lipped about. Then I asked myself if all of it combined was enough to make me walk away?"

"Erica, I know where you are going with this but there's more to this than..."

"Daddy that's the point that I'm getting to, couples are allowed to work out their issues in private and make individual decisions as to how they want to proceed. In the spirit of protecting me from unforeseen heartache, I have not been given that space, and privacy, because you made the decision for me."

"But sweetheart, I could never stand-down with the things I know. When Telly came to me, I did reject his request, but Telly knew my reasons…"

"And I love you for that. For once, someone other than my mother was looking out for me, but I also ask that you respect my decision should I decide to move forward with Telly." Erica reached for my hand and squeezed. "Daddy I know you have information about Telly that you've accumulated over the years, just as all friends know each other's dirt, but whatever that some-thing is… I don't want to know."

"I can respect that, but Erica, at least let me share what I know about Reebie."

Just as Erica was about to speak, Crystal charged in the room and rushed to the screen that monitored Telly's brain activity. On the pages that printed out below there where several peaks and valleys on the reports, several of the peaks were nearly off the page. It was then that Erica's hands blocked her words from escaping, which left her only option to point at something she couldn't convey.

When my eyes followed her eyes, I saw it too. Telly fingers were moving and his eyes were flickering, and after a few more minutes his toes, ankles, and neck began to wake one after the other.

"No, it's not a malfunction, nor has the surge protector reset. I need a physician in her now, the patient's vitals have rapid-ly changed and continue to improve by the second." The nurse yelled in the intercom.

"Come on baby come on, come back to me Telly, you can do it." It was a struggle to prevent Erica from leaping on to the bed, but I did my best with one leg, and a crutch on my shoulder.

In the blink of an eye the room was filled with several medi-cal staff and two on-call doctors, but not Dr. Martinez.

"Guys, I have to ask you to step out, this room is about to get very crowded and we'll need the space." Crystal said with a voice full of joy and tears. "Erica, I told you. I told you…"

"Telly if you can hear me wiggle your finger." One of the doctors yelled. "Please record that the patient wiggled his fingers at 9:10 A.M." Was the last thing I heard as the door closed. Three weeks after Mrs. Ned said he would, Telly woke up.

CHAPTER 49

August 5, 2018
1:45 p.m.

ERICA

He is a miracle in every sense, not only in his recovery but also in the person who woke up over a month ago. It was miraculous, and I've never won a 5k marathon, but what I feel today has to be that equivalent. To go from hospice arrangements, and the possibility of a lifetime trapped in the body of a breathing mannequin, to watching him regain his equilibrium and move about unassisted, my faith was awakened when Telly's eyes opened.

To celebrate his month of recovery I decided to cook a Sunday dinner and invite a few folks over. The first to arrive was my dad with an aluminum covered pan, then Mrs. Ned and Phaedra – with four aluminum covered pans, followed by my mom with two aluminum-covered pans. I also invited his buddies but on such short notice, only my dad was able to make it. Though his voice hadn't returned to full strength, he was overjoyed by the gathering.

In the kitchen, I arranged a serving order. First was my mother's oven baked chicken, the crawfish mirliton, next to my dad's shrimp fettuccine, dirty rice, Phaedra's shrimp pasta, and Mrs. Ned's baked fish down on the furthest end. The dessert in the second pan my mother carried in was banana pudding from an old family recipe, after I made room in the refrigerator the meal was set.

I served Mrs. Ned and Telly a plate, but everyone else was more than happy to help themselves to as much as they wanted.

"Erica Gurrrl, you put your foot in this crawfish mirliton...I need this recipe."

"...*ummm, you mean my recipe*" my mother interjected "I still may press charges on her. Talking about, *she's going to compete on the food network.* I said not with my recipes... you're not."

"Whatever momma, you know I added my own pizazz to your recipe."

"As long as you know, any pizazz you got came from me we'll continue to get along." My daughters' laughter was above the entire room. The conversations at the table shifted back and forth from Telly's recovery, and constant jokes about how I was *a sad little puppy* during the time he was in the coma, but I didn't mind at all.

I know this may sound like a horrible thing to say but Telly's memory hasn't fully healed to the point where he remembers that night, and that makes me elated. I don't want him to remember the fight we had leading up to the shower. I am comforted to know that he has no recollection of me pitching that toothbrush holder, or the emergency room, not even the days I sat by his bed. He can't recall. None of it. The good news is he remembers people, places, and things prior to the accident, and but the months of June and July are blacked out.

Thank God.

After the meals, we all sat around and talked, but none more than my parents. She can't hide it. She loves him so much. Everything he said is either really funny to her or the most interesting thing she's ever heard, which is her way of flirting within a contained area. I had to remind her again that he's married, and the only reason he's back in her life, to some degree, is because of me.

"Momma, you have already caught up. If you're still chatting twice a day, then you two are catching up on something else."

"No, it isn't, and it's not my fault he enjoys my conversations. I don't see nothing *wronnnnnng... with a little–*"

"Mother!"

"*With a little facetime.*" She giggled like a teenager. "Gotcha, didn't I?"

I know Diana gave my father the impression she's no longer interested in being his wife, but I can only hold my mother off for so long. She is a goal driven woman, and my dad has become a new goal.

She felines and purrs around him.

She is a master of subliminal targeting.

I think he's enjoying the flirtatious energy.

Diana, you better get over it quick, before you might find yourself getting served first. That's all I'm saying.

"They tried to pronounce my son dead in that hospital. I told those doctors not tonight." Mrs. Ned voice boom through the house. "Then I looked down at Phaedra rolling and sliding on that floor like a mop bucket, and what I'd said Phaedra...?"

"*Phaedra get off that floor... before you catch something they can't cure.* The first thing I thought about was herpes. I popped up off that floor like a lottery ball and started checking myself." The room burst into laughter with her, even Telly enjoyed hearing all that happened while he slept.

I loved his family.

Suddenly my mother waved her hand, and moments later Rosa and Parks appeared with their cellos. With my mother playing in the center of the trio, they treated us to a tune from The Pirates of the Caribbean, and then Lion King. It was masterful and eloquent. After the performance was over Mrs. Ned rushed the living room stage to show her appreciation, kissing all three on the cheek repeatedly.

Standing at the rear of the performers was Biyell, who extended the applause. Telly met him halfway as they embraced, and shook hands, and chest bumped as best he could. After Biyell greeted the entire room, I wasn't surprised to see him make a straight line to Phaedra the moment Telly turned to find me, neither was Phaedra.

Should I tell him now? Was the look she shot me.

I nodded emphatically.

With a finger, Telly invited me to the bedroom, and so I followed.

"I wanted to pull you off to the side to say thank you..." He kissed me.

"For the dinner? You don't have to thank me..."

"The dinner is only part of my gratitude. To hear them tease you about how you never left my side made a brother cry in front of his momma. I tried to hide the tears but couldn't. You really love me..."

"Telly I love you more than I can express in–"

"You don't have to say it because everyone knows it, and most of all I feel it. The reason I wanted to invite you back here is that I need to get a few things off my chest and come clean."

"Telly no, this conversation can wait. You're under doctor's orders to remain at a low-stress level."

"Erica what I'm about to say isn't stressful. Carrying it around is what stressed me out for years."

"Before you say it there is something you should know. On the day you opened your eyes, my father and I had a conversation about the argument you had with him. My position was clear – if his rejection was because of the person you were prior to the accident, and I still want to marry you. Of course, he persisted, and was about to mention someone name..."

"Reebie..."

"Yes…but how did you know?"

"Because I heard you."

"You heard us…? But, but… how could you hear us if…"

"All throughout that morning, I started to hear sounds, like the beeping of the monitors, and a man's voice I recognized as Uncle Glenn, *keke-ing* with a woman I now know was your mother. Then I heard both of you. It was an echo chamber of voices that boomed between my ears. Then everything became crystal clear, and he was about to tell you about Reebie."

"Yes, but I no longer care about her, or what she was to you, or if you were seeing her while we were together. The only thing that matters to me is *Telly & Erica. Am I, enough?* If not, then let's keep our friendship. As long as I can still have you in my life, I'm happy."

"Erica you're more than enough for me, and I've had time to think and dream about the type of man I am, and I'll say it definitively – the man I was before the accident died in that shower. I have been given a second chance to love you the right way because you deserve the best." This time I kissed him.

"The first step in being the best me, is to open every door in my life to you. I will no longer compartmentalize your role in my life, and I will trust you completely for the first time. Part of trusting you means telling you the whole truth."

"But Telly I don't care about this woman Reebie…"

"But you should because Reebie is my daughter…"

"You have a child…?"

"Yes, she's sixteen and the reason I never told you about her because I have been absent from her life. I send her mother financial support, but that's it."

"This was the woman in Lafayette when you were a pastor?"

"Yes, who told you?"

"Rasta, but only up to the part where you thought she had an affair…he never mentioned anything about Reebie."

"It's all true, my ex-wife tracked down Phaedra who in turn told my mother I was avoiding her, so my mother pops up on my job with the last person I wanted to see again. When Phaedra, my mom, and Cutina finally cornered me, I didn't want to believe any of it and insisted that she was pregnant for my assistant pastor. My mom stopped speaking to me until I owned up and took the paternity test. The results came back and Reebie was my daughter. I was so angry that I wanted to rip that entire chapter out my life, but my mother and Phaedra collected those thrown away pages, and they maintained a relationship with my child."

"Telly I appreciate your openness and…"

"…there's more"

It was then that I braced myself for the Heather part because I knew he was still seeing her. I knew about his second cell phone that he hid in the trunk of his car, under the spare tire. One day when I had to take my car in for service, Telly needed a ride to the airport. On the way home from the airport I caught a flat tire. It was the roadside assistance tech who found the hidden phone and handed it to me.

"Telly, sweetheart, let's have this conversation at another time, we have guests." It was then that his cell phone sounded – it was a text – more than likely from Heather. Quickly he replied to the text.

"… follow me."

Telly pulled me into the living room and positioned me next to his mom and Phaedra. We all looked at each other and shrugged, that's when he opened the front door and stepped out onto the porch.

Parks abandoned tablet played alone on the coffee table.

When he returned, two individuals I did not recognize trailed behind him. The women directly behind Telly caused Phaedra to gasp, but the one who followed her caused Mrs. Ned to scream.

"My Grandbaby, it's my grandbaby!" They ran to each other's arms.

After two minutes in Phaedra and Mrs. Ned's embrace a formal introduction was made.

"Erica, Uncle Glenn, Momma D, Biyell, Rosa and Parks, this is my daughter Reebie and her mother Cutina."

She was beautiful and huggable and so happy to meet everyone.

"Momma her hair is so long and pretty." Parks loved long natural hair.

It was then that I believed him.

Telly who woke up a month ago was a different man. I knew why he hid her away from me, and never wanted to have a conversation about having children – and God. These pages of his life did not gel with the carefree single bachelor lifestyle he projected, but this Telly is the one I've wanted to meet from day one. This is the Telly I hoped for, because I never expected a perfect man, only a man who was responsible, accountable, and loved us. Telly reintroduced himself, and today I want to marry him more than I did when he proposed. One more note, Reebie hardly resembled her mother because she was the spitting image of Telly.

Nice to finally meet you… Reebie.

CHAPTER 50

August 6, 2018
9:05 a.m.

UNCLE GLENN

On radiant mornings like today, I would often bend the blinds on the kitchen door and see him standing out there long before any of the workers arrived: inebriated by the incense of fresh construction. When Rasta and Biyell built my home, I may have visited the site twice at the most, but for Biyell, admiring the progress of his new home at the crack of dawn is to him what the first cup of coffee is for me.

He modified the plans for my *French Country* design by moving the garage to the left side, and a fountain up front, but it's basically the same house. Not bad for a guy who was living in a one bedroom closet this same time last year, but hey…he earned it. Our company is a well-oiled machine, with two construction teams, and the cash is rolling in from three different directions, thanks largely to Tiffany.

Dammit, I love her multiple house selling-ass-self!

If I had my other leg, I would break out into a sanctified praise dance. She's that awesome. Biyell better get his shit together and fast. He will not find a better one than Tiffany, that's all I'm going to say about that.

If only my marriage was as effortless as my business, this would be my best life thus far.

Bylisha slept over at Tyra's house.

Diana was slow to rise.

Not that our interaction would have been civil. I wanted to tell her about what happened yesterday at Erica's house, but Diana doesn't give a shit, because my daughter is connected to Derinda. How fucked up is that? Is that fair?

Every day it's the endless loop of rolling eyes, talking around me and over me, ignoring what I've cooked, non-stop calls with her sister, and when she has nowhere to go, it's the fuck you housecoat and polka-dot scarf. I hate that scarf and she knows it.

It's her *Fuck Glenn uniform*.

From down the hall, I hear the sliding of those pink slippers.

"And good morning to you too."

I greet her every morning the same way. I know it annoys the hell out of her, but so too does that polka-dot scarf.

"Biyell will do a partial move in this week, he's no longer wasting money in that extended stay. Isn't that great news?" She ignored me.

She started humming an old tune that has a new meaning. *Keep On Walking* by Ce Ce Peniston.

"You don't have to throw that pot of coffee out, I just made it ten minutes ago. Diana don't throw…" She threw out the fresh pot.

Welcome to the *Braxton Home*.

Where neither one of us is willing to find other accommodations despite having enough money to live anywhere in the world. This is no way to live. She may have accepted this as our new norm, but this ain't living. I shook my head, that's all I could do.

Turning away from Diana and back to the front of the construction site, I saw a white BMW sedan park next to Biyell's truck, it was Jarvis. They sat on the tailgate of Biyell's truck and marveled at a home that was nearing the end of construction. With a cup of coffee spilling on my wrist I walked out to join them.

"If you fall your ass down, I will leave you there until Saturday," Biyell said as I hopped towards them. "My house isn't even finished yet, and he already has a one-foot trail from his kitchen to my side door. I can tell right now, we ain't gonna make it as neighbors."

"Both of you can kiss my black ass – slide over." Reluctantly Jarvis made room for me on the tailgate.

"Uncle Glenn we're having a two-legged conversation, you don't qualify."

"Fuck-you Biyell." I struggled to keep air in my lungs.

"Why not use the motorized scooter like disabled people… with common sense."

"Jarvis why don't you mind your business, if I want to hop then I hop!"

"Keep on hopping like that your other leg gonna catch a flat…" Jarvis said as Biyell ran in a circle in laughter.

"They got a Used Leg shop on Claiborne, you can get two for fifty." Biyell returned to the tailgate and fell backward into the bed of the truck.

"Oh, I get it, it's *fuck with Glenn day* this morning, alright."

I couldn't complain because it hadn't been *fuck with Glenn day* in a while, but the one thing for certain, any day is a good day to roast my ass, and no one is exempt.

After the cheap shots, we updated Jarvis on Telly and his daughter, but he wasn't surprised. After Telly, we talked about everything from our future *Madden Thursdays*, to Jarvis buying the lot in the next block – that is when he reached into his inside suit pocket.

"Oh shit, he got the long white paper…which could only

mean somebody wants some money or she's trading you in."

"I figured you would be familiar with the white paper, how much Tamara dragged your ass to court, but here it is." Jarvis handed me he paperwork while Biyell leaned in for a closer look.

NEW ORLEANS CIVIL COURT

BRIANA NAPOLEON vs. JARVIS NAPOLEON

"My Dawg, she really went through with it? I mean, it's over for real for real? Like me and Tamara over?"

"Like Diana about to be if she doesn't..."

"Uncle Glenn ain't nobody trying to hear that bullshit...this is about a real break up, not *I'm mad with you, no I'm mad with you first, so that's why I don't like you, and that's why your booty stink...*" Biyell mocked in a whiney voice. "But anyway, Jarvis when did you receive this?"

"This morning, I was packing up the rest of the furniture when dude knocked on the door. Talking about getting blindsided – I thought once she blew off steam and the thrill of Mr. Anchor subsided, she would come back but..."

"The Anchorman anchored your pussy down to the ground... dude was like *clink clink.*"

"Fuck you, Biyell..."

"That anchor man was like *and in other news, reports are coming in that I, took that nigga's pussy...now back to you.*" I couldn't resist getting in a free shot.

"Fuck you too, Uncle Glenn."

For the second time, Biyell rolled around in the bed of the truck in laughter "he said- he said, *and in other news, I took that nigga pussy.*" Biyell laughed so hard he became mute.

"That's enough Biyell" I'm trying to give this matter with Jarvis and Briana the serious attention it deserves." I can't lie, that joke was pretty funny.

"...but anyway, Jarvis how are you feeling about this?"

"Uncle Glenn it's like I'm..."

"My stomach, oh lord, the anchorman said *reports are coming in, Jarvis pussy is gone, and the person fitting the description is… me, Carl Nash. I took your shit"* Biyell held his stomach as tears appeared in his eyes. "I'm about to piss on myself…"

"Biyell that joke was over last week, but anyway, you were saying?"

"It just hit me this morning. I can't believe I'm going to be on my second divorce with two sets of kids from failed marriages. That's the part I hate. I'm officially a baby daddy times two."

"Welcome to my world" Biyell wiped his eyes with the mid-section of his shirt "when you meet women and say *I have three kids by two different women,* they will look at you like your breath stink. But here's the kicks part, they have kids for another dude."

"…and that's the bullshit I never wanted to deal with, that's why I stayed with Monica for as long as I did."

"I stepped to a chick the other day. She said *so in other words you're asking me to go for a ride in your 4x4?* I was like huh? I don't have a 4x4? *Bitch said, not yet, and I won't be that third or fourth Baby Mama, keep it moving dude."*

"Bruh she handled you like that?"

"Jarvis, that's what I get for being honest, that's why you have to lie to these women. They want that lie, they will believe the lie in half the time, and you'll fuck'em quicker."

"*No-no-no*, we're not going back there," I interjected before one contaminated the other. "Jarvis this is a point in your life to spend some time alone, strengthening your will power, and ex-amining where you went wrong. All of this is your fault, and you need to fix that component of your brain that allowed Monica to fuck you in a van like a twenty-dollar trick."

"Uncle Glenn you're right, but I didn't look at it that way. She was also my wife at one time, so I gave myself a Day Pass to enjoy all the rides in the park. I wasn't counting on a paparazzi and a blogger."

"…and if it wasn't for those pictures you and Monica would still be at it wouldn't you?"

"No, because it was just –"

"Boy stop before God pop you in those lying lips, you know damn well it wasn't going to end until you two got caught, just like I got caught with Tyra."

"Okay, you got me."

"Thank you, now that we're getting to the truth of things answer this simple question: are you happy?"

Jarvis pondered for a few seconds "I'm not happy my marriage is over."

"But that's not what I'm asking, are you happy?"

"No, because my wife is with another dude..."

"The Anchorman went LIVE in that *puuuusssssssy*..."

"Biyell, chill dude..." I yelled "leaving the wife out of the question altogether, I'm only dealing with you, are you happy with Jarvis? I don't want to hear anything about marriage or kids, you're on an island alone right now, are you happy?"

"No..."

"Here's the rest of it...I don't want you entering into another relationship until you're happy with Jarvis. I mean, overjoyed with Jarvis. The reason you fucked Monica so quickly didn't have anything to do with the issues within your marriage and everything to do with Jarvis being miserable with Jarvis. You fucked Monica because you needed to feel better, you fucked Briana for the same reason, and for a little while it made you feel better. But even the best pussy has a twenty-four-hour shelf life if you need a woman to make you feel better about Jarvis."

"...but isn't that the role of a woman, to pleasure her man? To please me? That's what Tiffany would always say to me that she's my *Help-meet*."

"Yes and no...just as I explained to Rasta after he was discharged from the hospital, for a woman to help you, is not the same as making her solely responsible for your happiness."

"I KNEW IT," Jarvis leaped off the tailgate excite like a contestant on *The Price is Right*. "That's where Rasta got that from, trying to sound all deep and shit. He got it from you."

"It doesn't matter where you heard it just as long as you listen. Obviously… you didn't."

"…because I didn't know where the nigga' was coming with all that philosophical shit…"

"What Rasta tried to get you to see was it wasn't Briana's job to make Jarvis happy, he should've been happy when he entered the relationship. And that's why I don't want you approaching another woman until you're happy with you as a man, and loving your life, and accomplishments, and happy with the relationship with your children: only then do you find a woman to share your happiness."

"Jarvis… or you can do what I'm doing?"

". . .and what's that Biyell?"

"**Number One:** Admit you're not good at relationships and marriage. **Number Two:** Get a Tesla…"

"What?"

"Jarvis don't pay Biyell any mind. Tesla is this married woman he's fucking, instead of working things out with Tiffany."

"Call it what you want, but I don't have the headaches, the husband ain't fucking her anyway so it's *Pussy on Demand* for me. No stress, and none of the additional expenses that comes with a single woman. That's why I'm happy."

"So, what's number three?" Jarvis asked.

"Oh yea, number three… release the dick and let Tesla drive it!" Biyell reclined into the bed of the truck and started convulsing. "This is how I be when Tesla driving and that nut shooting out – check it out Uncle Glenn." Biyell flopped around in the bed of the truck like a catfish out of the water.

Suddenly Jarvis phone rung – he stepped a few paces away to answer.

"Oh, that reminds me" Biyell removed a key from his chain "I wanted to give you the key. This way, if I'm out in the field you can lock up after the crew leaves."

"Not a problem…"

"This one key will open every door but I'm having a cement walkway laid for you to make it easier to enter the side door."

"Is there an alarm code?"

"That door will not have an alarm on because the only way to enter is through your yard."

"Now back to you, Biyell listen to me, leave that married woman alone and fix things with Tiffany. You've made her suffer long enough."

"I'll think about it."

"I'm serious, and the fact that she helped design this interior and selected the floors. You know as well as I do that Tiffany was anticipating being in your life forever. Do me a favor and give her another chance. Stop being a supplemental dick for different women and settle your ass down."

"Uncle Glenn, you don't think I listen when you speak, but I do. And I do miss her, but I have to hit Tesla a few more times. Ya heard me."

"Guys I need to head over by Telly and have a chat with him…"

"Don't go stressing him out…"

"I'm not, and he said a legal discussion is just the thing he needs to mentally tune-up."

"Well I didn't bring up my issue with him on yesterday, but before you leave remind him: we still need to talk?"

"Talk about what?" Biyell face wrinkled.

"MANNNN, UNCLE GLENN: leave all the old shit in the past, and let that man reestablish his credibility?" Jarvis suggested.

"Just let Telly know we still need to talk…. okay."

"I will, with your petty-ass. That's why Diana cracked you in the eye, you don't know how to let old shit go." Jarvis said, as he closed his car door, and reversed out to the street.

CHAPTER 51

August 6, 2018
10:05 a.m.

DIANA

As soon as he entered the side door I reached for the remote, powered off the television and made my way down the hall. He has that look, and I'm all too familiar with that look. I'm not in the mood to talk.

"…so, you're gonna walk off without answering me." He tried to make small talk about touring Biyell's house – but real estate is the furthest thing from my mind.

My life as of late feels like one of those dreams where you're surrounded by people you know and love, but when you engage them in conversation, they can't hear you. Glenn knew my position, and he still befriended her. That's basically saying he could care less.

Prior to this nightmare, if he had a concern or something, he didn't want me to do – I would respect his wishes. If there would have been a man that he felt threatened by, not that there ever was, then I damn sure wouldn't be chatting it up with that guy.

I will not co-exist with her.

The more of her that's in his life, the less of me he will see it's the only way to protect myself. Men love to be in control, and the head of this or that, but the first time a woman wiggles one tit, all of a sudden, they've lost control. Cheating is never an accident, it's always a deliberate act, the only thing that's accidental are the convenient excuses.

I'm not the one.

And I'm not saying he's cheating with that bitch, but I will say this, from the calls I did tap, Glenn could have her whenever he gets good and horny enough. Which according to my calculations should be any day now. Not since his accident, have we gone this long without knocking boots, therefore its just a matter of time before their conversations shift into something sexual.

Twice last week I entered the guest room while he was sleeping and conducted a quick phone check. She's texting him all throughout the day about miscellaneous crap.

TEXT: *Can you believe what Trump said today, OMG, we have to get out and vote.*

TEXT: *Here's a video of our grandbaby practicing her cello. Less video games, more Cello.*

TEXT: *I am thinking about wall mounting my television do you have anyone you recommend? When it comes to technology or electronics, I am so behind in the times. LOL.*

Do you see it?

She never crosses the line but tap dances right down the middle. On the surface, it appears innocent, but Glenn would always say a *dog can smell a dog*, but a cat can also smell a cat. She's appealing to his natural instincts to help, provide, and comfort. She knows him because he hasn't changed much, if she plays helpless then he will come. But I'm ready for whatever. When the shoe drops, I plan to emotionally detach from Glenn and all of this bullshit.

My sister said *"Girl don't be like that with your husband, be-*

cause of some fly by night fling. Break a broomstick and chase her ass away from your husband."

But that's part of the problem as well, why is it always up to us (the wives and girlfriends) to chase away a fly by night fling? If Glenn was sold out for me – the fly by night bitch would have never found a place to land. I'm not spending a single day of my life chasing away someone who should have never been in his space. Glenn will police Glenn, and if he lacks the situational control required to handle her, then I was obviously with the wrong man.

"Diana, I see it your way but try to see it my way. We're not talking about the same Glenn from the '80s, this Glenn is a millionaire. Half of that money belongs to you. You're not going to like knowing she's enjoying his half."

And that's when a nerve was struck.

Part of me wants a divorce and the other half is leaning towards staying and chasing that bitch away from my husband.

I cannot believe I said that, my husband.

Glenn hasn't felt like my husband in a while, but he remains my husband unless I do what my heart is telling me to do. But what if he marries Derinda.

"FUCK!" I said her name. I need to get out of this house for a while, feels like I'm losing my mind.

"Are you okay? I was coming from the bathroom when I heard you scream." He spoke through the cracked door.

I nodded.

"Diana, I understand you're angry, but the way you're choosing to communicate it is childish."

"Fuck you, Glenn! What's childish is the way you have allowed this woman to reappear and destroy everything that we've built."

"Diana we've gone over this too many times, I'm tired of saying the same damn thing. You listened to the calls, nothing happened between us. I apologized for the conversations, but what else do I have to do?"

"I want you to leave me alone...and close my door."

"HAVE. I. FUCKED. HER?" He pulled the comforter off my bed, rolled it into a ball, and then threw it back at me. "Answer me dammit."

"If you did, I wouldn't know, and I doubt seriously if you would confess, but it sure in the hell feels like you have had sex with her."

"Oh, *noooooo my sista* – you need more than that." His eyes scanned the room for something else to throw, but there wasn't anything soft within reach. "Nope, ah ah, you've destroyed our marriage with a bullshit accusation that's based on a bullshit gut feeling, and you think that half-ass answer is sufficient?"

"...Glenn close my door please."

"You refuse to answer because you know I haven't laid one finger on her. I have been committed to you and only you, and I'm rewarded with accusations and a *funky-ass attitude.*" Then I watched him deescalate by self-coaching. "Diana, in anger you have said you wanted a divorce, in fact, you said it twice. I still want this marriage and I still love you, but I'm not going to beg you to stay where you don't want to be, not another day. For real Diana, this is it. Are you ready for the divorce filings to start?"

I didn't answer.

"Diana do you want a divorce? If that's what you want, then say it right now and I will serve you within forty-eight hours."

My mind wanted to say yes, but my heart wouldn't allow me to speak freely. It hurts so bad, to hear him laugh with her, the way he once laughed with me, to watch him light up when she calls, the way he once lit up the moment I walked through that door. It hurts so bad, that in thirty-five years of marriage, I could not give this man one child.

I was so desperate to have what she has – I have adopted a child, and it still doesn't count, because Erica looks just like my husband. He's right, I've never had to share Glenn.

"Diana I am not leaving this room and you will have no peace until you answer me, I will follow you in the bathroom, even

366 / TJ SPENCER JACQUES

if you have to shit – you will answer me. Should I call Attorney Larry Aisola, and have him draw up divorce paperwork? I can cut you a check for half of everything in that account right now…"

"Before I answer you, I need to know."

"What is it…"

"When I divorce you… will you marry her?"

"Who is her…?"

"Glenn…"

"Why does that matter?"

"Because it matters to me…will you?"

It was then that he hopped from the seal of the door and came to rest on the corner of the bed. Distantly he contemplated his answer and searched for the correct verbiage to resolve this argument. I know my husband.

"I've told the guys that the best way to handle situations like this is with the truth. If you decided that you know longer wanted me, then the answer is yes. I would marry her because I know her and I'm way, way, waaaay too old for dating sites. That is my honest answer."

"I appreciate your honesty, could I ask for a small concession?"

"What is it?"

"I would like to implement your 3N3 rule."

"Three days or three weeks or three months to make a major decision?"

"But I would only need three days…that's more than enough time."

"I will grant you that request if you grant me one concession?"

"As long as it doesn't involve sex…"

"Could you hear me out first?"

"Okay, what is it?"

"In case you decide on the divorce. While we're being civil. Can I have one kiss, just in case this is goodbye?"

I thought about it for a moment.

"Just one kiss Diana…?"

"Glenn…I'm sorry, but I can't."

CHAPTER 52

August 6, 2018
4:05 pm

BIYELL

We are in the same location, the same bed, but at a much earlier time in the day. When you're *'supplemental dick'* for a married woman, unfortunately, you have to work within and around her schedule. Today she only has ninety minutes for me to the exact, and I made the most out of the first half. We were both pleased and used the remaining forty-five minutes to swap the same sweat, breath, and the same heartbeat.

An airy voice said, "You are a master lover."

"If I'm a master lover then you are Cleopatra of Cumming." She blushed face flat into my chest. "Seriously, that was the longest I have ever lasted inside of you, but make no mistake about it, I wanted to bust ten minutes after I clocked in."

"That's so sweet, you denied yourself just for me. Well, aren't I special?"

"You are very special …" After a deep breath, she kissed the side of my face.

"Did I ever tell you that you're the only man I've enjoyed other than him?" Whenever she referred to her husband, it was simply *him*.

"…you have, and at first I didn't believe it. I only slightly believe it now."

"And why would you think it's not true?

"Because men lie about who they're sleeping with, and women lie about who they've slept with. Asking a woman for an accurate number of who they've slept with, is like asking a random woman how much she weighs."

"I said, you are the first man I have enjoyed."

"There was another man you've had during your marriage?"

"One, but he was much younger."

"Well, it's obvious you fired him because I have the job. So, let's hear it."

"There isn't much to tell, the sex came at a time in the marriage when I was starving for something strong inside of me, and for a while he delivered.

"…so, what happened?"

"He became a local celebrity overnight, and I couldn't risk it. He was good, but no one compares to you Mr. Veiny."

I assumed I was her first affair, but I wasn't, not even close. It was then that I started to feel sorry for her husband, all this time dude had no clue. I recall one time we were having this same discussion on Madden night and Telly basically ended the debate when he said.

My life, the way I make my living is in failed marriages, and when I first started out in Family Law, the husband was always the one caught cheating. Fast forward fifteen years, and sixty percent of the men have caught the wives with someone she connected with on Facebook. In the Friends list and Blocked list, backing out relatives, are a snippet of the men she's fucked with or will fuck with – at some point.

Well, Rasta didn't believe Telly's theory until he broke into Shameka's phone. She was under the influence of flu meds that day, and that's when he saw it firsthand: three previous boyfriends in her blocked section, and the ex-boyfriend in the current friends. However, as it relates to Tesla, I'm the one enjoying all of her today, and that's all that matters.

"If you were free to be with any man you choose, who would you pick out of the two of us – Popular dude or Mr. Veiny?"

"Mr. Veiny all day every day." She said emphatically.

"Are you sure you don't need a minute to think about it?" She laughed out loud.

"The last thing I want to do is inflate your head any bigger than it is, but the first time you entered me, I thought you were going to rearrange all of my organs. The pressure was unbearable, but I adjusted."

"So glad you did adjust because I was about to write you up."

"Write me up?"

"Yes, write you up and put you on a 30-Day probation."

"What for…?"

"For the wait-wait…"

"… why did you have to bring that up?" Tesla blushed into her palms.

"Wait-wait-wait-wait okay I'm ready, I'm ready, but don't push in too deep okay, wait-wait-wait-wait-wait, okay, okay, now a little bit more, hold up a second wait-wait." That is how she controlled my thrust, with both hands on my thigh.

"That's not fair, and I admitted on day one that you had the largest one ever…" She giggled up to my lips.

"I know our lives are complicated, but this right here" I gripped a hand full of her ass "this is effortless."

"It is…and it's beautiful." She rested her head on my chest.

"I'm single as we speak, but I'm not sure for how long, at some point I may want to do the full-time thing again."

"…you're certainly taking the long way home bus driver."

"I know, I know, but this is the first time I have ever asked this question…"

"Well you certainly know how to get a girl's attention." She whipped her hair left to right, then again, like one of those AKA chicks. "Let's hear this never before asked question."

"Have you given any thought to us…you and I, me and you, going full time?"

"…having sex with you full time?"

"You know what I'm getting at, do you think you can be with me full time, every day as your man, or am I better for you in this role? Wait, before you answer, as long as you're honest I can handle the truth either way…"

With the manicured nail of her index finger, she drew figure eights in the moisture on my abdomen. Her heart rate returned to a normal thump, and her body cooled to room temperature.

"It's like this, and I kid you not, I, oooh, oooh, hold up."

"…is that another one?"

"A big one." she whispered.

Although our love making session ended about ten minutes ago, periodically she would get a jolt between her legs, a spasm of the sort, then her eyes would squint like a brain freeze, as the sex continued without me. Once the shivers were over, then she would resume her sentence.

"Ahhhhh, all right… I'm back."

"Are you sure because I have all day…?"

"Yes, as I was saying…the special things we do to each other during our special time together is all I know for sure. You've presented me with options I've never considered."

"So is that a yes or…"

"Ugh! My words are sputtering *because-because…because,* I've never fathomed a single thought of living with another man full time other than *him.* It would be a major adjustment for me and add to it the social pressure, no one has ever seen me with anyone but him."

"I understand this dilemma is new, but I also have a home that's going to be ready to go in a few weeks, and for now this works, but I know me. At some point, I'm going to want you in the bed with me all night."

"...but it was you who said, you were taking a break from the marriage thingy, and doing the single thingy, because you've failed at being a husband. Those are your exact words... minus the thingies. You're switching up on me?"

"I wouldn't call it that, simply letting you know up front that I'm single right now, but that could change, and you're someone who could inspire me to step back in the full-time relationship thingy."

"Because... I suck a really good dick?"

"No, that's not it, because you're –"

"Biyell you don't know what I'm like every day, you only know this." With my hand, she smacked her ass cheek. "You may decide once we're together that I was better as a sex partner, but not as a wife."

"And you could decide the same, that I don't measure up to him full time."

"...that's why this has worked so well for the past two months because we never complicated it with expectations that exceeded this room. Don't get me wrong, I'm obsessed with you and would experience major withdrawals if I couldn't get to you, and would burn down your grandmother's house, but I can't make any promises when it comes to a relationship with you. This is the first time we stopped making love long enough to discuss anything."

"I see, not a problem..."

"Biyell don't go negative on me after saying you can handle the truth. Would you like me to start over from the beginning, and tell you lies like: I would make the best wife ever? I don't know what life is like with you or if I could sustain you beyond this bedroom." She kissed my neck, then launched into a search for her panties and bra.

"I appreciate your honesty, but I have one more question."

"What's with you and these questions today...? But fire

away."

"What if I decide on a full-time woman to move in with me, can I still count on you?"

"Count on me for what…?"

"Can I still count on you to carve out time where you and I can be together?"

"Like this…?"

She headed into the bathroom with her panties on and bra in hand.

"I don't know, I would have to think about that…"

"What's to think about?"

"That's a change in your status, and what turned me on about you was the fact that you're single. I don't like that drama that comes with married men."

"But you're married…"

"I know…but you said in the beginning that even if it's a tiny little bit of me, you wanted it. Since then I have made it a point to come here at least three times a week. Haven't I?"

"Yes, you have…"

"I've even fucked you in my house that I share with him. Didn't I?"

"Yes, you did?"

"I'm glad you have acknowledged that I have gone far and beyond, to make sure you were taken care of. If you have someone at home, then that changes your status. You know longer need me at that point, and I like feeling needed. I'm not sure if this answers your question but it is the most honest answer, I could submit… I don't know how I would feel about continuing with you, if you have her."

I chuckled "Biyell, meet Mz. Cheeky Black… Mz. Cheeky Black meet Biyell."

"Not cheeky, but I'm spoiled, and I like things as is."

"…But you can't make me any promises, which makes me month to month." In the bathroom mirror, she fingered through her hair.

374 / TJ SPENCER JACQUES

"Let's make a deal, if you don't force me into a yes or no answer tonight, then we will continue as we are. The only thing I ask is should you decide to go full time with Tiffany then you promise to come to me so we could have a conversation. Deal?" From the bath, Tesla extended her hand for a shake.

"Only if you promise one last romantic visit if I decided to go full time with Tiffany. We have a deal?"

"Sounds like it's going to be Tiffany, so here's the promise I will keep. I will still christen the house with you as my parting gift. Do we have a deal?" She extended her hand again.

"Woe, that's tough…"

"Biyell you can have me on every countertop, on every piece of furniture, and in every bedroom in that beautiful home. I promise." She spoke with a seductive voice then hurried back to the bathroom carrying the rest of her clothes. "…but once Tiffany is there full time, I'm out."

"Well that settles it, you have a deal, but there's one more thing I need to make you aware of…"

"…and what's that?"

I sat on the edge of the bed and waited for her to turn away from the mirror.

"And what's that…?" From my face down, her eyes scanned my body and zoomed in on the part she loves.

"He's hard again?" She wondered.

"Yes, he is, and I still have twenty minutes. I would like to redeem my time please."

"You're serious?" Timidly she approached me.

I removed her panties and slung that fist full of lace to the other side of the world.

"Get your ass in that bed…"

"But-but…"

"What we have here, is over, when I say it's over…" I pushed in hard and deep. "Yes, I'm taking Tiffany back but I'm still holding you to that final promise. When I call you, I expect you to come to me immediately. Have I made myself clear?" With-

out warning, I pushed in deep and long.
"Have I made myself clear?"
"Yes…yes-yes…yes Mr. Veiny"

CHAPTER 53

New House Living Room
8:45 p.m.

BIYELL

I still can't believe this is my house, sometimes I come here just to smell the newness in each room. I never understood why people buy existing homes when you could build one from the ground where every detail is to your specifications. My ass was first to shit on each toilet.

But I can't take credit for a single doorknob in this house, it was Tiffany who handled it all.

Being that the home was livable minus a few minor trim issues, I decided to grab an air mattress from Target, a few snacks, and a bottle of wine. From Uncle Glenn, I jacked a few towels, a roll of toilet paper, some bedding and two wine glasses. Once I had my bed set up, I chilled the wine in one of the ice chests my crew utilizes throughout the day. After another shower, I called her.

"Hi, Biyell…" The phone rung once before Tiffany answered.

"Did I catch you at a good time?"

"It's always a good time for you."

"I know it's late, but can you come over...I would like –"

"On my way...be there in ten minutes."

"The garage is open for you..."

Her car pulled into my garage seven minutes later. Tenderly she approached from the garage entry into the house, across the kitchen, and stopped in front of the mattress.

She wore a white Delta Sigma Theta shirt, with a long red skirt underneath. Her hair was adorned with a red satin scarf that she fastened into a bow at the top. Her lips matched her bow, her fingernails matched her lips, and her toes matched her skirt.

"So...you had one of those sorority meetings tonight?"

"Yes, it was my turn to host."

"You look very pretty..."

"Thank you, and I like what you did to the place. Nice furniture choice." She teased about my air mattress in the living room.

"Have a seat please, it can hold both of us."

Reluctantly she sat on the mattress.

"Thank you for coming tonight."

"Thank you for inviting me."

"Are you dating someone?"

She rolled her eyes "No..."

"I had to ask, I didn't want to assume."

"I'm not dating anyone. How could I? I've been waiting night and day for you to call me."

"Tiffany I'm going to cut right to it." She deeply inhaled, then held it. "You hurt me, and you know that but I've had the valuable time to think things over, and I miss you. Earlier today, I was with someone, she's married, and it was during that conversation I realized I didn't want to be the old Biyell, I changed my life to prove to you the kind of man I could be, and I like that Biyell better than the old me. I accept your apology and would like to have you back as my woman again. Every day, the way we were. Let's move forward."

Tiffany crawled up the middle of the mattress, but my chest was as far as she could make it before the tears fell.

"Sweetie, what's wrong?"

"Someone else is giving me another chance that I don't deserve, I will never hurt you again, I promise."

I pulled her the rest of the way and spoke into her eyes.

"I'm not perfect, far from it, but I want to move forward. I don't want you carrying this guilt. There may come a time in the future that I need you to forgive me and that's why I wanted to say this face to face. I have been with someone, it was just sex, but I don't want a fuck buddy anymore, and I don't want to live here without you."

I slid my hand under the pillow where I hid the black box.

"I was going to give you this the night of the reception, but Telly punk ass beat me to it with his proposal." I got down on one knee on side of the air mattress as Tiffany's hands converged over her mouth and nose.

"Tiffany, I'm happier with you in my life. I still have a ways to go, but I promise to always tell you the truth and be the best man I can be to you. Tiffany Arceneaux will you be my wife, will you marry me?" I slid the ring on her finger.

Her yes was an endless nod. Once the ring came to rest just below her knuckle, her lips attacked my lips and her arms attacked my body.

After about an hour of catching up, it was time to ask her one more question. I walked over to the ice chest and removed the wine bottles and glass. The moment Tiffany saw the wine bottle, a dimmer wiped away her smile. But I expected it.

"I know about the drinking thing and I'm asking you to do something very special for me. I want us to drink this bottle of wine…"

"Baby I can't…you know I can't –"

"Shhhhh it's just us here, no one else." I handed her the glass of wine and pulled her to the middle of the living room floor.

"This is the last I will ever mention this, and that's why this wine is so important. That *Josh fucka* enjoyed a side of you that I never knew existed, and that's what hurt me the most and my ex-wife spoiled that *Mike fucka.* No other man should ever enjoy a part of you that I hadn't, so tonight, just this one time, I'm asking for the honor of meeting Taffy. Would you do that for me?"

After a pause that was a month long, she slowly raised the glass to her lips, and we enjoyed the wine together. Right around the third glass, just as she was past tipsy, I connected my phone to the Bose speakers in the ceiling and pressed play.

If you're horny, let's do it
Ride it, my pony
My saddle's waiting
Come and jump on it.

"I'm the pony tonight, come ride me baby." I undressed. She undressed. She mounted me. When the ride finally came to an end, we collapsed...all was forgiven.

I may not need that last round with Tesla after all.

CHAPTER 54

New Orleans Civil Court
August 9, 2018
9:35 a.m.

RASTA

His name was Attorney Leo Franklin, and he was the legal counsel RemoveSlander.com hired. Telly said they went head to head a few years back, and when it was over, he was beaten up pretty bad. Though Telly couldn't be here this morning, that bit of information gave me peace of mind because Telly hates to lose, and he lost to Attorney Franklin.

On the right side of the courtroom was an elderly couple. They appeared straight out of central casting for the church scene in The Preacher's Wife. The husband depended on the wife to confirm if he heard what he thought he heard, even if nothing was said. They were here this morning to pursue his lawsuit against the Housing Authority of New Orleans, for damages to their rental properties. That's what he mumbled at the top of his voice.

"Trifling bastards. I should have followed my first mind but you, you wanted the money from Section 8, but I told you it ain't worth it. Is it worth it now? Huh, Shirley. What did you say? It ain't worth it now huh? You can't give people shit for nothing…"

"Hush it, Harold," the wife popped him on the thigh "We wouldn't have the houses in the first place if it wasn't for me. You hush it right now or I'm leaving you here to deal with it on your own."

Harold then turned towards our bench.

"Young man, are you paying attention? This is how they treat us when we're up in age?" He said to Jarvis nosey ass who couldn't look away or mind his business. "If I had two good ears and a working prostate, I would be in a bar right now." Harold roared in laughter as his wife popped him on the same leg, but much harder.

As he and Jarvis chuckled at each other from across the center aisle, I watched Jarvis take out a note pad and describe Harold all the way down to the peppermint tubes socks he wore.

"I love her though, been married fifty-two years. How bout' you, is that your husband next to you?"

"Oh no sir, that's like my brother."

"Well, I had to ask, because you never know these days. The menz' are with the menz' and the womenz' are with the womenz.' We passed one of those *Morphodites* on the way up here, didn't we honey?" Harold roared again.

"Sir, please excuse my husband, I'm so sorry." The wife said as she popped him on the thigh a third time in three minutes, while I bent over in laughter.

From several huddles throughout the sparsely filled courtroom, came a constant hum of whispers, in which none of the words could be deciphered. Directly behind Mr. Harold was a pregnant looking guy who sported a comb-over, that failed miserably. I wonder if he was the owner of HoeLeaks.com?

Uncle Glenn couldn't be here this morning because of a meeting with his attorney, and Biyell paranoid ass hates courtrooms even when he's the defendant. Today, it's just Jarvis and I, with an anxious LaDeisha in Washington, sitting on pins and needles.

"I've just spotted an old buddy from college; you guys hold down the bench…I'll be right back." Attorney Franklin's basketball analogies were endless.

On the right side of the courtroom, Attorney Franklin greeted his old attorney friend with a cheerful hug. The air in the room was somber like the viewing period before a funeral, and the busiest person in the room was a clerk who never lifted her head. Nearing time for the judge to take the bench, our attorney returned to our side for a final pre-trial walkthrough.

"There's not a lot for you guys to do this morning, because this is merely a formality to determine if we should prepare for a jury trial. I hope the owner of that website doesn't show, this way we can get an *alley-oop* off the tip."

"Meaning what exactly?"

"If they fail to show, then I can obtain the court order today and have the site taken down within twenty-four hours. We're second on the docket, behind my buddy who is here to provide a status on his client. All in all, I say they have about an hour, if not then we run a full court press."

The judge blew into the court in full authority and power and just as Attorney Franklin predicted, the first case was over in less than twenty minutes. We constantly scanned the room for any new faces, but none entered. The pregnant looking guy was actually next, then it's our turn, followed by the landlord couple.

"Huddle up and make it tight, with the next three-pointer we can win the tournament." Attorney Franklin was also a college basketball coach who was in between gigs. "Once the Judge is done with a few legal signings, I will take the shot and then it's Champagne in the lockers." We even broke the huddle with a team handshake.

"Next case on the docket this morning is Jarvis Napoleon vs. FelSafe Media. Council please state your name and who you're representing."

"Good morning Judge LaCouture, I am attorney Leo Franklin representing Jarvis Napoleon. My client is present your honor."

The judge never lifted her head.

"Legal counsel for FelSafe Media please step forward and present the defendant in this matter." Judge LaCouture called out a second time for the attorney for FelSafe Media, but once again, no one answered.

"Attorney Franklin is there a motion that you would like to file at this time?"

"Yes, your Honor, we are seeking a court order to have the website deleted from the hosting company servers. We're also requesting that the orders of this court apply to all domains that may have circulated the content, including but not limited to Facebook, Instagram, and Twitter. Your Honor, being that the defendant has ignored the orders of the court to appear, our final request is regarding the judgment that should be awarded to my client."

"…and what request is that?" The judge asked but continued to sign documents she was handed by the clerk.

"I ask that the judgment awarded also include all personal property owned by the executors of FelSafe Media." It was then that Attorney Franklin produced from his briefcase additional legal forms.

"Your honor attached you will find deed information on private property owned by the proprietors of FelSafe Media, this includes a residential home. Please apply a lien on all property and earnings until the orders of the court have been fully complied, and my client has been made whole. May I approach?"

"Yes, you may."

Jarvis and I fist bumped.

Judge LaCouture flipped through each page of the filings, then appeared to sign on three of the pages. While the Judge was distracted, a brunette-haired woman entered the room and continued up to the clerk's desk.

She wore a deep navy suit that wanted everyone in the court

to know how proud she was of her bubble shaped ass, and legs. The Clerk gave her a nod, that's when she addressed the court.

"Your Honor I am Attorney Leslie Parker, and I am on the docket as the attorney for FelSafe"

As she slowly raised her head, Judge LaCouture reminded me of CBS Morning news anchor Gayle King. "Attorney Parker, you've been in this court too many times to count, what time do I take the bench?"

"Always at 10 a.m. promptly your Honor."

"Let the record state that the attorney representing the defendant was aware of the day and time her client was due in court. Is your client present?"

"Your Honor, my client is not present and –"

"Your client was served six weeks ago!" Judge LaCouture's voice boomed around the wooden panel walls. "Before I conclude this matter – state for the record why your client has chosen to ignore my summons?"

"Your Honor, I'm appearing this morning for the record. I was prepared to represent my client; however, I have not received the remainder of my retainer due to a financial hardship. I also ask for a continuance of this matter."

"Objection your Honor to any form of continuance. The defendant is not present."

"Your Honor my client is not in court today due to a family emergency."

"What sort of emergency?"

"His mother died this morning your Honor."

Judge LaCouture eyes bore down on the filing from our attorney and after about a minute she addressed Attorney Leslie Parker.

"Attorney Parker your client has the deepest condolences of this court, but I will not grant a continuance on a last-minute walk in. This court has a protocol that I..."

Suddenly, I became distracted by the whoosh of the courtroom door. I was the only one who noticed. I felt the moment I stopped breathing. I felt the juncture at which my heart jammed, the zenith at which my nerves snapped, it all happened in the split second he walked through that courtroom door. Like the little lady across the aisle from us, I punched Jarvis on the thigh, because I was too staggered to speak.

"...you're a lowdown little bitch." Jarvis whispered.

"Your Honor, it appears my client Timothy Feltus of FelSafe Media has arrived, may I have a moment?"

"I will grant you a fifteen-minute recess, and then we will resume." After the bang of the gavel, the court was in recess.

"Good, because that's all the time I need to fuck him up," Jarvis said as the Judge left the bench.

"Guys no worries on this, being that his attorney made his financial situation known to the court, I will ask the judge to set a court date for trial within two weeks."

"...his financial situation was always known to us."

"Do you guys personally know Mr. Feltus?"

"He was one of our closest friends before he stabbed me in the back."

"This time around he stabbed all of us and cost me a marriage. He was the one who put those pictures of me and Monica on that website." Jarvis tried to get Timothy's attention. "Hey, homie, what's up Timothy? *Let me holla at you one second.*"

"Jarvis bruh, I need you to calm down."

"Fuck the money, I'm about to bust his ass right now."

Attorney Franklin and I struggled to get Jarvis to calm down. I wanted to kick his ass too but not now, not while we have him on the ropes.

"Jarvis what he did to you guys was a flagrant foul, but as your Attorney, I'm asking you to trust me. Let me handle this for you. If a fight breaks out in this courtroom, you could get ejected out of the game."

"I mean no disrespect Attorney Franklin but fuck this lawsuit. I'm about to kick this nigga's ass. Bail me out later."

I pulled Jarvis down to the bench by the sleeve of his suit

jacket. "Bruh listen to me, you don't think I want to walk over there and fuck him up? Have you forgotten what he cost me? I damn-near took my own life. If I'm chilled, then you chill. Mr. Franklin will deal with Timothy. Don't fuck this up for us, too many people are counting on that site coming down this week."

We managed to get Jarvis to calm the fuck down, but his eyes remained locked on Timothy the entire time. Timothy was focused forward, but I know he felt the blowtorch heat from Jarvis.

Once again it was Timothy.

The one who always appeared to be two blocks ahead of us when it came to dirty underhanded shenanigans. Timothy existed on a level of wickedness and pettiness that was beyond anything we could have concocted. Once again it was Timothy, but instead of a single target this time he came for all of us.

Biyell
LaDeisha
Briana
Monica
Jarvis
Tiffany
Telly

But not my wife? Not even in the context of being married to me did he attack Kayla, which raised even more suspicion.

For nearly three months, Timothy stalked us like a jilted little bitch and uploaded personal information on a website. He has built an anonymous community that logs in to that website every day, hungry for new gossip, and it was the fallout from our bad decisions that he served on a silver platter.

When Judge LaCouture returned to the bench and court was back in session she left little doubt who was in control.

"I have taken into consideration that there are certain life events that are beyond our control, therefore, I will grant a thirty-day continuance, in which we will resume in full session and resolve this matter that day." While Judge LaCouture leaned over to her clerk to confirm the best day next month, Attorney

Parker seized that break in the proceedings to make a request.

"Your Honor, request for sidebar."

The request was granted.

After a five-minute discussion, the body language of our Attorney suggested that he only agreed with half of what was deliberated. Without any announcement from the Judge, our attorney hurried to us for another huddle.

"Here's where we are, Mr. Feltus doesn't want to go to trial. He would like to settle the matter today."

"Okay, so what is he offering?"

"He will delete the entire site and all associated links if we agree to drop the suit."

"Fuck no..." Jarvis objected before I could speak. "I want to go all the way. I want him to pay for what he did to my family."

"I understand Mr. Napoleon, and my goal is to make him pay, but we could win a national championship right now with the takedown of that website."

"With all due respect, he doesn't get to cause all of this hell, then get off with a slap on the pinky finger. I was served with divorce papers on Monday, my wife is gone, and my kids will soon live under the roof of another man. I've lost everything. I don't have anything else to lose. Nah, I want my day in court with that pussy-ass creep."

"And what say you, Mr. Roderick?"

"On this one, I have to agree with my brother, we want the site down today and proceed to trial. Timothy is the most conniving piece of shit in this city, and the only way to prevent him from building another website is to make him pay for this one."

"Not a problem fellas, I work for you. Be right back."

After another ten-minute deliberation, Judge LaCouture announced the agreement in court, and the website was ordered down until the next court date on the eighteenth of September. During that time, both attorneys were encouraged to continue settlement discussions.

In true Timothy fashion, his lawyer requested a police escort

388 / TJ SPENCER JACQUES

to his car, because he feared for his life. Even though he was the one who declared war on us, we were held in court until the clerk received the call that Timothy had left the premises.

Less than Two hours later, HoeLeaks.com went temporarily offline.

404 PAGE NOT FOUND

CHAPTER 55

6:15 p.m.

UNCLE GLENN

It has been a while since I've heard the boisterous ruckus of my crew, God I missed having them all together. Diana and Bylisha will not make it in for another three hours, which is enough time to get as loud as we used to. On the Bose system is Lil Wayne who never sounded better – *Damn I Missed My Dawgs*.

We sat around the pool for a test run of this new brand of weed I picked up from this new medical marijuana dispensary. A group of white guys are legally in the weed business, selling the same weed Rasta caught a charge for, but fuck it, we needed some weed.

"Uncle Glenn, where did you get this weed?" Rasta stared sideways at his blunt. "I'm about to pluck this shit in your pool and go get a pack of Camels."

"It's called *Carpet Burn* and it's mild, I'm saving the *Hunky-dory* for when you all leave."

"Ain't that some shit, all the good weed I've given you over the years, you have the audacity…"

"Say it again Rasta," Biyell yelled.

"You have **THE- FUCKIN- AUUUDACITY** to roll up some Wal-Mart parsley, and call it weed, Uncle Glen you ain't shit." Rasta and Biyell dapped and laughed.

"Well if you want the good shit then, grow the good shit. I don't like this new law-abiding Rasta anyway. Old Rasta would've come through the door, with a pound, but Jehovah Witness Rasta shows up empty-handed and talking shit."

"Let's hurry up and smoke this eucalyptus bullshit. I invited a guest tonight."

"Bruh we haven't played in three months and you invite someone on the first Madden Thursday? In the preseason? Since when we invite a guest in August?" Biyell complained.

"Stop whining, the older you get the more you whine…" Rasta said.

"Damn…what's that funky smell?" Jarvis asked as he made his way poolside.

"White boys sold Glenn some dried mustard greens, and called it weed." Biyell said.

"I heard they had to hold you back from catching a murder charge in court?"

"Uncle Glenn you have no idea how close I came." Jarvis was handed the tray of mustard green weed. "The only reason I didn't knock his teeth out was because his mother died this morning."

"Damn, I'm sorry to hear that."

"See there, God don't like ugly…" Biyell said.

"Oh well, the site now says 404 PAGE NOT FOUND. I'll take today as a partial victory. A full win would have been gouging out his beaded eyes and pissing in his face."

"My goodness Jarvis, we've never heard you speak with such anger? Point to where little Timothy hurt you?" Biyell teased.

"Dude I'm serious, Timothy was the lone asshole who went

on the attack and had the nerve to ask for a settlement without paying a dime. Oh no *podnuh,* you will take the site down, and he has a house in his name. Drop it like it's hot!"

"Whatever that is y'all smoking smells like ten-day old piss!" Telly said as Erica escorted him through the patio. They hugged us one after the other – I was last."

"Hey dad, I have a delivery for you."

"Thanks for dropping him off, and if I ever get sick, I want the same *Erica Care Health Plan* you provided for Telly… with transportation."

"Me too…" Rasta said.

"Sign me up for the Erica plan as well. You sat by his bedside like a prison guard."

"I was honored, and I would do it again in a heartbeat." Erica kissed Telly and then waved at us as she headed out.

"Fellas, I didn't come over here for weed that smells like Kermit The Frog farted in my face, I came here for a game of Madden." Telly complained.

"For real Uncle Glenn, you should call the cops on them for selling you this weed. That's false advertising." Rasta suggested.

"If syphilis had a scent, it would smell just like this," Biyell said.

"Yea Uncle Glenn, do us all a favor and never offer us weed again for the rest of our lives, this one time I will *Just Say No.* Now fire up the game!" Jarvis yelled.

In a single file line, the guys made their way to the living room with Telly's wobbly-ass, and my crippled-ass in the rear. "Oh Biyell, Kayla dropped off your deed, don't forget it on the counter."

"Thanks, Uncle Glenn, I've been waiting on it."

"Telly let me holla' at you one second," I said once inside the doorway.

We sat across from each other in the wicker seats, and I could tell he was bracing himself for a continuation of our last argument.

"I have to give credit where it's due, you really impressed me at dinner. Your daughter Reebie is precious. I could have hugged her all day."

"It felt good, it really did?" Telly smiled with pride.

"It felt good for me too. I was glad to witness the new Telly do something the old Telly would have never allowed."

"I'm not supposed to be here right now, not amongst the living. You might say this sounds like bullshit but for the first time, I am content. I'm not hiding a child because I'm embarrassed by the situation. I'm sick of that old life, never going back."

"And that's why I asked my daughter to drive you over here, I wanted to have a word with you."

"I think I know where this is going and I –"

"Telly just hear me out for a minute. Before this accident, you know how firmly I was against you marrying my daughter. Hell, even before I knew she was my daughter I thought Erica was too good for you. But after that dinner, I saw you in a different light."

"I appreciate that, I really do. I am a new man and you will see it in my actions. I guarantee it, Uncle Glenn."

"Just call me Father-n-law."

It was then his head fell into his lap, then came the sound of sniffing. I saw the weight of guilt leave his body, I saw him struggle to forgive himself for all the lies he told, all the women he hurt, I saw a man who was ready to walk a new walk, and I was more committed than ever to walk with him. I never made a claim to be perfect, but I tried with everything in me, to always keep my word.

"I want you to make me a promise, and that is you will honor her, love my grandkids, and create the family you always wanted to have. You have been given a second chance to live a life of integrity and enjoy it to the fullest. In your second life, please take care of my daughter. Can I count on you to be the man I know you can be?"

"I promise you…" He sniffed into his lap again.

"You have my blessing to marry my daughter… son n law."

I grunted upwards and made my way into the living room, leaving Telly alone with his thoughts. As soon as I made it to the kitchen there was an unfamiliar knock at the door. It was Rasta's special guest, a face I never expected to see."

"Guys I would love for you to meet someone who has brought me a mighty long way, and he claims to be a hell of a Madden player. Please welcome a new member to our Madden Night, Dr. Morton from *West Jeff Behavior Management Clinic*."

I see what you did here Rasta, you're not so slick. Since we refused to make an appointment with a mental health therapist, you have integrated mental health therapy into our weekly get together. I see what you did there you sneaky little dawg you, and I love it.

CHAPTER 56

August 9, 2018
10:05 p.m.

BIYELL

It was so good to be together with my crew, all in one room doing what we love, playing Madden, and roasting whoever happened to be the victim of the night. Tonight, it was Uncle Glenn turn again for paying sixty dollars for some dried-out maple leaves. Definitely wasn't the quality of weed we were accustomed to smoking – that homegrown bud from Rasta.

It broke my heart to hear Rasta say he's out of the weed business until weed is legal in our area, this new Rasta ain't shit. We don't like this dude. Rasta who always maintained four open possession charges was my nigga-for-life, but not this bunk-ass pussy whipped Rasta imposter.

Old Rasta was like fuck the police every day, but I guess the seven years of probation, and experimenting with dangerous masking agents, would wear any man down, so I understand.

And to our surprise Dr. Morton who we now refer to as 'Doctor Dre' was a baller for real – he dropped beat-downs with those Chiefs all night. It didn't take us long to figure out the real reason that Rasta added him to the group.

To study five Hoe Rats.

I excluded Uncle Glenn from the Hoe Rats, because he's nowhere near our level of dumb-shit, but he still has some areas that need fixing.

Something really cool happened during the latter end of the evening. Dr. Dre and Jarvis decided to partner on a project aimed at men who struggle with commitment. In my opinion, it's the perfect partnership because Jarvis loves to write, and Doc is always evaluating the behaviors of those around him. Hell, the only time he wasn't studying us is when he was beating the living shit out of us on the game. But it's cool, and I think the name they settled on for the project was called

Curing The Man-Whore
Addressing The Melancholy That Leads To Male Infidelity

I think they should have named the book H*ow To Turn Off Your Dick* because that's my problem. Just cut right to the point without trying to sound all deep and shit. *Addressing Melancholy?* It means depression or sadness, I know this because I Googled it while no one was paying attention, then used it in a sentence like I know my shit.

Tamara use to aggravate my melancholy every day asking me all those questions, Ya heard me.

Then there was the situation with Timothy, and how it's always Timothy. I told Rasta straight up that he was wrong for holding Jarvis back, because the opportunity to bust his ass is hard to get. I've been trying to catch Timothy for two years, I even parked near his mom's house for two hours one day, could never catch him. Nevertheless, I'm happy the website is down. That Timothy is a *hoe-ass-Lil dude*, but I will run into him during Mardi Gras, it's guaranteed.

But the highlight of our first Madden Night of the 2018 season, was watching Uncle Glenn give Telly his full blessings to marry Erica. I've never seen my dawg so emotional. Glenn and I discussed it yesterday. I told him I've spoken to Telly every day since he was discharged, and several times during those conversations, I had to look at the phone to confirm who I called. He changed.

He really changed.

A few days ago, he told me during that time he was in that coma, his father came to him in spirit, and they set out on a hike up Interstate-55 all the way to Chicago, and then back.

I was like "bruh I know you miss your dad and all, but Dr. King didn't walk that damn far."

"B, it was a walk that I'd prayed would never end."

"What did you talk about from New Orleans to Chicago and back? You know I talk a lot, but I would have run out of stuff to say right around Jackson Mississippi."

"B, we mainly talked about life, and his relationships and where he went wrong with each woman. In listening to my dad, it helped me to process my thoughts. We talked about how restless he was at my age and said I got it honestly. He said many of my issues with women were due in part to the fact that I am competitive by birth because he was an athlete, but the difference is I made women the opponent."

I'm not one to get all spiritual but I believe Telly really did see his dad during that time he was in that coma. Telly told me he was embarrassed to have a child from a failed relationship, and that's when I went off on him. I cursed his ass post-coma.

Last month, while you were catnapping that judge denied my appeal to reinstate parental rights. Because of my actions, I was stripped of my rights with the kids I have with Tyra until I complete an evaluation. Here you are with a child you can see, but you're on some bullshit because things didn't work out with her mother? It was you who got a hair up your ass and left the per-

fect woman. You feminine-wash ass-nigga. Telly if you don't fix
that shit with Reebie, then you need to go back to sleep, because
you ain't shit. That's real nigga talk, Ya heard me.

That conversation was on Friday, and Sunday he asked me to
be there to witness it. At first, I was only going to see *loose boo-*
ty Phaedra, but I'm glad I was there to watch the circles come
together. I later asked him how did he pull it off?

"The first moment I had alone is when I called Cutina to apologize for divorcing her over dumb shit and denying Reebie. She
accepted my apology and the invitation to our Sunday dinner."

I'm glad all of those old issues were put to rest, like the Heather chick (who I thought was fine as fuck in that video) and now
he's working with a clean slate. I am too, right after I fuck Tesla
one last time. I know what you're thinking but this is it, for real,
and it's what she wants. Apparently, our little thing we had was
only spicy to her if I'm single, but not if I have someone. *I can*
be the other man, but she can't be the other woman?

Ain't that some shit?

When I called her to collect on my promise, she had already
settled in for the night.

"Biyell, you would call when I've already tied my hair up and
in the bed." She said in a discrete voice.

"Didn't I always drop everything when you sent me a nine-
ty-minute window?"

"Yes, but what about later this week? Saturday would be
more convenient."

"Tiffany is moving in on Saturday, and if this is our last time,
then I want to overdose on you. I want a night I will never forget.
A night only you can create. I want everything."

"Okay, alright, since you put it like that, let me put on something and fix myself up..."

"No, I want you just as you are right now, no makeup, no
nothing. I want my last memory of your body to be in its purest
form."

"You want to see me looking like this?"

"Yes, because you're always so flawless, with sweet smelling perfume and glitter lotion. I just want you."

"Your wish is my command this one last time…I'll be there shortly."

"The side door is open."

Somehow, I knew she would agree to come tonight, which is why I hurried into the shower and did my best to brush away that after taste from the gutter grass those people sold Uncle Glenn. I know she can't stay all night, but I plan to put so much dick on Tesla that she'll call me tomorrow begging for more. I'm not going to ask her for any, but if she calls me then…hey, it's my duty as a concerned citizen to help her during a time of need.

Wait, I think I hear her coming in.

Through my side door, she floated in.

"Stop right there," she was a few steps into the kitchen "What do you have on under that bathrobe?"

"Nothing."

"Remove it."

The bathrobe slid off her shoulders and formed a pile around her feet. I relaxed on my elbows and appreciated the dimly lit view of her body, the natural gleam of her skin. For her age, she was everything I loved about a woman.

"Do you like?"

"I love it, now remove that scarf so I can see your hair."

"My scarf too?"

"Yes, remove the scarf. Drop it, then slowly walk to me. I want the image of your sexy body permanently in my brain whenever I look in that direction. Every time I come through that door, I want to think about how happy you've made me over these past three months." Tesla did as she was told.

Once she arrived at the bed, crawled the rest of the way to my lips. We kissed like the world was ending at midnight, like two strangers who became lovers on a remote island. We belonged to one another. I hear Luther singing.

If only for one night.

"Thank you for coming, can I take my time?"

"You can, but for now just lay back and enjoy." She whispered, then slurped me into her mouth. My eyes roll up to whiteness.

After about five minutes, I wanted her to stop.

"Ride me," I tried to pull her up, but she refused "come up here before you make me..."

Her lips made a popping sound as she released that suction "Nope, you said you wanted everything this one last time, now you have it." She slurped me back into her mouth. My eyes rolled back to whiteness again.

Another five minutes sucked away.

"Baby, baby please, if you don't stop, I'm about to..."

Pop!

"Let it go Biyell...you know you want to."

"I do, but inside of you."

Pop!

"Give me the first one now, and if you behave, I might let you have your way..."

Then I felt her soft fingers caressing the sides of my balls and I couldn't fight her any longer, she had total control over my body.

"Oh baby, oooh baby, I'm, I'm about to..."

Pop!

"You're about to what... what Biyell?"

CHAPTER 57

The Night of Rasta & Kayla's Reception
June 2, 2018
9:35 p.m.

There we sat side by side, watching the moon swim laps across the pool, feeling mutually fucked over and equally rejected. I could tell the events of the night had left Diana deeply disturbed, because in all of these years I'd never seen her in a housecoat & scarf or anything other than a work uniform. But I was also traumatized by the events of the evening, and she had never seen me in a vulnerable condition. Nevertheless, I tried as best I could to remind her of the wonderful marriage she had, even though I no longer believed in the institution of marriage.

"If he thinks I'm going to sit around while he fawns and drools over that bitch then he's sadly mistaken." Her words slurred. "… but I'm no less beautiful. He might feel otherwise, but I know I'm fine." She hiccupped!

"Diana, please don't think like that" I stood and grabbed her arm before she departed "Don't judge Glenn on those twenty-two minutes you were outside alone. I knew you were out there because I followed you but stopped in the foyer. From there I watched you through the glass door – just to make sure you were okay. I saw when you pitched your keys across the parking lot, and when you picked them up. Each time you pumped your fist in the air or banged the hood of your car, I saw you. I didn't go beyond those glass doors – it wasn't my place."

"…and I saw you." Diana turned front and center.

"…you were more concerned about me than my husband. How fucked up is that? But thank you for caring about me during a time when I mattered to no one."

With the elegance of a ballerina, Diana tiptoed to my lips and kissed me.

Holy shit she kissed me.

Diana.

Astonished, I didn't kiss her back, but she continued until her tongue touched my tongue. I knew this wasn't Diana, this was the liquor, this was feeling rejected by Glenn, this was the reappearance of Derinda, and Erica again, the look on Glenn's face when he saw the mother of his only child.

This was also Diana.

Her lips against my lips, her hands on my face, all of this public display of affection was merely an outward expression of her inner pain, and the need to feel wanted. I accepted it. I was being used as a sedative. I tried to convince myself that this wasn't happening, even while it was happening.

I didn't stop her.

The same way Josh didn't stop Tiffany. I allowed her to continue until she was straddling me on that pool chair. In a housecoat, black and white polka dot hair scarf, and black lace panties.

Lil Glenn: Don't do this Biyell, she's drunk and your taking advantage of her.

Pimp B: *Mannnn fuck that, she kissed you first.*

Lil Glenn: This is Glenn's wife Biyell. Stop this now! It has already gone too far.

Pimp B: *Remember that time you beat your dick thinking about fucking Diana on their kitchen table? Remember at the old apartment when you had to use the bathroom in Glenn's bedroom, because the guest bathroom was occupied. Remember you opened her dresser drawer, and saw those leopard printed panties? Well, this is your chance to live it out. She's safe because she's married. Diana will never kiss and tell, she has too much to lose.*

Lil Glenn: What about the code? You are breaking rule #1 and if you don't stop this now there's no coming back.

Pimp B: *Didn't that nigga' Josh snatch your lady tonight? Fuck that code, if Diana gives you that pussy – you better take it.*

"Diana-Diana-Diana, you don't want to do this..." I separated our lips.

Inches from my nose she said "unlike Tiffany I can hold my liquor. I know what I'm doing, and with whom I'm doing it to. For years, I've felt how you've looked at me. I knew you took pictures of my panties. I knew how bad you wanted to fuck me. I tried to resist those thoughts, but after tonight...fuck it. This might be your only chance, and if I were you, I would take it. I'm just saying."

Pimp B: *Biyell you remember the last time you tried to run from some pussy, and you pulled a hamstring? Don't miss this opportunity. Get the pussy Biyell. She's giving it to you.*

About two minutes later she took me inside of her and rode that pony poolside, it was a liver shivering nut when I exploded. I didn't have to move a pinky finger, Diana did it all. Since the night of the reception, I have enjoyed my hands free, self-driving Tesla, without a single regret.

CHAPTER 58

August 9, 2018
10:35 p.m.

UNCLE GLENN

What a night this has been, all the guys together and the addition of Dr. Dre! I think this Madden season will be the best one we've had in years. The only down part of the evening was the discovery that Timothy was the one who created that website and posted all of those videos.

And the nerve, to request a police escort?

That coward.

Doc listened in as we posthumously roasted Timothy in retaliation for all the headaches he caused, then he offered a perspective I hadn't considered.

"Do you think Timothy made the recent series of choices because he misses being a part of the group?"

"He was a part of the group until he did the other back-handed-back-stabbing thing to Rasta. He's out of the group due to

his own actions. Making a move on someone's girl is a no-no."
Jarvis said.

"True but what if he asked each one of you for forgiveness,
could you?"

"I speak for the entire group when I say...hell no. There's no
coming back from that, wives and the main girl is off limits; but
the side chick is free game." Jarvis laughed.

"Oh... really" Rasta paused the game "so you're saying I
could have made a move on Briana?"

Jarvis ignored him..."

"Did y'all see that? He became instantly pissed off when I put
a name to all that dumb shit."

"If you would've touched Briana, we would be in here fighting like Popeye and Brutus in this bitch."

"I thought so, ...and remain silent for the rest of the night
before you get called out again." Rasta laughed. "Wives and
mistress were all off limits, and don't forget that. Now back to
kicking your ass."

Surprisingly, Biyell was quiet for the rest of the evening.

Strange.

Very strange, Eerie.

Once Diana came in around nine o'clock, we shut it down
and made plans for next week at Biyell place. This year Madden
Night will float around even though I love hosting and cooking.
Even Dr. Dre wanted in on the hosting, so the locations for the
next three events were set. Once everyone was gone, I washed
the dishes, fixed Diana a plate, and put the rest of the catfish and
shrimp pasta in the fridge, then headed to the shower.

After my shower, I tapped on Diana's door.

"Hey, I left you a plate on the kitchen counter", as usual she
didn't answer.

"I'll put the plate in the refrigerator in case you get hungry
later, okay Diana?" Her television rumbled the walls, but the
door was locked.

Not that I wanted anything, but why lock the door?

"Good night Diana." I then mumbled my way back to the kitchen.

She asked me to give her three days to decide if we were going to work things out, but three days came and went. I had an appointment with my lawyer today. He started divorce paperwork and updated my estate plan.

"In case anything happened to you, Erica wouldn't beg Diana for her fair share. Let's remove that decision completely by cutting Diana a check for half of the funds in your account. Let's buy her out on the real estate firm from the life insurance policy you guys placed on each other. Biyell and Rasta will receive full ownership of the firm, Erica will receive about six-million plus. Diana will receive nine million, plus an additional two million from the policy. Finally, there's one million going to Jarvis for his publishing company. With your signature that completes the update to your Estate." Attorney Aisola recapped and sealed my updated will. Then he printed my divorce papers.

All I need now is her signature.

That conversation was twelve hours ago.

This is not the route I want to go. I still love her, but all of this fighting we're doing is over catty little issues. I owned up to my role in all of this with the phone calls and failing to mention the ring, but I've never cheated on Diana, not once. She got the best of me every day of this marriage, but I can't make her want me.

Here I am, fresh into my fifties and having to start over again. I never thought we would end this way.

"Is that what I think it is?" The large gold envelope was still sitting on my counter.

"It sure is, Biyell left his deed, even after I reminded him."

I know why he forgot this deed, when pussy is on his brain that boy is worthless. I'll go walk it over and place it on his counter. Their filming a commercial for the construction side of our business in the morning, and I don't want the blame to fall on me if his deed comes up missing. And quiet as kept, on the way back from Biyell's house, I plan to sit poolside and smoke the rest of this pine-sol weed.

I grabbed the extra key Biyell gave me and headed across the yard.

At the halfway point between our homes, my t-shirt had already began to cling to my chest, but I refuse to concede to that motorized scooter. Finally, I made it to the side door – it was open.

I know this is a safe neighborhood but why leave the door wide open?

Once I entered the house, I only made it a few steps past the dryer when I saw a familiar pile of clothes.

Pink housecoat

Polka-dot scarf

Pink plush slippers.

I had recognized them because each item was a gift from me at one point. The housecoat was last year's Valentine's Day gift, when I hired a massage and nail tech to give my wife a day of beauty in her living room. The black and white polka dot scarf wasn't any old hair wrap, but a part of a Gucci blouse and scarf outfit, I gave Diana during her fiftieth birthday bash at the Sheraton Hotel. I didn't need any more confirmation that it was Diana's clothes because I heard him.

"Oh baby, oooh baby, I'm, I'm about to…"

Pop!

"You're about to what…?"

"Diana I'm about to cum."

That's when I hopped three more times to the kitchen. They didn't see me, but I saw them. I saw my wife of 35 years between his legs. My beautiful wife, whom I worshiped the ground under her feet, was ass in the air naked, with her head bobbing for an apple.

"That's it Diana, catch that nut baby. Get it. Good girl. That's that hands-free nut I brag about, my little Tesla. Thank you, baby, get all of it, every drop."

That's when my good leg, old *Mr. Reliable*, the leg that never accepted any excuses, that leg, it buckled just as Biyell roared in Diana's mouth. Everything from that point happened in flashes of white lights.

VOOOOOSH

I heard him say oh fuck it's your husband. I heard her make a sound that could have been a scream of concerned that I was on the floor, or fear because I'd caught her in the act of adultery.

"Glenn I'm so sorry, I'm sorry, I'm sorry, fuck I'm sorry, I never meant to hurt you." In my peripheral, she gathered her housecoat, scarf, and slippers."

"Awwww man, I fucked up, man I fucked up." He said.

Then I felt her hands under me, as she tried to lift me off the floor. I couldn't feel my body, but I still had my vision, and could still smell the vapors from my wife's breath that reeked of another man's dick.

There are things in life that require natural sweeteners to make them taste better.

Diana said the night of Rasta's wedding when I found her out by the pool. Biyell was that sweetener. I'm not sure if it was the lotion thick moisture in the corner of her mouth, or the view of Biyell's naked body, or the thought that my dick wasn't on his level, or finally having an explanation of where Diana was on the day's she vanished for two hours; but one of the before mentioned induced the first palpitation in my chest.

VOOOOOSH

I'm in the back of an ambulance, I know that much for sure, and I hear Diana somewhere near the lower left side of the gurney. The State Trooper who arrived on the scene and the EMS guy both knew Diana, I wonder if she also sucked their dicks? In the stairwell of the hospital, perhaps?"

"Mrs. Braxton is your husband allergic to any medications?"

"No…"

"And you found him where?"

"In our living room on the floor."

"How long has he been unresponsive?"

"I lost pulse right before you arrived, but I continued to give him mouth to mouth resuscitation, while his best friend assisted with the "chest compression."

"Brian, I need you to step on it we're losing him." He yelled at the driver.

"ETA two minutes. Trauma staff is waiting on the ramp."

"Brian cut it to one-minute ETA even if you have to push cars out of your way, we're losing him."

VOOOOOSH

I'm calm because my thoughts just shifted to my beautiful daughter, and my two precious grandkids. I got to meet them and enjoy them, and it was thoughts of them that provided the morphine in my veins once the heart attack peaked. I'm also comforted that Telly is a changed man and I no longer have to police him.

That toothbrush jar through that shower door was the best thing she had ever pitched in her life. And then there's the Real Estate business, which is in good hands, and never really needed much input from me.

It is for that reason I followed the advice of my lawyer this morning and placed Erica as heir to my share of the community property.

VOOOOOSH

I tried my best to convince the men I considered my dearest buddies to change, though I fell short of that goal, I still feel that their lives have been impacted in a positive way because of my life. As for Diana, she can go forward and raise Bylisha without anyone knowing what led to my heart attack, and at the end of the day, it's a private matter between us.

VOOOOOSH

Why me? Why Biyell? How long have those two flirted right under my nose? Will Diana marry him and live together as a family with Bylisha? When the first responders rolled me to the ambulance through the curious eyes of my neighbors, was that Timothy's Lincoln Navigator parked across the street? When did he arrive? Did he see my wife tiptoe across the yard to Biyell?

So little time.

So many questions.

So much to ponder.

Nevertheless, I leave you with the burden of these questions. I'm no longer worried or troubled by the actions of my wife. The good news is, I can rest in this fancy black lacquer casket (with the gold plated handles) in peace knowing that I wasn't Infallible, but I was the best Glenn I could be for thirty-five years of marriage. On that note, you can lower me down fellas.

For none of us liveth to himself, and no man dieth to himself. For whether we live, we live unto the Lord; and whether we die, we die unto the Lord: whether we live therefore, or die, we are the Lord's.

Damn I miss my dawgs already.

Yours truly,

Glenn Braxton

THANK YOU

Thank you so much for supporting me through another installment of Infallible. Since Volume 1 of this series, I have received so many encouraging emails from readers who shared how this book entertained and affected them in ways they never expected. Those emails are priceless, and inspire me to continue on this journey as a writer.

I decided to self-publish my novels because I wanted to tell a story that has never been told, in a voice that has never been spoken. Most importantly, I wanted to say what needed to be said, as only I could say it. Thank God, I followed my gut. Your support has proven that my books are fully capable of finding a place in this crazy literary world, and a slot on the most important bookshelf of all – your heart.

In several places throughout this novel, I hid in broad daylight clues to that scandalous affair, and now that you know the ending, I think you might enjoy reading Infallible Volume 4 again.

Like most affairs – all of the signs were there the entire time, and I only wish I could be there to see your expression when the truth smacks you in the face.

If you have enjoyed Volume 4 of Infallible, please leave a review on Amazon, and make sure to follow my website at TJnovels.com for new release updates. I am also creating a fan page of video reactions to this novel – please post your video reaction on my Facebook page or send your YouTube video to writeTJwrite@gmail.com

Thank you

TJ Spencer Jacques